River, Diverted

River,
Diverted

Jamie
Tennant

Palimpsest Press
1171 Eastlawn Ave.
Windsor, Ontario, N8S 3J1
www.palimpsestpress.ca

Printed and bound in Canada
Cover design and book typography by Ellie Hastings
Edited by Aimée Dunn
Copyedited by Theo Hummer

Palimpsest Press would like to thank the Canada Council for the Arts
and the Ontario Arts Council for their support of our publishing
program. We also acknowledge the assistance of the Government of
Ontario through the Ontario Book Publishing Tax Credit.

LIBRARY AND ARCHIVES CANADA CATALOGUING IN PUBLICATION

TITLE: River, diverted / Jamie Tennant.
NAMES: Tennant, Jamie, 1969- author.
IDENTIFIERS: Canadiana (print) 20220280371
             Canadiana (ebook) 2022028038X

ISBN 9781990293276 (SOFTCOVER)
ISBN 9781990293283 (EPUB)
ISBN 9781990293290 (PDF)
CLASSIFICATION: LCC PS8639.E644 R58 2022 | DDC C813/.6—DC23

For everyone who has been through the wormhole.

*In memory of Tanaka Kazumasa and
Nakadaira "Nax" Yoshihiro.*

No one ever steps in the same river twice:
it's not the same river, and you're not the same person.
—Heraclitus

KENICHI AND THE KAPPA

I'm holding a book that cannot exist.

That's not a philosophical puzzle or an obscure zen koan. This book should not, *cannot*, exist. Yet here it is, as impossible as the sound of one hand clapping.

The book is titled *Kenichi and the Kappa*.

What the hell's a *kappa*, you ask?

Kappa means "river-child," but that's a literal translation, and not a helpful one. The *kappa* is a creature from Japanese folklore. A malevolent spirit, likely invented by parents to keep their children safe from harm. I can imagine those children, listening as their mothers describe the sordid creature—its putrid fishy aroma, its nasty fondness for kid-meat—sons and daughters with their eyes wide, breath stolen from their lungs. Maybe parents hoped stories of the child-hungry *kappa* would steer children away from the river. By today's standards, that's crappy, near-pathological parenting. Then again, you don't play by the river if you're scared of the river monster. And if you don't play by the river, you don't drown in the river.

Maybe it's best that I don't have children. They would be *so* messed up.

At some point in Japan's postwar history, the *kappa* underwent an image makeover. It's as if they fed the legendary river imp to the nation's *kawaii* machine. *Kawaii* means "cute." I imagine the *kawaii* machine as a giant Dr. Seuss-meets-Rube-Goldberg contraption, all pulleys and levers and bellows, powered by the giggles of Japanese schoolgirls. You insert an item, there's a flurry of animated activity, and *kawaii!* Out pops the item in its cartoonish form. Cute has copious currency in Japanese pop culture, which is why *kappa* no longer eat children. *Kappa* have become Sanrio toys and mascots for sushi restaurant chains. Nothing about today's *kappa* would keep you away from the riverbank.

But, okay—this impossible book.

There's an illustration of a *kappa* on the white cover, a pencil sketch dashed off by Reiko one night at work as we waited for customers to arrive. In her rendering, the creature seems to be looking past me, over my right shoulder. Its back is hunched, its beak raised—yet its eyes are soft, as if it were smiling. A creature caught between its past and its future, between its cruel history and its comic present. Above the sketch is the title, written in a bright-orange font. The letters look sewn together, like felt stuffed with cotton batting. It wrongly suggests the story is for children.

At the bottom, in a simpler font, it says "By River Black."

But, okay—here's the thing. My name is Helen Olinda Delaney—but it is also River Black. *I'm River Black.* But I didn't send this manuscript to a publishing house, work on it with an editor, or even show it to my sister, and I make my sister read *everything* I write. I don't even possess a copy of this manuscript. There was only ever one, and I burned it down to ashes.

Yet here it is. In my hands, as real as the cup that holds my coffee or the chair that supports my widening forty-something behind. It showed up three days ago—the book, not my widening behind—in a plain brown padded envelope. It has lain on my kitchen counter, untouched, since then.

Oh, and—not only did I not publish this book, I didn't technically *write* it either. I transcribed it from a notebook onto a computer. I embellished it, gave it a bit of colour. If it were a comic book, it would say *inked* by River Black.

This is Daniel Truman's book. Daniel, whom I got to know in a tiny kitchen at the back of a hostess bar in the mountains of Japan. This story was for him and me alone. He would be mortified to know it was published.

That's what I think, anyway. No one knows how Daniel would feel—about anything—because Daniel is dead.

FIREWORKS

Memories diminish. They fray into hazy fragments, become like a disjointed dream remembered two days later. Individual moments flash and flicker like sunlight on a calm ocean. These sparkling, disorienting moments belie the fact that beneath them, something murkier, yet more monumental, floats in silence. Like the back of a blue whale spotted just below the ocean surface: you can't really see the whale, but you feel its presence, its strength, as it glides beneath the sun-dappled plane. That, to me, is the true memory. Not the images you can recall, not the sparkling sunlight, but the elemental power that lies beneath them. Some of my memories conjure dread—there are shapeless Lovecraftian horrors underwater that I'd rather let sleep—while other memories lead me to the whales. To life itself.

Memory diminishes. My aging brain displays some memories as though shot on grainy film stock. But even faded and cracked, they are powerful. A cluster of friendly faces at the bottom of an escalator. The smell of cigarettes and filthy shag carpeting. The sequence from Binzuru weekend, when we drank Jim Beam in apartment 301, glass doors open to the mad chorus of crickets in the hills behind us. A rich, humid mountain breeze. Nicolle took red nail polish and adorned

Daniel's toes to much laughter, knowing the locals would be amused by his *gaijin* feet, their fire-engine-red tips displayed prominently in his sandals. When we wandered out into the night, I felt the sweetest drunkenness I had ever felt. We wandered to a parking lot and sat on the pavement, Toby's head in my lap as we watched fireworks crackle and spark, for what seemed like hours, across the night sky.

And threaded through these memories, the delightful thought that rose out of the laughter and intoxication, the thought, *this is how River begins*. Bliss, potential, the future a blank page and my mind conjuring the words to fill it.

That bliss is the true memory beneath the images. It is the happiest memory I have.

ZOMBIES AT THE DOOR

"Three days ago?"

My sister Sheila, her voice thin on my cell's speaker-phone, like a baseball announcer on an old-fashioned transistor radio.

"Yeah."

"And you haven't read it yet?" My sister Sheila, incredulous and encouraging in the same sentence. It's an old trick of hers; she'll repeat my words back to me in a tone that somehow suggests both a challenge and a genuine expression of disbelief.

"No, I haven't read it yet, jerk." I glare at the phone on the faux-marble counter, next to a half-empty bottle of faux-French wine. "When did I have the time to read it? I have a script on deadline with the ex, and you know what he's like when I don't meet his deadlines."

"Oh, please. Yesterday your Instagram story featured a dozen horror-movie screenshots."

"Watching horror movies is research."

"If you have time to post pictures of grindhouse flicks, Hel, you have time to read the book."

Sheila's right, of course.

"I just don't understand how it can exist, Sheel. It's like

fifty-seven pages of cognitive dissonance. I know it can't exist, but here it is. The thing *scares* me."

"Scares you?" Incredulous again. "Nothing scares you, Hel. Your pen name is River Black. You write movies with names like *Legacy of Brutality* and *Sixteen Ways to Strangle.*"

"I never wrote a movie called *Sixteen Ways to Strangle.*"

"Well, you should, it's a great title."

"Noted."

"Just read the book, Helen. It wasn't conjured from another dimension. Someone obviously found your old computer, discovered the file, printed it...published it, and mailed it to you, and...yeah, okay, when I say it out loud, it does sound pretty impossible. But it's a *book*, not some arcane tome of doom."

"*Klaatu barada nikto.*"

"Exactly not that. Exactly *not* the Necronomicon."

There are thousands of reasons I love Sheila, and one of them is she never fails to get an *Evil Dead* reference. Well, neither do Evrard, my movie biz friends, the kids at the fan expos, the horror bloggers...but, okay, they're *supposed* to get those references. They're all showing off their trivia knowledge, trying to secure their standing in some imagined nerd-boy hierarchy. I don't care if they get those references. Sheila's another story. When Sheila gets my references, it matters.

"My point is that wherever it came from, it exists," she continues. "It's real. Buck up, read it, and move on. Then you can go back and concentrate on *Pinned XVII* or whatever it is."

"It's the fourth installment, not the seventeenth, thanks."

"It's quite an accomplishment, wringing four films out of that series. One movie about a murderous psychopath displaying dead women like butterflies? A cinch. But *four...*"

"You can't imagine my pride," I deadpan. There was a time when I would have defended these films, but that time has long passed.

I scan the book cover for the seventy-sixth time. "I'm not scared of the book itself," I say. "What terrifies me is that by opening the cover, I'm opening a door. A door that's been locked for a long time."

"What door?"

"You know. The Door. Locked. Boarded up. I smashed up the furniture and nailed the broken pieces across the door frame."

"Ah, right, so now it's a *Night of the Living Dead* reference."

"Yeah."

"Wait, who are the undead in this situation?"

"I, uh…I think the undead are my memories."

"So you nailed the doors shut against your memories… but your memories come from inside, not outside…"

"Right. It's not a perfect metaphor."

The glass of wine in front of me has left overlapping grape circles on the counter. I raise the glass, swallow quickly, place the glass in a new spot, wipe up the old circle. Repeat. I've been gulping back impressive amounts of vino since *Kenichi and the Kappa* showed up in my mailbox. It doesn't seem to be helping much.

I haven't allowed myself to think of Daniel Truman in years. Okay, that's not true. I haven't allowed myself to dwell on him. To dwell on the memory of his face, his claustrophobia and purple fingers, his sweetness. In a different way, though, he is with me every day. I feel him rise up from the crevices in my brain, wispy like sidewalk steam. I acknowledge him as one would acknowledge a ghost in the hallway—a polite hello to recognize that yes, I see you, you shouldn't still be here but I do see you.

"Are the zombies your memories of Japan?" Shelia is preoccupied with dismantling my admittedly weak metaphor. "That doesn't make sense because you talk about Japan a *lot*. I mean, the fireworks alone. Everyone in your life has heard you talk about the fireworks at least a dozen times. If your memories are the zombies, you walk among the undead pretty regularly."

"I don't dwell. That's the point. The more I dwell on the

memories, Sheel, the more I bump up against the real night-mare ones. I don't want to think about Daniel and I don't want to think about..."

"About?"

"He Who Shall Not Be Named."

"Ah. Toby."

"Don't say the name of He Who Shall Not Be Named, Sheel!"

"Yes, yes, okay, Daniel and the other one. So, they're the zombies outside the door?"

"Yes. One of 'em already got inside. Through the root cellar, I think. Stupid cellar doors are never secure enough. I heard thump thump thump and then a crash, like he fell through it."

"You heard all this from the twenty-first floor."

"Then it was like, he reached the top step and was thumping on the door—"

"Your Vancouver condo has a root cellar?"

"—and before I knew it, he was in, somehow, with these rotten limbs that shouldn't have been strong enough to break through the plywood, I guess, but—"

"All that to say...?"

Sheila indulges me in my horror similes (or metaphors, depending), but eventually she shuts me down. My flights of gory fantasy eventually make her flip the switch, and my big sister becomes my Big Sister. She worries about my mental and emotional health. Rightly so, I suppose.

"All that to say, I don't want to think about Daniel." I pause for another gulp of wine. "When I talk about those days, I think about how much fun we had. But those memories look like a redacted CIA report. There are big black rectangles blocking out the boys' names."

Daniel was the most unlikely friend I ever made. Other than Sheila, he was the first person with whom I shared my stories. In return, he shared with me the most unlikely story I'd ever heard, about a razor-beaked river god and the boy who tried to tame him. For many months, he let me into his private tale, let me polish it, let me be part of it.

Then one day, Daniel evaporated.

I choose that word on purpose. The Japanese have some fantastic words that you can't really translate into English. Consider the word *natsukashii*. You could say it means "nostalgic," but nostalgia is a hollow, sentimental thing, mined for marketing and bad television programming. It's how I feel watching *Stranger Things* or listening to *Forever Young* by Alphaville. If something is *natsukashii,* on the other hand, it suggests a return of the departed, a hole temporarily filled. *Natsukashii* is the word I'd use when I watch the original 1954 *Godzilla*. I can almost see the yellowed plastic television with its postage-stamp screen, and smell steak pie wafting in from the kitchen. When the feeling of *natsukashii* passes, I am emptier than I was before.

But, okay—Daniel. Evaporation. The Japanese word for "evaporation" is *jōhatsu*. Yet *jōhatsu* also means "unexplained disappearance," or what happens when one has debts, or an unhappy difficult marriage, or wants to avoid the mob. Possibly it's what happens when you *don't* avoid the mob— you don't evaporate, you *are evaporated*. In most cases, though, the *jōhatsu* are people who cannot not face their lives anymore, so they erase themselves. That's what happened to Daniel, for a time. As we would have said, bastardizing the Japanese, he "went *jōhatsu*." Eventually they found him in a canal, his lungs full of water, his heart full of holes. No longer *jōhatsu*; gone just the same.

He Who Shall Not Be Named evaporated, too, but it was less of a surprise. He was never really there in the first place.

I'm in touch with a few people from those days in Nagano. Nicolle and Allie, mostly. We'll tag one another in old pictures that remind us of one another. It's all very casual, but the truth is, it's bizarre how much I still care about these people. They passed through my life as I passed through theirs—as blinding flashes, with searing intensity. Despite the brevity of our initial relationships, we marked one another permanently. We were bound by a shared experience and a shared language, and we forged friendships in the improbable heat we generated together. I haven't seen any of them in more than twenty years, but they still matter. When I look at old photos, the flame burns a hole in my chest, and I soon have to put the pictures away. It's a literal, physical pain that protects me, keeps me from unearthing too much happiness and, with it, the despair that comes with knowing it's forever gone. The old Japanese saying rings true—*ichi-go, ichi-e.* Once in a lifetime; never again.

There are others who mattered even more. Yet for some reason they're no longer part of my life. Why do we lose touch with people? Facebook welcomes the lapsed letter writer, the big fat jerk who can't be bothered to make a phone call. What about those who aren't on social media, though? Like Babette, my former roommate. Like Sora, my former student. Like Reiko, Masa, and Nax. I wonder sometimes: does Rei-chan still draw? Did Sora grow up and have a family? Does Masa still cobble sentences together from rock'n'roll lyrics? Would Nax still look at me the same way, something sparkling in his sleepy eyes? Would He Who Shall Not Be Named still be a duplicitous son of a bitch?

I drift away from the phone and towards the window. It's nighttime, and I can see the black rift of the harbour between here and Vancouver Island. Above it, lights twinkle at one another silently. Below me, a stack of lives lived in green-tinted glassed-in blocks assembled on top of more green-tinted glassed-in blocks. Surrounding it all, the nonstop horizontal glide of headlights.

On the counter, underneath the book, lies the envelope in which it came, with that word featured in its smeary postmark: 長野. Nagano. The city I called home for two years. I lived in Sanyō Heights, a decrepit pile of plaster and rat traps that has probably been gentrified by now. For those two years, I worked at a bar called J.J. International. Most of the customers' names have disappeared from memory. I wrote those names on dozens of bottles, stored in our "bottle keep" for the customers' future enjoyment, but those names no longer connect to faces. I have boxes of photographs filled with strangers I can't remember.

I remember Nax, though. He sold J.J.'s years ago. He probably still sits in his floor chair, jotting inscrutable numbers into his battered beige ledger, surrounded by his art collection—not hung on walls but wrapped in less-battered but equally-beige paper, stacked sideways against one another, sixteen frames deep.

The package came from Nagano. Who else might still be in Nagano? Masa, for sure. I'm not sure about Rei, or Babette, or Sora, or He Who Shall...

Sigh. Okay. *Toby.*

His name fills me with cold resentment, which is why he oughtta remain unnamed. In my head, he's one of the zombies out on the lawn, half-rotten jaw swinging beneath his upper lip, an unholy moan rising from his throat. I can hear him banging on the window now. It's amazing, considering we're twenty-one stories up. Maybe he's part vampire? Maybe that it, he's a vampire, not a zombie, and he's here to drain my soul—but, okay. Toby could still live in Nagano.

Which of them could be responsible for this book? It has to be Nax. The Sanyō Heights apartments were his; he rented them to house his staff. Nax would have sorted through the remnants I left behind: weathered old paperbacks with tea-coloured pages, piles of half-knitted scarves, an assortment of euchre decks, and most pointedly, my *wāpuro*, a monstrous computer that was little more than a typewriter with a screen, something you might have seen advertised in a 1981 edition of *Omni* magazine.

Anyway.

Kenichi and the Kappa. It's in my hands before I allow myself to reconsider.

"Stupid book," I tell it.

"If you're going to talk to the book, that's cool, but this is a long distance call," Sheila says. I'd forgotten she was still on the line. "Are you going to read it or not?"

It is cool and smooth and weighs almost nothing.

"Is it giving me a choice?" I ask. As I open the cover, I glance at the front door, half expecting to hear the bump and moan of the undead. Instead, there is memory. In the darkness, shadows; shadows that both hide mountains and *are* mountains. The sound of a metal beast on its rails, and the scratchy sensation of fine ballpoint on paper, two words spinning and twirling out of my fingers and along the plastic length of the pen. The words *River Black*.

THE SHARKSKIN SALARYMAN

River Black. River Black. River Black.

Cursive, lowercase printing, formal block letters. Fat cartoon balloon fonts. A version where the R was an enormous upper-case *kaiju,* its leg raised and ready to stomp the lower-case letters into dust.

I was practising. A new name required a new signature.

The train bucked and swayed, rendering much of my work illegible—*Lovei Hlack? Rivir Boack?*—but even the wobbliest scribbles made me grin. My New Signature. After all the autographs I would sign someday, *River Black* would flow from my fingers as easily as *Helen Delaney* ever had.

Giddy, delirious from jet lag and Japanese chocolate bars, I slumped backwards and smiled to myself, thinking about the last few hours. The blurred confusion of airport concourses and unintelligible signs. The soothing voice of the Skyliner train and its gentle reminder not to forget your belongings: *o-wasuremono gozaimasen yo.* The baffling intensity of the three-minute walk between Ueno train stations: crowds like

schools of fish, darting and twirling without a single colli-
sion; chirping traffic signals like battery-operated sparrows;
low-hanging bridges against high-rising neon. There, on the
train, the deliciously electrifying culture shock was muted
by the darkness outside. But even in the darkness, there
were shadows. The mountains, the sky, the trees and shacks
and houses and roads were all there, even if they had been
reduced to silhouettes of silhouettes. I wanted to see those
shadows, so I pressed my face against the window. Behind
me, a salaryman in a sharp blue sharkskin suit watched me,
amused; I could see his reflection in the window. His amuse-
ment would not dissuade me. I had been briefed on sixteen
dozen Japanese *do*'s and *don't*s. Don't stick your chopsticks
vertically in the rice. Don't tip. Don't eat or drink while
walking down the street. Don't pass food from chopstick to
chopstick! There was no rule about pressing your face against
the train window. I was going to fit in here and respect this
culture, but I was still going to be me.

A confusing proposition, I guess, since I'd come here to
become someone else.

A high school acquaintance named Katya started
the wheels turning. She had worked at place called J.J.
International in Nagano, where she sat at tables with men,
poured drinks, lit cigarettes, and made conversation. "It
sounds sketchy," she'd admitted, "like it's some kind of pros-
titution thing, but it isn't. It's just talking. I can see if they've
got any openings, if you want."

"Boy, do I!" I joked. "Sounds great."

Yet here I was, in another hemisphere.

The window vibrated in its casing, causing my top teeth to
rattle against my bottom teeth. I opened my mouth to end the
chattering and stared, gape-jawed, into the invisible Japanese
countryside. I let a long, low aaaaahhh stretch its way out of
my throat. Sometimes I do things that feel good and look
weird. The juddering motion of the window gave my voice
a rapid vibrato, and I wondered what the sharkskin-suited

salaryman must have thought about this strange foreign chick bleating into the night like a bewildered goat.

I stopped watching the nothing and honed in on Sharkskin's reflection in the glass. His hair was mostly grey, buzzed over the ears. Hints of wrinkles, splayed like fingers, sprouted from the outer corners of his eyes, but he didn't exactly seem old. Every few minutes he glanced in my direction. It was an aloof but amused attention, and it reminded me of my father. All his gaze lacked was the thin wateriness of the seventh-brandy stretch.

My father. In my world, the most talked-about movie of 1995 was *The Death of My Father*. It was also the most over-hyped production; it was emotional, yes, but God how I wished people would stop talking about it.

Scene: Sad young woman experiences anxiety attacks after the death of her father.

Montage: Scenes that suggest a troubled father/daughter relationship.

Shot: Sad young woman's sorrowful glance at a photograph of, you guessed it, happier times.

Cut to: a newspaper obituary displayed on a refrigerator door. Please note that the fridge magnet sports a photograph of Igor and the Count from *Hilarious House of Frightenstein*.

That summed up Helen Delaney, circa 1995: sad, confused, fascinated by pop cultural ephemera, enthralled with goofiness and spooky, horrible things.

That sums up River Black, circa now, too. Though with less sadness and more confusion.

As I stood up to hit the vending machine, the train seemed to make a perpendicular shift on the tracks. I felt like a surfer on an erratic wave. With surfing on my mind, I spread my arms out for balance and launched into a mostly off-key approximation of the *Hawaii Five-O* theme. No one in the car seemed to notice.

At the end of the car, a row of vending machines shone with the promise of so many garishly packaged pleasures. Beer!

Cigarettes! Boss Coffee! I opted for a Pocari Sweat because, I mean, it's called Pocari Sweat. What's a Pocari? Why does it sweat? Neither the milky translucence of the bottle nor the blue-and-white label provided this pertinent information. As I hung ten down the sideways-shifting aisle, Pocari Sweat in hand, we barrelled into a tunnel. The train shook and I shot my arms out with a short squeal, flailing for a grip on the backs of the seats beside me. The bottle leapt out of my grasp, fell onto the aisle, and rolled to Sharky's shiny-leathered feet, where it stopped with a bump against his toe.

I stepped forward, embarrassed, and kneeled to retrieve my beverage.

"*Sumimasen.*" I looked up at him apologetically. Excuse me. A phrase I was likely to need with some frequency.

Sharky raised his hand in front of his face, vertically, in line with his nose, and waved it back and forth slightly while shaking his head. It clearly meant "no worries" and he clearly still found me amusing, which was a relief. When people don't find my antics amusing, they find them annoying, and I never know which way it's going to break.

Back in my seat, I had swig of the Sweat. It resembled a sports drink, but sports drinks at home are the colour of crayons and salty enough to curl your tongue into a Twizzler. They kind of bully you into thinking you've been refreshed. This was more subtle and did not, despite its promise, taste like the sweat of anything.

In the window reflection, it appeared that Sharky was nodding off. His head lolled forward, his chin bouncing off his collar bone. The way my dad used to get after the fabled seventh brandy. Used to get. Past tense. Former tense. Dead tense.

"Dead." I said it aloud, as if to remind myself. I looked at the mirror surface of the window and said, to Sharky's sleeping reflection, "My dad is dead."

"I'm sorry." His eyes flicked open and he fixed me with a gaze that was no longer detached or amused. In the reflection, his eyes appeared sympathetic.

"Thank you." I was genuinely moved. "Thank you so much."

"Death is a part of life, but that doesn't make it easier for anyone. Even Buddhists grieve, and they believe we're either coming back or going to heaven." He spoke clear English, with a mild accent.

"I bet they do." *Ugh, insightful, River.* "I, ah, had a complicated relationship with my dad."

He raised both eyebrows, a subtle request—or perhaps permission?—for me to continue.

"But, okay, it's hard to explain. I kind of thought I was finished grieving, because I never really think about my father, but here I am, in Japan, to try and get away from his ghost."

Not to be at peace with his passing but to *get away from his ghost.* Sharky's eyes widened; he seemed to like that phrase.

"Relationships are complicated." Sharky fixed me with a serene gaze. "Most of them have an afterlife of some kind."

"Oh, that's good. I'll have to remember that one."

The Limited Express blasted into another tunnel. I turned around and climbed onto my knees, to look over the back of my seat at the man himself, instead of his reflection. I towered over him, which seemed impolite, so I came around and plopped down in the empty seat across the aisle from him.

"I started to have anxiety attacks," I spoke as if talking to myself, which I sort of was. Honestly, half the time I'm talking out loud, a listener is optional. "They began about six weeks after my dad died, but they stopped yesterday when I got on the airplane."

Sharky nodded silently. Across the aisle, a woman in a yellow blouse nibbled at a boiled tentacle treat, her mouth working shamelessly against her apparently resistant snack.

"You are going to Nagano?" he asked.

"Yes!" I smiled "When I started to have these attacks, my sister thought it would be great for me to take a break from my life and go do something interesting, so I'm here..."

Wait, I thought, what if this guy is an immigration agent? A cop? Coming to work at a hostess bar in Japan was probably not exactly legal.

"...to teach English," I finished.

"Why Japan?"

"Because I've been fascinated with Japan ever since I was a little kid. Godzilla movies and anime and all that. I mean, I don't think Japan's all marauding *kaiju* and Hello Kitty, that's all just, like, clichéd nonsense, even if it's cool clichéd nonsense. I have a lot of respect for the culture. I even studied the language a little bit. And it helps that Japan is far away from Canada, in just about every way you can imagine. I need to go through something transformative right now."

"Excellent!" Sharky was delighted. I suppose other foreigners probably answered that question with a grunt and a shrug. "What does it mean, transform...forma...?"

"Transformative. Something that will change my outlook on life and help me become a new person."

"I understand."

"No, I bet you don't." I rested my right foot on my left thigh and turned towards him, my hands held out as if preparing to catch a ball. "I'm changing everything. I'm a chrysalis—no, that's way too hard to translate, your English is great but chrysalis I dunno, but, okay—I got ahead of myself. All my life I wanted to write movies, right? But I never did it. I just sort of wandered through a boring university degree I didn't want and wandered into a boring job I didn't care about, and then my father died and I started having anxiety attacks. My sister said to me, now's the time, go away, go be who you want to be, so I thought, why don't I go away, do something different, start writing, and even change my name? So that's what I did."

I wondered how much of that he understood. Turn the linguistic tables and I would have been lost by the second sentence.

"What is your name?" Sharky asked.

"My name is River Black," I stuck out my hand with

jokey formality. "And you, sir, are the first person in history to meet me."

Sharky did not play along with the handshake, but he did bow gently towards me. I dropped my hand and tilted towards him in return.

"River," he smiled. "In Japanese, river is *kawa*. I think people will call you Kawa-chan, if they are your friends."

"Well, I hope they do!"

"May I call you Kawa-chan?"

"Of course you can. You're my very first friend!"

"Kawa-chan, will you also do private lessons in English?"

Talk about non-sequiturs.

"I'm sorry?

"My daughter," he continued. "Her English school is no good. We would like her to have private lessons. Would you be interested in teaching English to her?"

"Hm. I don't mean to be rude, but I'm nervous about committing to something before I even step off the train. Maybe. What's her name?"

"Sora."

"Sora?" I laughed. The name Sora meant "sky." "Of course I'll teach her! River and Sky…that's fate saying hey, yo, *do* this thing."

The train rocked hard as the tracks veered to the west. My head snapped forward as if my neck were suspended on a spring. Out in the black, a sparkle of dots appeared. Civilization! Clusters of white, pink, and orange stars in a galaxy of streets. A bright-red warning light like a giant dwarf sun floated through space just outside the window. A brief trill of electronic bells filled the car, and a woman's voice spoke a few sentences in Japanese. "We have reached our final destination of Nagano. Please remember all your belongings; *o-wasuremono gozaimasen yo.* Thank you for traveling with Japan Railways."

"Well." I stood. "Thanks for letting me talk. And nice to meet you."

He handed me a business card, which I took in proper style—with both hands. It couldn't decipher much as it was entirely in *kanji*, but I agreed to call within the week.

"Good luck, Kawa-chan." He lowered his head forward slightly in a nod, like the suggestion of a bow. It was the first time anyone had ever called me River, even if it was in a different language. I beamed, bowed slightly and said, as I had been taught, "*Hajimemashite. Dōzo yoroshiku onegaishimasu.*" Nice to meet you, please treat me kindly.

I forgot to ask his name.

My suitcase resembled a nylon sausage, stuffed as it was with one hundred pounds of lifestuff. I wheeled it off the train and onto the platform, following a wooden construction barrier wallpapered with posters. Station staff stood in the warm, moist air, wearing clean white gloves and austere expressions. Voices on loudspeakers made secret announcements beyond my comprehension. A stooped farm woman worked her lower jaw from side to side with the palm of her hand. The worn plastic wheels of my suitcase whirred against the polished stone floor. After twenty hours of travel I should have been an exhausted pile of carbon-based garbage, but everything infused me with light and energy.

I was River now.

The concourse ended in an atrium that looked out into the city night. I could see a jumble of lights: solid white, neon red, roman letters in yellow, *kanji* in blue, reflections in reflections, windows brought out of darkness by electric flicker and buzz. Lights and signs were crowded together, at once cluttered and chaotic but somehow forming a natural pattern. Their own perfect asymmetrical symmetry, or so it seemed to me. A wild luminescent garden.

From behind the bright blocks and blinking towers, a pulse seemed to emerge. As I approached the rail, looking out over Nagano *ekimae*, that pulse seemed liquid. It rose to envelop the rail, the floor, my mind. It was real! I heard the sound of drums and hands clapping in time. There was a melody threaded through it all, punctuated by cheers and shouts as though a vast and adoring audience were heralding my arrival. Celebrating me. Me!

When I reached the rail overlooking the station square, there weren't any roads to see, just a river of men and women that flowed around a large fountain. They wore white and blue summer kimonos that wafted in time with their movements, movements forward but also upward and downward, hundreds of souls as one living thing, their hands rising and falling to meet with a clap in midair.

My pulse quickened until finally it stopped, and my heart burst into my veins, filling my body with heat and wonder.

TELEPHONE CALL TO NAGANO-SHI

Right now, I feel the opposite. I have finished reading the book, and my veins are filled with cold dread.

Kenichi and the Kappa. I knew what these pages contained the moment I saw Reiko's sketch on the cover. To read these words again, though. Words I typed, as close to the spirit of the story as possible. Transcribing them from Daniel's Blessèd Blue Notebook to the computer screen. That's what an editor does; she takes the story and makes it what the author hoped it could be.

Given the low word count and the puffy title font, I half-expected a picture book, but no. There are no illustrations aside from Reiko's *kappa* on the cover. Wide margins and spacing of the text make it seem written for a child. The language is simple enough that it could have been, perhaps, though it's a bit dark for today's kid-lit audience. There is a dead child and a tragic climax. I am suddenly horrified that I allowed little Sora to read it. Most of it, anyway.

There is no title page, no author's biography, no ISBN, no publisher.

Impossible.

As I was reading, I finished a glass of wine. In the fifteen minutes since, I have guzzled the rest of the bottle and stared at my phone. The indicator blinks at me like an accusation. There's a text from Sheila—

ARE YOU SURE YOU'RE OKAY?

—and guilt lands on me like a falling piano. There's a text from Evrard's assistant—

EVRARD WANTS TO KNOW HOW THE DRAFT IS COMING—MEETING WITH PRODUCERS NEXT WEEK!

—and a second guilt-piano plummets out of the heavens to crush me. Then there's a text from Evrard himself—

ARE WE GOING TO TALK ABOUT THIS OR NOT? – E

—because Evvie's the kind of person who adds a signature to his texts, as if they could be coming from someone other than him. The text from Evvie engenders just enough resentment to alleviate some of the guilt. The film reverses; one of the pianos reforms, reconnects to the rope, and rises back out of the frame.

What is this book, Nax? Why did you do this? Why did you go through my word processor and extract this story? Out of all the rambling letters to Sheila and half-finished screenplays and crummy drunken poetry, why this? Such an enormous gesture for…what, exactly?

The wine makes suggestions. Terrible, terrible suggestions. In my front closet, there's an old Rubbermaid tote filled with years of sentimental sediment. Burrowing into it like a drunken gopher, I rummage through epic volumes of letters from Sheila, sepia-toned photographs from disposable cameras, half-finished screenplays and crappy, crappy drunken poetry until I find a yellow scrap of paper. As I exhume it, I also see, in the mess of artifacts I've jumbled around, a pale blue cardboard cover. It's the Blessèd Blue Notebook. The original draft, Daniel's draft, of *Kenichi and the Kappa*. As I stand, blood rushes into my skull and the floor tilts. Deep breath. I'm okay. I return to the chair, drop the last sip of wine directly into the back of my throat, and pick up my phone. This has to be done now, before the nerve disappears and I sit here, drowning into the night.

I dial the number printed on the yellowed scrap. It will be morning in Nagano. The familiar ring, sounding somewhat distant, disconnected from the line. It sounds older, more analogue, as if I am calling into the past. Three rings. An answer.

"*Ee, moshi moshi.*"

I know the voice. It is Misaki, Nax's daughter.

"Misaki-san?"

"*Hai, Misaki de gozaimasu.*" She is polite, unsure who I am. A tremble in her voice.

"Misaki-san, I don't know if you remember me," I say in English. "This is River. River Black."

"Kawa-chan?"

"Yes," I say, not expecting this familiarity, not wanting it, not wanting this to be a reminiscence or a conversation. "River. I called to speak with your father. Is he there?"

There's an odd silence, odd in that it doesn't sound entirely silent. There's a swell in the silence, an expansion, as if air pressure is changing in the room.

"Your father," I repeat. "*Otōsan. Sensei. Irrasshaimasen ka?*"

"*Irrasshaimasen,*" she says, and then there's the unmistakable sound of a sob. "*Irrasshaimasen. Kino shinda.*"

He isn't here.

He died yesterday.

J.J. INTERNATIONAL

Nax is gone.

Nax came for a drink at J.J. International, the bar he owned, at the end of every night. I saw him six nights a week for two years. He sat on a barstool with a scotch and water, a warm laugh, and a story or two. Yet my most vivid memory of Nax is my first one, from my first night at J.J.'s. The train ride, the sharkskin salaryman, the festival at the train station, Nax—a collection of vivid images, and beneath that sun glittering on the water, there is a leviathan that is neither whale nor elder god. It is a breathtaking creature, a hybrid beast of emotion, and it is *huge*.

Overlooking the station square, upon my arrival in Nagano. Blue and white kimonos, dancing figures below forming one stream as steady as the throb of drums and the chant, which sounded something like *so-rei, so-rei*. I could have stood there forever, but a different sound cut through the ruckus, a sound directly aimed at me.

"River!"

Gathered at the base of the escalator was what appeared to be the entire staff of J.J. International. Two young women, teenagers really; a slightly older, slightly disinterested girl with blonde curls; an impossibly tall and even more impossibly handsome boy whose *yukata* barely reached his knees. They all wore the same patterned headbands, *yukata,* and *geta* sandals as the swirling figures who danced and clapped and circled in eddies around the *ekimae.*

"You probably didn't expect such a celebration," said the tall, striking boy as the escalator carried me towards them. His name was Toby. He looked, puzzlingly, like a six-foot-four Asian Aryan in his *yukata*, sandy hair, and blazing—I mean, ferocious, backlit, *blazing*—blue eyes.

"Not really," I replied after a moment's gawk. "This is how they greet me in every country."

Toby threw his head back and laughed. I didn't think people actually threw their heads back when they laughed, but Toby's bounced backward like that of a puppet. A disturbingly sexy puppet.

"But seriously," I continued, "What is this?"

"Binzuru festival." Toby placed a hand on my back as we walked, in a way that seemed more like physical guidance than inappropriate grossness. "Big festival, beautiful dancing, lots of noise, and some fireworks tomorrow. Glorious sound and fury, signifying nothing."

The curly-haired blonde, Babette, mimed a finger down her throat and said, "Baaaaaarf."

"Okay, that's fair," Toby replied. "Binzuru's not about nothing. It has a history."

"I didn't barf at your facts, mate," Babette smirked. "I barfed at you."

Toby either didn't hear Babette or pretended not to. "It's named after Binzuru, a doctor who was one of the followers of the Buddha. It's mostly a commercial venture now, though, supported by business. Another insidious interweaving of spirituality and rampant capitalism. Welcome to Japan, where religion, culture, and business are one and same."

"You mean they didn't arrange this just for me?" I said.

"Sure, they did," Toby replied. "We are each the centre of the universe."

"Baaaaaaarf." This time, all three women simultaneously mimed the finger down the throat.

"I love your name," said the young woman called Nicolle.

"Oh, thanks. I wasn't sure it was going to work."

"What do you mean?" asked the other young woman, Allie.

"It's not my real name."

"I knew it wasn't a real name," said Babette.

"My real name is Helen, if you wanna know." I shrugged. "I probably shouldn't have told you that because now it's going to be super weird at all times. Maybe just call me 'Hey! Dude!'"

They all laughed, except for Babette, who increased her pace. The pulse of drums and the chant of voices, *so-rei, so-rei*, faded into the background.

"Don't be put off by that one." Nicolle dropped her voice and nodded in Babette's direction. "She's difficult."

"She's a bitch," whispered Allie. "Sorry, she's your flatmate."

"Not a problem," I grinned. "Difficult people are my speciality."

"Why River Black?" Toby interrupted.

"My last name is Delaney. It's Irish. It means 'black river.'"

"It's a dark and beautiful name, River Black. Surely you didn't settle on that just because of the literal translation."

"Actually, no, I did not settle on that just because of the literal translation."

I enjoyed the way it hung there, as everyone waited for the explanation.

"She wants to write horror movies!" Nicolle grinned. "Sorry if that was a secret. Nax told me."

"Yeah," I admitted. "It's a pen name. Helen Delaney didn't really have enough cool danger to it."

Toby took the news with great gravity. "Tell me about this."

"Why?"

"That's really unusual, for a girl—"

"Girl?"

"—woman, of course, woman—to even like horror films,

let alone get involved in them."

"What are you talking about? Women directed *Humanoids from the Deep* and *A Night to Dismember* and *Pet Sematary* and *Slumber Party Massacre* and *Buffy the Vampire Slayer* and *Near Dark—Near Dark!* With Lance Hendrickson! Her name's Katherine Bigelow, and she's gonna be huge—"

"Okay!" Toby backed away, eyes wide in mock fear. "Okay!"

"Besides," I continued, "I don't want to write slasher flicks. I want to write about giant radioactive creatures that crush cities underfoot, or werewolves, or demons from the ancient netherworlds."

"That sounds fun," Toby said. "Is there a market for that?"

"Of course there's a market for that!" I said, and just like that, I suddenly believed there was. What did it matter if there was or not? I'd torn myself away from my cherished sister, my mother, forfeited my job, and moved across the planet—all to become River Black, and River Black wrote monster movies. I had to believe there was a market for that.

"Taisei Abinasu," Toby said, pointing to an unremarkable building on the corner.

"What's a Taisei Abinasu?" I asked.

"No one knows. They name their buildings here."

"I know. Apparently I live in Sanyō Heights." I pronounced it incorrectly, as everyone at J.J.'s did, *Sun Yo* instead of *Sahn Yo*. "I'll live with Babette in 301."

"A fine room. A room with a storied history of travellers passing through. Taisei Abinasu, though, is where your indentured servitude begins."

"He's kidding." Nicolle said without looking back.

"I'm not!" he protested. "You're all kept women! You're—"

"Shut up, Toby," Allie sighed.

"Baaaaaaarf," yelled Babette from the front of the pack.

Several windows up on the third floor of Taisei Abinasu appeared to be made of dark-red glass and were emblazoned with the characters "J.J. インターナショナル."

"J.J. International." I smiled sideways at Toby, proud of

my elementary *katakana* comprehension. "Sounds more like an ill-defined import/export business than a watering hole."

"I think Nax was going for a stylish, intercontinental flavour." Toby fished a white-and-blue cigarette package out of the wide sleeve of his summer kimono and flicked a finger decisively against its bottom. A stark white cigarette snapped from the package's open end, which he plucked from the package with his lips. It was an impressive trick, I thought, but he only got away with such a showy display because he was cute.

"Nax wants J.J.'s to be sophisticated," he continued. "A romantic hotspot where beautiful foreign women mingle with salarymen as well as gentlemen of distinction. Just so you know, off the skip? It is not that."

"Ah."

"He dresses it up with semi-rare artworks, and last month he hired a weekly jazz quartet." Toby punctuated the statement with the sandy flick of his lighter. "But there's still permanent grime everywhere and a family of roaches nesting in the telephone."

"You don't even work there, what are you complaining about?" Nicolle thumbed the elevator call button as Babette held one finger near her nose, stared me in the face and whispered, "Baaaaaaarf."

"No one here should complain about anything whatsoever," she said as we piled into the narrow elevator like a clown car in reverse. "Full-on hostess bars, with Japanese staff, are bananas. I've heard rumours. The hostesses can't say no to a drink, and they have to encourage customers to buy them as much booze as possible, to raise the customer's tab. If they have to go to the bathroom and puke to continue, they do. But they only get to use the bathroom once in a night. And customers are allowed to take the girls out on 'dates,' whatever that means."

She must have seen fear in my face.

"Don't worry," she said. "This isn't anything like that. You can drink what you want and pee freely."

We took the elevator to the third floor, Toby puffing away contentedly on his cigarette. We exited into a hallway with a heavy black lacquered door. When opened, a chorus of voices shouted at me in cheery unison. I would learn later they'd shouted "*Irasshaimasse!*" Welcome, customer. A phrase I would go on to utter, in joy and defeat and boredom and excitement but mostly in an automatic monotone, at least sixteen thousand times.

"Hey!" I shouted back, as my pupils dilated into the dim.

My first impression of J.J.'s was one of expectation-based awe. At the time, I didn't notice the room's odd blend of "businesslike jazz bar" and "setting of a 1980s TV drama in which everyone wears shoulder pads." The walls were beige, decorated with oil paintings and tall rectangular mirrors bisected by dark diagonal wooden panels—decorative, mostly useless as mirrors, but quite suitable for jazz and shoulder pads. There were three tables on the left side of the room and one table on the right, at the foot of a mammoth oak-and-glass cabinet filled with what seemed like hundreds of liquor bottles. The bar was on the opposite side of the entrance, and beyond the bar, in the northwest corner of the room, a modest kitchen. J.J.'s was both shoddy and chic, though not intentionally so. It was more like a nice room that had grown long in the tooth.

A gentleman seated at the bar revolved on his stool and smiled at me. He was Japanese, perhaps in his sixties, in an old brown suit. The suit's former crispness was rounded and sunken—well worn, but not worn out. It suited him and seemed to match the surrounding interior design. The man's hair was styled short and square, almost a flat-top, but longer, which give his head a triangular outline. His temples were whitish grey, the colour of cigarette ash.

"Ah," said Nax. "You are...River?" It sounded like ree-bah.

"*Hai*," said a young Japanese woman next to him. "River, this is Nakadaira-sensei."

"Nice...to meet you." His voice was coarse but his cadence measured, with pauses and lingering vowels. He spoke with the rhythm of someone who had once studied English with careful attention, and who still retained a certain refinement.

"I am Nakadaira. Staff...call me Sensei. When I am not here, they call me Nax!" He laughed, entertained by his own nickname and the fact that his foreigners had coined it. I liked him already.

"River *de gozaimasu*," I recited. Toby flashed a goofy grin and gave me an over-enthusiastic two thumbs up motion. "*Hajimemashite. Dozo yoroshiku.*"

"Ah!" Nax smiled. "Very good, very good! You...speak good Japanese..."

My new friends exploded with gleeful laughter. I raised an eyebrow.

"That's just what people say." The explanation came from a boy standing behind the bar.

"What do you mean?" When I turned to him, he quickly looked down at his hands. My gaze followed. His hands were freaky. It looked as though he'd been squeezing handfuls of grapes, the fingers stained purple. His fingertips bulged, bulbous like the tips of drumsticks, and his nails curved up and over the tops of them.

"Oh, ah, you know." He didn't notice my involuntary gawking, because he didn't look up at me. "They're just impressed when someone even tries, so they'll tell you your Japanese is great, even if it's not. You'll hear it a lot."

"You must be Daniel." Daniel, I had heard, was the lone male staff member. Before I could embarrass myself by asking about the hands—and I absolutely would have blurted out a question about the hands, believe me—the woman next to Nax leapt off her stool and bowed.

"My name is Reiko, and I am sort of like your boss! I am the Mama!" Her introduction was like a snippet of a Broadway number, half-sung and half-spoken. Her smile turned her cheeks into golf balls of flesh and created dimples big enough to hide your valuables in.

"So you run the place, Mama-san?" I asked.

"Yes! Thank you for coming to here! I am happy to get to know you." She was almost fawning, yet she didn't seem insincere. "So, tonight, after work, we will go to India for drinks. Will you stay here, and then come to India?"

"Seems like a long way to go for a nightcap. All the way to India?"

"No, India is a bar!" She laughed, and I didn't bother to explain it was just a crummy joke.

Going out for drinks after a dozen hours of recycled air and cold airplane sweat, after crossing the date line and managing a three-hour train ride in the humid remnants of the summer swelter, was not a sensible thing to do. It was also obviously the only thing to do.

"Sure, I'm in."

"Good!" Reiko's grin seemed to bounce her dimples up and down. "Now you have met so many people, but you should meet Masa. He's our best customer. Come with me!"

Reiko guided me to a wooden table, its surface nicked and dented by countless evenings of ice buckets and ashtrays. Allie sat there, her blond bob unnaturally luminous in the dim light. Across from her was Masa, who leaned towards me, propped on his elbows.

"Ah, new staff!" he said. "I am Masa. Where is your country?"

"Canada."

"I see." His face was round, and his hair was shorn almost to the skin. Something about his expression seemed melancholy, despite an oddly mischievous grin.

"One time, I was in Canada. I got out of the airport and was very surprised. I saw caribou prostitutes! They had short skirts and shaved legs. I felt so lucky."

"Masa-san, you're such a weirdo." Allie teased him, then turned to me. "When I met Masa, he told me he felt lucky he came across a brush fire and was able to score barbecued koala bear for dinner. It's a running joke. Caribou hookers, though, that's gold, mate."

"Can I have caribou prostitutes in Canada?" he asked me. I was unsure how to answer this, but I wanted to keep the joke going.

"Sure," I advised, "but if you're going to do that, there's one secret."

Masa leaned forward expectantly.

"Beaver fur condoms."

"Oh my God!" Masa brought his hands together over his face. "I was making a joke! I am so embarrassed."

He was clearly not embarrassed.

"I'm sorry," Masa continued, his face sunken with faux-humiliation. "I am always making bad jokes. Nice to meet you. River is a good name. What's your full name?"

"River Black."

"What?" He gazed at me in animated disbelief. "No, it's like, black river? Black water! One of my favourite songs. *Old black water, keep on rollin', Mississippi moon wontcha keep on shinin'.* It's the Doobie Brothers. I like rock'n'roll. So I can't believe it. You're black river. Oh black river, keep on drinking! What do you want to drink?"

"Ah, what are you having?"

He was having bourbon and water, so that was my first alcoholic beverage in Japan. The first of hundreds. Thousands. To think about it now, it sounds sad and sordid, the amount of alcohol we consumed, but it never felt that way. It was beautiful. It was warmth. It was how we melted into the world. For the next two years, most of my evenings were measured out in flashes and blinks, in the clinks of glass on glass, of ice in tumbler, time skipping forward and back like a surrealist film edit. We sat. We watched. We laughed. We laughed and drank and sang.

Then it all ended, and no one would ever take the Limited Express to J.J. International again.

LIMITED EXPRESS
(HAS GONE)

The Limited Express run, from Tokyo to Nagano, took approximately three hours. The sparkly new Asahi *shinkansen* makes it in half the time. It glides smoothly, comfortably; when you head to the vending machines, you don't feel like you're trying to stay upright on a surfboard. The front of the train looks duck-billed, a design that reduces wind resistance at high speeds. Compared to the rickety Limited Express, the *shinkansen* is an improvement.

But it's also not.

Two Boss Coffee cans and a Crunky bar wrapper litter the seat beside me. The combination of sugar, caffeine, fear, and excitement is like a Mentos mint; my head is a two-litre bottle of soda. My brains feel like they're going to fizz out my ears. It's the opposite of what happened to me twenty years ago. Twenty years ago, when I first came to Nagano, I calmed down. Now, I'm freaking out.

I remember telling Sharky about my father on that old train. I also remember telling him about my anxiety attacks.

The feeling, as Sheila and I referred to it, because *anxiety attack* suggested an elevated heart rate, sweating, panic. I never suffered that. My attacks were like a sensation of burial, of entrapment. Though I've never been clinically diagnosed as claustrophobic, I know what it feels like. I suffer what you might call *sporadic* claustrophobia, and it isn't caused by enclosed spaces, though enclosed spaces don't help. At the height of the attacks, I would rush to stand in the most open outdoor space I could find, but the sensation of being buried alive would remain. The only thing that worked was fleeing to Japan.

Now here I am again, but with the opposite sensation. This time, as the train climbs into the mountains above Tokyo, I fear the feeling will come back.

"If Nakadaira dies, you must come to his funeral," Masa once told me. In response, I simply grunted in the affirmative, as good as a handshake. Proper respect would be paid to the man who gave me a job and an apartment. He often fed me, occasionally clothed me, even loaned me money. Agreeing to this theoretical future show of respect was the right thing to do. It was also the *Japanese* thing to do, and though I wasn't Japanese, it felt natural and decent. Twenty years later, I have lost that sense of connectedness to the culture, to the people, to myself. All that remains, for whatever reason, is this strong sense of obligation. That's not out of character. I always think I have to do everything that's expected of me. Those expectations are astronomical, and of course, they exist only in my head. I argue with myself about it daily. In this case: Masa wouldn't remember that I promised to come to Nax's funeral. Yes, he would. Masa won't care if you don't fly thirteen hours to pay respects to a man you haven't seen in twenty years. Yes, he will. Why do you care. I don't know, I just do. You're an idiot. Shut up, you're an idiot, and you smell.

Sheila thinks I use this overdeveloped sense of duty as an excuse for self-flagellation. A reason to beat myself up. She says it's why I'm still working on a script for Evvie, a man I recently described to someone as, if I recall correctly, "a sentient puddle of bile stuffed into a pock-marked bag of skin."

Sheila has told me repeatedly that I should see a counselor, a psychiatrist, or someone with some kind of professional degree, to talk about my innumerable issues. Naturally, when I bought that breathtakingly expensive last-minute airline ticket, I neglected to tell Sheila. She has no idea that I'm here. Sheila would be wrong in her analysis this time, anyway. Guilt and obligation are only background players. The real reason I'm here is that stupid book. *Kenichi and the Kappa,* the McGuffin that set this whole story in motion. If it wasn't for the book, it's possible I never would have known Nax died. No, I'm here because of the freaky book from the Twilight Zone. If it hadn't weirded me out so badly, I would have read it when it arrived, before Nax died, and I would have called him then. Nax himself might have answered. He would have explained the book. He would have asked how I've been. He would have been blissfully ignorant of the fatal stroke that lurked around the corner, and I would have learned about his death too late for the funeral, if at all. If the book's intention was to get me back to Japan, its timing was impeccable.

The *shinkansen* bursts out of the mountain and onto the valley plain on which Nagano City rests. Something twinkles at the back of my brain, and for a moment I forget the anxiety, the uncertainty, and remember *so-rei, so-rei,* a mantra that seemed held aloft by the pulse of drums in the air.

There is no street festival to celebrate my arrival tonight. Even if there was, the chant and throb would be muffled by the new walls and windows that enclose the once-outdoor atrium. Why do such mundane places—bottoms of escalators, entrances of shopping malls, Starbucks—end up being attached to all the heart-wrenching, life-changing moments? Break-ups, announcements, beginnings, ending, arrivals, departures. Here, at the bottom of this particular escalator, I met a young blonde giant with electric-blue eyes.

I see them all in my mind, as if it were twenty years ago, except now they are ghouls. They are at the bottom of the escalator, eyes sotted with dark, dripping ooze. Instead of waving in wide circles, Toby's arms reach up toward me, ready to render my flesh from my bones. He stumbles forward, jittery as though from an unnatural dimension.

Geography has influenced my fantasy life. Back home he was a zombie, and here he's the gnarly demon kid from *The Ring*. Except much taller. There is, of course, no one at the bottom of the escalator, except for a lone young Japanese boy, squatting against the wall with a cigarette dangling from his pillowy bottom lip. I don't know why my brain invents monsters to rattle me, especially when there are real ghosts all around me. They've taken the form of tight-faced women in business skirts, middle-aged men in wire-framed glasses, doddering grandmothers in a floral-print blouses. They all look so familiar.

I need a smoke.

I haven't bought a package of cigarettes since the '90s. Smoking is like drinking *shōchū* or sleeping until 4 pm, something that only happened during the Nagano years. Yet now, here, the urge pulses through my body with pack-a-day doggedness. There's a *conbini*—convenience store—across the road. I stare at the shelves behind the clerk. Mild Seven Light. Probably the most popular cigarette in the country, at least around here (and leave it to the Japanese to name their product in English that includes consonant blends, Ls and Vs, so difficult to pronounce for Japanese folks. "My-roo-doh Seh-ben Right-oh.")

"Mild Seven Light *onegaishimasu.*"

The cashier shakes his head and gives me a questioning look.

"Uh...my-roo-doh seh-ben right-oh, *onegaishimasu?*"

"*Moshiwake arimasen.*" He shakes his head again. "*Arimasen yo.*"

They don't have Mild Sevens. It's like if a Tim Hortons stopped selling coffee—if a *conbini* doesn't carry them, it means they don't make them anymore. The station, the cigarettes, these should be insignificant changes, but instead they throw me, rob me of much-needed comfort.

My suitcase drags behind me, noisy on the cobblestone walkway; the rumbling smooths out as I reach the asphalt of the road beyond. The streetscape beside Nagano Station appears unchanged. There are small cafés, recognizable from the uniformly-sized white plastic signs placed out front. There's a hotel on my right, marked by a placard that is modest to the point of invisibility. Up ahead, on the corner, just past the parking garage, I see it.

Taisei Abinasu.

It stops me in my tracks. It is exactly the same, except J.J. International's red-tinted windows are gone. J.J.'s is gone. Now there is only Taisei Abinasu, another futuristic four-story commercial building, clad in white squares that look like spacecraft ceramic. At home it would be an unusual structure. Here, unremarkable.

J.J.'s closed years ago, but being here, seeing black glass instead of red, has a finality to it. Like seeing someone's gravestone for the first time. I'm a bit shocked when a valve turns in my chest, tightening it, forcing tears into the corners of my eyes at the realization that I will never set foot in J.J.'s again. Yet...sure, I could have come back to visit Nagano before today. In fact, I could have even come back while J.J.'s was still open. Would it have made a difference? Would 'one more time' have been better, or would it be like taking a tour of your old summer camp after it had decayed into collapsed roofs and an overgrown shuffleboard court?

People, though, aren't summer camps. It would have been good to see Nax once more before he died. He didn't age a day after I left, because he lived entirely in photos and memory: wrinkles around his eyelids, a sleepy expression that disappeared with the sudden movement of his features. The rest of his face brought his eyes to life, and he always seemed so wise, even when he was being insufferable. Nax lived to be eighty-eight, but to me, he did it in the body of a 70-year-old.

The tears peek out from behind my eyes, but they don't completely emerge. I force them out with the heel of my palm, wipe them on my skirt, and walk. I reach Nagano *o-dōri,* the wide avenue that bisects what is, essentially, a smallish city. Has anything changed on this street? The Tokyu and Cher Cher department stores still dominate the nearest block. As I turn in the opposite direction, towards my hotel, memories sprout unexpectedly from the cracks in my brain. Where tiny roads intersect with the avenue, pedestrians wait for the light to turn green despite the utter absence of traffic. The public toilets are still there. Hotels and office buildings. Cars on the "wrong" side of the expansive road. The creek that runs through the centre of town.

Many Nagano streets are lined with canals, drainage ditches called *dobugawa,* the sources of which I presume are mountain streams or rain run-off from higher elevations. The one in front of me is more of a little river. It flows towards me, between houses and parking lots, and where it meets the avenue, it ducks into a culvert under the road. Above the entrance to the culvert, the regular sidewalk has been replaced by a promenade of red stone. In the centre of it stands a *kawaii* little statue of a *kappa,* about two feet high, carved from green stone. Its base is a round, squat pedestal. Its feet are flat, its legs squat. Its arms are leveled over its chest, one hand over a breast, the other below the other breast, like a woman caught stepping out of the shower. It has a tiny, conical human penis. Its head is oversized, like a doll's; a downward-pointed beak, wide eyes, pink circles on its cheeks, large, teacup-handle muppet ears, and dark-green hair that grows downward from the concavity in its skull. Its hair looks like some kind of water flower has flopped onto its head. It's cute. It's wrong. *Kappa* aren't cute.

"Kappa not cute."

It's a strangled sound, like someone who's swallowed a bowl of something glutinous, like maybe a cup of those tapioca balls you get in bubble tea. Did that statue just talk to me? Did—no. I see it now.

It's not the statue.

A knotted, dripping finger raises up from the canal behind the statue, pointing, first at me, and then at the cutesy green sculpture.

"Not *kappa*," it hisses. "Not *kappa*. THIS IS *KAPPA*."

Before the thing can show itself, I close my eyes. "Jesus. Stop it, River."

There is just a stupid cutesy statue here. There was never anything but. Still, even though I loosen the death grip on my suitcase handle, I pick up my pace. I look straight ahead, the way I do when I'm passing a group of neighbourhood men gathered on someone's stoop. I certainly do not look back to see if there are, in fact, wet handprints on the otherwise dry red stone.

My mother thinks I have an over-active imagination. Sheila has described my mind as a "perplexing clusterfuck of competing realities." They're both right. Some of my conjurings are intentional, but some of them are projected straight out of my subconscious, like someone snuck into the theatre and fired up the projector without permission. My id is like a dark Disney or, if we're going to be geographically relevant here, a darker Studio Ghibli. Being emotionally overwhelmed and jet-lagged probably isn't helping.

Left, down Shōwa *o-dōri*. The Royal Host, a sort of Japanese Denny's, hovers over the corner like a flying saucer that sells breakfast. A block farther, I look for the *yakiniku* restaurant where the smoke of barbecuing meat would fill our nostrils, settle on our clothes, permeate our hair. It's no longer there. I turn onto streets which may or may not have names. Unnamed streets are common here, but we were young and drunk and couldn't read the street signs anyhow, so who knows. We used landmarks for reference instead, arrogantly reinventing the local geography like entitled settlers. Sanyō Street after Sanyō Heights, Zenkōji Street after the temple, and India Street, after, well, India. India Street, and the Hotel New Yama, is my destination.

The lobby of the Hotel New Yama is the size of a small bedroom, all stark white paint and glossy dark brick. At the front desk, a gentleman with the air of a formal English butler nods and smiles faintly as I stumble through the transaction in a half-remembered language. He passes me a key attached to an eight-inch baton of opaque purple plastic, *Hotel New Yama* stamped in white on one side. One is to return this key to the desk every time one leaves the hotel. I will forget to do so exactly 100% of the time.

The doorframe of my fourth-floor room is smaller than usual—business-hotel-sized. Before I even open the door I know that, like all Japanese business hotels, the rooms will have beige walls and dark wood furniture. There will be a small window, hidden by a sliding rice-paper panel, that looks out onto nothing. There will be a bathroom right near the entrance, compact enough that I'll feel my knees pressing against my earlobes when I pee. There will be *just enough* room for me to walk past the bed to the desk, fitted against the far wall, as well as a modestly-sized television.

The door swings open and lo, it is so, except somehow even smaller than imagined. My brain begins to sag in the middle. Jet lag has mushed it until it feels like the flattened, fur-matted pillow your dog sleeps on. There is one foolproof way to overcome the westbound jet lag: go drinking until you can't stand another drop, go to bed, weather the hangover, and in the morning, presto, you're on Japan time. It always worked for twentysomething River. Fortysomething River, however, can't do that without risk of heart failure. I opt to fill a plastic glass with tap water and sit at the desk, knees actually touching the wall underneath. I pull over a pad of Hotel New Yama stationary and a pen. I open my laptop and proceed to ignore it, tapping the pen against my leg instead.

Tap. Tap tap. I fumble with laptop cords, plug it in, bathe the room in the bluewhite glow. I have two weeks to finish this blood-soaked disaster called *Pinned IV,* but my head feels mulched. I stare at the desktop screen until the icons burn into my retinas.

My window looks out onto India Street. I see a row of five or six bicycles in front of a now-shuttered shop and wonder if the bikes are locked up.

SANYŌ HEIGHTS

The first night, Allie and Nicolle gifted me a stolen bike.

We converged on India already drunk and rowdy; to Master-san, the owner and bartender, we must have appeared like a churning Katamari ball of *gaijin* and liquor, increasing in size and subsuming everything in our path. For years he put up with us, half-wasted from customers buying us drinks, full drunk by the time the sun came screaming out of the sky towards us at seven or eight am. He never complained and never asked us to go home. Maybe our bar tab put his kids through college or something.

When we poured ourselves out the door that first night, it was after sunrise; Allie and Nicolle headed straight for a row of bicycles, found an unlocked one, and wheeled it over to me with a grin.

"You'll need one of these, yeah?" Allie slurred. "This one looks gold."

"That seems like a bad idea," I replied.

"Eh, no one here bothers to lock their bikes." Nicolle flailed her hand around, a drunken facsimile of a dismissive wave.

"It's okay," Toby whispered in my ear from behind me. "I don't think it's cool either. This is how *gaijin* get a bad reputation. Take it. Save up, buy your own bike, put this one back where they found it, and the balance of karma will be restored."

"Okay," I said. "Hey, imagine just how much karma will be out of whack when thousands of foreigners show up for the Olympics. Bike lock futures are going to skyrocket."

"Let's start a manufacturing business! It's an untapped market! It's an un! tapped! market!" As I watched, Toby skipped to the top of the street, continuing to shout. Passersby on their way to work deftly stepped out of his way.

By the time Toby, Reiko, and I reached Sanyō Heights (Nax had dropped off my luggage hours ago) the giddiness had subsided. My head swirled with liquor and sunlight. I began talking, Reiko encouraging my rambling with enthusiastic interjections. Toby barely spoke, charmingly listening to me in near silence, except to poke and prod, to flush extra details out of the bushes. In this light, in this liquor, he was admittedly damned fine, six foot four if he was an inch, clarity in his eyes that I simply couldn't muster at this time of day, in this kind of drunk. I watched him in my peripheral as we passed vending machines and the narrow, open storm ditches, gullies like canals that hugged each curve of the road. I wouldn't learn the word for them until the following year.

"So you're just a J.J.'s regular, then, are you?" I asked as we reached the stairs at Sanyō Heights.

"A J.J.'s rat, that's me," he smiled. "I have a gig up in Iizuna. Construction. We're building a set of three log cabins. They call them 'Canada Style.'"

"I don't know a single Canadian who lives in a log cabin." I smiled at him, and he returned it with a strange little bow, one hand cupping the other fist.

"Good night, River. *Namaste*."

"*Namaste*?"

"It means, I recognize the divine within you."

"I'll take your word for it." Using yoga language to say

good night was intriguingly cheesy. Why use the most obvious signifier of fake spirituality available?

Reiko took me up the stairs and along the exterior corridor. There was another apartment building across the open courtyard, so close to Sanyō that it was like the structures were hugging. Apartment 301 lay at the end of the walkway. Babette had not come out with us, and was likely asleep, so we kept our voices low as Reiko produced a long, narrow key and let me into the apartment.

"So, one thing." Reiko looked at me apologetically. "You might see cockroaches sometimes."

After tonight, with the warm glow of the alcohol and new friendship, I welcomed the critters as happily as I welcomed anything else. King Ghidorah himself could come screaming down from Iiyama spitting gravity beams, and I'd ask him in for tea.

This warm glow did not survive. It lit out for the territories by the time I woke on the *tatami*-mat floor at 1:48 pm. I puked my spleen out several minutes later, all over the shower-room floor. I hosed down the room and returned to bed, feeling as though a spike had been driven between my eyes, through my pillow, and into the floor. Later, Allie brought me soup and I cried a little because I couldn't eat it.

When the hangover subsided, however, the glow returned, sparked by the warmth of the bright August sunlight that flooded my room. *My* room. Not a room in my parents' house.

"Babette!" I pushed myself off the futon. "I have a room!"

No response came.

"Should I have a party to celebrate my room?" I asked. Again, no response.

"I'm gonna have a party to celebrate my room," I told my room.

An hour later my futon lay folded in one corner with a small pillow, filled with soba husks instead of foam or feathers, set on top. A breeze swished through the open balcony door. I had managed to vomit on my skirt and top, so I washed them and some underwear in our wee plastic washing machine, the laundry equivalent of an EZ-Bake oven. Wet stockings and underpants dangled on a plastic rack, hung like a mute wind chime, the clothes secured by built-in clothes pegs. I could hear the occasional hum and buzz of crickets; I was told that at summer's height, the swell of cicadas and crickets was deafening here, a few blocks from the hills that lead up to Zenkōji temple.

The door opened and Babette stepped through into the upheaval. Our apartment had a small foyer, with bathroom and shower to the right and modestly sized kitchen to the left. Ahead, on both sides, were the two bedrooms, each with cardboard *shoji* doors. No wall separated the rooms from one another, just another, bigger cardboard sliding door. I had slid these *shoji* open to let the breeze freshen up the place.

Babette had a decidedly minimalist approach to interior design. Her room held only a futon, a small chest of drawers, a lamp, a fan, and a kerosene heater set upon the slightly frayed but otherwise immaculate *tatami*. My room, on the other hand, looked as though Godzilla had stomped Tokyo and his mother had come through trying to tidy up the mess behind him. It was as though each of Babette's five previous roommates had left their entire lives behind in 301. One pile of detritus, excavated from the back of the closet, contained three Australian westerns (in paperback), an empty bra package, a tiny faux-fur coat, an envelope of photographs of a mountain in New Zealand, not one but *two* broken hair dryers, an empty lipstick tube, a ripped blue blazer in a size 18, an empty plastic pail of unknown origin, three pairs of cheap slacks, a ratty brown teddy bear, several unlabelled VHS tapes, and a copy of Crowded House's *Greatest Hits* on CD.

"Please don't do that." Babette marched into her room and started to slide the doors closed in a mild, and I thought unnecessary, huff.

"I'm just letting some air flow through," I said. "It smells like if an armpit had halitosis."

Babette scowled and slammed the *shoji* shut. Maybe she had some strange personal space issue—I don't have any personal space issues, so such issues never made sense to me. I came around to her doorway. I was the picture of domesticity in jeans, untucked workshirt, tank top, and a strip of an old beach towel, also found in the closet, tied around my head to keep my hair back.

Babette settled into a cross-legged position on her futon. All was pristine around her, save for the motes of dust that had poured into her airspace from when I shook out and ripped up the aforementioned beach towel.

"I need a computer." I pushed up the sleeves of my workshirt. Babette didn't respond. "Do you have any idea where I can buy a computer? I mean, they have personal computers here, don't they?"

Babette raised her head and gave me an inscrutable glare.

"Yes." Her New Zealand accent turned the ess into an iss, "Yiss." For a moment I thought that was the end of her reply, but then she turned her attention to the chest of drawers, looking through them while she spoke. "They're not popular here like they are at home, though. And it'll all be in Japanese. You should just pick up a *wāpuro*."

"A whatchanow?"

Babette rolled her eyes. "A word processor. It'll be a computer that does nothing else but word processing. You can probably pick one up at the Hard Off."

"The *whatchanow?*"

"Hard Off. It's a second-hand electronics shop. Please don't make the joke you're about to make."

"Am I that obvious?"

"Yiss."

I sat down in the doorway, back against the wooden pillar that constituted a doorjamb.

"What's going on with you?" I asked.

"I don't understand the question."

"Oh, you know. I'm new. I'm getting to know people. I have been told things about you, but nothing *real,* you know? Why are you in Japan?"

"To make money."

"Ah. Good idea. Yen is *really* high right now."

"Yiss."

Silence. I removed the makeshift bandana, twisted it around in my hands.

"What were your other roommates like?"

"Quiet."

"Ah, well, too bad for you, then. Your luck was eventually going to run out."

"I guess." *Giss.*

"You've been on staff the longest. How do you like the current line-up?"

Babette's shoulders slumped. I was already wearing her down. She stopped pretending to sort underwear and sat facing me.

"They're cliquey bitches, right?" Babette scowled. "Nicolle and Allie and Reiko. But that's fine. I'm used to it."

I nodded as if in agreement, though I wasn't in agreement at all. "What about the boy?"

"Daniel?" Babette's scowl softened. "He's a mess."

"A miss," I mimicked.

"A mess," she agreed, either ignoring or not noting the mimicry. "Nicest, politest, kindest boy you'll ever meet, but he's a wreck. Didn't you notice?"

"He didn't say much, but he seems pretty quiet. And there's something up with his hands. They're...unusual."

"It's because of a heart condition," she replied. "He's one fragile lad. On top of that he can barely speak, he's nervous about everything, and he's monumentally claustrophobic. He can't even go into the snack closet."

"What kind of heart condition?"

"I don't know. Daniel doesn't open up much. He acts like

a puppy that's been whipped about some. Someone asked him once what on earth made him come here if he was so sick. He told 'em yeah, I kind of hate it here, but I hated it in America, too, so what's the difference."

"Cheery."

"He's a larf," she agreed. "But I like him twice as much as the others. Or Tobias."

I must have grinned because Babette looked suddenly stricken.

"Oh, fuck, not you too."

"Well, he's cute."

"Ugh. Let me make the joke I asked you not to make earlier. Tobias Handler gives me a hard off."

"Nice one."

"Yeah, well."

"He is pretty—"

"Stupid. Pretty stupid. That half-assed philosophical shit he comes up with. I don't trust him, and you shouldn't either."

"Oh, you have some inside information?"

"No. I just get an immensely fake vibe from him. It's not just me. My boyfriend sees it too."

"You have a boyfriend? What's his name?"

"Shinji."

"A local! You're dating a local!"

Babette looked as though she was about to spit poison at me like a cobra. "Why is that important? Are you bloody racist, mate? What the hell."

"No!" I was mortified by how she took it. "No, of course not. I just mean, well, I was told we wouldn't get to know too many *Nihonjin* outside of the customers."

"He wasn't a bloody customer. He's never been to J.J.'s."

"All right, all right. Sorry, that's totally not what I meant anyway. How'd you meet him?"

Babette's tension slacked a little. She simultaneously seemed to want to tell me all about him and yet also throw me off the balcony.

"I met him at a host bar," she replied. "He was a host for a while."

"They have hosts here? I thought it was just hostesses. That hostessing was a full-on retrograde sexist tradition."

"Oh, don't worry, it is."

"So what's he like?"

"Shinji? Comes across as a bit aloof, but he's just quiet. He's a softie."

"Kind of like you."

"Yeah, well, there's a reason I'm seeing him, and maybe that's it."

"Hey, can I make a deal with you?" I asked.

"What?"

"Well, if you help me throw away three years' worth of Australian relics and remainders, I promise I won't let a soul into your room during the party."

Babette's facial muscles drooped.

"You're having a party?"

"Yeah! I have a room! It's my first room, and I want to celebrate!"

Babette smirked at me, but beneath the smirk was the kernel of an actual grin.

LEPIDOPTERA

Tap tap. Dot. Line. Squiggly line. Sketch sketch sketch. A face, mouth yawning, fangs piercing the air between me and the page. Mega-Mamushi, the monster snake *kaiju* I invented in Nagano. A leviathan-level snake monster wasn't entirely original, but back then, it seemed brilliant. I haven't drawn her in years. She's not looking so good these days; her eyes aren't the same size, giving her the appearance of a frog looking through a magnifying glass. I used to be a better doodler.

My father used to draw. In fact, he was a fantastic artist. He kept some of his work in a drawer, a drawer for special things. Sometimes, it's hard not to suppose, he must have opened that drawer, taken out the items, laid them on the bed, and glanced them over with either pride or, much more likely, regret and bitterness, as those emotions were more his speed. Three excellent pencil sketches of world leaders (Churchill, JFK, Gandhi). Two first-place medals for high-school track and field. A book of Yeats' poetry, the kind that fits in your palm, not that he needed the text, as he'd committed many of them to memory. Things treasured, a life left unpursued.

I can remember, very clearly, the first time I recognized that my father might be some kind of artistic savant. We were in the yard, in Toronto, at the house Sheila and I grew up in by Yonge and Eglinton, an old Victorian two-and-a-half story that today would fetch far north of a million dollars but, in 1975, was no more impressive than the next near-identical home. I was playing with plasticine at the picnic table, where we used to sit in the summer, eating butter-dripping corn on the cob speared on either end by plastic corn holders also in the shape of corn. We'd joke that we should drink milk out of cups shaped like udders. Yellowjackets darted under our elbows to get themselves some of the barbecue action. My father in one of those classic '70s lawn chairs with the plastic weave. It was the near-beginning of my monster days; no full-blown obsession yet, but, as with most kids, I'd begun to learn the canon: Dracula, the Mummy, the Wolfman, and, of course, Frankenstein (sorry, horror nerds, I meant to say "the Monster"). I had fashioned a lumpy, poorly-proportioned body, but the head—the head was impossible. I marched over to my father with a lump of the vaguely oily material balled between my palms and presented him with the raw materials.

"Daddy, can you make me a Frankenstein head?"

I didn't know my father was an artist, I just knew he was Daddy, so if anyone could do it, he could. And he did. He pinched the lump between his fingers, forming the classic forehead-heavy Monster, and then fished a toothpick out of his breast pocket. He began to nick and carve, etching lines of hair, edges of ears, ridges of eyes. When he handed it back, my breath hitched in my chest. It was beautiful. It was the Monster. It was perfect. I wish it had been Play-Doh instead of plasticene. I would have let it dry and kept it forever.

Most of my memories of my dad are not this sweet.

I give up on Mega-Mamushi and awaken the laptop with a swish of one finger.

By now, the screenplay for *Pinned IV* should be 87 pages of creeping dread. 87 pages of misogynistic mutilation, punctuated by dark quips from our "hero," the murderous

Leo Pardpeti. Why 87 pages? That's "finished." 87 pages is 87 minutes, and running time means more to Evrard Frederich than plot or character development. Too long and it's "a fucking art film." Too short and it's "a fucking short film." His window is precisely 85 – 90 minutes. I usually shoot for 87 pages. This is not 87 pages. It's about 15.

Scene: Young woman's too-cool, self-consciously edgy horror blog and meagre screenwriting credits catch attention of notorious German filmmaker.

Montage: German is less insane than public image suggests; whirlwind romance begins.

Shot: Woman at computer, aglow in its blue light, working on her first screenplay for German.

Cut to: Oh hey wait German is absolutely bonkers after all. Woman looks lost, probably a litre of wine deep, as she works on her fourth screenplay. Please note the file on the desktop titled "P4 Final." It's actually 87 pages of the phrase "All work and no play makes Jack a dull boy." She emails this to the German one day, and his text response is "You're not funny—e."

Pinned IV, the fourth film in the reasonably popular *Pinned* series. *Pinned* was my attempt at smart, subversive horror. Under Evvie's directorial hand, it has curdled into repugnant swill. Repugnant swill with a cult following. I should own this, as Tommy Wiseau owns *The Room*. Pretend it came out exactly as I intended and enjoy the admiration. Except I can't. The *Pinned* series is Grand Guignol blood-splash goresport torture-porn that my bullying ex-boyfriend browbeat me into writing. With every fanboy at HorrorCon celebrating what I consider to be my artistic nadir, my soul dies a little.

Years ago, I told Toby there was a market for monster movies. It wasn't exactly true. I rhymed off female writers and directors in the genre, but I had to dig pretty deep. Jesus, I think I named *A Night To Dismember* as an example. *Nobody's* seen that.

Today, there are so many hip, talented women I call contemporaries, from Jennifer Kent to the Soska Sisters, but as much as I love and admire them, they kill my soul a little, too. They direct their own movies. They have directorial talent, production skills, cinematographers, professional actors, interest from studios or the financing to shoot independent.

I have a laptop, three moderately successful productions that I loathe, and crippling self-doubt.

Ugh. *Pinned.*

The original *Pinned* is almost a defensible film. It centres on Leo Pardpeti, played by Estonian actor Meelis Kuusk. I have nothing bad to say about Meelis Kuusk. He is gold, as Allie used to say. He plays Pardpeti as a skittish, awkward, koogly-eyed near-silent creep who is clearly a serial killer from frame one. He lives in former funeral home because, well, serial killer. No one likes him because he gives them the willies. He even has a willie-giving hobby—pinning butterflies. Apologies to those who pin butterflies, but if you're not lepidopterist, you're a creepo. Says the lady who writes about murder all day.

Anyway, Pardpeti is visited by a realtor. When she inevitably gets creeped out and flees, she is struck by a car. Pardpeti carries the injured woman back to his house. Just as we think he's going to care for her, maybe nurse her back to health, he drives an enormous metal spike through her abdomen and "pins" her to the wall. It's sloppy and gruesome and darkly hilarious. He starts trying to pose her like a butterfly—while she's still alive—and she rips at the new pins. Eventually she slumps forward and falls to the floor, dead. He tries to pose her on the floor but can't drive the "pins" into the concrete. Realizing it hasn't worked out as planned, Pardpeti freaks out, screaming and moaning and smashing his own face against the wall. I'll give Evvie and Meelis credit, it's a super distressing scene. Evvie may not know how to light a set or mic a set or shoot a set or even build a stupid set, but he has his moments when it comes to actors. I think it's because he scares them, so the pain you see onscreen is real.

So. Pardpeti is secretly in "love" with Dr. Dorothy, his general practitioner. This is established via an over-abundance of unsettling psycho-male-gaze camera shots. Evvie loves those lingering freakshow voyeur moments, thinks they give the horrorboys a chub. I shudder to think they do, even though I know, sometimes, they do.

So, yadda yadda yadda, murder murder murder, finally he kidnaps the doctor, but not to kill her. He keeps her in a guest room and tells her he wants her to help him with his "project." He starts to show her all the butterflies and bugs, enthusing how beautiful they are—and credit again to Meelis, God bless him, he's so good as Pardpeti, it's as memorable as Deiter Laser in *Human Centipede,* as shitty as that film was.

Anyway, she gets freaked, on account of the insect pinning and the abducting, and breaks free. She bursts through a door and into his "Museum of Beauty." In the funeral-home parlours, he has arranged a display of corpses—rotting, slumping off their pins, scarred, faces frozen in fear. It's the film's big reveal, and it's a horrific nightmare sequence. In spite of cheap design and random camera angle choices, it's effective.

Pardpeti catches Dr. Dorothy, he tells her she's the most beautiful of all, and pins her up. He looks around the room at his other "artworks" and has a bleak epiphany: that it wasn't her physical beauty that he loved, that he can't make her the crown jewel of the collection, that she will simply rot and stink like all the others. He grows despondent and has another meltdown. Suddenly, Dr. Dorothy's eyes snap open and she gulps at the air like a drowning woman surfacing. She peels herself off the wall, pulls the spike out of her stomach, and buries it in Pardpeti's throat.

Except no, that's not what happens. That's what happened in my original script. In the finished film, after he affixes her to the wall, he uses scotch tape to pull her lips upward into a smile. He steps back, as if admiring a pleasant Matisse, and says "The crown jewel of my collection." Fade on him pumping embalming fluid into her or something stupid that Evvie came up with.

"But if she dies, it's not the movie I wrote!" I screamed in a Tallinn hotel room, three days before production. "I don't *want* another film where the bad guy lives. I want him to die with the realization that he was wrong!"

"If he dies, the realization is, no sequel!" Evvie shouted, his hands flapping about his face. "How can we make *Pinned II?*"

"I don't give a damn about a sequel, Evvie. I didn't write this to showcase eviscerated Estonian extras. It's disgusting and it's scary and it's fun, but in the end, it's gotta be about something, whether it's him getting his, or him understanding the difference between—"

"I am the director!" Arms pointing in six different directions at once, his madman approach, which surely he knew wouldn't work on me. "I'm not goddamned Tom Six. *Pinned II* cannot be about a fan of the first *Pinned* movie or some such meta fuckery. No! He lives to kill again, we live to make another movie. *Verstehst du?*"

It wasn't the fake fury or the nearly convulsive hand gestures that punctured and deflated me like one of Pardpeti's pins. It was the all-too-sane look in his eyes. The eyes of a man looking through a woman at the pile of money behind her. My body withered and I sat on the corner of the bed. He took that as permission. Not that he needed it, contractually speaking.

What does a psychotic monster to do next, if there's no redemption or repercussion? Well, he becomes increasingly ridiculous. He decides to turn on tourists, as in *Pinned II,* cashing in on *Hostel* several years too late. In *Pinned III,* he has a showdown with a second psycho who doesn't appreciate the "artistry" of what he does, but simply kills for killing's sake. It's serial murderer as staid establishment stand-in, chiding the surly, reckless, unnecessarily butcher-y young upstart.

It really is a very stupid movie.

Pinned IV? Oh, where to begin. Evvie wants Pardpeti to buy a motor home and take his museum of mayhem on the road for the pleasure of rich maniacs around Europe. This may be Evvie's worst idea of all and a continuity nightmare for the franchise itself, given that Pardpeti's house and collection were burned to the ground at the end of *Pinned III.*

Everything I have written, deleted, and written again is abysmal. *Pinned IV* is not my *Troll 2,* so inept it's hilarious. It's not my *Evil Dead 2,* playing off tropes and subverting the genre. It's just my *Jason X. Friday the 13th* in space. It's dumb, it's uninventive, it's a cash grab. Were Roger Ebert alive to read my script attempts, he would say they suck on so many levels, and I would concur.

I'm tired of writing about women captured and killed, tortured and maimed, for the pleasure and profit of my ex-boyfriend. I'm super relieved that Evvie and I are on the outs, to be honest, because he's not beside me, pressuring me to see treatments. Honestly, as a boyfriend, he was better than you would expect. There was a wild, anything-goes-and-any-thing-can-happen feeling, dating a German filmmaker who spends his days on eastern-European movie sets finding inexpensive new ways to spill fake blood. In the bedroom he was far less of an animal than he appears in interviews, which, believe me, counts as a good thing. But, God, professionally, what an asshole. I don't have a contract anymore, but I need the money. Vancouver is expensive, even in a condo rental, even one with a deep discount thanks to one of Sheila's law clients. The *Fangoria* notoriety and HorrorCon appearances, the guest-authoring graphic-novel segments and the cameo in the James Wan movie, they're all based on my atrocious work for Evvie. I don't even have an agent. Evvie talked me out of it.

Besides, I said I'd write it, so I have to write it.

I'm a horror writer. The term "horror" conjures up different things for different people because it *is* different things.

It's confronting your darkest fears. It's expressing your wildest imaginings. It's expressing the fears of the times we live in through allegory and metaphor. *The Brood* is about Cronenberg's divorce and custody battle. *Eraserhead*'s about fatherhood (or being scared of it). *The Shining*'s about, well, I dunno, according to a documentary I saw it's about a whole bunch of completely ridiculous things at once. But that's the point—everyone in the documentary was adamant that they knew what *The Shining* was about.

Horror movies can be about viscera and violence for their own sake, true, but the more that's the case, the less I care. But even those movies have impact. I once saw a movie where the heroine finds a dead body in a bathtub. As gore goes, it was tame, but it was the detail that stuck with me. I guess the bathroom was cold, because there was a brownish-red slush on the surface of the water. The body's head was lolling backward, the limbs and torso fat with bloat, flesh mottled like chicken skin, blackened, yet almost translucent in places. Sheets of skin stuck to the sides of the tub. It was gross, but that was the point. I still think about that image. I can almost smell the unholy stink of death. I can't remember the name of the undoubtedly terrible movie, but the image still horrifies me. Every few years, I have nightmares about it. There's a power in that, isn't there?

When I came to Japan in the '90s, I tried to write my first *kaiju* movie. *Kaiju*: monsters like Godzilla, Rodan, or those beasts in *Pacific Rim*. My *kaiju* was Mega-Mamushi, the Godzilla of snakes. She was a Japanese pit viper that mutated after a tsunami-provoked nuclear accident unleashed her from the deep. I never tried to make that film. I never finished the screenplay. She could have been my Cloverfield, my tribute to Toho Studios. Instead, she's a memory that I've drawn to resemble a lopsided amphibian.

I'm almost fifty. There are so many women kicking ass in this industry, writing, producing, and directing films. They are not almost fifty; if they are, they didn't start their careers recently. I wouldn't know where to begin. So I type out garbage words for a garbage person named Evrard Frederich. The thought makes me want a drink. I close the laptop, lock the door, and march for the elevator before I can change my mind.

No need to go farther than next door. We called this India Street for a reason.

On the outside, India is the same shaggy dog it always was. An immovable curio festooned with smaller curios. Neon beer displays, wooden shutters, posters, an old wagon wheel, and the familiar brownish-yellow sign promising Bourbon and Eats. It also promises Every Spirits, whatever they are, and features, puzzlingly, a likeness of Betty Boop.

When I pull the door open and slowly crane my neck inside, I'm shocked to see that the interior is also unchanged.

Some watering holes in Nagano sport sophisticated but bland interiors, the design equivalent of smooth jazz: black tables and red walls, clean mirrors and shiny chrome, leather seats and karaoke screens assaulting you with their cartoonish fractal images. India looks like art hippies fashioned a hovel out of vinyl records and dusty tchotchkes. And it appears that no one has touched one single bauble since I left. I know memory is tricky, but I swear they're all here. The beer steins painted with floral designs. Bottles of Early Times whiskey with Japanese names scrawled vertically down the label in black magic marker. The rough wooden walls like pages of scrapbook—not a fussy modern "scrapbooking" scrapbook, but an old-fashioned messed-up things-pasted-every-which-way scrapbook. Coke trays and East Indian plates and a Marker's Mark mirror and graffiti everywhere, initials and names and salutations from drinkers past. A Johnnie Walker statuette still hangs from the ceiling, doffing his hat and clutching his cane as if it were a wizard's staff. Toby called him the "mage of the blended malt."

The knick-knacks, decorative hangings, graffiti, the rows of books and piles of vinyl records that lilt forward and away, always threatening to topple—all here, as if by magic. Surely only magic could have held it all together this long. Magic and the ever-busy hands of Master-san, who spent his evenings moving back and forth, somewhere between a distracted scurry and a dead run, picking up ashtrays, dropping down drinks, whipping himself into a lather of spilled bourbon and pieces of yolk from his famously greasy egg sandwiches.

"Tamatsuki-san *wa...?*" I ask the youngish woman behind the bar, using Master-san's real name. I don't directly ask where he is; what I say is more like saying "Hey, so, Mr. Tamatsuki?" and raising my hands in an exaggerated shrug. If I ask directly and it turns out Master-san is sick or deceased, this young woman might collapse into paroxysms of social mortification. Well, no, but she'd be plenty uncomfortable trying to find the balance between truth, privacy, and polite consideration.

"Not here," is all she says, which was an encouraging sign that he's still with us.

"*Hai.*" I say. "*Mizuwari kudasai.*" Whiskey and water, please. When in Rome, drink like a Japanese businessman. I sit at the bar, on a rickety stool made of wood and prayers. I read the mashed, frayed spines on the record sleeves piled two feet high beside me. So many Allman Brothers records. It's shocking that nothing has changed in so long. Then again, maybe *everything* has changed? How could I be sure that the knick-knacks and coasters and posters and records are the exact same ones that were here in 1996? Maybe Master-san rotates the tchotchkes on a semi-annual basis. With the exception of Johnnie Walker, of course. He was the *tchotchke première*, at least in our books. Surveyor of our early-morning drunkenness, Toby would say. Benevolent god listening to our confessions and stories, offered up like squalid little prayers.

We drank at work, and at India, we drank after work. We drank to celebrate, we drank to cope. I'm pretty sure what I'm doing right now falls under the latter.

HANABI

We drank Jim Beam and cola from a hodge-podgey assortment of coffee mugs. Proper glassware wasn't a high priority at Sanyō Heights. Everyone thought it was a welcome party, or even a birthday party for the newborn River. I insisted we were there to celebrate My Room, and no one declined to play along.

"To my room!" I raised my Hello Kitty mug high.

"To your room!" Up went six other mismatched mugs, and then we drank.

Babette perched on a small stool in one corner of my now-proper room. It had been less like decluttering and more like deforesting, but the *tatami* was clean, the windows sparkled, and the closet floor had been exposed to the air. After tossing the last garbage bag of miscellany, Babette and I struck up a verbal contract: a party was fine, but Babette's room was strictly off-limits, so the seven of us were crowded onto the four *tatami* mats that constituted my bedroom floor. It smelled of old straw and new dusting spray and humid summer nights, the sound of crickets and cicadas louder than the music on the tiny CD box I'd discovered, along with my monstrous grey beast of a *wāpuro*, at the Hard Off. The CDs came courtesy of Hard Off's cousin, the less suggestively named Book Off, where I'd scored used copies of random Japanese acts like Puffy and Yen Town Band for a hundred yen a disc.

I wasn't much of a partygoer in my younger years, but now I wondered what I'd been missing. Did partying always produce the weightlessness, the ease, I felt that night? It was like floating in a warm saltwater pool. Even Babette's caustic tone softened into something less corrosive.

"Hey, folks, hey." Toby raised his arms, bent at the elbows, palms out, as if appealing to a larger crowd. "I would like to make another toast."

"Baaaaaaarf."

"Thank you, Babette, for that thoughtful and gracious introduction. Raise your glasses!"

We obediently ensured our glasses were full for the toasting. Somehow, this took us about ten minutes. Somewhere in the midst of it, Nicolle found some old nail polish I had unearthed from the closet and began painting her toes a bright red crème.

"All right," Toby eventually continued. "I know this party is to celebrate the sanctuary and sacred place known as River's Room. However, I think all of us would also like to welcome you, River Black, to Nagano, and to the world."

"Gold!" Allie yelled.

"We all came here for different reasons, some of them simple, some of them not so simple." Toby spoke to me directly, despite the tone of public address he had adopted. "What you're doing is far braver than what we have done. It might seem unusual to some, that you've come around the world and decided to change your name, as if you're trying to break from your past, or maybe even hide from it. This isn't true. You're here to move forward, not to leave behind. You're here to step far enough outside your world to be able to achieve your dreams, and it's a far braver thing than anything most people will do with their lives, and I salute you for it. To River!"

"To River!" they shouted, except Babette, who reiterated her baaaaaaarf but clinked mugs with me all the same. I rolled my eyes a little in solidarity with her, but even if his speech was fragrantly cheesy, he had laid his finger on it perfectly.

"Do you have any words for us, River Black?" He looked directly at me, and I found myself wishing he would never stop.

"Uh, okay?" I stood up, a little whiskey wobble in my knees. "Day after day, I used to wake up, go to work in a restaurant, come home, feel sad, watch a movie, go to bed. It was time to do something enormous, so here I am."

I mimed a curtsey and sat down to enthusiastic applause.

Babette learned toward me. "You don't think changing the name is a bit much?"

"No way."

The room hushed. Even the crickets seemed to take a quiet breath of awe. Daniel had spoken. Out loud. To a room of people.

"I think it's cool," he continued, "and takes a lot of courage."

"Yes!" I raised my over-full cup of bourbon and cola and knocked it against Daniel's shyly raised glass of orange juice and orange juice, then watched him gingerly sip from the cup. One of his eyes seemed slightly lower than the other, and shaped differently, longer and tilted downward towards his cheek. The asymmetry was subtle, but it made his face seem askew, especially when he raised his eyebrows, which he was doing right now, as if his beverage was too hot. I thought to myself that if anyone in the room knew anything about courage, it had to be this guy. Daniel was as skittish as a neurotic cat, and still, he was here.

"Toby, it's your turn." Nicolle was at his feet in seconds, left foot in her right hand, inspecting the nails.

"Do what you must," Toby said in a mock-high-handed tone, then amended it to the more in-character "Follow your bliss. —I know, I know: baaaaaaarf."

By the time Toby's toes matched Nicolle's, we had all imbibed more bourbon than was technically necessary. We soon filed out of 301, a *gaijin* procession marching down the Sanyō stairs, along the street, though the night. It might have lasted a minute, it might have been twenty, the evening flickering and shifting, my eyes focusing on new sights and sounds and smells. The way the *dobugawa* widened as we reached the main east-west road. The Two Horses Boning Store, a tiny sex shop—more like a kiosk—that was never open and whose sign proudly displayed the aforementioned horses *in flagrante delicto*. The red lanterns, the narrow streets, the smell of fried food and earthier, umami aromas. Jokes and laughter, laughter and jokes.

We reached our destination, a parking lot crowded with families, where we gathered like gregarious cattle. My brain felt light and warm, like the air around me, like my body itself, as though I could lift into the breeze and float away. Toby, with a sly smile, noticed me staring at his painted toes and he extended them once for my benefit, which made me laugh again.

"How did you get here?" Daniel asked, suddenly serious.

"By air."

"That's not what I mean."

"I know, Daniel, I'm messing with you." He stared at me earnestly and I grinned back at him. "I found a sign. Literally, a poster on a telephone pole. It shouted at me. Learn Japanese! Private tutor available! $15/hour! I'd been watching Japanese TV and movies since the mid '70s; how could I refuse? That sign wanted me so badly!"

I leaned towards him on a ridiculous angle, pushing my forehead close to his. "Learn Japanese, Helen!" I shouted. "Learn it!"

Daniel laughed nervously, so I pulled away and resumed at relatively normal volume, which, after a gallon of Jim Beam, was still fairly loud. "About three months into lessons,

I bumped into this girl I knew from Jarvis, that was my high school, named Katya."

Daniel nodded. "She left J.J.'s just before I started."

"Right. She told me all about this gig. I was pretty miserable, so when she said Nax had an opening..."

"So you just sorta fell into it."

"Yyyyyyeah," I fudged. "Sorta."

"Sorta?"

Walk softly, River, or he's going to think you're a lunatic.

"I, uh. Well. You ever hear of Ultraman?"

Ultraman was a Japanese TV show they licensed and dubbed into English for the North American market. I used to watch it on the crappy off-white plastic box that my parents called a television in the early '70s. So Ultraman, in all its grey-scale glory, was my favourite show forever. I went as Ultraman for Halloween once.

Daniel nodded.

"Okay," I began. "I'm not saying this happened for real. It happened in my head. I saw that Japanese lesson poster, and then I saw, over the horizon, Ultraman's head. That smooth silver fin back to front that makes him look like a sleek robot fish, those yellow oval eyes. Then he, uh, gave me a thumbs up. So, yeah, it didn't *happen* happen, but..."

"I make up weird shit like that all the time," Daniel said. "It's what gets me through the day."

What a wonderful reply.

"Yes!" I lowered into a cross-legged position on the asphalt and Daniel sat beside me. "You, sir, are going to be, like, my new best friend."

"What about me?" Toby had lain on his back on the pavement, and now shifted to rest his head in my cross-legged lap.

"Sorry, Toby, you're too late. You can be my new best bud, but you can't be my new best friend."

"I'll take it!" Toby smiled and, at that moment, there was a crackle and burst above us and a million purple flowers bloomed and fell from the celestial trees. They were followed by blossoms green and red and white ripping open the darkness with beauty as they burned through the sky with a sizzle and hiss.

"You have the most comfortable lap." Toby looked up at me, upside down from his vantage point, and smiled. A silly boy with a silly attempt at flirting. My heart fluttered.

Bliss, potential, the future a blank page and my mind ready with the words to fill it.

This is how River begins.

AN UNEXPECTED GUEST

And this is where River ended up—alone inside a dusty memory, the fiery flowers long extinguished and turned to ash. Just like the promise of that night twenty years ago. Alone in a dusty memory, surrounded by dusty Allman Brothers records and bottles of corn-mash liquor.

I start to cry. Johnny Walker looks down at me without judgement, promising me distilled benediction. I'll take it.

"Mama-san," I call. She looks up at me with a strained, extended *hai*. "Jim Beam, *ippon kudasai*." She nods. She ignores that I'm weeping to myself. She brings me a tin kettle full of water, a bucket brimming with ice, a black magic marker, and a familiar bottle with a white label. Before I open it and begin to drink, I draw three lines on the label – one downstroke curved slightly to the left at its tail, one shorter, straight line, and a final vertical stroke, longer than the other two.

川

Mama-san watches from behind the bar. "*Kawa?*"

"Yes," I agree. "River."

I throw back a shot, neat, then pour myself a whiskey and water to sip. I try reading more titles from the stack of albums, but the spines are too frayed with age, the names and titles erased.

Daniel was born in Missoula, Montana. He had an over-protective mother and a partial atrioventricular septal defect. A hole in his heart, of all things. The kind of condition ready-made for tragic teenage romance movies because it's so meaningful, man. It was also responsible for the cyanosis and clubbing of his fingers.

Daniel didn't show up for work one night. I went to check on him, and he wasn't there. I panicked because his health had recently taken a turn for the worse. He had been assaulted by a local scumbag named Kogawa, and the strain on his heart was too much. They found him later; no one could say if he tumbled into the *dobugawa* after he died, or if that's what killed him.

I exist in the present, but this room exists in the past. I'm living in both timelines at once. Thinking of Daniel hurts too much, but this room insists. It has its own spirit, like the evil hotel room in Stephen King's *1408,* except instead of being malevolent, it's socially inept. It keeps putting its foot in its mouth. It doesn't mean to kick at the bruises, but it can't help itself. Sitting in this room is a masochistic act. Bottoms up.

People ask me why I choose to write horror. I tell them it's because I love the freedom of imagination, the powerful metaphorical ability, the feeling of catharsis, the rush of fear and shock. Fewer ask me why I chose to become River. When a blogger in Vienna asked me that, via email, my flippant response was *Because she was going to come out eventually.* When Daniel asked, I told him everything. All of it.

It wasn't that I was unhappy. It wasn't that Helen Delaney's life needed to be discarded. She was merely a shell I had outgrown. Changing my name, moving to Japan—at the time it was all so sensible. When you're in your twenties, the ordinary business of living is fraught with drama. I was a well-mannered, outgoing, socially over-engaging weirdo. No poverty, no drugs, no abuse. I didn't need saving. I only thought I did. I thought I needed saving from boredom. I needed to shake off these anxiety attacks, yes. I was sad about my father, yes, but his cancer had been deemed terminal years before. We weren't close, my father and I, and I had no illusions that I could have done something to better our relationship while he was alive. There was no guilt, there were no deep-rooted, troubling emotions to reconcile. There was just a vaguely sad girl with too much time on her hands, a mother who didn't know what to do with her, and a beloved sister who was busy becoming a lawyer.

There's a puddle on the floor behind the bar, sticky and red. Candy-like. The aroma that wafts up from it reminds me of the sunroom in Sheila's old apartment, the sick sweetness of a dozen empty, unwashed red wine bottles. Wine that I used to quell the anxiety that would crush me, like a giant boa constrictor, until I could no longer breathe.

Before I left for Japan, I worked at an upscale hipster bar called The House of the Spirits; a pun on spirits, the drinkable variety, yes, but the place was actually named after the Isabel Allende novel, which is either clever or eye-rollingly pretentious. My high school friends had moved on, and my sister was busy articling. I went to work, watched movies, ate take-out shawarma in my bedroom at my mother's house. Sheila's apartment was on Bathurst Street, across from the TTC yard above Dupont. I took to staying at her place frequently, and she didn't mind, having semi-relocated to the Yorkville apartment of a new man whose name escapes me now. Both Select Video and After Dark video lay on the route from my work to Sheila's apartment. The number of berserk B-grade horror films on the shelves! Sometimes I went in just to look at the box covers. "This Holiday season, the slay ride begins!" shouted *Black Christmas*. "At last! The truth about demons!" cried *The Demon Lover*. And how could I not rent *Shriek of the Mutilated* after reading, "A frenzied hunt for a hideous beast uncovers an evil cannibal cult and death is the devil's blessing"? *Shriek of the Mutilated!* What a title. I rented that one. It wasn't very good.

That was my life. I don't know what would have become of me, but I would have lived that life indefinitely, but for the death of my father and the anxiety attacks that followed.

Daniel didn't share or understand my love of the horror genre. Sometimes Daniel would come to Sanyō 301 and we'd watch movies on VHS. I tried a few modern ones, but the boy couldn't handle it. *The Fly*, with its oozy drippiness and acidic vomit, actually caused him to hide his face behind his fingers like a five-year-old. After *The Fly*, we watched classic monster movies only.

"How did you ever get into this kind of thing?" he asked, peeking bravely at a disintegrating Jeff Goldblum.

There was a simple, if messy, answer: the movies, the writing, the career, were all based on an aggregated heap of childhood interests. The *kaiju*, the sci-fi, the tattered cardboard cases of old videotapes in a milk carton in the corner. Godzilla, of course, and his usual crew (Mothra, Rodan, Gammorah), but Kumonga, and M.O.G.U.E.R.A., and Hedorah, and eventually The Giant Brine Shrimp and all the other obscurities that led to an obsession with Japanese monsters, then Japanese horror, then Japanese gore, and then everything else.

Man. I am drunk. It is the better part of a bottle of bourbon later, and I barely noticed the passage of time, lost in my own thoughts.

"Mama-san," I call, and make a gesture like writing cursive in the air, a signal for her to bring the bill.

Back at the Hotel New Yama, I manage to find the lock with my key, but it takes two hands. I almost trip my way into the vestibule. I have barely regained my balance when I hear it.

"Pfft."

The sound of a scornful breath. A hissy dismissal.

"Mah."

The voice comes from the bathroom, where the light is on and the fan is running. A chill doesn't run down my spine— my spine *becomes* a chill, the nerves like brittle strands of ice that might shatter when I shudder. Having lost the bulk of my motor skills to the bourbon, I slide along the wallpaper, feel its smooth ridges against my arm, until I stand a few feet shy of the bathroom door.

"Bah!" It is a horrible sound, a choked, bleating voice. "Why are you here?"

Then I look.

My brain registers the creature as everything at once: turtle, monkey, bird, fish. Its body is an uneven shade of blackened green, the colour of deep places choked by weeds and algae. Its skin glistens with an oily sheen and is speckled with bulbs and bumps like half-formed scales. Its hands taper into long knotted fingers with rotten-yellow nails, fierce like talons. A membrane-thin webbing links its digits.

Its visible foot has three toes; an extra nail sprouts from its heel. I say "visible foot" because the creature is perched on the edge of the bathtub, as if about to dry its hair after a shower, and the other foot is submerged knee-deep in the toilet bowl.

"You don't want to remember," it says, as if I'd asked.

I push myself off the wall and feel my internal gyroscopes sputter and fail. I slump towards the doorjamb and catch it with my hands. In front of me, the creature shakes its head as if disappointed by my life choices. Its belly is a sickly yellow compared to the rest of its oblong body, and its dark, sinewy neck protrudes from the shell, supporting that simian reptilian monkey frogface.

"Simyan reptilian monkey frogface," I mumble, my lips smushed against the doorjamb.

It has a cruel, pointed, beak-like mouth and blackened but hearty teeth. A pink wormlike tongue. Its eyes are black and round.

"Mah. You not want to remember!" It shouts at me.

I stare at it dumbly, taking in its twig-like fingers and the long, slimy hair. Its hair surrounds the depression in its head, a moist, disgusting concavity, as if its skull were caved in by a bowling ball. The top of its head looks like a dirty birdbath.

The thing gestures at me. "Different."

"You don't know me."

"Look different. What?"

"Canadian."

The thing raises an eyebrow. "Canadian is what?"

"A person from Canada. It's a country."

"Mah!" it says, turning away. "Maps! Useless."

"Okay," I say. "What are you? What...species?"

It leans towards me with a ravenous leer.

"Species is persons. *Kappa* eat persons."

"Ah, you *are* a *kappa*."

"What else?" It gestures towards itself. "Look like panda?"

"Sarcastic little muppet, aren't you."

"Mah!" it shouts. "Persons! *Kappa* suck their innards out through their asses!"

"That's a crappy way to eat dinner," I say, listening to its ragged breath.

"Mah." It leans back again and crosses its arms like a judgemental guidance counsellor. "Bad pun. You think funny. Can't talk drunk person. *Kappa* come back."

When I open my eyes, it is gone.

I am on the floor of the bathroom, curled around the bottom of the sink. It's something dark o'clock. My head feels like an axe-throwing target after a competitive lumberjack event. The elfin dimensions of the bathroom add a unique quality to my headache, like a steel band contracting around my head. The room is closing fast around me. Is it morning? The funeral is today. I have to get ready.

My body, however, has other plans. My horror-hardened gag reflex is no match for the alcohol. I am in too much agony to pull myself to the toilet bowl or the tub, so a gushing stream of puke splashes against the tile and back into my own face. I feel it, a warm spray that is instantaneously cold and clammy. The smell does its best to draw out more of my insides, but my guts stay put for now.

This is not the Japan I remember.

THE MIZU SHOBAI

The Japan I remember must have included vomit. I wasn't a hair-trigger puker, never have been, but surely it happened. Yet other than that first day in the shower, I can't recall the details of any terrible hangovers or vomitous consequences. Unlike the memories I intentionally keep at bay, memories of illness (self-induced or otherwise) are banished to the fringes by the countless sunny ones. There was boredom and anger and frustration and sickness, but those things are whitewashed by the memories of delight. Evenings spent listening to Masa ramble, joke, and sing karaoke. He was especially fond of the band America: "Sister Golden Hair" and "Ventura Highway." He lamented that "Black Water" wasn't on our karaoke system, and thought it should be, in my honour. When it was time to close for the night, he would give us a mournful look and sing his version The Cars' old hit, "Drive." "Who's gonna drive me home..." he would croon, before adding, "Nagano taxi!"

The staff were like the Borg. Once I was assimilated, I was at one with them. Even Babette, who professed to hate everyone, seemed happy in her peculiarly cranky way. Over the years I was at J.J.'s, new staff would arrive and assimilate in the same way. Employment at J.J.'s was based on character witness and word-of-mouth; like an exclusive club, you had to know somebody to join, but once you were in, we had your back. No one stayed long—three months here, six months there—except for the core few. Every few weeks, someone new arrived, someone old left, but through it all Allie, Nicolle, Babette, Reiko, Daniel, and I remained. Newbies referred to us as The Lifers. No one was going to spend their life at J.J.'s, but in some contemplative moments, other possible meanings took shape in my head. What were we doing, if not condensing as much life as we could into these months? What was I doing, if not leaving behind one life for another? I was writing the first film. The origin story of River Black.

Nax didn't just open up a bar. He ripped apart the fabric of the universe, allowing a few of us to slip through the subsequent wormhole towards an otherwise inaccessible life. When he sold the place, the wormhole closed back up again. We shared a rare experience at J.J. International, and for that alone, those days are irreplaceable. Especially for me. Those days melted my pain away, the way a hot bath dissolves caked-on dirt. Life seemed golden, and what didn't seem golden in the moment became so from the vantage point of the next afternoon, when viewed backward through the murky miasma of whiskey, water and cigarette smoke.

On worknights, Reiko was in charge. Nax would stroll in after midnight to enjoy a drink, but rarely did he direct our operations. We deferred to Mama-san. Who should sit with which customer? What should we do about this half-wit who complained about his bill? I need a bottle for Mr. Yamaguchi, but we have four bottles that say Yamaguchi. Which Mr. Yamaguchi is this? Reiko always knew, her memory stickier than the rat traps that lay around Sanyō. "That's Mr. Yamaguchi from Hakuba," she would immediately reply. "He was drinking Wild Turkey three months ago, he works in construction so you drew a crane on the bottle. It's up on the second shelf."

Daniel was our Master-san, but really, he was a token male presence behind the bar. This fragile, frazzled kid was supposed to be the muscle should there ever be trouble? We took care of ourselves, thank you. If a customer's hand slunk beneath a table and pawed at a knee, if a proposition went from comic to serious or crude, you could count on Babette, Allie or Nicolle and, after a time, me, to proffer an "Oi, bugger off, mate" and end the situation *tout suite*.

Customers came to drink and talk to 'exotic foreign girls.' Baaaaaarf. Half our evenings were spent in the empty bar, waiting for these exotica-craving gentlemen to arrive. We were all dressed and dolled up by seven pm sharp, but most nights, there wouldn't be a soul in the room until after nine. We would sit, Reiko's choice of compact discs on the stereo, chewing gritty-tasting shrimp chips which dissolved into a vaguely fishy paste that glommed onto to the backs of our molars. Custom-invented card games, gossip, hair braiding, laughter, hand-written letters home; ways to fill the quiet gap. Reiko would sketch the room, us, anime characters, or anything you requested. You hoped to avoid the brusque middle-aged businessmen, or gross men barely concealing perverted fantasies about white girls, or men more interested in muttering to one another for two hours, leaving us to feign interest in their impermeable conversations. You hoped for Masa or another favourite customer, for friendly faces, for men who chose J.J.'s because they thought we were cool folks, not potential girls on the side.

One of my first nights on the clock, early evening. The door opened and we all called *irrashaimase* in unison. It's what one says to welcome a customer, and it's mandatory. It always seemed like a call-and-response between us and the vacuum-gasp sound of the door opening. This night, it wasn't a customer, it was merely Toby; our chorus devolved into something akin to "*Irrashaimashoh*, hi Tobes."

"Don't I get a full-on *irrashaimase*?" Toby pouted.

"You're not a customer," I said. "Wandering minstrel,

transient jester, errant cousin, really tall surfer, giraffe groomer—"

"And once again, the esteemed River Black manages another height joke."

"Babette, pass me a Tissue of Kitten," I said, ignoring him. Babette passed me a box of tissues, the brand name of which was Tissues of Kitten, and I loudly blew my nose.

"Gross." Nicolle frowned.

As I stood to dispose of the tissue, I noticed Daniel as he approached the narrow shelf-lined pantry where we stored dry goods and snacks. At the doorway, he paused and craned his head forward around the doorjamb, even as the rest of his body continued through the door.

"He's legit claustrophobic," Allie whispered confidentially when I sat back down. You'd think she was telling me he had cancer, from the gravity and secrecy in her tone. "When Rei buys food, she puts the snacks right by the door so he doesn't have to go into the room."

"Food?" I joke. "Can you call overpackaged cheese, frozen chicken chunks and vaguely fishy polystyrenish French fry-shaped shrimp chips 'food?'"

"How does he go to the bathroom in this country?" Nicolle asks.

"I hear he keeps the door open," Allie replied.

Babette stopped knitting long enough to roll her eyes.

"And which of his non-existent roommates told you that?" she said. She had a point. Daniel didn't even live at Sanyō. Reluctant to force girls to live with a boy, Nax had offered to pay the rent on a separate apartment along Chūo-*odōri*.

The vacuum seal around the door broke again, and *irrasshaimase* leapt from our mouths. I'd only been here a few days, and already the greeting was second-nature.

A trio of thirty-something men in beige company coveralls walked into the room, tentative and uncertain for a moment, until Reiko bounded at them, chattering and smiling and leading them to a table.

"This is an unremarkable drinking hole on the third floor of an unremarkable building tucked behind the train station and a parking garage." I shook my head slowly. "How does anyone find us?"

"Couldn't tell you mate." Allie said. "Come on, let's take up first shift, yeah?"

Nicolle put a hand on my leg as I started to rise. "I got it. You relax, newbie."

I watched the scene from across the room. Daniel handed each of the customers, now seated, a hot steamed towel wrapped in a loose plastic sheath. We kept these *oshiburi* piled in a special warmer that resembled an over-sized toaster oven. Reiko retrieved a bottle from the bottle-keep cupboard without asking for their names; she remembered their faces. Daniel ferried a glass bucket of ice and a cylindrical carafe of water to the table and lay down three coasters. Coasters, it seemed, weren't actually to protect tables. They were to highlight, in some arcane fashion, the importance of the customers. Hostesses were not to use coasters.

The men were previous customers but strangers to Allie and Nicolle. The conversation began with the usual simple introductions. A short-term, vaguely defined friendship would form, or not. Any tenuous connection helped. Allie talked about the Gold Coast and Brisbane. One of the construction workers excitedly told her he'd been to Sydney once. "Opera house!" he said. "*Sugoi na.*"

One of the construction workers, a pokey-looking fellow with a country boy haircut, smoked incessantly. Nicolle lit him a cigarette, cupping her hand around the lighter flame, every other minute.

I pulled out a tattered, brown-hued paperback from my satchel, a Linda Howard novel salvaged from the Sanyō 301 purge. All due respect to her, but after four pages, I realized it wasn't my thing. I replaced the book in the bag and removed an envelope instead. I took it to the bar and sat in front of Daniel.

"Letters from home already?" Daniel asked.

"Yessir. This is from my big sister." I lay it on the counter in front of Daniel, as though he had never seen this mysterious item called a "letter" before. "She must have mailed it three days before I left. She's so cute. She wants to know how I'm doing."

Daniel looked up, dish rag in hand, shiny black ashtray in the other.

"I know, that sounds like a normal question from a sister, but she doesn't mean it like a normal question. It's not, how are you settling into a foreign society where you don't speak the language and the food's unfamiliar most of the time? What's it like eating tuna and squid on a pizza? Are the customers sketchy or are they nice guys? Nothing like that. She wants to know how I'm *doing* doing. Like, my mental health, my grieving process, my reinvention."

The rag hung, motionless, as Daniel's head listed towards one shoulder.

"Okay, I know, that's a normal question too. I'm just saying, man, I don't know. I'm doing great? Can I write back just one sentence in block letters, I'm Doing Great?"

"People asked me about my health all the time." Daniel's gaze falls on the bar as he talks. "Mental, physical, emotional. I'd just tell them I was doing great. They never believed me."

"Well, Daniel, you just need to improve your acting skills."

"You used to have panic attacks, right?" He said it quietly, as if this was information he wasn't supposed to possess, though I was certain that not only had I told him directly, I'd told a room full of people, loudly, on several occasions since my arrival.

"Yeah. Those seem to have stopped."

"How are you doing with...." Personal questions seemed to cause him intense unease. "You know, like, the grief thing."

"My father was a cold man with a drinking problem. He wasn't abusive but we weren't close. When he died I was sadder than I thought I would be. I never would have guessed my subconscious would start messing with me. I mean, it's not like an image of my dad comes to mind and *blammo* my heart rate goes up. I'd freak out *a propos* of absolutely zero, a couple times a day. He died almost a year ago, and only now has that stopped. I guess quitting my job, flying around the world, and meeting new wicked cool people like you guys was just what the doctor ordered."

"And here you're River."

"I am!" I beamed at Daniel, who continued to dry and stack the black ashtrays, like little ceramic flowers of doom. "I mean, yeah, I'm River. But I'm Helen. It's not as dramatic as I make it sound. I haven't drawn up a list of character traits to embody. I'm not taking six months to learn to talk like a lady in a florist's shop."

" . . . "

"That's from My Fair Lady."

" . . . "

"I mean, I'm still me, just me trying to go in a new direction. Plus, River Black is a much cooler name than Helen Delaney. Observe."

I flipped the last page of my sister's letter to the blank side, where I messily wrote,

GODZILLA VS NAX THE MERCILESS
By Helen Delaney.

I paused, gave Daniel a dramatic look, which he didn't see because he never met my gaze, crossed out my name, and wrote my other name.

GODZILLA VS NAX THE MERCILESS
By ~~Helen Delaney~~. River Black.

"See? One is decidedly cooler than the other." I glance furtively over to Nicolle, Allie and their customers. "Say, country boy over there is going through cigarettes like there's no tomorrow, you'd better go replace those ashtrays. More than two butts makes Nakadaira nuts."

Daniel delivered fresh ashtrays and returned.

"Are you writing?" He asked, smiling at me or, more accurately, smiling into the middle distance, just shy of my right shoulder.

"Ah, well, no. I've been acclimatizing. Did you know they speak a different language over here? So crazy!"

"..."

"That was a joke."

"Oh."

"Oh. Ahem. Okay, collar pull, tough room. Anyway, I do have some writing ideas. I've been jotting dark and disturbing ideas into my Cursèd Black Notebook for years."

"Curse-ed?"

I reached into my bag and held aloft a tattered notebook on which I had painted, in drippy red nail polish, Cursèd Black Notebook.

"Master-san!" Allie half-sang at Daniel. "Potato fry *kudasai*!"

Daniel's face fell a little. He stepped towards the kitchen, parted the curtain and grimaced.

"Open the window," I suggested, referencing his claustrophobia without referencing it.

"It's not just that. This room is disgusting. It's greasy and dirty and awful."

"Want me to make the fries? It's just dumping a bag into oil."

"No, no, it's okay, I'll do it."

I watched him steel himself as if he were a hockey player hitting the ice on the final power play. Before he disappeared through the *noren,* though, he turned and gave me a thoughtful look.

"Hey, so, all that stuff you just told me? Why don't you tell all that to your sister?"

"Damn, son, you make a lotta sense."

I came around the bar and stood just outside of the kitchen, holding the grease-imbued curtain open as we continued our conversation. Daniel took my advice and threw the window open wide anyway. He tiptoed delicately around the microscopic space as if afraid to touch any of its surfaces.

"Have you always been claustrophobic?" I asked, after a moment, with what I hoped was a direct gentleness.

Daniel stooped to pull a plastic bag from the freezer, digging his nails into the thick material and pulling sideways until the bag came open.

"It's one of the things that gives me anxiety," he told the fries in the bag.

"It must be tough."

"Everything's tough," he said, barley moving his lips. The roil and sizzle of frozen potato hitting hit oil almost drowned out his reply.

"There are people with zero anxiety who never do something as brave as this," I told him. "You came to a country where you don't speak the language and you took a job in a bar."

"My mother freaked out," he told the oil. "She doesn't think I'm well enough."

"Like..." I tried to weigh my words, but still managed to insensitively blurt out, "mentally?"

To his credit, Daniel laughed, one short, sharp bark.

"No. I was born with a congenital heart defect, which should have been corrected. My mom never really told me, because she's embarrassed, I think, but it seems like the doctors downplayed it because they knew we couldn't really afford the surgery. So now I have Eisenmenger syndrome."

"Eisen..."

"Eisenmenger syndrome. My heart and lungs are a mess. I get shortness of breath. Pulmonary hypertension—high blood pressure—in the arteries in my lungs. I can even faint if it gets bad. And then, of course, there's the cyanosis." He held up his hands, his fingertips inked bluish purple in the florescent light. His twitchy expression and gentle voice made him seem like someone who had been fingerprinted for crimes he never would have had the fortitude to commit.

"It's why anxiety attacks scare me. They make my heart race, which always makes me think I'm dying. Truthfully, a heart and lung transplant is about the only thing that would fix me up for good. I'm lucky I'm still around."

I sat on a low metal stool and noted how correct Daniel was about the kitchen. The appliances looked like someone had gathered years' worth of dirty stove grease in a jar and spread it around the room with a butter knife.

"Dude, that's intense."

"Yeah, it can be."

"So why are you here?"

"Because," he said, "like I said, I'm lucky to be around at all. It's like a gift from the universe or something. So I'm not gonna waste it, you know? Also, this place pays pretty well. I send money home a lot. Makes me feel better about abandoning my mom."

"Dude, you did not abandon your mom." The oil blurps once, threatens to splash out of the pot, but then subsides. "How did you find out about J.J.'s?"

"I met Toby on the street one night."

"You came here without a job or a place to stay?"

"Yeah." Daniel pinched two enormous chopsticks in his fist and used them to swirl the sizzling French fries around the dank oil.

"Daniel, you're not just brave, you're kinda stupid about it!"

Daniel grinned at me, in the direction of my face, though he still averted his eyes from mine.

"It was super scary," he admitted, still grinning. "But you know. Here I am. Keeping my monsters at bay."

"Here you are," I agreed. "You appeared out of nowhere, totally unsuited for the surroundings, completely unprepared for the experience, and it's all working out okay."

He swizzled the oil and smiled down at it, nodding in agreement.

"Yeah," he said. "I feel pretty okay."

PAYING RESPECTS

I do not feel pretty okay.

For all the drinking and mild debauchery of my J.J.'s years, I have never awoken in a puddle of my own sick on a bathroom floor.

Gingerly, I pick myself up off the tile, turn on the shower, and step into the tub, where last night a *kappa* scolded me for being hammered. I crank the hot water up enough to burn but not quite enough to blister, and scrub away the ick. I feel the headache and queasiness balance themselves. One careless move and I could trigger another upspew.

What *did* I see last night?

My brain, a kaleidoscope of drunken wackadoo, wanted to reinforce a message. Fear. Daniel. All of it represented by this gnarly little munchkin in my brain. I suppose I must have been subconsciously embarrassed by my drunkenness, too. It's not every day that a product of your nightmares dismisses you as too drunk for a conversation.

Well, brain, mind your own business. I have respects to pay.

I'm unfamiliar with Japanese death rites and rituals. I'm not sure if today's event is officially a funeral or a wake. Either way, it's at the Nakadaira residence, not in a funeral hall. I used to go to that house monthly, to help Nax fold his newsletters—inscrutable vertical rows of *kanji* and syllabary photocopied on stark white paper. The newsletters were for his investment clients. Or maybe his art clients? His business was always nebulous and puzzling.

Every time I move too quickly, it feels like an act of aggression against myself. I try to refocus that aggression against the hangover, but the best I can do is swallow two Excedrin and chug a bottle of the sweet Sweat I tucked into my bag for emergencies just like this one. Hangovers grow mean and mangy the older you get.

A familiar but unexpected sound buzzes out of my bag. I grab the phone. It's Sheila.

Oops.

"Hey, sis." I drop onto the bed, the phone pressed between the pillow and my ear.

"Morning, Hel. You just waking up from a nap?"

"No." I glance at the bedside clock. "It's ten-thirty a.m. here."

Laughter.

"No, really, it's ten-thirty a.m. here."

"…"

"I'm in Nagano."

"…"

My head throbs with pains, alternately blunt and stabby. I have an unwanted yet vivid image of my head busting open, *Scanners*-style, and my guts, usually immune to gore-induced nausea, do a jerky pirouette in my abdomen.

"Nax died two days ago," I try to say, but it comes out as a pathetic sob.

"Oh." There's a different tone to her silence now. "Oh, I'm sorry, Hel. That's awful. But…you know, it's been…a really long time, and it's not like you kept in touch. Did you even—"

"I made a promise," I insist through my tears. "I know it was a long time ago, but I promised to come back to pay my respects. I had to fly out immediately. The only reason I made it in time for the funeral is that they were delayed a day.

Something about inauspicious days for funerals. Otherwise I would have missed it completely."

"Hel, honey, you don't sound good."

"I'm not good! I have a hangover! Crying with a hangover really hurts!"

"Does this have anything to do with the book?"

"Sheel, the book didn't give Nax a stroke."

"You sound like *you're* having a stroke. Don't you have a screenplay to write?"

" . . . "

"Helen?"

I sigh, expressing a combination of pain, exhaustion, and exasperation.

"I have a screenplay to write, but first I have a funeral to get ready for, and I look like a beast. I'll message you later, okay?"

Reluctantly, Sheila lets me go. I dry my hair, apply enough makeup to hide the fist-sized bags under my eyes, and head out into the belligerently sunny light of the morning.

Out on India Street, I am shocked by the dreamlike familiarity of everything I see now that the sun is up. Images seem to rush into my corneas as though there's a vacuum in my head, sucking it all in. Round convex mirrors edged in orange-painted steel protect a near-blind intersection. Bulbous, almost elliptical trucks, laden with plastic cases of slender-necked lager bottles, idle in front of restaurants with English names: Do One's Best, My Gold, Snack Donkey. Ancient temples nestle alongside modern homes, each with its own version of the traditional Japanese tile roof. Above me, dangling lanterns of white glass and steel, red ribbons tied to green trees, *kanji* and *kana* raised high beneath a slanted, irregular grid of electrical wires. All around me, I know, the mountains are there, hidden now by the shops and bars and buildings beside me. Off to the west, Mount Asahi, and the fox shrine, *sakon inari.* The setting of our story. Where a boy met a *kappa.*

I make my way along the Gondō, a lengthy shopping arcade intersected by tiny streets and covered by a convex glass roof. It's kind of like half-indoor, half-outdoor. It is ablaze with the flashes and blinks of glittery ribbons that dangle from the ceiling, red and gold and yellow and green tendrils that cascade down from larger spheres of ribbon, themselves suspended from the metal lattices of the glass roof's frame. My brain sees the ribbons as some kind of psychedelic, abstract squid; one of them raises a tentacle and salutes me, though I'm pretty sure it's the wind. I remember the Gondō as a bustling shopping zone—clothes, pharmacies, food, specialty shops, anchored at the south end by the Itō Yōkadō department store, with its clothing and toys, its family restaurants on the top floor and grocery section in the basement. I remember how the Gondō whizzed with bicycles and pedestrians. Today, it's nearly empty. It's hard for me to know—is this the vision of a dying city, one that was over-primped into unsustainability for the Olympics? Did the bullet train not sufficiently tether the roof of Japan to the foundations of Tokyo? Or am I just here outside of peak hours on an off day?

Muzak fills the air like gaseous syrup floating above me, pooling in the spaces between the storefronts and the ceiling. The electronic blips and sharp bells of the *pachinko* parlour cut through it like sparks through space. I reach Itō Yōkadō and enter through its automatic glass doors. Someone from the perfume department, in the upper register women must reach to be true customer service professionals, calls *irrashaimase!* I stumble and trip through an inquiry about funeral envelopes.

"Hai. Hai. Koden bukuro de gozaimasu ka? Ah, go-shūshō sama de gozaimasu."

She leaves her perfumey post and leads me to the second floor, where she smiles, indicates the funeral envelopes, apologizes for something, and dashes back to her station. I don't even have time to thank her.

Outside, on Nagano *o-dōri*, I make for a line of taxis. The first in the row opens its automatic passenger door in my direction. I offer the driver a slip of paper with Nax's address on it.

The house is somewhere in the Miwa neighbourhood, which I couldn't find on my own in a thousand years, despite having been there dozens of times. The streets in Miwa twist and circle, their names concealed and unavailable to me should they exist at all, and so many of the houses seem identical.

My head beats harder than my heart. I am nauseated and sore, but I feel a little better.

My mind wanders to Sheila, so concerned that I'd flown off to find the origins of the book. She wasn't entirely wrong. It's just that the origin of the book is dead, as dead as the author.

Why this book, Nax?

North of the city centre, Nagano mimics a western suburb, with its minor highways and major thruways. Suburbs in Canada depress me; there is too much space and too little character. They're cookie-cutter corporate blocks pasted on the edges of every city. Now, racing up the wrong side of the road past a Circle K and a JAL office and an Applebees, a blue calm is released into my veins. It's like a homecoming of sorts. It comes at me like sun though the window, a gentle warmth that I hope will stay with me, pull me through what's coming.

The taxi slows in front of a walled front garden, indistinguishable from the walled gardens on either side. We momentarily block a few other cars, makes of Mazda and Nissan unavailable back home. The road is barely a lane and a half wide, with no sidewalks.

I pay and step out of the taxi. Two elderly Japanese folks shuffle their way up the drive. Nax's house is spacious and lies barely thirty feet from the street, yet somehow it is nearly invisible, obscured by cherry and persimmon trees, walls, and cars. It is modern but uniquely Japanese, with a roof made of some space-age polymer but designed to look like old clay tiles with *kanji* stamped on the bases of the exposed cylinders. I can see heads and shoulders through the open front door. The vestibule is filled with shoes; as I watch, the elderly couple ahead of me slip their footwear off and glide into slippers without touching their stockinged feet to the floor. The women wear identical funeral outfits—austere skirts with business suit–like blazers, or for the older ones, midnight kimonos. Suddenly my modest black dress is too little, the sleeves too short, the neckline too wide. Even as I tell myself not to worry, I'm already spun around, headed to the road, feeling a recognisable cultural inadequacy; I don't belong here, I'm stupid foreigner with no right to this ritual, my participation in it is inappropriate, presumptuous, an embarrassment.

The ground drops away underfoot, a shallow step, but enough to confuse my feet as they tangle beneath me. As I stumble, two hands appear out of the ether and steady me by the shoulders.

"*Ah! Gaijin da!*"

His tone, his voice, his inflection. They obscure decades. I expect to look up and see him calling to me across the road, strange little half-smile on his face, cigarette burning in one hand, standard-issue work tie askew, sweat beading on his forehead. I'm a bit kerfuffled from almost falling face first into him, but a warmth spreads out from inside my chest and forces my lips into a smile.

Masa.

"What are you saying?" I joke, my Japanese so rusty you could crumble it in your hand. "There's a foreigner here? I can't believe it!"

"*Watashi mo shinjirarenai.*" I can't believe it either.

I throw my arms around his neck in spite of myself, knowing I'm making a show of things, an inappropriate show of physical contact in a society where they bow, not hug, but I don't know where else to go with the momentum.

"You can't touch me, please," he jokes, his accent heartbreakingly familiar. "I'm Japanese!"

"I can't help it," I say, reverting to English as well. "I'm so excited to see you, Yamada-san."

"Oh my God. I can't believe your mindness. My name is Masa. Please call me Masa."

"I thought maybe after all this time, I should be polite."

"No. Masa! Masa-chan! It's okay."

"We never called you Masa-chan!" I laugh. "That's what you'd call a ten-year-old. How have you been, Masa-san?"

"I am always thinking of you."

It's an old joke. He doesn't mean it. His expression is inscrutable as it always was, with the tiniest hint of a smile, as if you can see the muscles in his face *about* to smile, but they're just trying to fake you out. "*O-hisashiburi desu ne.*"

"Yes. It really has been a long time."

"Are you leaving now?" he asks.

I look back over my shoulder, into the foyer.

"No, I just got here, but I don't think I can go in. I don't know what to do, I'm not sure I brought a big enough gift, I'm not dressed right, I'm...I'm scared."

"River Black is scared? I can't believe it. Nothing is scary for River Black."

Why do people think this about me?

"Come with me," he says. "Just follow me. Your dress is okay. It's black. That's enough."

We head into the foyer. I slide out of my shoes and into slippers. I'm strangely thankful for the sombre atmosphere, as it alleviates the need for small talk. Where would we even begin? Masa was a customer and a friend, but we haven't stayed in touch. I wonder if he married. Perennially single, sometimes noticeably lonely, none of us would have bet on him finding a wife. His lack of traditionalism was one strike against him for serious women in serious pursuit of serious husbanding.

"Follow me," he says.

"It's always the best way," I reply. We always followed Masa. If we were served a tray of assorted sauces and food-stuffs, we watched Masa to see what sauces went on which foods, which items you could pick up with your fingers. We always followed his lead.

First, we stop at the small table in the hallway, sign a register, and present our ornate paper envelopes with their white-and-black ribbons. There are probably words to be spoken during this exchange, proffering the gift with both hands, but I stay silent. No one expects the white girl to speak Japanese anyhow. I scan the register out of the corner of my eye, curious to see if I can make out the signatures and messages, but they're all in Japanese except for one name scrawled illegibly in cursive. It looks like a rudimentary illustration of a bumblebee.

The family has set up an altar, flanked by a modest row of flowers, in one of the sitting rooms. There are a few offerings, apples, something that looks like *mochi*. In front of that, a small table is set with a ceramic bowl of incense powder and a hot black stone. The smell of the incense used to make me think of an old country library on fire down the road. Now, I think of Japan.

On one side of the room the family sits in a row of folding chairs. My heart squelches when I see how small that family is: a few men I do not recognize, Misaki, and her mother, Nax's wife. She was never more than an apparition to us, floating along the corridors of this house as we hand-folded Nax's newsletters. Today, though her countenance is ghostly pale, she has never seemed more like a living being; she weeps continuously, sniffling and swallowing as she stares into her lap.

Misaki, on the other hand, looks blank, decimated. Her hair hangs down in front of her face, and it seems that if she could disappear entirely behind that curtain of hair, she would. Her face is bent towards her knees.

I watch Masa nod to the altar, pinch some of the powder and drop it onto the stone, where it begins to smoke. He repeats the action. Then he puts his hands together with his prayer beads, bows to the shrine, and then to the family, who, in their seated positions, return the bow without looking up. Masa then crosses the room and leaves.

I repeat his actions verbatim, hoping no one will notice the missing prayer beads.

As I follow Masa deeper into the house, I am surrounded by strangers, mostly elderly men. It's possible some of them were J.J.'s customers, even regulars, but after two decades, their faces are no longer the same. Would a customer know me? Masa recognized me, but we were friends. My hair is still the same, my face mostly free from wrinkles. I am roughly the same size, though my hips have widened, the heaviness of existence sinking into my behind. I tell people I'd rather carry the weight of the world in my booty than on my shoulders. Most find it funny,

I turn a corner, into a parlour of sorts, and stop short with a gasp.

I expected to see an urn. Instead, I see Nax.

Corpses aren't frightening. They're just people with the lights off. There's no point in being afraid, or even letting it push you down the grim spiral of contemplating your own mortality. You know you're gonna die. I certainly do. I get paid to spend hours imagining new and more sickening ways for a person's ticket to get punched. So it isn't Nax's corpse, exactly, that shocks me still and silent. It's the sight of his face. It's the peaceful expression, cheeks slack, the tiniest almost-smile on the corners of his lips. It's the expression that settled over his features when he would sit at the table, cigarette in one hand, a particularly poignant passage of jazz in his ears. It's a face of transcendence. It occurs to me that there could not be a more suitable expression on his face right now.

In another large room, there is a table lined with assorted snacks, *sembe*, small sandwiches, that sort of thing. A door on one side is open to the garden.

"I can't believe I am seeing you, Kawa-chan," Masa says. "So many years! Nakadaira was the last person I still saw from those old days at J.J.'s. Except maybe Babette. I saw her once, maybe two times. She married Shinji."

"She did?" Babette is one of the folks who does not do Facebook, Instagram, or any other social media. Nicolle and Allie have also lost track of her. I immediately feel an unpleasant guilty sensation in my chest. If Babette were here, I'm not sure she would want to talk to me.

"Do they live in Nagano?"

"I think so."

Babette is still here.

"So what are you doing today?" He means "these days."

"Oh, you know. Working on the next *Pinned* movie."

Masa looks surprised. "*Ah, Pinned da?* I know him."

"Evrard Frederich."

"Yes. He's popular in Japan. But, please, I'm sorry, I think he kind of..."

"Stinks?"

"Yes. Why not make a new movie? You are good!"

I don't respond to him. Out in the garden, I can hear a tiny voice that rises and falls, the way a hummingbird's buzz swells and retreats as it circles your head. Masa continues to speak, but I don't really hear him. A cold hand has wrapped itself around my throat, and it's trying to wring tears out of my eyes. The tiny voice is so familiar, even though she would be...oh, dear God, she'd always joke that she was thirty, and now she'd *actually* be thirty. This day has shaken loose all kinds of unexpected bits of debris, shaken the bugs from the log, and my head is suddenly lighter than the rest of my body.

"I...I have to step outside for a minute."

"Okay."

As I make my way towards the doors, he calls to me. "Kawa-chan."

I turn.

"Thank you for coming. I think you have Japanese mindness."

"Thank you, Masa."

He means my sense of duty, of *giri*. He thinks that's what brought me here. He doesn't know about the book. I stare out into the garden, at the source of the hummingbird sound. A little girl, about same age Sora was when I taught her.

LITTLE SKY

I had been in Japan two weeks when I started teaching Sora—two weeks during which the world was a swirl of new colours. I had the overwhelming sensation of a city, a culture, a nation rising up to swallow me. I wanted to be devoured that way, to sink deep into this stomach, but I was still tethered, albeit reluctantly at times, to my previous life. I made phone calls home, mostly to Sheila, sometimes to mom. The three apartments at Sanyō—306, 303, and 301—shared one landline, connected to the wall in my bedroom. At least once a day, I would respectfully linger in the kitchen, trying and failing to not eavesdrop on conversations with parents, boyfriends, airlines, or English students. I learned to unplug the phone when I slept, because I had also learned that family and friends had no grasp on date lines and time zones, nor did they understand that we were freakish liquor ghouls who went to bed between six and nine a.m.

Babette and I were still circling one another like suspicious cats. Well, maybe it was more like Spike and Chester in the old Looney Tunes cartoons. She tried to swat me away, but I was just so gosh darn persistent. And perky! I must have made her so very angry in those first few weeks.

Babette had the most experience in Japan, so I asked for her thoughts on Sharky's offer. She thought it sounded odd but legit, so I picked up the landline and dialed the number on the business card, which was the only part of the text I could translate. Someone answered with a measured *moshi moshi* when I realized I didn't know who to ask for.

"I, ah, I'm looking for…Sora-san's father?"

Pause.

"Is this Kawa-chan?"

"Yes! This is…?"

"Sora's father, yes. I'm happy to hear from you. You are getting comfortable in Nagano, yes?"

"Slowly. I love it, but…it's a lot to take in."

"I can understand."

We made arrangements. I was to teach Sora every Saturday morning at 11 am, at his sister's home, which was close to the other two schools she had to attend on Saturdays. The idea of doing three classes on a Saturday, on top of regular school, was an affront to everything I believed in regarding childhood, but hey, this wasn't my country.

A few days later, I hopped on my ill-gained bicycle—I told Babette that riding it felt like spending blood money, which made her laugh—and headed east, beneath the train tracks, towards the Kazama neighbourhood. It was close to Chikuma-gawa, the longest, widest river in Japan, which rose out of the Japanese alps and flowed through Niigata to the Sea of Japan. Some of the streets were narrow, almost unfinished, with scruffy tufts of grass emerging from the gravel on either side. The structures here were spaced out, unlike downtown, where unoccupied lots were nonexistent.

Both the 'burbs and downtown, however, shared one feature: continuous strata of signage. Vertical metal signs, framed in red steel piping, on the sidewalk. Plastic signs above shop doors. Signs affixed to fences with zip ties. Signs supported by wooden Y-frames. Signs on telephone poles, signs jutting out from telephone poles, signs adjacent to telephone poles. Was it an ad? A bus stop? A public service announcement? A geographical marker? Not knowing what the signs meant, not knowing what the buildings contained, was unsettling on some fundamental level. Even a sign in English could mislead you, as English was clearly employed to add cachet, not information. In downtown Nagano there was a shop whose sign said "…and meat." Would your first thought be "men's jeans"? Because they sold men's jeans.

Sharky's sister's house had a yellow-beige exterior, slatted shutters, a modern traditional roof. It was nestled between a doctor's office, a low-rise apartment complex, and a vacant lot. I kicked down my kickstand. No need to lock up. We thieving foreigners mostly stayed downtown.

An elderly woman answered the door. She wore a pink blouse and a surgical mask, which meant she was ill and trying not to spread germs.

"*Ah,* Kawa-chan, *dōmo!*" The woman offered several rapid, jerky bows. I slipped out of my shoes and into slippers as Babette had instructed. The woman led me down a smooth, sand-coloured hardwood hallway and continued to speak, a swift current of words I could not decipher. I worried that vital information was being missed but had no way to let her know, so I hoped for the best.

Towards the back of the house, she gestured towards a western-style door, held up a finger and said, in English, "One hour…thirty minutes."

"You got it."

I opened the door. The room beyond was compact and bright. There was no decor to speak of, other than the sheer white curtains on a wide south-facing window. Most of the room was occupied by a round wooden table upon which sat a sweaty pitcher of ice water and some glasses. Next to it, beside the window, was an easel that supported an over-sized pad of drawing paper. There was a waist-high bookshelf on which you could see four rainbow rows, the brightly coloured spines of children's books. On the chair furthest from the easel was the actual child.

Sora sat with her hands folded in front of her, as though expecting me, but without standing or offering Japanese formalities.

"Hello," she said. She had spoken one word, and already I noticed she had better pronunciation than Reiko.

"Hello. You must be Sora-san."

"I am Noguchi Sora," she replied, giving her surname first. She wore pink cotton pants and a white sweatshirt emblazoned with the image of a glittery butterfly. She put out her hand, elbow locked in a rigid formality, and smiled. "Nice to meet you."

"Nice to meet you! Look at you, you're adorable."

Sora's face was set firmly into an impress-the-teacher mask, and she sat up straight, as if she were in a real classroom. As if I were a real teacher.

"May I call you Sora-chan?" I asked.

Sora nodded and said, "Yes, teacher."

"You may call me River, Sora-chan."

The mask fell away. Sora screwed her face up, bunching her cheeks around her nose.

"Teacher?" she asked.

"River," I replied.

"My father says your name is River Black," she replied. "I should call you Miss Black."

"I have an idea," I replied. "You can call me Miss Black, but later, when we are friends, you can call me River."

Sora grinned and nodded. Our first goal was already established: become friends. This was not part of the curriculum her father would think necessary, but it made me feel more comfortable already.

"How old are you, Sora?"

Sora held a hand upward as though she were admiring her nail polish. With her index finger, she began to count on the other hand, until she had counted four, when she stopped and looked at me.

"Thirty," she proclaimed, bursting into giggles.

"Thirty!" I played along. "You're older than me! You should be sensei."

I pulled out my textbook, several colouring books, and one children's book, all of which came from either the bottom of my tickle-truck closet or from Babette, who had been teaching at least ten hours per week of under-the-table English lessons since her arrival. Sora's father had assured me that Sora's English was "better than I would expect." We began by talking about the usual: names, places, likes, dislikes. She was astounding.

"I like vanilla ice cream, even though some people think that is boring."

"School is hard for me, but I study every day."

"My dog is named Aki. It means autumn."

The children's book I brought was miles below her skill level. The textbook was somewhat better. I spun conversations around the words she knew, until we came across blips in syntax or vocabulary she had never found need to learn: words for flavours, words for areas of study, words for emotions. We used words in sentences, formed complex sentences, paid attention to verb tenses and conjugations. She wrote notes with stern concentration, but then returned to me, all smiles. Eighty-five minutes later, we had done the entire lesson plan.

"Would you like to read to me for the last five minutes?" I asked her.

"Can we end early, Miss Black?"

In a country where trains arrived like clockwork and rice was eaten to the last lonely grain, new teachers probably shouldn't cave in to such requests.

"No, Sora, I'm sorry."

Sora didn't appear surprised or particularly bothered, as if she was used to trying, and failing, to get away with minor indulgences. She picked up the children's book and frowned slightly at the cover.

"Beh…Bessy?"

"Yes."

"*Bessy's Best Day*."

"That's right."

Sora held the book up to me with both hands. "The book is about a cow."

"Yes."

"Miss Black, I am so very sorry. I think this book might be for little kids."

"And you're thirty, so this book is probably not for you."

Sora giggled again. Her laughter was like a brook of joy, babbling over rocks in the sun. It was impossible for me not to grin back at her. For the first time, I understood why some people loved kids.

"Okay." I lowered the book cover and patted it in her lap. "*Bessy's Best Day* is just our beginning. We'll read it today because it's all we've got. I'll bring you something better next time."

"Can it be scary?"

"I don't know, would your father like that?"

"He won't mind. He knows I like scary things."

"A girl after my own heart. Okay, maybe a little scary. With scary pictures?"

"It doesn't have to have pictures, Miss Black. I'm old enough for just words."

Sora read me *Bessy's Best Day*. Bessy needed a life, it seemed, given that her "best day" involved finding some fresh grass to chew, and something about a honey bee, and a fence, and I don't know, maybe some chickens or something.

"Okay, Sora, Bessy's bumming me out. I think we can call it a day. Class is finished."

"Thank you, Miss Black." She closed the book demurely and placed it on the table in front of her. "It has been nice to meet you. I am happy to have a nice teacher!"

Obasan appeared on cue, as if she, too, had been watching the clock. She showered me with quickfire Japanese and presented a cream-coloured envelope with two hands. I took it with two hands and held it respectfully as I bowed, thanked her, and headed outside to my bicycle.

The envelope was plain, with the opening at the narrow end instead of lengthwise like a letter envelope. Inside were two ¥10,000 bills. Two hundred fifty dollars? For ninety minutes? It must be a mistake. I hoped it wasn't.

"Goodbye, teacher!" came the little voice behind me. I turned to see Sora grin and wave her hand at the end of a fully extended arm. "See you soon!"

DEVIL IN THE GARDEN

The girl in the garden brings all of it back. I recall how important Sora was to me. Sora reminded me there was another side to this country, one that didn't involve middle-aged men and their drinking habits. The girl in the garden reminds me that Sora, too, can be counted amongst my losses.

Misaki drifts into the room like a lost spirit aimlessly wandering the house in which she died. I cock my head to the side and offer her one of those apologetic funeral smiles. She manages a half-formed smile in return, one that barely turns her lips and gives her eyes a wide berth.

"Misaki-san," I say quietly. "*Go-shūshō sama de gozaimasu.*"

"Kawa-chan. *Dōmo.*" Misaki grabs my hand, quickly and firmly, and presses it tightly with both of hers, the closest she can come to allowing a hug. "I can't believe you came."

"I promised I would."

Her bloodshot eyes glisten as she scans my face. Maybe she's reading the years in my pores, the way you read the rings of a tree. She appears to find something there, after all; her face relaxes and her smile expands. It makes the next part, the selfish part, the inappropriate question, even harder.

"Do you know, Misaki-san, what your father did with the things we left behind?"

She looks at me, clearly puzzled.

"You know, when I left here, and I know it was a long time ago, but I left a word processor in the apartment."

"Oh," Misaki replies. I immediately regret asking this inane question, but she seems unbothered. "It was so long ago. I don't remember him ever bringing anything home. I would have seen a *wāpuro* in the house. We can check his office, though. Come with me."

Misaki obviously knows there's no colossal grey techno-relic in her father's office, but she seems happy for the distraction. We cross the foyer and mount the shallow stairs that lead to the upstairs hallway. At the door she slides the *shoji* open and, with a bow, steps inside. It's a heartbreaking gesture, possibly habit but more likely meant to honour the space that was once his.

When I enter, I bow as well.

The room is stuffy, closed up, and smells of paper—piles of newsletters, stacks of *Asahi Shimbun*, row after row of framed paintings still packaged in brown shipping wrap. I walk into the room as though it is a museum. Misaki walks to one of the rows, one item leaning against the next, and traces the closest package's corners with her fingers. There is no *wāpuro*. The only technology is a tiny transistor radio, from the 1970s, on a low table.

Two broken hairdryers and a faux-fur coat. If you left it behind, the farthest it journeyed was the closet. Nax never acquired my impractically oversized writing machine. Nax had no use for such a thing. In the end, Nax was an elderly man who didn't have time left to waste doing something as confounding and preposterous as printing *Kenichi and the Kappa*. I am suddenly shaken by just how wrong I have been. About everything.

The paintings sit as they always have, wrapped and dusty, but now something about them seems final, as if they are the last parts of her father being shipped away. Misaki abruptly lurches into tears, her entire body contorted by grief. I raise my arms and hold her, as this is no time to stand on ceremony, and she must agree; she squeezes me harder with every sob. I start to cry, too, but grief is only part of it. I cry at the realization that Nax is truly gone, that I have lost this place, that I am a selfish clod, and that the book has led me to nothing but a room full of leftovers from an old man's life. Misaki gathers herself more quickly than I. She apologizes, and I apologize back, still sobbing. There are some gentle words I cannot understand, and then she is gone, possibly embarrassed, back to the duties and rituals the day demands. I am left calcifying with guilt and self-loathing, unable to think or move.

Then I feel something shift in the muddy crevices in my brain. It reaches out like the evil hands stretching out of the muck in *Phantasm,* wanting to pull me into the mire. Into *the feeling.*

I try to outrun the anxiety attack, heading back down the stairs and towards the garden. Two small groups of men are gathered in opposite corners. They keep up the appearance of mourning-based propriety, but here on a smoke break, they allow themselves louder laughter. It's strange that I almost don't see him, standing alone between the clusters of smokers, facing away from me.

Hands claw at my chest, my face, my hair, and pull me backward into the filth until I am covered, buried underground. Mud fills my mouth and stills my tongue. Dirty water fills my lungs and wet, sticky clay sucks at my limbs. My heart screams in my chest, and I am unable to move, speak, or breathe. Welcome back, horrid old friend. The claustrophobic spell makes me want to run towards the nearest open space, but the nearest open space contains the cause of my claustrophobic spell.

Toby.

Toby, whom I haven't seen in twenty years, who disappeared without a word. Toby, who now turns, hands in the pockets of his black funeral suit, and looks up from the earth to spot me frozen on the polished wood floor, unable to move, encased in ice. His eyes widen briefly, followed by a silent laugh that's more shoulder shrug than guffaw. He glances back down at the ground, sighs, and returns his gaze to me. His head shakes as though he cannot believe what he is seeing, which maybe he can't.

The grabbing hands dissolve and I feel lighter. My head is above the muck now. My esophagus is still enflamed, so breathing feels impossible, but the attack subsides, as if waiting to see before continuing its rampage.

"Hello, River," he says.

I don't respond.

"It's okay if you'd like me to leave," he says.

It's okay if you'd like me to leave? He immediately assumes his presence matters to me? It does, but so what? So what if I want him to leave? I can't ask him to leave a funeral. Can I? How well did he know Nax? Did he know Nax like I did? Did he—

"It's also okay if you just want me to shut up."

I stand still in the hallway, looking like a statue but feeling like an idiot. The others in the garden have noticed Toby speaking, first glancing at him, then glancing down the hallway at me, where their eyes come to rest. Suddenly I am self-conscious, so I force my feet into motion, and walk the few meters to the open glass doors that overlook the sun-flooded yard. There are steps down into the garden, so I am few feet above ground, taller than him. It's my only true advantage at the moment, so I remain there, looking down at him, projecting a superiority I do not remotely possess.

"You can stay. It's a free country."

Holy Jesus, River. Weak.

Toby laughs, looks down, looks back up again. Did he always make, break, and re-establish eye contact like that? Did he always glance downward like that? It makes him seem thoughtful, less threatening. What new devilry is this, I wonder? The New Toby, arrogance and control replaced by supplication and contemplation. A front in either case. A carefully crafted and maintained illusion either way. Do I want an apology, which I would reject, or do I want his old, narcissistic defiance in the face of confrontation, which I would also reject? This, this almost doe-eyed expression, this quiet, thoughtful consideration, this I do not know what to do with. This lack of words, either. Toby never lacked words. He was a pressure cooker of words. Words would leak from his lips like steam, rising into his nostrils and ears—too many words, words so copious they lost all meaning. Every word a drop of water in the roiling river of his nonsense. A meaningless torrent, all rushing in one direction with one purpose—to further the agenda of Toby, to fulfil the self-projected myth of Toby, to get whatever it was Toby needed or wanted out of you, out of the moment, out of the world.

"For God's sake, Toby, say something."

Soft laugh, look down, look up. Still no words.

"I'm sorry, River."

I'm sorry. Now, that I can work with.

"Sorry?" I fold my arms and snort. Sorry! Tobias Handler is sorry. What is he sorry for? For being a liar? A cheat? A criminal? A fraud? A con man? For taking off without a word to anyone? Without a word to me? When I needed him the most?

"For all of it," he says, as if he can read my thoughts. "For hurting you. For who I was."

"You're sorry for who you were." I mirror.

"Yes."

"And now you're someone else."

Toby looks down again, but this time he does not look back up right away.

"I've been through a lot, River."

"Ah." Because the rest of us haven't in the last twenty years. The rest of us, of course, meaning me.

"I know." He continues to look down.

"You lied to us." I stand in the sunlight above him, offer him a righteous glare assisted by the height advantage. For the first time, I am six inches taller than him. Him and his grin and his guitar and his *namaste* and his absurd pontification and what he was really doing was, I don't know. I still don't know.

"I got involved in some sketchy business," he continues. It is not a startling revelation. I draw my pinky fingernail across my face, from my cheekbone to the tip of my chin. The colloquial gesture to indicate *yakuza*. I mime it quickly, as if brushing away a fly, hoping only Toby will catch it.

"That's not it," he protests. "I wasn't mob material. My most impressive talent was that I could play twelve Sublime songs on the acoustic guitar. No, it's just that things got..."

I can feel myself slipping sideways, and I know I need to hold fast, though if I break down, at least I'm in a place where the people around me are doing so themselves.

"Things got what, Toby?" My voice is quiet, but it feels like I'm shouting. The truth is that I want to shout, to scream at him, but I'm not sure what I want to say. I don't know which knob to twist inside my head, so as I fumble in the dark for the dials, my mouth keeps the volume at a whispery mumble.

"Do you know how things were for me?" I ask quietly. "I loved you, I needed you, and you vanished."

Toby doesn't reply for a moment.

"I'm sorry about Daniel," he finally mumbles at the ground.

"You could have said that twenty years ago, Tobias," I say. "It would have changed things considerably."

THE SAKON INARI

Toby wasn't just a con man. He was the P.T. Barnum of emotional swindlers. He listened to me talk and talk. I thought he was a wonderful listener because he was open-hearted, generous, kind. Turned out it was nothing but reconnaissance. The more intel he gathered, the easier I would be to capture.

I told him plenty, more than I should have, about my father. I didn't want that to be my defining biographical detail, or even a minor character note. The girl with the new name, the girl with the weird hobby, the girl with the dead dad. Yet when I opened up to him, I felt lighter with every word that gushed out of me.

One night, a few weeks after I'd arrived, Toby appeared at J.J.'s after closing time. The Lifers were there Monday through Saturday, seven through two. Toby didn't work with us, so his presence was erratic, the flight path of a blackfly; his appearances were irregular, though never quite unexpected. He was the wacky neighbour, Kramer or Lenny and Squiggy, suddenly inserting himself into the day's action.

"I like to think of Rosencrantz and Guildenstern as my role models," he said, when I called him on this.

"I like to think you mean in Tom Stoppard's world," I replied. "In Shakespeare's world, they're just dead."

The real reason Toby appeared at the end of the night is that many Japanese bars charge *setto,* or *sekiryō.* It's a cover charge. Toby always appeared after we'd stopped charging set for the night. He worked late, I said. He's a cheap bastard, Babette insisted. Both were true, in retrospect.

This night was different. For this night, Toby had something planned, blocked, and rehearsed. He had a scene in mind. I know they say show, don't tell, when it comes to storytelling, but no one wants me to transcribe the affectation-riddled tripe that Toby dribbled onto us that day. Or any day. Seriously, how much of this movie could someone sit through?

INTERIOR J.J.'s: Late evening/early morning. J.J.'s staff sits at table one, while Toby stands in front of the bar, pacing, gesticulating like a very white Baptist preacher.

TOBY

Which one of us doesn't owe a debt to family? (Pauses for effect). Our families, our bloodlines: we are the very manifestation of all those who came before, nurturing one before the other, taking—

BABETTE

Baaaaaarf.

Babette's mockery didn't dissuade him, of course. He continued for five more minutes as we squirmed with embarrassment, all so he could say, in far too many words, that it would be nice to pay tribute to my father. He had learned that symbolic acts, performed with either sincerity or irony, spoke to my love of rite and ritual, drama and gesture. What was coming to Japan and changing my name, after all? Personal pageantry. A gesture. The gorgeous new boy cared enough to help me honor my recently deceased father? He knew I would play along.

The next day, I walked the short distance from Sanyō Heights to Zenkōji Temple. I had started to visit the temple almost daily, rain or shine or that state in-between when the mountains were dimmed by the gathering rainclouds and a sheath of fog. Walking through the gardens at Zenkōji, through the chirp of birds and gentle clicking of crickets, I would feel as if there was no ground beneath my feet; I walked only on vibration, on the sound of the stones underfoot. Some days I wanted to abandon J.J.'s, River, the lot of it, and become a monk. I even stayed up all night to attend prayers at sunrise once, kneeling on the *tatami* of the inner sanctum with two dozen worshippers, our shoes in crackly plastic bags at our sides as the monks and priests came out to the altar. I felt their mysterious words flow through me, rich baritone voices I didn't need to understand in order to feel.

On weekends, I diverged from the streams of visitors to the east side of the main hall and walked through the trees to the pond, where I could sit and watch white koi float soundlessly like underwater clouds.

A cobblestone road led from the Zenkōji Road to the main gate, before you reached the main Zenkōji hall. The wide path was lined with vendor stalls—low awnings, bright vertical flags, swaying strings of red lanterns. Old women hunched over canes, men in suits prepared to do business, children in kimonos cried cross-legged on the ground while mothers laughed and shook their heads. On this road, I bought a pair of *waraji,* woven straw sandals intended for prayer. I'd had to convince the vendor that yes, the ones with the white straps were the ones I wanted. Yes, someone *was* dead. Japanese worshippers would tie their *waraji* to the Niō gates, a wooden arch-like structure, the wide pillars of which contained statues of the temple guardians, muscled and fearsome, with wild and watchful eyes.

I would not tie my sandals here, because we "ex-pats" had to do everything slightly wrong, personalizing rituals that weren't ours to personalize. We thought we were respecting the culture. Maybe we were creating our own. Either way, everyone ignored us, which was a blessing.

Nicolle and Allie, when they weren't funnelling vodka sodas until five a.m., were avid hikers. Up in the low mountains, on the other side of the Susobana River, they had stumbled across a small fox shrine overlooking the city. This was our destination on the modest slopes of Mount Asahi.

We hiked together, all of us, ascending streets and asphalt laneways and eventually dirt trails. We waved at farmers and listened to the bird bangers pop like air rifles; we watched the fluttering streamers of silver used to scare birds away from the orchards. The trees were now bent-backed with enormous green apples partially wrapped in tissue paper, which imbued their green skin with pinkish-red hues.

Toby led the parade like a babbling Sherpa, trying to guide us up the hillside with the sound of his voice. Daniel took frequent sips from his water bottle and called on us to rest every few minutes. Everyone knew his strength was easily depleted, and no one complained, but he must have felt awful, panting, walking at a snail's pace. I tried to distract him from his self-consciousness. When we stopped for him to recuperate, I would gesture to the little red bibs tied around the necks of stone Buddhas, comment on the reflective ribbons that fluttered between branches, point excitedly at the bulbous, blood-red bellies of the autumn dragonflies.

"*Shichinin no Samurai!*" Toby shouted at a farmer and gestured towards our crew of seven. The farmer took a second to confirm our numbers and laughed out loud in return. We turned up another narrow trail, past a decaying little shed. An enormous ewe stood under its roof, its wool sodden and mucky, its eyes trained on the distance, as if we were of no interest, which we weren't, I suppose.

"The final destination is upon us," Toby intoned. "Your spiritual journey for the day has achieved its physical goal. What remains is what happens within you!"

The shrine was in a small clearing beyond a set of red *torii* gates. Two stone foxes posed on stone pillars. There was a structure no larger than a shed, immaculately kept, locked up tight. Nicolle pressed her face to the small gap in its sliding doors. We were subdued; even Toby spoke in a low voice. Through the trees we could see Nagano below, like an enormous nest in the mountain plateau. This simple place felt every inch as holy as the grand hall of Zenkōji. It may have been me, or only in my own mind, a spiritual flux of my own creation. I felt that way in churches, too. I was an atheist swiftly humbled by the hush of divine places.

"Thanks for bringing me up here, guys," I said, but only Daniel heard me. Allie had joined Nicolle in pondering the contents of the shrine; Reiko stood, head cocked sideways, in front of a metal pillar. On the sides of this pillar—just a steel 4x4 driven into the ground, really—were various writings, including the English phrase *May peace prevail upon the earth*. Babette sat on a rickety bench picking at her cuticles.

"You're welcome, River," Daniel replied as I pulled the straw sandals out of their crinkly plastic packaging. He stepped forward and grabbed a branch from one of the trees by the edge of the clearing, overlooking the city. He pulled it down and towards me so I could tie the sandals to it. The straw straps were smooth and difficult to knot. I pulled firmly on the loose ends.

Should I say a prayer? No, a prayer was too much, too formal, too much an admission that perhaps there was something to pray *to*. I thought, instead, about how I had chosen to remake, rethink, move forward. My father—my poor, lost, miserable father, on the other hand—probably grew tired of himself too, but without the freedom to reinvent himself as I did. Locked in by his generation's definition of the word *possibility*. By the time he was 40, self-weariness had turned to self-loathing. When he died, we didn't understand that his anger and the pain were real and constant. We blamed him for poisoning the family. We blamed ourselves for not loving him enough. We blamed our mother for not making things better, as mothers are supposed to do. We blamed him and we blamed ourselves and we grieved and felt our hearts sour.

"And now I let that go," I said out loud, as I lightly released the branch between my fingers. The branch sailed upward, and the sandals dangled from the tree like wind chimes, knocking against one another in the breeze. Rite and ritual. I had made my own.

That's when Babette shrieked.

She didn't yell or scream, she shrieked. She shrieked the shriek of the mutilated. It shattered the contemplative silence and caused each of us to flinch and shriek a little ourselves.

Babette leapt on top of the rusty bench, which protested with an aluminum squeal, and pointed at the carpet of brown leaves. There was a faint rustle and shift before the triangular head of a snake emerged. It revealed itself one leaf at a time: over four feet long with a bright-green back that curved to a yellow belly. It seemed to hover, to move forward and sideways simultaneously, before it disappeared back under its brittle brown blanket. A second later, Babette's sketchy bench creaked and one corroded leg buckled. She yelped, terrified of being thrown down into the snake's path, and scrambled up the incline to the other end, arms flailing to find balance. Then, as if disheartened by the defeat of their comrade, all the legs gave way at once. The bench seat fell flat to the ground and somehow Babette, like a drunken surfer, kept her balance, emitting tiny shriekettes all the while. Reiko held one hand over her mouth and pounded the other against her thigh. The rest of us barely held ourselves together, although we knew better than to laugh at Babette's expense.

"Holy shit, mate, did you see that thing?" Allie wisely diverted our attention from Babette's panic back to the snake itself. "That was amazing."

"Who would win in a fight, the snake or the fox spirits?" Toby asked.

"Fox spirits wouldn't attack a snake," said Reiko. "A real fox, now, that fight I would watch."

"Oh! My! God!" shouted Babette.

Daniel and I looked at each other and giggled.

"Cool snake," he said.

"Very cool snake," I agreed.

Neither of us realized we would both take the creature home with us, tend to her, watch her grow, and release her back into the world again. As far as we knew then, she was simply gone.

"Thanks, Toby," I said as we began our exodus from Asahi-yama.

"You're welcome."

"Are you busking tonight?"

On warmer nights, Toby would busk on the Gondō shopping arcade, next to Shlomi, the Israeli guy who sold crafty necklaces laid out on a black blanket. Eventually uniformed police officers would tire of sitting in the nearby police box, wander over to them, and shoo them along.

"Yeah. Maybe I'll come by J.J.'s if Masa's there. I learned 'Ventura Highway' for him."

It should be noted that, on the nights Toby brought his guitar, Nax would never charge him set.

"He'll love that," I said.

"Can I walk you home after work?"

"I'd like that," I cooed.

Yes. Yes, I fell for it. I fell for all of it. Instead of seeing a con artist, I saw someone winging their way through reinvention, just like me. Unsure of the next move, taking missteps and allowing himself to stumble. A gorgeous man flailing helplessly while professing he had it all under control. I never told him how transparent it was. It made him vulnerable. Which made him adorable.

He would have hated to know that.

DARK SCARY STAIRS OF DOOM

Jesus H. Christ, did I just tell Toby I used to love him?

I tumble through the house, past the other funeral goers, into my shoes, and out the front door. I struggle to look composed when in my head I'm Sally in *Texas Chainsaw,* blindly and bloodily fleeing out into the dawn.

Don't make a scene. Keep it together. Don't let anyone see you shatter, or you might as well spit on the tatami and spray-paint Me! Me! Me! on the shoji. Today is not about you, River.

Another elderly couple arrives, and I dive into their taxi the second they disembark. I mumble a destination and the car begins to hurtle down side streets as narrow as a length of twine. The closeness of the laneways makes it seem as if he's driving at tachyon speed. We wind and whirl until I can see the massive shape of the temple, partially hidden behind trees. I mumble again, *here's good here's good,* and smoosh a fistful of yen coins into the driver's white-gloved hand.

It's too much, it's all too much. I need calm down, to focus on the cloudlike movement of the fish, to walk with the sound of stones underfoot.

The roof of the main hall crests the treeline, its dark-brown slope dotted with gold buttons. I think of Noah's biblical ark, cavernous and wooden. On Zenkōji' s east side, the gravel path crunches beneath my feet, but I am too distracted to be transported. Other than my footsteps, the grounds are nearly silent, the row of trees muting the sound of the street only metres away.

When the pond comes into view, something washes over me. I wouldn't call it peace, but it comes from the same mother. Not much here has changed. The pond is halved by a footbridge of flat rocks precariously balanced on underwater stones. On the west side of the pond rests the large rock I sat on for hours, writing bad poetry and letters home, watching turtles and koi ripple the surface. A koi peeks from the water now, absently and without curiosity, nibbling at air before it slips back under, its translucent white suddenly ethereal and cloudy.

The sound of an iron bell pours through the air, thick like an enormous drop of syrup, disappearing into the ground. I sit on my rock and stare at the pond. Over by the main temple hall, there will be pilgrims, monks, children, families, devotees, worshippers, elderly men in surgical masks to keep coughs and colds to themselves, young boys squatting against storefronts, tour groups led by uniformed women carrying tall banner-flags easily identified above the heads of a crowd in case someone becomes separated in the throng. Tiny shopkeepers in grey farmers' clothes or kimonos, selling umbrellas, pottery, chopsticks, clothing, hats, food, Zenkōji trinkets, and *maneki neko,* white porcelain cats with one paw raised to beckon luck. Austere ceremonial items, wooden slats with prayers etched on them, incense to burn, sandals used to honour the dead. Here there is only me and, at the moment, one fat koi gumming the edge of the rock.

I'll buy some sandals, I think to myself. I'll write Nax's name on them and hang them at the Niōmon gate, down by the old Zenkōji road that leads to Sanyō Heights. I'll kneel a moment, maybe throw on some sunglasses so nobody gets too unnerved witnessing a weeping white lady. I'll say, "See you again," like he and so many others said to us when we left for home, as all of us did, eventually. That will be my private memorial.

"Did you ever go down into the *okaidan*?" says a voice behind me.

Goddammit, he followed me.

I don't reply. I watch an exceptionally rotund koi float to the rock bridge and begin mouthing at the edge of the stone as if tasting his way to freedom.

"Probably not, I guess." Toby makes no attempt to approach me but talks to me from a distance. "Remember, you and I stood there at the top of the stairs," he continues, "where there's all that red-painted wood and that gold-painted metal railing leading down into the dark…we stared into the dark for what, ten minutes? You called them the Dark Scary Stairs of Doom. I wasn't going to push you to do it. On account of the claustrophobia."

He's setting up a story. It's like a shoddy, ineffective prologue to a film with a clueless, cliché-ridden script and a director who condescends to their audience. Something Evvie would direct, maybe.

The *okaidan*. It's a fascinating part of Zenkōji, but I've never had the courage to see it. Of course, you can't see it, and that's the point. Below the main hall of Zenkōji there's a sacred statue of the Amida Triad—Amida Buddha and his two attendants. Supposedly it's the first image of Buddha brought to Japan, from India via China, in the year 552. It is so sacred that no one is allowed to see it. Not even the head monk. Some believe it doesn't exist at all, that its container houses nothing but dust, like the Ark in *Raiders*. Pilgrims can approach the *hibutsu*, the hidden Buddha, by going down below the main hall, into the nothingness of the *okaidan*, to the pitch-black hallway that circles the room in which they keep the Triad.

Daniel and I would stand at the top of the stairs and egg each other on, bonding in laughter and fear. We'd offer each other money, favours, our first-born children, but it wasn't going to happen. I was terrified of my past claustrophobic spells, and the idea of Daniel willingly descending into a subterranean tunnel was absurd. The boy could barely use a bathroom stall. Why Toby never descended those stairs is anyone's guess. Lack of curiosity, lack of interest, laziness. All three could apply.

"I finally went down there after I came back to Nagano," Toby says. "I was on a sort of…okay, I know this sounds like the old me, but I was on a sort of spiritual journey. Becoming a different person. It was like…you know in John Carpenter's *The Thing*? Where it was like, this creature pretending to be someone else?"

I roll my eyes hard enough to pull an ocular muscle.

"'John Carpenter's *The Thing*'? Don't be an ingratiating prick, Toby."

"You're right." I hear him sigh. "You're right, I don't need to bullshit you."

The smell of still water, the soft rustle of the trees, the cloudlike koi—without these, I would feel frayed, unknotted, pulled apart.

"You might think you've been in darkness, but this is another kind of dark," he says, his voice slightly closer. "The *okaidan* is like you're taking a shortcut through a universe where light doesn't even exist. You wouldn't feel claustrophobic because you couldn't tell if the space was narrow or wide. The darkness strips away everything. Strips it down to you, you and the smooth wooden wall beneath your hand as you walk."

Toby steps up beside me, but neither of us look at one another.

"Do you remember the point of it all?"

I do, but I don't say anything.

"You're supposed to feel the wall as you go, to guide you

in the dark, but also because if your fingers come across the lock to the sacred chamber, you'll break the wheel of samsara and reach nirvana finally and eternally."

He pauses a moment.

"When I was back home in Halifax, I ran into some... legal issues."

"Of course you did."

"Yeah. Something like that makes you re-evaluate your life choices. I decided to come back here, and I told myself the first thing I'd do is visit Zenkōji and go into the *okaidan* and find the stupid door to paradise because goddamn it, you know? I thought it was going to inspire me or bring me peace or something. Either way, I built it up to be a really big deal. Except when I finally got there, I didn't find the door. At first, I was devastated, but then I realized. I'd just been just hoping for the easy route. No penitence, no reparations. I just wanted to grope around in the dark for the key to heaven."

It's a poignant story. It hits all the right notes. Regret, guilt, sympathy. I so desperately want to believe him.

"Just like the rest of us," I mutter.

"That's the point!" He's animated now, and finally I risk a sideways glance. He's not looking at me as he talks, but at the surface of the pond, following my gaze. His hands move like he's hosting a television show, but he's gesturing for his own benefit. "That's the point. I realized groping for a doorknob in the dark was stupid. I had to go up into the light. Earn forgiveness. Do penance, make reparations. Action. Self-determination through action."

Toby slides his hands into his pockets as he settles into silence, his head cocked slightly to one side, as if listening to the low *bloops* made by the koi as they surface and submerge. I stare blankly ahead, caught between sympathy and rage. Rage has had the upper hand for quite some years now. Sympathy will have to up its game considerably to come out on top.

"Let me see if I can piece this together." I pull my feet up onto the rock and tuck my knees under my chin. The shock of seeing Toby has dissipated; my nervous mumble has been replaced by mild sarcasm. "There's a bad moon on the rise, so you scurry home. Then you run into some legal issues, which even an idiot would translate to you went to jail for something. That gives you plenty of time to think about how you messed your life up. You come back here for an easy fix. You realize there isn't an easy fix. Now you're what, ladling out soup for Zenkōji monks at lunchtime? Cleaning up radioactive mudslides in Fukushima? Reading to the blind? You had a little time-out in a correctional facility and now you're improvising your own twelve-step program?"

"River, I know, it sounds like bullshit, but I really am sorry. I was young and messed up and—"

"That's not the problem, Toby." I pull myself to my feet beside the rock. My muscles feel tense, as though they're pulling into themselves. My lungs can't seem to get enough oxygen. "I don't care what you were doing or what happened when you left. What I care about is that you didn't exist. You were a creation. You weren't any more real than a character I invented."

"No," he says. "There was a real me."

My shoulders stiffen and my hands flap around at my sides. I want to toss him to the koi.

"I was in love with thin air!" It's as close to a shout as I'll allow myself in this quiet place. Facing him directly, I notice that a few wrinkles have crawled out from the corners of his eyes. Like me, Toby has grown old.

Good try, sympathy, now get the hell out my way.

"You were a used-car salesman." I try to manage my tone of voice, but it's like trying to smooth down waves with your hands. "You were one of those evangelicals on late-night television, preaching the gospel of whatever thoughtful, sensitive-guy baloney you thought would sell your religion. No! You were a carnival barker. You used words like *namaste* and talked about inner children and you had Maya bloody Angelou beside your bed and there's no way you ever cracked the spine on that, and you stole and YOU SAID YOU LOVED ME!"

Oh. There it is. It comes out in a tense, hoarse croak, but there it is.

Toby briefly glances towards my face, then back at the earthy brown mirror of the pond surface.

"I didn't love you," he says. "Back then, I didn't know how."

"You didn't know how?" I stare at him a moment. "Which one of you didn't know how? The you we saw every day? The you who shared a bed with me? The you who ran away?" I turn towards the rock bridge and prepare to storm away. "Come on, Toby," I say. "Don't you see? There was no *you*."

KITCHEN PARTY

Who were *any* of us then, though? Were any of us regular people? Nicolle and Allie were hard-drinking, free-spirited world travellers at the tender age of twenty. Reiko was prone to giggles and singing Skid Row songs on karaoke—yet she also managed a business at the age of 22. Daniel was as fragile as a dried-up maple leaf, and I was, well, I was a nascent River Black. Toby was like a shadow that travelled on the underside of daylight, slipping through the cracks and around the hours, as if regular time and space were of little concern. He could appear at India just before twilight and ghost, without so much as a whisper, before full daylight broke. He was supposed to be a labourer on construction sites in the north and east, but his hands seemed too pink, too smooth, to bear this out. When confronted about this matter-of-factly by Babette, he replied, "Gloves and moisturizer are nature's miracles," and we let it go without reminding him that neither, in fact, were natural.

Toby rarely let you inside. He could regale, amuse, and delight, but he couldn't tell you who he was. You didn't see his secrecy because he didn't come across as secretive. Instead, he was more interested in you than in himself. Once you started to discuss yourself, he could slide between your words, separate sentences with surgical precision, extract new meanings from the incisions; he could have you questioning your own thoughts, so he never had to challenge you himself. You were so wrapped up in looking at yourself in new ways thanks to Toby that you eventually forgot to ask about Toby.

It wasn't quite gaslighting. That came later.

I can't bear to paint too detailed a picture. We flirted into the fall, watched winter froth its way out of the mountains and into the city. Meaningful glances. Pointed innuendo. Late-night walks home. But just before he should have leaned in to kiss me, he'd ruin another evening by just going home. Then, one night, there was a break in the pseudo-philosophical psychoanalysis, an awkward silence, the kind of awkward silence that has the import of thunder, announcing that a kiss is imminent as rain. It happened quickly, and he was gone; not out of shyness—it was simply part of the role. The mystery man, keeping me off-balance. Keep 'em wanting more.

The kisses happened more often and grew longer, until finally, one night, I invited him upstairs. We walked along the landing and through the door, into a kind of dreamlike embrace, silent by necessity—sex so quiet it became more intense, the atmosphere bordering on surreal.

Everything seemed normal in the morning. It was normal for me to wake alone in an icy room, reach for a lighter, and fire up the frayed wick on my worn-out kerosene heater. Then I remembered I hadn't gone to bed alone, and my heart dropped. I lay under my duvet a few minutes before putting on my robe and sliding the *shoji* open with glum resignation.

Babette sat at the undersized kitchen table, coffee mug in both hands and her breakfast, square slices of white bread topped with toaster-oven-melted processed cheese, on the table in front of her. Her flat eyes judged me over the rim of her mug as she sipped.

"What?" I said.

Her eyes rolled sideways to the tabletop, where a Tissue of Kitten box had been dismantled and a note written on the cardboard in a nearly illegible hand. The pen strokes resembled fragile Nordic runes that had been shaken, broken, and spilled from a Yahtzee cup.

Early morning, didn't want to wake you. Talk to you as soon as I can. Namaste.

"Namaste." Babette's voice the aural equivalent of a child sticking out her tongue.

"Yeah, I kind of hate that too," I admitted.

Babette glared at me.

"You know I hate that fucking guy."

"Yeah, well, that's got nothing to do with me."

"It's got everything to do with you. I think you're making a big mistake."

"Yeah, well, duly noted."

Babette snorted.

"You know, there's rumours he does shady stuff for Takahashi," Babette sniffed.

"That would be more meaningful if I knew who Takahashi was."

"Local *yakuza* honcho."

"Please. You know as well as I do they're not gonna trust a white Canadian guy who thinks he's a guru."

Babette glared at me a moment. "I'm not going to talk you out of this, am I?"

"Nope."

"Fine." She put the coffee down and picked up a sagging piece of cheese toast. "Good luck, mate."

"Well, what about your mystery guy?" Indignance crept into my voice. "He doesn't come around. We don't even know him."

Babette put the toast down and hardened the glare.

"I know perfectly well who my boyfriend is," she replied. "You don't know who Toby is, and you never will."

A moment of tense silence.

"Tell you what." I reached out and grabbed her coffee mug, took a swig, placed it back in her hands. "I'll never ask about your mystery guy if you never bother me about Toby. I'll shut up if you shut up."

Babette stared down at her cup with disgust.

"Make your own damn coffee, mate." Then, with a shrug, she continued to sip.

"You know where I can buy cleaning supplies?"

"We've got some under the sink."

"No, I mean, like, enough to clean J.J.'s kitchen."

"There aren't enough cleaning products in the world, mate."

"Yeah, that room probably doesn't need cleaning products. It needs a cleansing by holy fire. I don't have access to holy fire, though."

"Downstairs at Itō, then," she said. "Why on earth would you willingly attempt to do this?"

"I feel bad for Daniel," I said. "It's like the world is one great big Mario game for him, except he's not playing it, he's actually Mario. It's gotta be terrifying. Thought I could do him a little kindness."

"Good luck," Babette replied. "Daniel will appreciate it."

I made my way to Itō Yōkadō along increasingly-familiar sidestreets. Orange railings lined the edges of the road, fencing off the canals. In the grocery store, I filled a basket with cloths, scrubbing sponges, and various cleansers. The cleansers were a gamble. I had to search every plastic bottle for telltale illustrations so I understood what was used to clean what. It was worrying that I didn't know the Japanese characters for "bleach" or "ammonia."

With my equivalent of cleansing fire in hand, I made my way down the wide avenue to J.J.'s. In the afternoons, it was common for the clouds to roll over the mountains and across the plain, trapping Nagano beneath an indistinct grey sky. This day was no exception. The bar was eerily dim and still, like a movie set after cast and crew have gone home. The energy from the night before remained charged in the air, as though the room were in stasis until the next moment could begin.

Daylight, however grey, revealed the true shabbiness of

the place. I could see the frayed bits of fabric on the couches, the inadequacy of our nightly "cleaning" regimen. I rounded the bar and strode into the kitchen.

"Okay, kitchen," I told it. "I'm here to set you free."

I went there that afternoon to free a kitchen, but freedom came at a cost. I finished, four hours later, feeling as though I'd angered Poseidon and he wouldn't let me get home to Ithaca. Forget an angry ocean god; try fighting the will of a quarter-inch of fry-vat grease splashed liberally onto an old stovetop over the course of a decade. My pores emanated the sharp scent of cleanser, my lungs tingled unpleasantly with the sting of noxious fumes, and my hands were wrinkled and moist from the rubber gloves. I ached and felt nauseated and couldn't wait to see Daniel's face.

It was Wednesday. That meant The Fantastic J.J. Band performed tonight. They were a jazz combo led by a tall, talented guitarist with the countenance of a sleepy librarian. For an ad hoc collective they were great, and the trumpet player Daikuhara could blow, as they say. The band brought in a few extra bodies, including Masa and Nax, who normally never appeared before midnight. It was loud and lively, and after a while it was overwhelming; if you were in the wrong mood, or a sensitive soul, the trumpet might seem like a hyperactive macaw screaming in your ear. Daniel was such a soul, and I knew he'd spend most of the night hiding in the kitchen.

I drew what everyone considered to be the short straw and sat with Nax and one of his art buddies. I didn't mind. Nax was sweet, and safe. New customers were the danger because they were unproven entities. Sometimes customers were curt. Other times, they were so antagonistic you wondered why on earth they ventured out into public. Why willingly pay steep bar prices, including a ¥3,000 set, to sit with someone and tell them they were ugly and stupid? What was the point?

Eventually I snuck over to the kitchen, where Daniel squatted on the stout metal stool, face to the open window.

The smell of ammonia still picked at the edges of my sinuses like nervous fingernails.

"You like?"

"It's fantastic." He smiled out the window. "Thank you."

"Well, you know, it wasn't just for you," I lied, resting my behind on the stainless steel counter. "It was needed. Badly. I swear, health inspectors pass by this place like there's blood on the doorframe."

Daniel raised an eyebrow.

"That's a biblical reference."

"Yeah, I got it."

Sticks rolled against the snare drum, the opening of "Caravan," and soon Daikuhara was exhaling madly into his horn, bending notes sideways with his mute. They flew out at perpendicular angles and scattered against the curtains of the kitchen door. Stragglers in the street, below the red windows, could be heard shouting goodnight to one another over the music.

"How's the writing?" Daniel asked.

"The Cursèd Black Notebook has been a little forlorn lately, I have to admit. Still, I have a seed of an idea. It's sort of a classic nuclear-bomb-makes-giant-lizard monster trope. I love *kaiju*."

Another eyebrow raise.

"*Kaiju!* It means 'strange creature.' Like Godzilla or Mothra."

"Okay."

"I started thinking about a legendary monster that mountain farmers muttered about in low voices. She's a giant snake. They'll call her *Mega-Mamushi*."

"She?"

"Oh yeah. Gotta be a she."

"The snake in the Garden makes Eve sin, but instead, your snake itself is female."

"I, uh, never thought of that? I just thought a kickass mom snake was a great idea because she's protecting her babies."

"That's good too. And you're really messing with tropes when your phallic symbol is actually female."

"Dude, you're on *fire* with the allegorical subtext tonight." I leaned against the wall and picked at a button of grease that I had missed on the stovetop. "You know, all this is because we saw that snake up at the fox shrine."

That's when Daniel, decidedly out of character, looked right at me.

"Me too."

"You too what?"

He looked away again, but there was still something unusually alive in his eyes.

"The snake. It gave me an idea, too. Like, don't worry, it's a totally very different idea. I started writing something."

"Daniel Truman." I mimed pushing him but didn't actually touch him. I was uncertain just how fragile his fragility was.

"Yeah, well, you know, I don't talk about myself much. But when you have a heart problem and a mom who won't let you out of the house, limits your television time, and thinks videogames are the devil's work, you find something else to do. I read and wrote a lot."

"This is awesome, Daniel. We can be writing buddies! What's it about?'

"It's about a *kappa*."

"Like, the little turtle-frog-bird hybrid dude? The mascot for *Kappa* Sushi?"

Daniel laughed. "Well, maybe a little more...traditional than him, but yeah. It's a *kappa*. A *kappa* named Soba."

"As in the buckwheat noodles?"

"I don't know. It's kind of stupid. I named him for the river, the Susobana. Like, *Soba* from the middle of the word."

"Right, yeah, okay, I get it."

"I dunno. I dunno if it's any good. Like, my grammar is fine, I always did okay in English class, I just don't know...I used to write really crappy stuff. Little-kid stuff. This is really different for me. I don't know if—"

"I'll be your editor!" I shouted loud enough to startle Daniel, even with the furious horn in the background. "Seriously, I would really like to help out. Have you written much of it? Why don't you give it to me when you're done?"

Daniel looked me again, then, with a sadness I hadn't expected.

"I don't want to wait until it's done because...what if I never finish it?"

"Why wouldn't you?"

Daniel didn't answer but stared at the tile. It took me a moment to realize what he meant. *You are not going to die soon,* I didn't say.

"Oh, come on, you'll finish it," I did say. "I can help you as you go, too, if that works."

Reiko poked her head through the curtains and grinned apologetically.

"I'm sorry." Her head tilted to the left. "But we are—"

"Busy, of course, yeah, super sorry, Rei-chan. Be there in thirty seconds, I promise." I turned back to Daniel. "I'm excited! I'm stoked!" I bounced a little on my toes as the band blared louder. "Let's talk later!"

Instead of taking me back to Nax, Reiko ushered me towards a table of customers I'd never seen before. In the end, the band made conversation impossible because both men were low talkers. We watched the Fantastic Band instead. Daniel's nervous-kitten demeanour weirded some people out, but I found it adorable. I felt almost protective of him. Also, I had a partner! A comrade-in-arms! Someone to trade manuscripts with, to come to with plot concerns, to inspire me. Even if none of those things came to pass, even if he was too shy to comment or to show me his work, the very notion of this would kick me in the behind, ferment my own creative juices, maybe pop the cork on some of my own ideas. Daniel would tell the story of Soba, and I would bring *Mega-Mamushi,* in all her ferocious glory, to life.

EVRARD ON TELEVISION

Over twenty years later, *Mega-Mamushi* remains asleep in her lair. Instead of birthing her into an unsuspecting world, I found myself a midwife to another monster entirely, one that was also asleep until he appeared on my doorstep on the cover of a book that can't exist.

Then there's my *other* other monster, Leo Pardpeti. I am his hapless mother. His scheming, malevolent father is in front of me.

It's four am, and Evrard Frederich is on television.

It's your standard Japanese television stage set, vertical banners of *kanji* on a bright-blue background. Dozens of flower arrangements positioned on stands behind a table of women who cover their mouths when they giggle. They're giggling now, as Evvie, seated at another table with two blue-suited men, shovels a pile of ramen noodles into his mouth with chopsticks held awkwardly in one ham-hock fist. You can see his crimson skin fighting for visibility through the pancake make-up. The missing incisor completes his look—that of a third-tier German-American boxer at the end of his career, a scrappy bruiser with a hot temper.

What you don't know is that's the look he's going for. When he's not on television, he wears a partial denture. In fact, he can be a bit prissy about the shine of his shoes or the crispness of his shirts. That's not normally something to make fun of, but I mention it because it would make him so angry if people knew. Almost as angry as when I call him Evvie.

At the more reasonable hour tonight when I tried to sleep, my brain bubbled like a sauté on high heat. I imagined a steady hiss, grey matter browned, sticking to my skull like burned egg in a pan. Toby and Daniel spun around my brain in an awkward, lurching shimmy, doing a zombie tango together. I prefer my thoughts to dance gracefully like Rogers and Astaire, or at least Grey and Swayze. These lumbering oafs, these awful memories and frustrating emotions, are ruining the entire production. Here I am, back in Nagano, the source of so much *natsukashii* for me, and these two idiots are wrecking the whole thing.

Sorry, Daniel. I'm just angry.

"You can't go home again" is a truthful cliché. A dark one, if you meditate on it too deeply. You know you can't go back because things won't be the same, and even if they are, *you* aren't. Japan was as much "home" as anywhere else I lived. I was really happy there, at that age, that time, in that place that no longer exists, with those people. If I think about it that way, I have to face the truth that I'll never feel that happy—at least, not that specific sort of happy—again. And that's heartbreaking.

Tobias Handler does not help the situation. I'm finally back in Nagano with some of the old gang, and goddammit, it's the worst.

I turned on the television to forget these ghosts, only to find one of my current demons eating noodles on a TV show. The channel guide promises it's the beginning of a Evrard Frederich late-night movie marathon.

Evrard stupid Frederich. The existence of his career is the triumph of a stubborn amateur's enthusiasm over anything resembling skill. Poor lighting, wooden acting, laughable effects, and yes, grim and dismal scripts. Before *Pinned,* I touched up his screenplays about alien lesbian zombies and murderous satanic cycle cults. Now, three films deep in skewered and dissected women, I would give an ovary to work on something as gleefully abysmal as *Space Station Sappho*. At least that crap was fun.

This movie marathon contains no *Space Station Sappho* or *Harleys Bound for Hell* (renamed *Motorcycles to Hell* to satisfy the legal department of an unimpressed Harley Davidson Motor Company). No, tonight's marathon is dedicated to Evvie's finest misanthropy, courtesy of yours truly: *Pinned* through *Pinned III*. Ugh.

Evrard became a minor cult figure in Japan because he challenged a kendo master to a duel. They don't "duel" in kendo, of course, and Evvie knows it; he just thought duel sounded more badass than competition or match. It began when he and Tatsuya Nakatani, a professor at Kansai U, had a disagreement over the sport, which Evvie dabbles in at best. Nakatani is a fifth dan. That didn't stop Evvie from saying, and I quote, that his "masculine fire burns hotter than any Japanese man's" and that "if we used real swords I'd serve you Nakatani sushi."

Yes, I dated this man. Remember, though, I knew about the partial denture. I knew about the box of wet naps in his shoulder bag. I knew how much he wept during the last twenty minutes of *Return of the King*. His absurd persona is partially an overzealous attempt at branding. When you see an Evrard Frederich movie, you are buying into a whole worldview, the way some buy into tough-guy writers for the author's image as much, if not more, than for the work itself.

Nakatani, however, is not a construct. He is a tough guy, despite being a fairly meek university professor. Evvie spent most of the match on the floor, both literally, and, as Nakatani mopped said floor with him, figuratively. Even though Evvie lost, the crazy *Doitsujin* with the bulging rage-eyes found a certain level of infamy here as a result. He is repeatedly invited to go on programs where he eats ramen with pretty young women dressed like office ladies.

"The noodles are too chewy!" He dramatically allows some half-masticated ramen to tumble from his mouth, much to the stage crowd's delight. Evvie brings the enormous bowl to his face so fast the broth runs down his chin, which makes him grin his mischievous yet also half-psychotic gap-toothed grin. "This is the worst yet!"

"Pfft."

The creature stands beside the bed, one hip resting against the wall, as if it had come into the room and became unexpectedly interested in the television programming. There is a glistening sheen of water on its murky skin. It looks like a demonic tortoise, yet it's standing there casually, like it's Sheila asking me what I'm watching on Netflix, distractedly tracing the water-filled hole in its head with two fingers, the way I might twirl my hair around my pinky. Holy God, LSD has nothing on exhaustion and stress. If I close my eyes tightly, shake my head a few times and look back again, the thing will be gone. It isn't really there.

Instead, I talk to it.

"He's quite a prize, eh?"

Soba, if indeed the thing is Daniel's *kappa*, scrunches up its already-scrunched face and closes its eyes.

"Stupid."

"Oh, no, not really. He just looks and acts like he's recently been dropped on his head."

"Mah. Humans stupid. This human extra stupid."

"Not stupid. Just broken."

That's when I notice that the creature's right leg, on the side that's not leaning casually against the wall, rests in the plastic wastebasket from the bathroom, which has been filled to the rim with water. As it adjusts its position, water sloshes up and over the edge and lands on the worn carpet with a *splat*.

"So you're Soba," I say. Its hand, still tickling the edges of the recess in its skull, freezes.

"You don't want to remember," it says.

"You said that last time." I push myself up into a sitting position, back against the headboard. "But you're wrong. I do want to remember. You're Soba."

Soba turns its frown into a grimace. "Stupid name."

"The river you lived in was called the Susobana, so Daniel called you Soba. You followed a boy up to the shrine to eat him, and he fed you cucumbers instead. That's how it happened, yes?"

It doesn't reply, exactly, but somehow in its stillness, it answers in the affirmative.

"Why are you here, bothering me now?" I ask. "Are you real?"

"Look forward!" it hisses.

"I don't know what that means."

It screeches. "Look forward! At TEE VEE!"

I turn to the television. The opening sequence of *Pinned III* is happening, the slow pan, down a dark alley, towards Leo Pardpeti's house of horrors.

"You," it says.

"Not me. I was only part of this mess."

"You," it repeats.

"You know, when this movie premiered in Vancouver, I didn't show up at the theatre. For two weeks, River Black was *jōhatsu*. She was gone, and Helen Delaney was left in her place. Helen Delaney wanted no part of this."

"Soba know," it says.

"Ha! So you are Soba."

No response.

"Well, you know, it's hard for me to tell. I know you're not *real* real. I don't have a history of dealing well with trauma. The first time I had panic attacks, I fled the hemisphere and tried to reinvent myself. The next time, I spent two weeks hiding in my apartment weeping, having nightmares about Evvie—that's the stupid human on screen, the one who looks like he walked onto a highway and tried to kiss the grill of a moving Greyhound bus. Once I dreamed that he rolled up a copy of the *Pinned III* script and drove it through my sternum. A little on the nose, but that's my subconscious for you."

Soba is not interested in my ramblings. It appears to be squinting at the television.

"Mah. Lighting bad."

"The worst! He's terrible at that. Thinks you can fix everything with filters in post."

"If want to succeed, be open," it says. "Want to remember. Be open, accept death."

"Great!" I slap my hands against the mattress on either side of me. "Thanks! You're helpful! What the hell does it mean, though?"

Soba turns to me, and for the first time, there's a shudder that starts in my spine and radiates outward. Its eyes are malicious black marbles.

"See death!" it shrieks at me, and I almost scream. Its voice comes from darker places, places I've headed towards but thankfully never reached. Places I would not have come back from.

"See death," it repeats. "Then walk into darkness."

"Jesus, you're like a teenage goth girl reading pretentious poems at an open mic. Are you saying this trip was a mistake? That I shouldn't be here? Sorry, Sobie. It's a bit too late."

The impatience drains from its face; its cheeks slacken. Its skin is the colour of meconium.

"Book." It says this with resignation. "Soba try warn you, but you are stupid. If must remember, use book. Go through book."

As suddenly as it appeared, it is gone. The room is empty. It's like the laziest edit you've ever seen; it's there, and then it's gone, along with the bucket of water.

Fear suddenly overwhelms me. When I look back at the television, we seem farther into *Pinned III* than I remember.

You fell asleep, River.

What do these dreams know that I don't? What is this slithering subconscious freakshow trying to tell me? See death? Look forward? Go through the book?

The *kappa* knows one truth: Nax, rest his soul, was only an excuse. I'm here for other reasons. To revisit. To remember. And to find out how, in the name of all that is holy, this monster I birthed twenty years ago has come to be part of my life again, on the pages of an impossible book.

If must remember, go through book. That little freak frog monkey bird knows of what it speaks. J.J.'s is long gone. I'll go back again, but I'll go back through the book. Go back and find out where it came from in the first place. Like a snake that eats its own tail, it will lead me to itself.

BOYS OF BOOM

The *kappa* was always in Daniel's mind, but I admit, I helped him give it a face.

From the impossible book:

> The *kappa* was an uneven shade of black-green brine, the colour of deep places choked by weed and algae. Its arms and legs glistened with an oily sheen, its skin speckled with bulbs like half-formed scales. Its limbs were long, almost human, with hands that tapered into long knotted fingers with rotten-yellow nails. It had five fingers on a hand but only three toes on a foot; an extra nail sprouted from each of its heels. Both fingers and toes were fierce and talon-like, connected by thin webbing

"Yeah, that's way better." Daniel took the page back from me and inspected my edits.

Daniel hadn't used words like "speckled," but took my suggestions. When he seemed caught on describing the right shade of green, I suggested "brine" and he went with it. He wasn't precious about his writing. He was precious about his superstitions. He refused to write in anything but his blue notebook, joking that his notebook was the opposite of mine, not cursèd but blessèd, so it was the only safe place to write. It was in his backpack at all times in case inspiration struck. His other superstition was this doomsday-clock belief that he might not finish writing the story, so I had to edit as he wrote. The convoluted solution was to edit photocopied pages from Blessèd Blue. We'd go over them together, and then I would transcribe our work onto the *wāpuro* and print them.

In the end, Daniel did share a little of his work with someone else. Reiko asked if she could sketch his *kappa*, and he provided her with the descriptive paragraphs. She sat at the bar, shoulders hunched over her drawing pad, glancing at the paragraphs, asking Daniel for translations and further explanations. When two older gentlemen arrived, I leapt into the Mama role so she wouldn't be interrupted.

As I pulled out a chair, one customer nodded in greeting, while the other smiled at me blandly. We made the usual small talk as I dropped ice into their glasses, poured the whiskey, and filled the water.

"So, what do you do?"

"Eh?" replied the one who nodded.

"Do. Work. O-s*higoto wa?*"

"Ah," he responded, and pointed back and forth between himself and the other customer. "We are working for Olympic committee. *Eigo wa, ka naa*...logistics?"

"Sounds interesting!"

Which, okay, clearly not interesting. Still. You did the best with what you were given. Boring people weren't the worst customers.

"Where are you from?"

"Canada."

"Ah. Toront?"

"Toron*to*. Yes."

"Ah. Niagara Falls!"

"Yes, not far from Niagara Falls."

It sounds mildly torturous, this repeated small talk, but I wasn't going to complain. At least I had a rudimentary understanding of Japanese, which came in handy when conversation hit a translation wall. When my Japanese failed, dozens of terrible maps of Australia, Canada, and New Zealand were drawn, and when artistic ability failed us, the world atlas was employed. The worst customers showed zero interest in conversation or us as human beings. They talked amongst themselves or sat in silence while we smiled like idiots. Minutes ticked by like torturous drops of water from a leaky tap.

Okay, no; the non-communicators were the *second*-worst customers. The worst, without a doubt, were the thankfully-mostly-rare pervy customers: in Japanese, the *sukebe* ones. Pigs who leered and told you how pretty you were. Innuendo was common but usually light-hearted. Inappropriate, yes, but jokey. The *sukebe* idiots didn't employ subtlety. It was "Your tits are too small," "You have a nice ass," "Please come to my hotel." Nothing remotely jokey. Entirely disgusting.

It's difficult to imagine a woman in her mid-twenties suffering through this today. We just thought of it as the cost of doing business. Besides, if someone truly crossed a line, Nax encouraged us to eject the slimy oaf for good. Which, albeit infrequently, *did* happen—especially if they tried to touch us. Most of the time, we were seated with average salarymen with average jobs who asked us average questions.

When everything failed, we gave up on conversation and sang karaoke: Japanese enka, '80s hits, J-pop, and countless classic-rock songs. Especially when Masa was present.

Masa was unpredictable, though. He wasn't merely a customer, he was Nax's friend. It allowed him certain advantages. For example, only Masa was allowed to take the hostesses off-premises. One moment, we were sure-footed in the drudgery of an evening spent entertaining strangers, and the next Masa had taken us by the figurative hand, stolen us from work. Nervous, unsure of protocol, we followed Masa into taxis with automatic doors and right-hand drive. They took us through streets at once familiar and foreign, through the maze-like paths of the Nagano water trade. We followed

Masa into brick blocks three, six, ten stories high, on each floor mysterious doors you would never open without him. Inside, red satin and smiling faces, Mama-sans and restaurant owners and cooks and unknown Korean women and construction employees in their winter jackets, and of course hostesses, who never quite knew what to do with us. We, too, were unsure what to do with *them*, sitting on the other side of the table, their hands cupping flame to light our cigarettes, our glasses remaining full no matter how quickly we drank, drinks refreshed by stealth and magic, karaoke machines blaring enka tracks, vocalized by drunken men in solid-coloured suits. We were awkward and excited, nervous and uncertain, drunk on all of it, and then, suddenly, there was a scramble through hallways and taxis and we were deposited, bewildered, back inside the Taisei Abinasu, unsure if what had happened had happened after all.

When Masa arrived later on Rei's *kappa*-drawing night, he was greeted by an enthusiastic, relief-soaked *irrashaimase,* as there were no other customers in the room.

"Ah!" Masa grinned. "It's my private party!"

Masa sat at the largest table and gathered us around. At 40, Masa was new management at a sizeable engineering firm, responsible for building most of the bridges over most of the rivers in the Nagano area, as well as the environment at the infamous Jigokudani monkey park.

"You like pizza? I will order pizza. You want a drink? Beer? Beer? Have a beer. Everybody. Reiko-san, *minna, nama biiru kudasai.*"

"Masa-san, you want the karaoke book?"

"No, not yet. After pizza. I need energy. Hey! So, are you happy tonight? You should be happy. Happiness is a warm gun—it's the Beatles, you know that—yeah. Reiko-san *domo.* Everybody has beer? Good. It's good."

Masa talked like this. I see, now, how it comes across: listen to how funny he is when he talks! Ha ha, silly English, isn't it hilarious? No. I'm not making fun of him. He wasn't a clown; this is merely how he spoke. We laughed, but *with* him, not *at* him. Some days he was stone-faced and serious, others giddy and ridiculous, but there was more there, something you couldn't see, something he revealed only in off-handed remarks he expected would be forgotten. He would sift through his limited English to find metaphorical ways to express difficult concepts, concepts that were often at odds with what you expected from a middle-aged Japanese man. Once he told Allie she drank so much because "a corner of her mind" was lonely. She told him to get lost, but we all noticed her switch to orange juice for a few weeks. Another time, criticizing Japan's treatment of Koreans, he told me, "We used to go to Korea with guns, but now it's with money. When I'm in Seoul and I see a ¥1000 bill, I see a bullet."

Very much not a clown. He said more in his "silly English" than most fluent people.

"*Kanpai!*" He repeated the word with a clink on each of our glasses. "Drink. Some time pizza will come soon."

"Masa, we're going to BOOM tonight after work!" Allie clinked his glass a second time for extra cheeriness.

"I see," he replied. "What is Boom?"

"BOOM!" Nicolle was excited. "It's a host bar! Reiko has a bit of a crush on one of the hosts."

Reiko, comfortable with Masa's presence, had returned to sketching the *kappa*. She blushed and continued scratching with her pencil.

"Do you want to come?" Allie asked.

Masa laughed. "Host bar? No, thank you."

"Ah, it's fun, you should come," I told him. "After we close, we're meeting Toby downstairs and heading over to the Gondō."

"Toby is your friend?"

"Of course!" I laughed. "You've known Toby for, like, at least two years!"

"Ah, yes, but. Take care."

"What do you mean?"

"*Mikakedaoshi*," Masa shook his head and raised his eyebrows. "His mindness is always Toby. Only Toby."

"Okay," I frowned. With Babette as my roommate, the last thing I wanted to hear was another slight against Toby. Toby was ridiculous and mercurial, but Toby was sweet and god *damn,* gave me quivers in places I wanted there to be quivers. I was in my twenties. I didn't care what this 40-year-old man had to say. I didn't ask him what *mikakedaoshi* meant.

Pizza arrived. Mayonnaise, tuna, and squid on an otherwise normal pie. I made a show of squinching up my face in disgust, but secretly I found it delicious. Karaoke was sung. Masa made us laugh again and again. Eventually Nax arrived for last call, and when it was clear no more customers were likely to arrive, we set about our closing rituals. Nax sat at the bar as we began to wipe and vacuum and sweep, working outwards in concentric circles, removing grey clumps of ashes and shrimp-flavoured rice cakes crushed into the shag. As a rule, this was done poorly, hastily, and drunkenly.

After Nax and Masa left, we locked the door and Nicolle poured us a row of shots. We shot them, then shot more. Soon, we tumbled out into the night, where we spilled onto the sidewalk like a sack of newborn kittens, stumbly and bleary-eyed. We sang Yen Town Band at the top of our lungs as we made our way to the Gondō. *Watashi wa / ai no uta de / anata wo sagashihajimeru.* With this love song, I'll begin to look for you.

BOOM's signage, at least two metres high, featured photographs of pretty boys with angular, gravity-defying haircuts. The point of a host bar is not much different than a hostess bar's—boys paying attention to girls to part them from their paycheques. BOOM was dim, all black walls and red accents, the recessed lights on the lowest possible setting, the karaoke screen on the highest. The hosts were cute Japanese men with more conservative haircuts than the poster promised. The inverse, the upside down, of our life, on every level, from inside out; unlike some of our customers, we were never there to ogle or demean, only to sing karaoke and laugh at the antics. Usually one of us had a crush on one of the boys. Reiko was fond of Kei-chan, who was paying his way through hairdressing school. Allie fancied a fellow named Ryō-chan. These infatuations were sad, in my unspoken opinion, like a boy with a crush on a stripper. These men were paid to flirt, to laugh, and to lie. False hope was Babette's cursèd gift to the girls, as she'd met Shinji at BOOM. This, they thought, proved that you *could* date a Boom Boy, and the girls clung to that like a love life raft.

"It was his last fucking night, mates, that's why it worked out," Babette would repeat, but it didn't matter. As long as she was with Shinji, Babette was keeping the dream alive.

Sodden with drink, our volumes turned up to eleven and judgement dialed back to about two or three, we arrived at BOOM, where we immediately requested tequila. Allie pretended not to notice Ryō-chan, burying her face in the karaoke book as though the songs were written in the fine print.

It was an unremarkable night in most regards: fun, but of the standard drunken variety. Reiko and Kei-chan were wrapping up a rendition of "Don't Go Breakin' My Heart" when the door burst open, startling everyone. Stomachs dropped. When a door slammed open in a bar, we had learned, nothing good was about to happen.

And nothing good happened.

A thirtysomething man barrelled in, head a-swivel, taking in his surroundings like a cop on a bust, checking the corners for armed combatants. He wore a blue suit so shiny it could have been made from aluminum foil. He sported sunglasses despite the dim, and he had a terrible damp-looking perm that reminded me of a Jheri curl.

I could feel the ions in the air reverse their charges. Eyes darted to the floor; even the eyes of the two women across from us, young girls in tight dresses with bored, blank expressions. Young man, shiny suit, bad perm, worse attitude. Nicolle eyed me quietly and touched her pinky to her cheek.

She didn't even have to complete the whole motion for us to understand. I immediately clutched at my bag, should we need to make a quick exit. No one wanted to suffer the unwanted attention of a gangster.

Jheri sat on a velvet bench beside us as the hosts scrambled to bring him his bottle—Courvoisier, of all things—and he spread his arms across the back of the seat as if taking in a show.

"Ah, shit," said Babette to herself. "So much for the mood."

As if he had heard her and understood, Jheri turned towards our table.

"Sing karaoke!" he said.

Reiko sat with her hands politely in her lap and stared at the floor. Both Nicolle and Allie looked alarmed, but Babette was having none of it. She stared straight ahead and down, into the centre of the table, into the ashtray that sat there, shiny and unused.

Jheri leaned forward and placed his hands on his manspread knees, his forehead jutting out as though he were trying to make her look up with the power of his mind.

"I can sing karaoke!" sang Ryō-chan, in an attempt to lighten the mood, but no one paid attention. Jheri spoke to Babette—yelled, really—but she refused to engage. She looked more worried than assured or self-possessed.

Jheri maintained his odd sitting-sumo forehead-forward pose a moment before he muttered the Japanese equivalent of fuck off, *bakayarō,* and turned away.

The synthetic cheer of fake keyboards erupted into the room and Ryō began to sing "Top Of The World" in what could be charitably described as a neighbouring key.

"Oi," Nicolle leaned over conspiratorially. "What the hell was that, mate?"

Babette shrugged.

"Reiko?" I turned around. She hadn't budged. "Would you be so kind as to tell us what just happened? What was that guy saying?"

Babette glanced at Reiko. Reiko glanced at Babette.

"I don't think Babette wants you to know," Reiko replied.

"See," Allie said, "That's the kind of guy I'm always afraid is going to come into J.J.'s. If we were at J.J.'s, we would have had to sing for the wanker. I bet he works for Takahashi."

Allie dropped her voice as she said the name. We had all heard it, whispered with fear and reverence. Takahashi, supposedly the Don Corleone of Nagano.

Babette smirked.

"His name is Kogawa," she said. "I know him. He's a wanna-be gangster asshole with a bad haircut, and he was just trying to bust my ovaries. No need to be worried."

Babette cocked her head and regarded Ryō, wavery voice chasing Karen Carpenter's melody, an anime-like expression on his face, like a children's singer as directed by David Lynch.

"Now this," she said, gesturing with her drink, "*this* worries me."

RIVER, DIVERTED

Now, courtesy of teeny tinny speakers set into columns along the Gondō, the Carpenters' classic is once again in my ears. I find myself humming along in spite of myself. Something in the wind has learned my name.

Scene: Hotel window is open. My laptop is also open. The documented titled *P4* is open on the screen. It was, about an hour ago, fifteen pages of text. That was until I read those fifteen pages of text and placed my finger on the delete button, watching the terrible, terrible words disappear one line at a time. There is nothing left but a blinking cursor. Not even an opening scene.

Where do you take a character that's no longer yours? Meelis Kuusk has a better grasp on Pardpeti than I do. He no longer belongs to me; he belongs to Meelis and, even more so, to Evvie. Evvie excised the last remnants of brightness from Pardpeti's blackened soul, all to bleed him dry at the box office. Or, more accurately, on streaming services. I have no idea why Leo Pardpeti is still killing and displaying women. It barely made sense in the first movie. Why on earth is he still doing nonsensically monstrous things all these years later?

Cut to: My fingernails are too long. I've always marvelled at people who can type with those dark red knifey things other women wear. I clip them. On television, yet another program about which I understand nothing. They are filming a woman in a restaurant, eating different types of bread. The scene is punctuated with voice-over remarks and plenty of word graphics, few of which I can read, other than the words for "delicious" and "bread." In the upper-right corner, a small window shows the reactions of a panel in a television studio somewhere. They react with great enthusiasm and amazement to the woman who eats bread. It's perplexing, all of this nonsense without context. What are they doing, and why are they doing it? Who knows? But it's logical, it's almost expected, that someone from outside the language, not to mention the culture, would ask these questions about a Japanese TV show. I shouldn't be asking the same questions of my own character—but I am. What is he doing, and why is he doing it?

Shot: The page is still empty. Maybe this time Pardpeti meets his match. The cops would be on to him by now. Maybe they've nicknamed him something, the way they nickname serial killers all the time. The Lepidopterist? Nah, awkward, plus it makes the anagram a little too obvious. The Entomologist? Hm...maybe. Pinner? Ugh. Horrible.

Cut to: There are items on the ceiling. One is a fire sprinkler. I can't figure out what the other two are. A white square the size of a matchbox, a half-circle plastic node that may or may not contain a light. Even the amenities on a hotel-room ceiling leave me alienated. There was a time when it didn't matter that I couldn't understand the language, the television, the paraphernalia affixed to hotel-room ceilings. It meant I was somewhere different. Today it just reminds me that I don't belong.

Cut to: I open the browser, struggle with intermittent WiFi, and fire off an email to Sheila, who was more than slightly concerned about my taking a last-minute trip to Asia to honour a man I hadn't seen in two decades. I Google "entomology slang." Unsurprisingly, the results are not relevant.

I shut the laptop. I close my eyes. I let myself think about last night.

Other than making fun of Evvie and me, Soba had few words to say. See death. Walk into darkness. I don't want to remember. Be open with death. The *kappa* was quoting cut-rate black-metal lyrics, apparently. I don't remotely understand any of it, but my own brain came up with it, so the answer's got to be in this head somewhere. What does Soba know that I don't? I could rephrase that question as, what do I know that I don't? The matter here is, what do I know, truly, that I have yet to admit to myself, to say out loud?

You don't want to remember things you have forgotten.

But I do. Passing backward through my life, exploring this part of the map of myself, might be something I need to do. I don't truly understand why. Before the book arrived, my days at J.J.'s were pleasant, hazy memories. Now it seems important, crucial somehow, to be present in this past. To slip into it the way one slips into a bathtub. Let it surround me, warm me, scald me, drown me. Where do I begin?

My subconscious has always been my undoing, so why listen to it now, especially when it speaks to me in such a hideous way? Through Soba, my subconscious seems to be telling me to be wary, telling me that I should be scared. So to hell with my subconscious. I arrived in Nagano with a poorly considered, hastily reached conclusion—that Nax must have printed the book. It still makes very little sense that anyone else would have done it, but the only clue that remains is the book itself. As clues go, it's a bit of a dud. I can't dust it for fingerprints.

So we must go farther back.

Nax never acquired the *wāpuro,* so my former roommate would be the last person to see the machine. Babette, Shinji, and Rei are likely somewhere in Nagano. Now where the hell do I start? I know how I don't start. I don't start by sitting and moping at a Lilliputian desk in cheap business hotel.

"Let's go get some ramen," I suggest to myself. I wish that

it was 1996. I would call Masa, and when he answered, I would sing *Hello, it is me you're looking for?* He would laugh, and we would meet for dinner. It is not 1996, though.

The Gondō is not as deserted as it was before. Shoppers, commuters, kids with faces aimed at phones. As I exit the east end onto Nagano-*odōri*, memories loosen at the back of my brain like rocks threatening to tumble down an escarpment. There is something else, though; an unpleasant sensation, an uncertainty like jelly, surrounding and isolating the memories. The shops and offices that line the road are same as they were twenty years ago. Exactly the same…maybe. Yet maybe not. How can you remember everything and nothing at once? How can a place look the same while you're not sure that it's the same? The dissonance creates a feedback loop; I imagine I hear the soft sine wave build into a high-pitched squeal, so I'm scrambling with the dials, hoping to fix it before it explodes and tears through my ears. The answer is to keep my head down and walk, to stop thinking *my God how this place has changed* and *my God how this place hasn't changed* simultaneously.

Doubling back, I take one of the streets that intersects with the Gondō and duck through the sliding doors of a weather-beaten brown building. Inside, on the left, a wooden bar surrounds an open kitchen; a raised *tatami*-matted seating section is on my right. Baskets of dishware, pots of cutlery, various plates and trays line the top of the bar. It's an *oden* restaurant. Boiled food. Sounds good.

I sit at the corner of the dining bar with an absent wave to the owners in the kitchen.

The owners fawn over me a little. I am, after all, a lone white woman with passable Japanese (*your Japanese is very good!*) who can answer questions she'd rather not be asked (*where are you from? How long will you be in Japan?*). All I want to do is order a plate of poached vegetables, a cold draft Asahi Super Dry, and not have to explain that, yes, Toronto is not far from Niagara Falls. I feel unkind about it, though. If I were a purveyor of foodstuffs in Canada, I'd be all, "Oh, you're from Japan? Oh, Saitama? Is that near Tokyo?" They're the same stupid questions.

My mood begins to soften. Everyone is so polite. Everyone seems to take genuine interest. We begin to joke a little, inasmuch as my oxidized *Nihongo* will allow. The cook is explaining to me how Americans seem wary of *oden* and how he's amazed by my willingness to order these spongey obscurities. I am about to dazzle and amaze him with my love of *oden* when the door jostles, the curtain rustles, and in steps Toby.

Our eyes lock the moment he steps through. Mine tighten; his widen, his expression turning wary. I picture him backing out the door on his tippy toes, as if he'd stumbled across a bear and didn't want to spook it. Yet now, after a day of wrestling and reckoning with the unexpected existence of Toby in my life, I feel far less angry. In fact, it's possible that I may have overreacted. You know, saying *there was no you* and whatnot. What I experience now feels more like the resigned acceptance of an unpleasant aroma—I don't like it, but I can deal with it.

"Of all the *oden* joints in the world, he walks into mine," I say as he approaches. Toby snickers and takes the joke as an invitation to sit, which, well, I guess it is.

"I promise I didn't follow you," says Toby.

"Shush," I say. "*Nama-biru kudasai!*"

Oh, how I've missed being able to just call out for a beer.

Set into the top of the bar in front of me is a shallow stainless-steel vat, partitioned into sections filled with various foods in broth. I remember the first time I saw *oden,* octopus tentacles protruding from brown soup in trays on the 7-11 counter. I had no idea it was so delicious.

"You got a lotta nerve, sitting next to me after what I said yesterday," I say.

"Don't worry, I don't expect you to actually talk to me."

He orders. His Japanese has a flow, a grace, that mine has lost. He even has that low-throated, guttural resonance that thickens the voices of older Japanese men. The cook, who is probably the owner, motions for the woman beside us to attend to us. She has blonde-accented hair and wears a billowy flowered blouse. It's sharply familiar, the way she repeatedly tops up Toby's *mizuwari*. I forgot how tiresome it was to watch a woman—any woman, in the water trade or not, on the clock or not—be expected to fall into the culturally prescribed service role. Then I remember that gender roles in Japan are more complicated than they seem. Just like anything.

Dinner arrives, each plate or bowl in succession, daikon radish and tofu and fried seafood paste and something beef-like from a part of the cow I cannot identify but eat anyhow because it is delicious.

"How's your meal?" Toby asks.

I grunt like a disinterested salaryman.

"Oh, absolutely," he replies. "The radish *is* delectable."

I grunt again, but this time I'm being funny.

"You think?" Toby studies a slice of daikon at the end of his chopsticks. "I prefer it sliced thinner, myself."

For some reason that makes me giggle.

"Ah. Made you laugh."

"I thought you didn't expect me to talk to you."

"Yeah, well." Toby pops the daikon into his mouth.

I lower my face towards the beef bits. "Well, don't get your hopes up, Tobes. There's an entire DMZ between the two solitudes of laughter and forgiveness."

But he's on to something, damn him. That small joke, that ability to slip a pry bar into the gaps in my defences just enough to make me laugh. Suddenly Toby seems more friend than enemy. If I'm going to solve the mystery of the book, he might be of use. I'm not about to tell *him* that yet, though. I remain silent, except for slurps and sips, for the duration of my meal. Toby is still cautious, and he keeps his mouth shut, too. Finally, draining the last of my second draft Asahi, I turn to him and break the slurpy silence.

"I want you to come back to my hotel with me."

Toby raises an eyebrow.

"Don't be a goof, Tobias. I have something…" I sigh and close my eyes. "I have something I need to show you."

He still looks incredulous.

"Look, I don't know if I like it either, but you're all I've got."

"Thanks?"

We call for the cheques. Toby makes to take mine, but I smack at the back of his hand with a chopstick.

"Ow."

"Stop it, then."

We pay our separate bills and make our way out into the night, around the corner, and back to the Hotel New Yama. I no longer feel the dissonance between the streets I see and the streets in my memories. Planning what I am planning to do, I have no memories at all.

BOYFRIENDS AND BANK ROBBERS

Which isn't entirely true. There are always memories.

The way *takoyaki* tasted from the back of a food truck at three a.m. The way mornings would break clear-skied before clouds would gather, crest the mountains, and turn the day monochrome. The way Nagano submerged itself in winter like a snowy-bearded monkey sinks into a hot spring.

I'd always been an enthusiastic four-seasons gal. Winter was the yin to southern Ontario's long hot summer yangs, even if those winters were occasionally a bit too yin. In Nagano, though, winters were perfect. There was always snow, and if there wasn't, you could find it by boarding a train and heading a few stops north. That year, a few months after I arrived, the slopes at Shigakogen, Iizuna, and Iiyama were well-groomed and welcoming as they prepared for the coming Olympics. None of us knew our way down a hill except Babette, who would disappear on weekends to go snowboarding with Shinji. The temperature averaged a reasonable -3° or -5° C and never dipped to the -20° nonsense you occasionally saw in Toronto.

Before long it was Christmas. The Lifers gathered in Sanyō Heights 306, along with a few new girls and Toby. We celebrated by baking individual turkey parts in what amounted to a glorified toaster oven. We laughed, raised glasses, ate a soggy approximation of stuffing improvised from our combined pantries. We raised more glasses, and then we went to J.J.'s. It was a work night. The Japanese do not celebrate Christmas. They do love to decorate for it, though; department stores and post offices alike were festooned with silver tinsel garlands and Sanrio Santas.

They installed a *purikura* machine, short for "Print Club," in the arcade by J.J.'s. It was a photo booth that ejected your images on tiny stickers with wacky backgrounds. Our Christmas *purikura* is so crowded you can only see thirds of faces (and Reiko's fingers, splayed in the V of a peace sign, in the bottom left corner). Over time, these stickers ended up affixed to walls and books, mugs and envelopes, letters and tables, popping up in the nooks and crannies in all of our apartments. Babette and me in sunglasses; Nicolle, Rei and me with our tongues out; Toby with a grin and an unlit cigarette between his teeth. The country slid into a recession, and we didn't notice.

To our horror, Nax removed the karaoke machines from J.J.'s. "The focus should be on good music and conversation," he said, clearly misunderstanding his clientele. Masa bemoaned the fact that he could no longer sing "Drive" as an exit cue, but after a week, he braved an *a cappella* rendition that soon became choral. The new sing-along became a ritual anytime Masa departed.

Without karaoke, we needed more tools to break up the boredom. Sheila mailed us another Rand-McNally Conversation Saver. It arrived in a large, heavily-duct-taped cardboard crate along with Kraft Dinner boxes, deodorant, bras that fit, and VHS tapes of *The Simpsons*.

Once a week, even in snow, I rode to the other side of town for Sora's lesson. Once, in ferocious hail and sleet, I received a phone call from Sora's father, who offered to send a driver. I was picked up by a triangle-faced chauffeur with a spritz of hair over his forehead, like a host-bar employee who'd forgotten his styling gel. He drove an absurd Mercedes-Benz the size of an ocean-going vessel; by now, having grown used to Japanese cars, it was off-putting to be in a right-hand passenger seat. I told Sora to tell her father never to send a car for me again. It made me feel kept, somehow, and besides, I liked the journey. The Mercedes never appeared again.

Sora was a model student, polite and precocious, her English outstripping that of her peers by a mile. Not because I was any kind of gifted instructor; no matter the lesson's depth, Sora understood on the first pass. Matters of grammar, verb tense, pronunciation, the odd irregularities of English—none of it fazed her, so every 90-minute lesson was over in 60.

One morning, grey and dreary but for the luminous mantle of white on the ground, she and I chatted over sliced Nagano apples, giant orbs of green bled through with red, the size of a large man's fist. It was early 1997.

"Did you bring a story for me to read, River-sensei?"

I raised my eyebrows and dropped my jaw. Sora giggled. *"River-sensei?"*

"Yes." Sora grinned and folded her hands in front of her on the table. "In September you said I should call you by your first name when we were friends. We're friends now."

I wasn't sure what criteria she'd used to measure. Was she waiting for a specific action, a specific moment? The eating of sliced apples? It didn't matter, it was cute as hell.

"I think we were friends months ago, Sora!" This made her giggle again.

"What will we read today, River-sensei?" She seemed to enjoy saying River-sensei, like she was getting away with something innocuous but nevertheless improper. She looked up to me, I think. I was a *gaikokujin,* a foreigner from the west, and a grown-up. My heart would melt when Sora turned those wide, trusting eyes towards me with a grin. I hoped I could live up to whatever modest status the girl afforded me.

"I'm sorry, Sora, I forgot to look for a new book. I know you weren't very excited about the last few."

"You promised me something scary."

"Do you know how hard it is to find scary stories in English aimed at ten-year-old Japanese girls?"

"Yes. I like to read them, and they are hard to find. But you are my teacher. I thought it would be easier for you."

"Why don't we do conversation practise for the next half hour?"

Sora rolled her eyes in the way children do when they forget you're looking right at them. I was definitely not living up to the modest status the girl afforded me.

"That's what we did last week, River-sensei."

"I don't have any..." No. I did have something she could read.

I had printed the first chapter of the story we were calling *Kenichi and the Kappa*. Daniel would have balked at sharing his work with Babette or Reiko, but a ten-year-old girl whom he would probably never meet? I reached into my bag, pulled out a black folder, and laid it on the table in front of her.

"It's not a book," she said.

"No," I replied.

She opened the folder to reveal some off-white 8½" x 11" pages, slightly dented around the edges despite my best efforts. The cover page announced the title in the only Roman font my *wāpuro* could create.

KENICHI AND THE *KAPPA*

"Why doesn't it have a cover?"

"My goodness, when did you get so demanding? Good thing you're my number one student."

"I'm your only student." Sora picked up the cover page, turned it over, and looked at page one.

"Go ahead. It's not really written for kids, but you should be able to handle it."

Sora sat up straight and tilted her head towards the first page.

"There was a monster in the river," she read along, and then looked at me. "This is better already."

"We thought it was a good way to open a story."

"This is your story?" Sora looked up at me, impressed.

"Not really," I admitted. "My friend is writing this story, but he's never written before. So I guess we're sort of writing it together? I am more like an editor. Do you know that word?"

"No."

"An editor takes a story and fixes it up. Makes corrections and suggestions to make it better."

Sora nodded and turned back to the page.

"All the kids in the..."

"Nay-burr-hood."

Sora nodded and continued. "All the kids in the neighbourhood knew this. Their parents had been warning them for years. A monster with the face of a monkey, the shell of a turtle, the talons of a bird, the hunger of a bear. A monster that ate children."

Sora read on, stopping occasionally to frown and sound out syllables. I interjected only with the occasional pronunciation or definition.

There was a monster in the river.

All the kids in the neighbourhood knew this. Their parents had been warning them for years. A monster with the face of a monkey, the shell of a turtle, the talons of a bird, the hunger of a bear. A monster that ate children.

The older kids, wise to the tricks of parents, would clamber down the steep embankment to the shallow water, even hop from rock to rock as the water sparkled and danced in the sun. The younger kids, however, stayed at the top of the riverbank. They would stare excitedly into the valley, looking for signs of the monster's hungry beak or its dark-green shell. Occasionally they would yelp and point, but all anyone ever saw were the dry tops of stones basking in the sun.

Across the bridge, on the other side of the river, the world looked different than it did in the city. There were hills. The houses had room to breathe. There were daikon fields and, most importantly, apple orchards. Kenichi loved apples. Sweet, juicy Nagano apples, so big they dwarfed his fist. He wanted one so badly he could see one, a green apple ringed in gold. So badly he could taste it: Kenichi's tongue twitched as he imagined the slightly sour edges of the fruit's sweetness.

Such a little thing to want. An apple! He wasn't asking for a bowl of ice cream or an expensive chocolate bar. Still, there were no apples at home. Apples—any fruit—were a rare treat in his family's two-room apartment. Money was a rare treat too, and pocket money for snacks was the rarest of them all. Yet if he could just cross the bridge and hike the steep roads up Mt. Asahi, he could have a mouth-watering apple right now. He only had to cross the bridge.

Kenichi sat alone at the top of the bank, near the bridge over the river. He could see flashes of silver from the metallic streamers in the trees. He could hear the soft *pop* of the bird-bangers meant to scare away winged scavengers.

The story is a bird-banger, Kenichi told himself. There is no monster.

So Kenichi stood, stared along the asphalt road, put his head down, and ran.

It only took seconds, but his heart had never raced so hard. He crossed the bridge and kept running until he landed on green grass, where he stopped, gasping for air, his hands on his knees, and looked up. It was the same view along the asphalt road, except now he was staring at the city, not the hills.

He was across the river, safe. Uneaten! There was either no monster or it wasn't hungry—or Kenichi had been too strong, too fast for it.

"Ha!" he yelled into the riverbank. "*Ososugi, kappa!*" Too slow, *kappa*!

Kenichi started ahead, elated, almost triumphant. He skipped along the trail, upward and upward, past green fields and trees heavy with pale-red apples rimmed in gold and yellow. He left the main road for a crumbling asphalt trail that led around the perimeter of an orchard. From the hillside came the insistent buzz of insects. A farmer stood among the trees, perched on a short ladder, inspecting what appeared to be green tissue paper wrapped around one of the fruits. The farmer grinned at Kenichi, watching his progress along the trail. When Kenichi was close, the farmer smiled, reached into a tree, and plucked the largest apple Kenichi had ever seen. The farmer swung his arm and pitched the apple underhand towards him; Kenichi needed both hands to catch it.

"*Dōzo*," the farmer grinned.

"*Dōmo*," he grinned back. "*Itakadimasu.*"

The apple was everything Kenichi had hoped for. He stood, rooted to the spot, and felt how each bite of the enormous fruit seemed to expand in his mouth. Sour juices curled his tongue, and his mouth felt prickly. Kenichi grinned, waved, and continued to eat as he went further along the path, until the asphalt had disappeared and only dirt remained.

Soon, he found some wooden steps that led up a steep hill. Curious, he climbed them to find a neglected Shintō shrine nestled into the side of Asahi. Its fifteen-foot *torii* gate had sloughed off its red paint, and its white flagpole flew nothing. Benches that once overlooked the city now lay broken by the edge of the precipice. A bright silver post shone in the decay. On one side it said simply, in English, May Peace Prevail Upon The Earth.

There was one lone structure, no more than a shed. A broom leaned against one side of it. Beside the broom lay a stone—coloured a blackish, brackish green.

Kenichi dug his teeth into the core of the apple, determined to scrape out every last morsel. As he finished eating, he noticed something shift in his peripheral vision. A shadow flickering across the leaves, a branch tossed by the wind. Startled, the boy stepped backward, away from the shadow—and tumbled directly into the shadow's source.

He only felt it a moment—round, damp and rigid—before it hit the ground with a thud. Cold liquid splashed against his calves. There was a yelp, as if something cried out in dismay. Not someone, some *thing*. It sounded like the twisted gurgle of a larynx unused to speech. The horrible sound continued—a choked bleating, like a goat imitating the temper tantrum of a child.

It was the stone. The stone that had lain by the broom, beside the shack.

It was not a stone. It was a creature with a stone on its back. No, not a stone; a shell. Yet it was not a turtle. Nor was it a monkey, a bird, or a fish. Yet all these were partially true.

Kenichi screamed. The monster. The *kappa*.

The boy scrambled to the shack, grabbed the broom, and held it out like kendo stick.

The *kappa* was an uneven shade of black-green brine, the colour of deep places choked by weed and algae. Its arms and legs glistened with an oily sheen, its skin speckled with bulbs like half-formed scales. Its limbs were long, almost human, with hands that tapered into long knotted fingers with rotten-yellow nails. It had five fingers on a hand but only three toes on a foot; an extra nail sprouted from each of its heels. Both fingers and toes were fierce and talon-like, connected by thin webbing.

Though its appearance was horrifying, it seemed too preoccupied with itself to threaten anyone. Kenichi watched as it fussed and gasped and rolled about on its rounded back, its sickly yellow belly to the sky. The blackish, brackish green of its shell appeared at once damp and cracked like sun-baked earth. A dark, sinewy neck protruded from the shell, atop which sat a face at once simian and amphibian, monkey and frog. It had a cruel, pointed, beak-like mouth that opened and closed, exposing blackened but hearty teeth, pointed and ferocious, with a pink wormlike tongue. Its eyes were black and round. It kicked at the air, slammed its fists into the ground, and gasped.

"Mi," it gargled. "Mi!"

Kenichi gripped the broom and raised it higher. Fear coated his throat in copper and sent an electrical current through the air. The monster continued to shout.

"Mi!"

It spread its twig-like fingers and smacked its head against the grass. Long, slimy hair grew in a ring around its skull, surrounding a moist concavity on top of its head.

"Mi!" Its voice had grown plaintive. "Miiiizzzz..."

Mizu? Thought Kenichi. Does the monster want a drink of water?

As if it could hear him, the creature's eyes grew wide and its beak snapped open and shut as it nodded.

"Miz...*mizu!*"

Kenichi was amazed to realize that the monster was asking for help. This was the hungry, horrible beast he had been told to fear? It was ugly, and angry, and dangerous, but it was also vulnerable.

"*Mizu!*" It raised one bumpy finger and bent it, gesturing inside the cavity on its cranium.

"You want water," Kenichi whispered. "...on your head?"

"*So!*" it barked.

The thrashing and flapping grew weaker, and Kenichi had another thought, that the monster might be dying. Everyone knew that if the water spilled out of a *kappa*'s head, it could die. If he allowed that, it would never terrify him or his friends again. If it died, then the stories about the monster would be nothing more than that: stories.

Yet something turned inside Kenichi at the sight of the thing. Watch it die? It was a living creature. He could not imagine letting something, anything, die. Was there another way? A way to...live with it?

Kenichi reached for his satchel and removed a bottle of spring water. The creature now lay limp, panting, eyes blinking slowly.

Its hair felt cold and greasy on his fingers, the skin beneath colder, greasier. He tilted the thing's head and poured water into the depression on it.

"*Kono yō na?*"

"*Hai.*"

Its head seemed to grow lighter in his hand. The creature's breathing relaxed, and soon it was strong enough to lean forward. The thing blinked three times in succession, turned its head left and right, and suddenly it bounded into a squat and stood upright.

"Ah!" it exclaimed. "Ah, ah, ah-hah!

Standing, it was four feet tall. Its eyes narrowed in suspicion, as if sizing him up.

"You're persons," it said. "Eat persons. Suck their innards out through their bums!"

It lunged forward with another "mah!" and water sloshed over the rim of its head and piddled down over its eyes. The thing stopped short.

"Go! Now! Before I eat you." The thing's voice, though, sounded half-hearted.

"So, you need water in that crater on your head, or you get sick?"

"Piss off!"

"You're a *kappa*," Kenichi said.

"Yes *kappa!*" It was angry now, but impotent somehow, unable to avoid his questions or send him away. "*Kappa kappa kappa!*"

"Well," he replied, "Nice to meet you, *kappa*."

The *kappa* made a dismissive sound. Pffft.

"*Kappa* is god," the thing replied stubbornly. "River god."

"We're not near the river," said Kenichi.

"Mah!" A look of superiority lit its eyes. "I am god. Live in river, but can go everywhere. Will go everywhere."

"Why?"

"To eat," it said.

Kenichi stood still and watched the *kappa*. He knew

that, if the legends were true, the *kappa* might not be able to eat him, now that he had helped save its life. But who knew how much of the legends were true? What if he turned away and the thing landed on his back and sunk its teeth into his neck?

"What's your name?" Kenichi asked.

"Pfft." It looked away. "No name. *Kappa*. From Susobana-gawa."

"I see. Well, then, what about Suso? Or Bana? Or Soba? I like Soba."

"Soba is buckwheat noodle," muttered the *kappa*.

"Well, unless you have a better idea, I'm going to call you Soba."

"Mah. Piss off! I don't need name."

"Well, maybe you don't, but I like my friends to have names."

"Friends?" Soba laughed, a husky barking sound. "Mah! No person can be friend. Persons! I eat you."

"You've said that. But I know that there's something you would rather eat, and I'm willing to go get them for you."

"Eat people," Soba insisted.

"No, people aren't your favourite."

Soba's shell lifted slightly; a shrug. "Children."

Kenichi, a child himself, shuddered and hoped his plan would work.

"What about *kyūri*?"

The *kappa* glared, but Kenichi noted the way its face twitched at the word.

"*Kyūri*," Kenichi repeated.

"Cucumber, yes." Soba's voice was tentative, uncertain. "*Kappa* love cucumber."

"Well, can I make you a deal?"

"Mah."

"I bring you some cucumbers, and you promise not to eat me or any more children in this city."

Soba *pffft*ed and *mah*ed a few times, shaking its head, but soon stopped fussing and looked at him.

"*Kappa* hungry. Bring Soba cucumber. Soba eat cucumber."

"Soba has taken to his new name, I see."

"Pffft," it said. "Mah."

"What do you think so far, Sora?"

Sora stopped reading and cocked her head in consideration.

"I think it's okay. It isn't very scary, but maybe it is going to be scary. The *kappa* is mean." She giggled again and repeated the word that had stood out most for her, which of course was *bums*.

"If you like it, we can keep reading it. There is a lot more story to come, but it's a work in progress. We might not have new pages every week."

"That's okay," Sora said. "I think I will like it."

"I think you are my favourite thirty-year-old," I replied. "But it's time to get going. Let's pack up."

"I have a boyfriend," Sora stated out of the blue as I slid the folder back into my satchel. "His name is Tetsuo."

"Congratulations," I replied. "You seem young to have a boyfriend."

"Everyone has a boyfriend," she insisted. "It's normal."

"Well, I'm glad to hear you're normal, then."

"Do you have a boyfriend? I have a boyfriend question."

"Unfortunately, Sora, at this moment, I don't know if I have a boyfriend."

This clearly perplexed Sora. Her face contorted the way it did when I used too many big English words in a row; she was sorting out whether she didn't understand my English or didn't understand the concept in any language.

"There is a boy, but I do not know if he is my boyfriend."

"How can you not know? Do you like him?"

"Yes."

"Does he like you?"

"I think so. Yes."

Sora tilted her head shook it a little. She was probably

looking for a polite English way to say that grown-ups are complete idiots.

Toby and I had been walking one another home—yes, that's absolutely a euphemism—for weeks. Yet his presence was too mercurial, his personality too slippery to grasp. Boyfriend was too solid a word for this relationship. I needed a liquid word. Maybe a gaseous one. Toby showed none of the eagerness that usually accompanied a new relationship. He showed up a couple nights a week, ducking through the doorway at J.J.'s, guitar slung over his shoulder like he thought he was some sort of wandering Buddhist Springsteen. Or he'd appear in the doorway of India or even BOOM, lobbing *hello*s around the room like softballs, making the rounds, saying hello to friends, acquaintances, and strangers alike. Everyone knew Toby, the tall handsome *gaijin* who played the guitar.

Toby lived in a hotel room above a pharmacy on the Gondō shopping arcade. When you looked out his window, you saw the pedestrian-only promenade below: the tailor, the croquette stand, the curry shop. Above, you saw a massive stretch of steel framing around the seven rows of windows that spanned the convex structure, like a half-pipe of metal and glass turned upside down, frosted and treated to diffuse the sunlight. At night, he closed the thick hotel drapes to block the electric lamplight. He had a real bed, not a futon; its low frame of black-laminated wood seemed to rise wholly from the floor, as if the room had been designed around it. The floor between the bed and the window was a repository for random items: rolls of socks, scraps of paper, boxes of tissues, some assorted fastener hardware, a book of Maya Angelou poetry, a pair of work gloves, empty money envelopes, a travel toiletry kit filled with an assortment of pill bottles, overdue VHS tapes of Japanese anime, three CDs (Silverchair, Green Day, and Goo Goo Dolls), all scattered on the carpet beneath the incandescent glow of the Gondō.

His sheets were black, and the bed always unmade, a surface of dark furrows and thick folds. In the evenings, when we fell into those folds, panting and scratching away at one another, it felt as though we were swallowed whole by them, as if we were falling through to another place, as though everything—Japan, River, everything—were leading to the moment we were in. By morning, Toby was usually gone, leaving little notes somewhere in the detritus, explaining how he'd gone to do this or that thing, have a wonderful day. I lay almost swaddled in those dark sheets, beneath the hiss of the electric heater on the ceiling, the faint background music of the Gondō permeating the glass, gently filling my ears as some sort of comforting green glow rose from my chest, something that said, this, this is where I should be, in this bed, in this apartment, on this continent.

None of this was suitable to explain to Sora. She was utterly convinced of her thesis: if I didn't have a real, official boyfriend, there was just no use in talking to me.

"Sora-chan, can you be my Japanese sensei for a minute?"

Sora grinned as if to show me her missing front tooth. "Yes! I want to be *sensei!*"

Adorable.

"What does *mikakedaoshi* mean?"

Sora picked up a marker and, with a bounce in her step, went to the white board. She turned to me with wide eyes and a loose-necked tilt of her head. I laughed aloud. This was her impersonation of me.

"*Mikakedaoshi,*" she said. On the whiteboard, she wrote the word in kana. みかけだおし. "This means, *ee, nan dake?* Maybe something is not so good as it looks on the outside. Like if someone pretended to be nice, but they were really a bank robber, you could say *mikakedaoshi.*"

That was the word Masa used about Toby. What had he been trying to say? It wasn't likely Toby was going to turn out a bank robber.

Was he?

A RELUCTANT ALLIANCE

Toby doesn't duck so his head can clear the undersized door-way of my hotel room. Instead, he bends at the knees and walks through as though he were doing the old "going down the stairs" mime routine. Inside, I kick off shoes, grab my carry-on, and heave it onto the bedspread, where I sit, cross-legged.

"You know, they say the bedspread is the dirtiest part of the hotel room."

"The dirtiest part of this entire venture is convincing myself to work with you."

Work with. In my head, we're already a team. We're a badly matched former-lover buddy-cop duo in Japan. *Tokyo Temptation?* Nah, too sexy. *East Meets West,* because they were a married couple named West? Ugh, River, but, okay—

"Sit," I order.

Toby pulls the desk chair over. His legs are too long; his knobby knees project skyward.

"Can I trust you?" I ask.

"You need to trust me with something?"

"I'm asking the questions."

"Is this an interrogation?"

"Kinda. Twenty years ago you had some kind of drug problem or something, I don't know what, and I don't care. Can I trust you?"

"Uh…" Toby pauses. Deciding where to start. "Well, when I left, I went home. I put Japan out of my mind. I started working at a local lumberyard. Started selling weed again."

Mikakedaoshi. Maybe not a bank robber, but still.

"I got arrested, did a little bit of time. First offense and all. It was terrible, of course. That's when I realized I was alone and in jail, so obviously something had to change. Problem was, I'm a coward."

I snort like an aggravated bull.

"Yeah, that's fair," he replied, as if I'd spoken actual words. "I was too afraid to approach my family, because they'd have none of it. The…I dunno, the finality of losing my family was too much to bear. Instead of running around apologizing to people, I came here. I went down into the *okaidan*, and when I came out again, I knew what to do."

"Your enlightenment as a woke Buddhist doesn't convince me."

"I'm not Buddhist. Remember how you mocked me behind my back about saying *namaste?*"

"Uh…" I feel squirmy, realizing he knew about that all along.

"I actually studied yoga," he continues. "For years. So, you know, you were kind of being an ass."

"Yeah, Toby, it was *me* being an ass."

Toby smirks at my sarcasm but doesn't disagree with my implication. "I needed to find work so I could pay back some debts," he continues. "I went to work making log cabins again."

I laugh, hard enough to feel a sharp pain in my diaphragm.

"No, it's true," he says. "It was actually what I was doing. I had…stolen a few things. From a few people. Borrowed some money from some people and never got around to paying them back."

"Got around to?"

"Okay, never intended to pay them back. I made it right, though. I even tried to pay Kogawa back, but I couldn't find him, and he has no friends to help me find him."

"You borrowed money from Kogawa? Given his connections?"

"Connections?"

"I don't wanna talk about that guy." Kogawa, the gross, bossy wannabe gangster from BOOM. The one who killed Daniel. Indirectly. In a manner of speaking. Maybe.

"Fair," says Toby. "Okay. So. I wanted to do more. I started to teach English as a volunteer. I helped Nax with the newsletters. I helped build a few homes for charity. That sort of thing. I don't know if I've made amends. There's no, like, karma meter to tell you when you've balanced it out. I just know that I'll be here a while longer, because I'm still trying to work up the nerve to go home and see my family."

If there was one thing Toby had, always, in triplicate, it was nerve. It's strange to see him like this. Seeing how far he's fallen and his pathetic attempts to be a better person, it's almost endearing. The whole story, if true, suggests legitimate contrition. It suggests I can, indeed, trust him.

"Ah, maaaaaaaaan." I lean forward with my chin against my chest. "Okay," I say to the floor. "Okay, sure."

"I have no idea what is okay or what you're saying 'sure' to."

Without raising my head, I reach into the bag I've placed on the supposedly germ-suffused bedspread.

"A little while ago, this came in the mail."

I offer up the book. It really is an offering, now. A peace offering of sorts. Offering, invitation, secret pact.

"Is this what I think it is?" I glance up to see him open the cover gingerly, as if picking up a dried, pressed leaf.

"What do you think it is?"

"The story. The story you wrote with Daniel."

"Daniel wrote it. I just helped. It's about a boy who discovers a *kappa* on the hillside."

"*Kappa* live in rivers."

"Yes, that's the point of the story, you jerk," I continue. "The boy thinks that too, but unfortunately for him, he finds out the *kappa* can go anywhere. The boy feeds him cucumber so he won't eat him, or any other children. But the *kappa* is demanding jerk and wants cucumber all the time. The boy ends up spending all his time feeding the thing. Then the boy meets a girl who, for some reason, can't see the monster, so he and the girl become friends, but yadda yadda yadda soon terrible things happen, anyway, the plot's not important. The point is, we had just finished writing the first full draft when they found Daniel."

Toby looks at me with a squint, as if I'd said something confusing.

"I had only printed out one copy, and I burned it."

"Why?"

"I don't know. Rites and rituals and symbolic gestures and whatnot. You know I'm a sucker for that sort of thing. Anyway, I kept his original manuscript, but this isn't that. This book is what I typed. This is the edit. And *that.*"

I gestured towards the cover art.

"That's the sketch Reiko did," Toby remembers aloud.

"She gave it to Daniel, but he insisted I have it. It was pinned to the *shoji* in my room. So."

"So?"

"So. This picture, the word processor. These were left behind, in 301."

"So." Toby regards the book carefully, as if searching its cover for the logic of its own existence. "How does this exist? Someone must have found it on the *wāpuro?*"

"Right."

"And then they published it and mailed it to you twenty years later? That's..."

"...like something out of a Murakami novel?" I ask.

"I was going to say screwed up."

"It's that, too." I raise my head slightly but avoid Toby's eyes. "Which is why I want to solve this mystery. I know it sounds like a stupid movie cliché where there's a McGuffin and a mystery and non-professionals somehow crack the case and we triumph in the face of a lost cause. So I gotta ask, is this stupid, Toby?"

There's more pleading in my voice than I'd prefer.

"It's a little stupid," Toby admits. "But if you're gonna

circumnavigate the globe to play Veronica Mars, you've gotta have your reasons."

"I didn't circumnavigate, I got on a plane."

"That you're bothered by 'circumnavigate' and not 'Veronica Mars' is telling."

"Know what's telling?" I extend my middle finger. "This. Know what it's telling you?"

"I can only assume it's telling me you want my help."

I glare at him. He smiles.

"Okay," he says. "I'm in."

There we go. The accord has been signed. My heart reels from trying to process competing emotions. What does a partnership with Tobias Handler look like? Where does one begin?

Those are questions, and questions are how you begin.

"What do you think about all this?" I fix Toby with what I hope is a professional, appraising look. He responds with pursed lips and a sideways glance.

"I don't know. It's all pretty unlikely. We can agree on one thing, though. The two things that comprise this publication, the sketch and the computer file—they came from your old room."

I take the book back from Toby's lap, staring at the pencil drawing on the cover, at the creature's placid eyes. "Yeah. That's why I thought it was Nax. They were Nax's apartments. I thought he was reaching out to me."

"Wouldn't a phone call have sufficed?" Toby says. "Instead of, you know, finding a bookbinder to print a one-off edition of something buried on a twenty-year-old computer?"

"It did seem a little extreme. He doesn't seem to have the *wāpuro* anyway."

"What, you searched his house?"

"I didn't search his house, I simply walked around it with a heightened sense of awareness."

"You searched his house."

"Sort of. Misaki more or less confirmed it, though. I should have given up there. But it's just so…weird. It's just surreal enough, just mysterious enough, to be cause for obsession. I don't know how much time I have for sleuthing, though. I can't afford to stay in Nagano too long. I've got a screenplay to finish—"

"You still work for Evrard Frederich?" Toby asks.

"Oh sweet Christ on a cracker, no. I've written for him. That's not the same as working for him. Please and thank you."

Toby looks down at the floor.

"Sorry," I say, "it's a sore spot. You couldn't know."

Toby nods, but we continue to sit in silence, the air between us heavy with years of unspoken thoughts. Making peace with Toby was not on the original agenda. All I know is the gates to my dark places have been kicked open, not by angry Cenobites or the satanic rituals of a Paemon cult, but by a stupid book. Now questions pick at the folds in my brain, kick at the back of my stomach.

"So what do we do?" I stand for emphasis, but the space between us is negligible, and his face bumps against my stomach. Flustered, I sit back down and stare at the disease-ridden bedspread.

"How on earth do you find out anything about a book? How do you find out who printed it? Who do you hire, a forensic librarian?"

"You were already on the right track." Toby moves to place his hand on my knee but thinks better of it. "The *wāpuro*. We know Nax didn't have it."

"It was a stupid idea, thinking Nax sent it," I sigh. "I found fur coats, several lamps, and a small Russian automobile in that closet. Nax never cleared out *anything*. Why would he have the *wāpuro*?"

"What about Babette?"

"You think it was Babette?" Suddenly, the idea of involving Babette feels intimidating. I never said goodbye to Babette. To anyone, really. Still, skipping out on my roommate without notice—even if there was no rent to pay—was probably not appreciated.

"The idea of anyone creating and sending you the book is bonkers. The idea of it being Babette is even more so. But she stayed there after you left, River. Of all the people we knew, she's really the only one who might know what became of your *wāpuro*."

"Where is she now?"

"I don't know. I bumped into her about four or five months ago in front of the train station. She didn't say much."

"She didn't like you."

"She was no ray of sunshine herself."

"She was fine if you got to know her."

"I couldn't be bothered to get to know her. Not everyone has the need to crack the hard cases, River."

"What do you mean?" I'm pretty sure I know what he means, but I feign irritation anyhow.

"I mean you made it your mission to break through to difficult people," he explains. "You treat friendships like you're a dedicated therapist who refuses to give up on their patients."

"That stings, Toby."

It doesn't actually sting, though. He's right. I close my eyes and exhale as if blowing hair out of my face, though I have no bangs to blow on. I was uncertain about including Toby in my impulsive, absurdist Asiatic Nancy Drew exploits. Now, I realize I might actually need him. I've made more progress in the last ten minutes than in the last week.

"So how long can you stay in Nagano?" Toby asks.

I squirm a little. "I...bought an open-ended ticket."

"Ooooh, fancy Hollywood screenwriter makin' the big bucks."

"No," I say. "Decidedly not. It was a ridiculous thing to do. But...I dunno. I..."

I don't want to admit that while yes, I have a deadline, and yes, I don't have unlimited funds, my obsession is strong enough that I bought an open-ended ticket. Just in case.

Toby sees that I continue to squirm and, bless his scuffed-up heart, he lets it drop.

"Okay. So how do we find Babette?" he asks.

"That I don't know." I give my non-existent bangs another blow. "Babette and Shinji could be in the phone book, though probably not, if they're still as secretive as they used to be. We really need someone who speaks and reads Japanese."

"And someone we can convince to follow us on this damn fool idealistic crusade."

"*Star Wars?*" I scoff. "You're quoting *Star Wars?*"

"Sorry it wasn't obscure enough for you," Toby smirks. "Next time I'll quote a line from *Suspiria,* okay?"

"*Suspiria* is hardly obscure! It's, like, Argento's most known film, and there's a remake, but, okay—sorry, I'm sorry. Do you know anyone who would follow us on this damn fool crusade, idealistic or otherwise?"

"Yes," he says, "and so do you."

I raise an eyebrow. "Masa?"

"God, no," chuckles Toby. "Masa's a good dude, but he's in his sixties and president of his company. He's too busy. He'd dismiss this nonsense out of hand. No, I mean Rei-chan."

"Reiko!" It's so obvious. "You think she'd help?"

"I know she'd help." Toby smiles. "I see her every once in a while, and she's always talking about how bored she is. She always wants to get together for coffee, but I dunno, I don't really have anything to say to her; we weren't friends. You, however, were."

I stare at Toby and feel something like mirth brewing. Before I can stop it, it makes itself known though a brief, bulbous chuckle.

"Wow." Dammit, I can feel it: there's a genuine smile on my face. "Was Reiko asking you out on a date?"

Toby shrugs, but the answer is probably yes. As the scales of loathing drop from my eyes one by one, I have to note that the boy—man—is still striking. You know, for his age.

"So, where do we find Reiko?"

"We visit her at work."

"Which is…?"

"Jigokudani Yaen-Koen," Toby grins. "She works at the monkey park."

CLOWN SHOES AND VUITTON HEELS

Rei loved Jigokudani Yaen-Koen. The place Masa helped build, where snow monkeys lounged in the sulphur and steam of "Hell Valley," enjoying the hot-spring pools. Tourists mingled with the monkeys, taking photographs and avoiding eye contact with the wildlife.

We were at work. It was that in-between hour after the door was unlocked but before the first customers arrived. Reiko showed me her monkey photos from a staff trip to Jigokudani a few weeks before I had arrived. She slapped them down on the bar one by one as though playing monkey-photo gin rummy, her grin widening with each photograph. A macaque, her bleary-eyed baby clinging to her belly. Another with its eyes closed, his red face serene, hands stretched out of the water towards the camera, where they come to a rest on a rock as though he were praying. Another of several monkeys, expressionless, heads above the water and still as Easter Island stones.

"And this one!" she pointed, her cheeks flushed, her mouth taut with a broad grin. "Look! It's so cuuuuuute."

What can I say? The girl loved herself some monkeys.

Allie and Nicolle laughed behind me as Allie shuffled a deck of cards, its cardboard box worn and separated at the seams. They were playing Indo-Creamer. Indo-Creamer was a popular brand of coffee whitener. How a coffee whitener related to a card game was arcane knowledge; whoever invented Indo-Creamer did so long before any of us arrived at J.J.'s. None of us really knew the rules, but we taught ourselves to play based on the rulebook. The rulebook comprised two old napkins covered in faded pencil scratches, so the word *rules* was always in quotation marks.

Before the game could even begin, the door whooshed and a customer popped his head through like a puppy out a car window. We responded with a measured, cautious *irrasshaimase*. New customer. Unproven entity. Reiko greeted him with her trademark smile, the one that didn't just fill her eyes but also her nose and forehead, somehow. There was the usual scurry—ashtrays and water jugs and moist towels and whiskey—before Babette and the young man settled into the stilted beginnings of a conversation.

"What do you think, Rei-chan?" I asked. It was our habit to judge the books by the covers—that is, to make guesses about new customers based on their appearance. "My guess is 'exceedingly average.'"

"Mine is 'boring as hell,'" she replied. I snorted so hard I felt like I bruised my larynx.

"You can't know," she continued when the seizures of my giggles eased. "Maybe he has an interesting life."

"He looks young. Kind of cute. Probably doesn't need his fragile masculinity bolstered."

"Like yesterday."

The day before, Nicolle and I had been seated with a mid-level manager from the Japan External Trade Organization. We sat propped on our elbows, barely awake; if our eyelids had elbows, they would have been propped on them, too. My insides turned into cotton stuffing and my whole body threatened to flop forward; I had morphed into a rag doll, the metamorphosis driven by sheer ennui. JETRO man spoke in tumbling spills; halitosis and fragments of shrimp chips sprayed from his mouth like aerosol. He talked about nothing. Over and over again. He didn't offer to buy us drinks, which, beyond being tradition, would have made it more bearable.

"It was like his mouth was a disgusting spray bottle," I said. "but at least he wasn't talking about my tits. Or telling me I was fat."

Many of our customers had a habit of forthrightness that would have been considered rude at home. It wasn't only these men; people in general seemed quick to express unfiltered observations. You got fat. You look tired. It was no more than an observation; it wasn't even a judgement. Occasionally, though, a customer took it a step further in cruelty. You were ugly, stupid, you should be speaking Japanese. There was no discernable reason for this rare, repugnant behavior, either. You could choose to get upset, but there you were, sitting at a table, letting a total stranger get under your skin. You can't cry in a tattoo shop—it's your choice to allow someone to scrape you with a needle for an hour.

"River?" Daniel stepped out of the kitchen. He looked a bit paler than usual, but there was a grin on his face.

"Ah, Daniel-san!" Sometimes I couldn't resist the painfully obvious Karate Kid jokes.

"I wrote some more today," he said in his sideways kind of way. "I'll make some photocopies after work."

"Daniel is on fire," I told Reiko, which made him blush, splashing a little grenadine into his pale. I hadn't told him I'd shared his work with Sora, because I didn't think he needed to know. Truth was, it was working out incredibly well. Sora reading aloud gave me a different perspective on the work.

"Oooo, that's really coooool," Reiko crooned. "It's so great you are working together."

"No, it's Daniel, not me. I'm just brushing up some sentences here and there."

Daniel mumbled a disagreement, which was sweet of him. I stood, walked around the bar, and started rinsing some ashtrays as Daniel returned to the kitchen.

"What about your own?" Reiko asked.

Daniel dumped a playfully-decorated plastic bag of *karaage* into the pot of oil we called a deep fryer. The chicken clumps hissed and popped merrily as I watched white wisps of snow swirl around the streetlights outside.

"Yeah, have you been writing?" Daniel arranged wilted lettuce on a plate as artfully as wilted lettuce would allow.

"Alas, the Cursèd Black Notebook has remained closed of late," I said, doing a terrible Vincent Price impression. "It's so easy to be distracted, you know? I mean, I suppose if I didn't go out, and didn't…uh…didn't like boys, I'd write more. But…"

But I grew up a pathological extrovert. A pleaser. Too hyper, too loud, too brash, too weird. Even the new kids at school avoided me, the cheery girl in the Slayer T-shirt who chattered on incessantly. The cool kids were Ralph Lauren button-downs; I was an off-brand polyester Hawaiian shirt. They were Louis Vuitton heels and I was clown shoes. I was an obnoxiously effervescent force of will with indefatigable self-esteem. Instead of falling into despair, I fell into books, films, the love of my sister. I fought hard to befriend the lonely, the stragglers, the other off-brand misfits. I was good at it. I always had friends. Just weird ones.

Now I was older, settled into myself. People in Nagano accepted my wonk. Some even loved my wonk. The way I saw the world and how I expressed that vision—it all worked for me now. If I hadn't come here, I never would have learned how much I enjoyed discussing geopolitics with middle-aged businessmen, or singing Beatles on karaoke with Masa, or drinking until dawn with people who skipped across the globe like stones, this place merely another point of contact to propel them forward, leaving ripples on surface. I was aglow with giddy joy. I had a temporary but kinetic kinship with people who accepted me, and a boy who sometimes took me home to his urban treehouse looking out into the Gondō below.

"It's okay, Riv." Daniel lifted the nuggety chicken chunks out of the vat one at a time with his long chef's chopsticks, blotted the excess oil on a paper towel, and arranged them on the platter. I waited patiently, filling tiny pleated-paper cups with mayo and ketchup.

"Yes," Reiko agreed. "You have lots of time!"

Reiko nudged me back towards the stack of monkey faces. She was so excited to share these, to express her extreme enthusiasm for small, cute things. I was rather ambivalent about monkeys, to be fair, unless they were the giant building-climbing airplane-swatting kind. I suppose that's more of an ape thing than a monkey thing. So I watched Reiko instead of paying attention to the photographs.

I remember feeling sorry for Reiko. Standing by while the *gaijin* around her propelled themselves recklessly through the days and nights. This included myself, despite my comparative restraint. Reiko was supposed to somehow control this production, but it was like trying to conduct a film shoot with a cast and crew of, well, macaque monkeys. Nax bankrolled the whole thing, an elderly man fascinated by American women, Pablo Picasso, and Miles Davis. Nax drew us monkeys to his park with brown envelopes of crisp ¥10,000 bills. His one-room western empire was nothing more than a movie set in need of repair and a new shag carpet. Then along come the idiots, and it's lights, camera, et cetera. We drank alcohol and screamed to the heavens at six a.m. We entertained philanderers and those who wished they had the nerve to philander. We stole bicycles and complained about post office systems. We said no when we should say yes, we stuck our chopsticks upright in the rice, we acted as though this was our disposable wonderland, a natural resource to exploit.

I tried so hard to show more respect, but how self-aware could I have been? I was in my twenties. We didn't yet know the phrase "cultural appropriation" when a wealthy rich customer offered to drape us in silks so we could have our photographs taken wearing kimonos worth $30,000 apiece. I didn't believe there was a transgression, a cultural annexation, when I prayed at Zenkōji without understanding the heart of Zen Buddhism. Even at our most respectful, we were still foreigners storming their shores, basking in the strangely dismissive adoration, taking the money, and going home. That was why I worked at J.J. International. In service of adventure, exploration, boundary-pushing, expansion, reinvention. Rei, on the other hand, worked at J.J.'s because she needed a job to live.

She must have thought we were all such selfish, stupid children.

ABDUCTIONS AND ONSEN

Now two of these selfish, stupid children were going to ask her for help.

Early the next day, the phone in my suite rings. Actually, it doesn't ring as much as it titters like a tiny electronic schoolgirl. Even the telephone is pint-sized.

"I tried to get us a ride," Toby says into my ear. "Honestly, just a ride."

"Oh, no, Toby, what did you do?"

"I called Masa."

Uh-oh.

An abduction.

After decades of beheaded journalists, missing aboriginal women, and the sheer unpleasantness of my own stupid films, I wish we'd picked a word other than "abduction," but we didn't. It creeps me out to use the word abduction in the jaunty way we once used it. Even "kidnapping" would be better. At least that has a Robert Louis Stevenson vibe.

See, the joke here, if there ever was one, is that when it came to Masa and some of our other clientele, suggestions were often not suggestions. If Masa "suggested" an outing, you were going. It was rude—impossible, even—to say no. Sometimes Masa would appear without warning at nine a.m.

and off we went—not quite against our will, but not quite whole-heartedly, either. He would drag us up a dormant volcano, or to drive us six hours to an adjacent prefecture, or take us to eat *natto,* which tasted like a sumo wrestler's loincloth after a championship match. It didn't matter if you'd stumbled home two hours prior and fallen into a paralytic sleep. You allowed yourself to be abducted. You did what was expected of you. In a strange way, you wanted to.

I do not, however, want to go to Jigokudani with Masa. It's too much like the old days.

"So, the good news is that we have a ride. The bad news is we have an itinerary to follow now."

"Dammit." Way too much like the old days.

"Well, you know, there are worse things than having an old friend drop a thick stack of bills on a vacation-within-a-vacation. He doesn't know you're playing detective."

"Pluralize that, Tobes. You're involved now."

"Sure. And by the way, he'll be there in five minutes. Bye!"

"God *dammit,* Toby!" I drop the phone into the cradle. This isn't Toby's fault, not by a long shot. This is classic Masa. I'm annoyed…but I feel like I'm home. Way way too much like the old days.

Sure enough, seven minutes later the phone rings again with a sound like a plastic robot blowing a raspberry. I assemble an overnight bag and head down to the lobby. Masa's black Toyota Premio, already too wide for India Street, is practically parked in India's doorway. He leans against it in his light-green sweater and faded jeans, *shatchō* in vacation mode, smoking a menthol Pianissimo.

"Good morning, good morning, good morning," he chimes in an approximation of the Beatles song. "How are you?"

"Great, thanks, Masa-san. Ready for Jigokudani?"

"Tomorrow," he says. "First we need people's onsen, then we'll go to the monkeys' onsen!"

Ah. Yes. The itinerary.

We cross the Gondō and snake our way east of downtown, north of where Sora's classes took place, along side streets I've never seen. The day is clear with the kind of sunlight that makes you feel like you're microdosing on LSD, I guess, having never microdosed on LSD. Outlines are sharp and colours breathe. We float through the city as though we're sailing a regatta down the roadside canals. It's bewildering that a city so small can harbour so many spaces I've never seen, as if the town has hidden them from me, as if streets readjust their alignments before I arrive. I imagine asphalt streams shifting and curving like a series of snakes, resolving only when I lay eyes on them. When I take my eyes off them, they will come loose behind me like a poorly tied knot.

We are silent, Masa and me. A bizarrely familiar game show airs on his dashboard television, but he pays it no attention, thankfully. Dashboard television? Seriously?

Somewhere in the northeast, near Shinano-gawa, he swings the car into a cramped parking lot. Toby sits by the entrance, butt resting on a tattered carry-on suitcase, elbows resting on his knees. He's tall and gangly and resembles the Cloverfield monster in that position, all spindly knobs and limbs.

"Morning!"

I grunt at him with discontent as he climbs awkwardly into the backseat, his lengthy body bent like he's one of those inflatable advertising tube men with a weak-ass wind machine. He strikes up a hello-how-ya-been conversation with Masa. Toby's voice is familiar yet strange, still rich and sonorous, but so much slower, more measured than it used to be.

Suburbs keep pace with us for a few more minutes and then drop away like failed marathoners, watching us go as we sail upward along the low mountain roads. Though he seems more watchful and tentative then he used to, Masa still accelerates at inopportune times, as though he's confused by the pedals. The guard rails seem alarmingly insufficient; they might as well be road lines with a few extra coats of paint. Above them, the mottled texture of the tree canopy sinks into the valley and washes up over the next mountain, beautiful—but, when you're certain you're about to hurtle into the thick of it after the Premio breaches the rail, terrifying.

As Masa continues to gather speed, Toby sneaks a glance at me. I smirk back at him. We both know what's coming, and soon, it does; an acceleration and a corner so tight it's almost U-turn. The trees approach us like a green tsunami about to roar over the breakwall. Instinctively my hand shoots upward to the holy-shit handle on the interior of the car. Toby and I burst into laughter.

"There it is!" I laugh.

"Twenty years later and it still never gets old." Toby grins. "Welcome to Air Masa."

He never admitted it, but Masa loved it when we made Air Masa jokes. He'd been known to sing "Rocket Man" in karaoke and mutter, "like my driving" after every chorus. We never warned new staff about Masa's driving; experiencing the fear was almost a hazing ritual.

"I have complete control," Masa says, and breaks into half-mumbled, half-confident rendition of Foo Fighters' "Learn to Fly."

"A surprisingly modern selection for you, Masa," Toby says.

"Yes," I agree, "Though it's around twenty years old now, too. Foo Fighters played in Matsumoto, remember that?"

"Yeah," Toby says. "Dave Grohl was bantering with the audience and Allie yelled, 'Hey Dave, more rock, less talk!' He joked about that for the rest of the show."

"I forgot about that." I stare out the window as Masa tries to outrun the clouds. "You think you remember so much until you finally talk to someone else who was there. Then you realize you remember almost nothing."

The Senjukaku Onsen Hotel lies in a copse of trees on a hillside, like an egg in a nest. Designed to blend traditional and modern, Japanese and western, it features faux-field-stone walls on the first floor with exposed framing and stucco, almost Tudor style, above. Masa parks the car while we take our bags inside. Polished marble floors reflect our faces back at us. Masa enters, cajoles the check-in staff, and laughs heartily. We are led to two separate rooms on the third floor: one for Masa and Toby, one for me.

My room smells of fresh *tatami*. There is a low table with two legless chairs, a wooden balcony overlooking the misty forest outside. I walk over to the table and allow myself to collapse into a cross-legged position on one of the legless chairs. My tailbone yelps at me for forgetting my age; the table bounces on the floor and a few wrapped candies leap from a black lacquer dish to the tabletop.

I place the laptop on the table in front of me. Like the puzzle box from *Hellraiser,* no good thing can come from opening it.

In *Hellraiser,* the head baddie, nicknamed Pinhead, informs our ill-fated heroine that he and his kind are "Explorers in the further regions of experience. Demons to some, angels to others." The baddies are summoned when you solve a mystical puzzle box. I'm not saying if I open the laptop pale torture-demons in cyberpunk bondage gear will appear and tear my soul apart, but my level of trepidation is about the same. Angels to some? When is writing ever angelic?

Well maybe it was, once, but since I got on board with *Pinned,* it's all demonic, all the time. Yet there I go, opening the laptop puzzle box, summoning the horror of my own volition. I log in to the WiFi but before I can open the file, a familiar ringtone streams from the laptop's speakers. Skype is ringing. It's Evvie. Dammit.

"Hello, Evrard."

Evvie's face takes up most of the screen, but even so, I can tell he's sitting at the kitchen table in his Berlin apartment. His greying flat-top gives his head an elongated hexagonal shape. His skin, distorted by the poor WiFi connection, appears less craterous than usual.

"Where are you?" he barks.

"I said, hello, Evrard."

"Yes, yes, hello, hello." His eyes dart around the background, my background, avoiding my eyes entirely, though it could simply be that he doesn't really understand how web cams work. "You are in a Japanese room."

"Good eye."

"Are you in Japan?" He sounds alarmed.

"Yes, Evvie, I am in Japan."

He winces, but I can't tell if it's because of that information or because I called him Evvie. He really does hate that.

"I came for a funeral," I tell him. "Nax died."

"Nax?" Evvie has heard my J.J.'s stories before. "I am sorry to hear this."

"Thanks, Ev."

"What is happening for you now?"

"I've gone off to the country to work on the script," I lie, adding a touch of truth by saying, "I was just about to get to work."

"I hope it is close." He tsks at me like a cross schoolmarm. I note that his partial denture is in. "We agreed on next Monday."

"You'll have it."

There is no chance in hell he'll have it.

"Have we used the Winnebago idea?" He's talking about the stupid concept where Pardpeti drives around Europe showing off his corpses. In Evvie's mind, this happens via Winnebago. I already know that Evvie will find a cheap Volkswagon, jimmy off the logo, and replace it with a Winnebago logo.

"Evvie, a motorhome would hold a very small number of bodies. The smell would be concentrated so badly that a single traffic violation would have Pardpeti behind bars."

"Pardpeti's house is burned down at the end of *III*. His house collapses in fiery chaos, and he will be starting a new collection! Looking for benefactors! Patrons!"

"It's a terrible idea," I insist. "The entire series is a terrible idea, but this is, like, I don't know. You lost me at the end of the first one."

"I lost you at the end of the first one?" Evvie's eyes darken beneath his heavy, craggy pumice-like brow. "You wrote it."

I don't correct him. "I keep trying to push Pardpeti into corners. I had that stupid house burn to the ground because at least those women got a funeral pyre of some kind. Maybe it only looked like a tribute to me, but it was a tribute. I thought, great, this goddawful house is gone. If Evvie won't let me get justice by broiling Pardpeti alive, at least I can get rid of this horrible house."

"Exactly!" Evvie leans in closer to the webcam. "*Superb!* Now we can take him on the road! Send him to the world's most beautiful cities, gather the world's most beautiful women, and bring them to the world's richest sickos! If this is not what you are writing, I hope what you are writing is better. You must tell me. This is my movie. *My movie.*"

Sigh. My movie. Possessive of his films.

"You should go home and work," he says offhandedly, as though it's common sense. "You can't afford a trip like this. Why don't you come stay with me? Come back to Berlin."

"I can afford whatever the hell I want to afford." Possessive of his films, possessive of me. "We've had this conversation, Evrard, and I'm not having it again. We're done. After this, we're completely done. *Verstehen?*

"You speak German like an idiot."

"You speak German like an idiot, and you're German!" I stick my tongue out towards the webcam. "I'm going to write now. Goodbye, Evvie."

As I click the hang-up icon, I clench my jaw so tight my teeth might shatter. Even seeing his ruined pugilist face makes me angry. Why didn't I just tell him no, I have nothing for you, you're not going to get a script, get out of my life?

I open one of several Word docs that contain notes:

passing thoughts, fleeting images, ideas committed to cell-phone recordings or napkins, transcribed and forgotten again. There's nothing here.

Yet it has to be done. I told him I would do it

Out of guilt, River.

I will do what I said I would do. If I don't have my word, I have nothing. I reach for a candy, unwrap it, pop it in my mouth. It tastes like lemon wrung out of a raw cod fillet.

I stare out into the foggy forest, willing shapes and monsters to come out of the mist, trying to pinch a drop of inspiration from my brain. Nothing comes. Not even that stupid river god.

Dammit. Before that call, there was already a minimal chance of harnessing anything akin to creativity. Now, the idea of writing anything, let alone something for Evvie, seems absurd. I'll never get anything accomplished with my neck and shoulders tightening like steel cables. I uncross my legs and stand, ignoring the cry of protest from my hamstrings. I'm stiff and stressed and I think I bruised my coccyx when I collapsed onto that chair. The *onsen* seems like the way to go.

Signs in both Japanese and English guide me toward the hot-spring baths. It is early afternoon, and they are nearly deserted. In the change room, an older woman dries her hair with a towel, methodically, with long strokes from scalp to split ends. She glances at me as I strip off my robe, and I am immediately self-conscious about my *gaijin* body: the stubble on my legs, the nubbins of cellulite on my behind, and most of all, the sizeable tattoo on my right shoulder. Tattoos are still considered taboo by some Japanese. Some *onsen* probably still ban the tattooed from bathing because of the *yakuza* connection. I hope she sees it as a faux tribal tattoo, a pattern of knife licks and curved points circling outwards like the petals of a flower. If she has a keen eye, though, she might notice that it's actually a highly stylized portrait of *Gojira*. Yeah. Godzilla. It seemed like a super cool idea in

1999, when I wanted to commemorate my new career and the launch of my personal blog and website.

It seems less cool now.

There's a pink plastic bath stool in front of several shower heads. I sit and wash myself. The soap is oppressively fragrant, a chemical floral, but the smooth motion along my skin feels nice, as does the highly pressurized stream of hot water. The tension, like rigor mortis set into my muscles, begins to relent. I am coming back to life.

The pool itself is filled with hot spring water that drizzles into the bath through a bamboo pipe emerging from an indoor garden at the pool's far end. The garden is picturesque, but the rest of the *onsen* resembles a mini public swimming pool, complete with small square tiles on the deck. My skin squeals as it sinks into the scalding water, but only for a few moments, until it begins to adapt, to loosen, to give in. My muscles soon follow. I tilt my head left and right, hear the styrofoamy squeak of sinews as my neck stretches.

The back of my head rests against the tile as I close my eyes. The soft burble of water is the only sound. It stretches across the room, across the afternoon. Time passes unmarked, propelled yet also restrained by the sound of water. It is the interruption in that flow, the sound changing from burble to dribble, that makes me open my eyes.

The bamboo tube now empties into the saucer-like surface of Soba's head, which slowly rises from the water like Martin Sheen rising from the river.

"Ugh. Stop that. That's disgusting. Show some decorum. When's the last time you even *washed* your headhole?"

It frowns and appears almost wounded.

"Clean."

"You're greasy and disgusting. Also, you're a boy. You're in the wrong bath."

"Pfft." Despite the squinty raspberry face Soba makes, the thing moves sideways, out from beneath the water inlet. "*Kappa* not need gender. Stupid."

"I'm stupid, or the idea of gender is stupid?"

"Both true."

"Please. The first time we met, you had your foot in a toilet."

"No." The thing regards me like a potential snack. No, that's not true. There's no hunger in its eyes. It looks at me more like I'm looking at it, I would imagine. With wonder and horror and a large helping of disbelief on the side.

"Yes. You're a new kind of god now. Lord of the Crapper."

"*Suijin*! *Kappa*!" It shouts and feints toward me. Water sloshes up over the rim of the bath. "*Kappa kappa KAPPA!*"

"I know what you are." It's weird to have this conversation when I'm not blind drunk or half-asleep. Unless I just fell asleep?

"I helped create you," I say. The *kappa* makes its hissy dismissive sound. *Pffft.*

"God," the thing replies stubbornly. "River god. Universe create *kappa*, not boy. Not *Kawa-chan*."

Sighing, I close my eyes again, hoping it goes away, knowing it won't. I should be scared at what my mind is capable of, or at least scared of the creature itself, but neither flusters me. This is not my first hallucinatory rodeo.

"You are afraid to be away from the water now, aren't you?" I ask. "You only appear near water now. You almost died because you spilled your head-water, and then in the end...well. Things didn't end well for you, so I guess you're extra cautious these days."

The *kappa* sits with its arms folded, glaring at me like a petulant child.

"I don't really have time for this, Soba. I need my faculties intact, I need my imagination focused, not conjuring up an ugly little grumpypants who sits here and insults me."

"Focus."

"Yes."

"On story about bad man."

"Yes."

"For stupid man who eat stupid noodle on stupid TV show."

"Yes. For the stupid man who was eating stupid noodles on that stupid TV show, I have to write that stupid story about the stupid bad man. Because life is stupid."

Soba doesn't respond. It moves its mouth side to side, as if masticating a particularly chewy bit of gristle.

"I am contractually bound to finish *Pinned IV*," I tell the hallucination, but I'm not sure who I'm trying to convince.

"You don't want to remember, but you must," it says after a moment. "Unholy soup. Remember unholy soup."

"Listen, I appreciate this alternate-dimension warning, but could you explain what in hell you're talking about now? Unholy soup? What is that, like, the worst grindcore band in history?"

Unholy soup. From nowhere, two simultaneous sensations envelop me, as if I've fallen through into a dream. First, a wave of nausea that engulfs my entire being. Then I think of that movie I saw, the title of which I forget, where that body was found in the bathtub, the one I sometimes dream about. The water. Unholy soup. In this context, a disgusting thought.

"Remember, River Black," it sneers. Soba abruptly submerges, splashing water upwards over where its head had been, and then re-emerges through the swirl of bubbles. The unsettling sensations disappear.

"Why don't you remember?" I say, somewhat shaken. "Remember how Kenichi fed you cucumbers. Remember how he—"

"Mah!" it shouts. "*SOBA EAT BOY!*"

My body is being lightly poached in this *onsen*, and still a cold, crooked finger runs down the length of my spine.

"Shut your ugly little face. You didn't eat him. Daniel died of a heart condition and fell into the canal. They found him in the canal."

"Daniel." It eyes me smugly as it sinks back under the surface, slower this time, not breaking eye contact. "Why say Daniel? I talk about Kenichi."

"I don't know, I got confused, you little freak. I am certain about one thing, though. I'm certain that you AREN'T FUCKING REAL!"

I stand and leap the length of the bath, smashing my clasped hands down into the water where the *kappa* had been. The water rushes up over the sides as though I'd executed an impressive cannonball, but it then slinks back into the pool as if embarrassed by the outburst. I stay under the water a moment, feeling around, making sure there is indeed nothing there, before my lungs begin to ache and I surface with a gasp.

At the sliding door stands a small child, about ten years old, her eyes wide and a grin on her face. She looks over her shoulder, perhaps to discern the proximity of her mother, and back at me.

"Uh." I push my hair off my face and brush the water from my eyes. "Hi."

The girl points to her nose with her index finger, the way Westerners would point at our chests to indicate ourselves. She's asking, can I go now?

"Uh, yeah. Go for it."

The girl bounds from the door and leaps into the air as she crosses her legs. When she lands, the waves are as impressive as mine were. She surfaces, giggling, and I giggle, too. Her mother appears at the door, eyeing her daughter. She sees nothing particularly amiss and disappears again.

I point to my nose, and then turn the finger towards her.

"*Himitsu desu*," I say in Japanese. *It's a secret.*

HANAMI

"It's a secret."

"Right. Why is the *kappa* secret?"

Sora scrunched her face towards her nose, so teacher could see how much thought was going into answering the question. "Because people are scared of *kappa*," she answered. "And if people knew that there was a *kappa* on the mountain, they would be afraid." Sora paused and tilted her head. "Actually, I think this is *aregorii*."

Allegory! I shouldn't have laughed out loud at that, but c'mon. I knew people who really were thirty, and they wouldn't have come up with that one.

"How so?" I asked.

"I think Kenichi and the *kappa* are repenting something else."

"Representing something else."

"Yes."

Was *Kenichi and the Kappa* an allegory? Absolutely. Was it something Sora could understand? Not likely. Daniel didn't really discuss the themes in his work. As far as I knew, it was just something he was doing for a lark. No, no. Not a lark. A distraction. Though he never mentioned it, his health had destabilized. His hands were growing worse, low oxygen purpling his skin like dye from within. His breath came in shorter, shallower gasps. He moved as though surrounded by glass figurines. He no longer came along after work to ride the bourbon boat straight into the sunrise. He went home and slept, and when he couldn't sleep, he wrote.

The way I saw it was this: Kenichi was Daniel, and Soba was Daniel's illness. Kenichi kept the *kappa* at bay; Daniel tried to do the same with his ill health. I did not know if this allegory was conscious. I should have asked him.

It was spring of 1997, a spring that didn't announce itself but simply sauntered into our apartment one morning as a mild breeze, languid and snuggly-warm. We opened the sliding doors all across Sanyō, hoping it would sweep away a winter's worth of cold and kerosene fumes. Jamiroquai and Pavement were at odds with one another—and with Babette—on my portable CD player. The walk to work grew brighter as the days lengthened and we jettisoned winter boots and coats in favour of spring jackets. The crusted brown on top of the mountains cracked to expose forest green. Business at J.J.'s picked up, and new staff began to cycle through. Nicolle left for a month, returning to Auckland to visit family. Allie, too, left for most of the spring, to travel in Thailand, Taiwan, and Hong Kong before its reversion to Chinese territory. Even Reiko took a short trip home to Fukuoka for three days.

Babette and I joked that we were the true Lifers, proving our worth while the others fell around us. I think we may have made several terrible Highlander jokes: "there can be only one" and whatnot. Meanwhile, Nagano sprang to life around us. Cherry-blossom season fell over the city like a fragrant pink snowfall on the trees, the gentle smell settling like a sweet-scented invisible fog. Cherry-blossom viewing is a national pastime and, naturally, an excuse for the consumption of beer, *shōchū*, and *sake,* so when Masa "suggested" an afternoon of it, we were not likely to argue.

It was a breezy, clear spring afternoon. Masa led a procession of us from Sanyō and up the cement steps on the hillside, between gardens and hedges and houses, until we reached Joyama Koen, the park just above Zenkōji. He walked ahead in that strange, detached manner of his, nonchalant yet eager. In the park a flat-roofed one-story building sprawled across the lawn, its doors open to allow the cherry-blossom perfume to fill the room. The place teemed with people of all ages—hyper-adorable children like Sora, salarymen in their weekend casuals (often jeans and a golf shirt, as Masa sported that day), elderly women with enormous gap-toothed grins, a couple of women in kimonos. We drank and smoked and laughed and, for a moment or two, looked out onto the vast canopy that stretched around us, sloping gently towards the temple grounds.

Afterward we wandered, buzzed and floating two inches off the ground, winter's last breaths nothing more than the occasional gasp lurking in the warm wind. Daniel and I walked to the main Zenkōji hall; I let him lean on my arm as we mounted the steps. A little wooden man sat cross-legged on a pedestal, draped in paper garlands. Binzuru, the doctor, his face worn smooth and featureless by the countless pilgrims who were encouraged to touch him for good luck and healing. I was under the impression you were supposed to lay hands on him in the place you yourself ailed. His head was worn down most, polished to the texture of velvet. I suppose touching his heart was too metaphorical; his soul, too impossible. These, too, would be worn smooth if they could be.

Daniel ran his hand over both the heart and the head.

We walked into the sanctuary, slipping off our shoes and depositing them in plastic bags we carried out onto the soft *tatami*. We looked in awe at the golden leaves and candlesticks and fabrics and dangling ornamentation of the altar. A person could sit cross-legged for an hour and never absorb all of the detail before them.

We walked towards the *okaidan,* the dark subterranean hallway where the key to nirvana lay waiting. We cajoled each other, called each other names, made games of it, the claustrophobe and the woman who felt claustrophobic under bright-blue skies, neither of us brave enough to walk into the tunnel of pure night.

"I'll give you *ichiman* yen if you go down there." Daniel elbowed me in the arm.

"I don't need ten thousand yen." I elbowed him back.

"You could skip the cycle of reincarnation and head straight to Nirvana after you die."

"I don't want to go directly to the afterworld. I kind of hoped I'd come back as a cat. Always wanted to know how their minds work."

"How about if you don't, I'll tell Nax about that time you said you were sick but instead went to go see that hip-hop show on the Gondō."

"You wouldn't dare!" I elbowed him hard enough that he stumbled forward. He giggled and feigned horror.

"You're trying to push me!" He mock-shouted. "You're trying to bury me alive!"

"Yes, Fortunado, I have my bricks and mortar ready!"

"What?"

"Edgar Allen Poe. Never mind. My dumb references are for my own entertainment, really."

I realized, for a second, that Sheila would have gotten the Poe reference, and for the first time since arriving, I felt a slight pang of homesickness.

We stepped out into the gardens and strolled around aimlessly, enjoying the fading afternoon light. There were a few more Caucasian faces than usual amongst the pilgrims. Westerner numbers increased as folks from IBM and various telecommunications companies began to arrive to prepare the massive communications infrastructure necessary for the '98 Olympic Games. Construction on the Nagano *shinkansen* was almost complete.

"Have you been working?" Daniel asked as we headed for the pond.

"You see me every night. Am I that forgettable?"

Daniel shoves my shoulder gently, though he looks in the opposite direction as he does it.

"You know that's not what I mean. Writing."

"Nothing," I admitted. "Honestly, I'm having too much fun working on the *kappa* story."

I kicked at the stones on our path as we walked. I enjoyed the satisfying mineral crunch.

"I know you've been working, obviously, because you keep giving me new pages."

Daniel laughed a gently melancholic laugh. "Every day's a bonus for me. Just hoping there's enough bonuses for me to finish this one thing."

"Daniel, come on, you've got plenty of time."

"I'm going to add a new character," he said, ignoring my response. We approached the pond and Daniel stopped to stare at the murky mirror below us. "A girl."

"I look forward to it."

I thought back to my conversation with Sora. A girl. If Daniel was writing an allegory of his life and struggle, what role would the girl play? Who was she?

Me?

"There!"

Daniel pointed towards the pond. Out of the earthy gloom a streak of bright orange emerged as a koi appeared, nibbled at the plane of water around itself, and submerged again. It was like seeing an ant in the kitchen: once you see the first one, you realize they're everywhere. Orange-and-white fish like blushes of coloured vapour. Only occasionally did they surface entirely, as if stepping from one reality into the next, as they breached the surface and worked their tiny mouths in the air.

"Are they eating when they do that?" he asked.

I shrugged. "Did you ever have goldfish as a kid?"

"Nah, we couldn't afford pets."

"Even goldfish?"

"Food, tanks, time to clean the tanks, water bills."

"You mom sounds like fun."

"It wasn't her fault."

I held my breath a moment.

"I'm sorry, Daniel, I didn't mean—"

"I still send her money," Daniel's voice wavered. "To be honest, Toby kind of saved me when he found me the job at J.J.'s. I've been able to send her a pile of money."

It was hard not to wonder how Daniel would be if that money had come twenty years before, when he needed surgery.

"Ah. *Gaijin da*!" Masa stood on the other side of the pond, brown paper bag in his hand, grin on his face. "I couldn't find you before. Let's go, we're having dinner now. *Yakiniku*."

"Okay, just a sec," I turned to Daniel. "You…you all right?"

"Yeah." His voice, now back to itself, settled back into his own chest. "Yeah, it's all good. Let's go eat free beef."

"Free expensive beef," I correct him.

"Beef!" he exclaimed, and we both laughed. I don't know why.

THE HORROR OF HELL VALLEY

There's no beef on the menu at the Hotel Senjukaku today. Instead, it is a gorgeous *kaiseki* multi-course feast of local and seasonal offerings. There are root-like vegetables, light and crisp, that taste like forgotten joy. There are baked mountain crabs that would fit in your palm and are meant to be eaten whole, shell, claws and all; I defer with a scowl. Toby shrugs and pops mine into his mouth with a grin, licking his lips like an animated wolf. I suppose I should be pleased that compared to a few days ago, I see him more as cartoon evil than true evil.

We are both overwhelmed by the elegance of the table, the artistry of the plating, each item on a different suitable plate or dish. I suddenly long for Sheila to be with me. She's never had a feast like this, even with all her fancy law-talkin' friends. Especially not in summer *yukata* robes, skin still exuding the heat of the mountain hot springs in which we sat until called to the table.

Masa's generosity has always bordered on pathology. We considered it showy at first, but to whom was he showing off? He could have impressed us with a lot less. We were a box of kittens; a ball of yarn would have sufficed. He has not changed. The Senjukaku Onsen hotel does not have the Ritz-Carletonesque splendor of forty-foot ceilings or crystal chandeliers, but it is every inch as impressive, though in a more elegant, Japanese fashion.

We eat in a private room and use the privacy as an opportunity to flop backwards on the *tatami*, torpid and over-stuffed. Then Masa rouses us, herds us into the car, and whisks us to the nearby *onsen* town of Shobu. I want to change into street clothes, but Masa will have none of it. "It's a hot spring town," he insists, "you'd be overdressed."

He's correct. In Shobu, tourists wander the streets in a state of water-induced bliss, clad only in *yukata* and sandals. We stumble upon a rifle game in a storefront, take up air rifles, and fire corks at tiny Matryoshka dolls set against a red backdrop dolloped with painted yellow sunflowers. I knock over a few and win an aluminum Hello Kitty piggy bank. In Toby's enormous grip, the air rifle is like a toy handgun. He wins a plastic keychain in the shape of a 2-D monkey. Masa leans so far over the counter I am convinced he'll tumble over it, but he is as steady as a yogi in his one-legged stance. He mows down an entire row of dolls but waves off the middle-aged man who approaches with prizes.

We wander through dark, mostly empty streets, trying to keep up with Masa, who is fleeter of foot than even Toby, with his giant strides. In fact, Toby struggles to keep up, restrained by his blue cotton robe, which barely reaches his knees and threatens to loosen in all the most unfortunate places. Backlit shop signs and the occasional streetlamp give the cobblestones a soft yellow glow. We follow Masa through these steep, narrow streets until he leads us to a tiny hovel of a restaurant that smells of old wood and cigarette smoke and the steam of boiling ramen noodles. We gather in one corner, order *gyoza* though we are not remotely hungry, and drink Asahi Super Dry on tap.

Masa asks after all of us, the Lifers and the women who came to J.J.'s briefly like cultural window shoppers, intrigued but not interested in buying. I give Masa and Toby as much information as Facebook has provided. Toby smiles, and I feel something close to forgiveness—or at least neutrality—in this moment, in this light, in this familiar sort of place, with these smells that seem to have wafted across decades to linger here for me, to make me feel at home. I do not think about Daniel or *kappa*. When the *gyoza* come, they are fresh, hot, delicious. We go back to the hotel, and I lie in the dark and listen to the distant sounds of other guests through the walls.

Today. Today was full-on. Today was…there isn't an adjective. I need to find a word, a word for the magic you feel when you're far from home and you're doing things in places that look at once the same yet entirely different, where you're invited to partake but held at arm's length at the same time, where…but, okay. Maybe I don't need to name it.

When daylight arrives the next morning, the fog has thickened in defiance, but it can't hold out against the sun very long. As Masa packs us into the car, sunlight begins to permeate, then dissipate, the mist; by the time we reach the parking lot of the monkey park, it's as if the day has opened itself to us.

The *onsen* at Jigokudani Yaen-Koen is about a twenty minutes' walk from the lot, along a wide, maintained trail. Public vehicles are prohibited in the nature preserve. Masa, never one to dawdle when the next adventure lies ahead, doesn't bother to wait for us. He's off down the trail immediately, gait determined, body angled as though he's leaning into the wind. We jog up the trail behind him.

"I thought you weren't supposed to bring food with you." I gesture to the plastic bag stuffed with chips and yogurt cups that bomps against Masa's thigh.

"You're not," Toby agrees. "The macaques will let you ogle them in the hot springs, but out here, on this trail, it's monkey country. It's their turf. They know what a plastic bag in human hands means. It means breakfast."

"It's my breakfast!" Masa calls back to us with a shrug and continues his speedy advance. Toby and I scramble to keep pace even though we know it's a pointless, exhausting enterprise.

"We should get him to take us to the ninja park next," Toby jokes. "You loved the ninja park."

"The ninja park was awesome. You could rent ninja costumes and smoke cigarettes while seven-year-old-girls lapped you on treacherous obstacle courses. I mean, that is awesome."

"Do you think people get it?" he asked.

"I'm not sure what you mean."

"When you told people about it afterward, do you think they got it?" Toby stares into the trees as he walks, his face suddenly thoughtful. He knows the answer to his question is no. No, they didn't get it, not really, not most of the time. How could they?

"Slow!" Masa admonishes with a short laugh. He is probably fifteen yards ahead already.

"I never tried to make anyone understand," I eventually say. "It's like explaining the fireworks. They understand 'really amazing fireworks.' They don't understand how it felt."

Toby nods enthusiastically, as if someone has understood him for the first time in years.

"Exactly. You can't explain things. Like how the weather, the temperature, was perfect. You weren't sure where the air ended and you began."

"The Hello Kitty mug."

"The kids running around the parking lot."

"Nicolle painting Daniel's toes."

It was my turn to frown. "No, they were yours. I remember distinctly."

"And they're distinctly my toes. You don't remember? Daniel cracked a joke about it being the first time he'd ever worn sandals. Jesus, his toes were swollen, not as bad as his fingers, but still—you don't remember that?"

I feel something large and heavy shift sideways inside

me. It feels uncomfortable, as though it's a physical element pressing against my chest wall. A stone fallen to block the doorway of my cave, leaving me in darkness.

Anger begins to ferment in my stomach. This is my treasured memory. How dare he—

Our reverie is interrupted by an unexpected hissing sound. I look ahead, expecting to see that little green jackass *kappa,* but instead there is a monkey. It ambles sideways, facing Masa from the side of the trail, eyeing him. Its reddish pink hourglass-shaped face clenches and releases with a threatening sneer, its mouth dusted with fine white fur, as if the macaque is trying to foster an unsuccessful beard. Its mouth forms an O shape and releases an excited hoot.

"Masa, give it the bag," I caution.

Masa, however, raises the bag towards his chest as if to say "Mine!" The macaque braves the open pathway and approaches Masa, putting on a bit of a show, stomping its feet as it advances, huffing and blowing. The monkey knows damn well that tasty treats are in that plastic sack. The beast is small, smaller than Soba, but it's a goddamn monkey, and size doesn't particularly relate to strength. It doesn't have to be massive to tear your arms out of your sockets. As monkeys are likely to do. Right? Isn't that a thing? I'm suddenly sure that's a thing.

It stands in front of Masa and sort of half-hoots, half-shrieks at him, its face a rictus of murderous intention. Masa, to my horror, leans towards the horrible, feral thing, making strange hissing and chicking sounds with his lips and teeth, as if he speaks the monkey's dialect. Masa raises his hands over his shoulders and does a sort of "Thriller" dance as he ups the volume on the hisses and chicks. With the bag dangling from his hand, he almost seems to be taunting the creature. In my mind, I see the monkey lunge and bury its monkey hands deep in Masa's neck. But, of course, that's not what actually happens. Unbelievably, the monkey seems to slow, and it grunts in Masa'a direction like a surly teenager.

My stomach sinks. Sure enough, punchy monkey is not done. It's hanging around the playground now, looking for a weaker kid to intimidate.

I am that weaker kid.

The macaque scurries back to the side of the path, but now begins to size me up, baring its teeth and grunting.

"Masa?" I taste copper at the back of my throat as my insides cave into an internal sinkhole. Monkeys tear faces off, too, don't they? Yes, yes, this is certainly true as well.

"Masa, what do I do here?"

Masa, God bless him, does not respond, but keeps walking, plastic food bag clutched protectively to his chest. The macaque is on my left, so I keep walking forward. Will it attack me from behind if I look away? Will it perceive me as a threat if I don't look away?

"Go!" I shout at it. That's when it bares its teeth again and shrieks at me like a banshee. *The Shriek of the Mutilated.* That movie is, ridiculously, about a yeti. A stupid mountain dwelling snow monkey that kills people.

The monkey's screech seems to have piqued the curiosity of its monkey buddies in the trees. Suddenly there are three of them. Two monkey buddies have come to back up their pal, grunting while he continues to squawk. Without warning it leaps forward a foot. It's a threat pose, a fake-out, but I still cry out in what is, honestly, sheer terror.

"Go!" My eyes start to sting. *You're not scared of anything, Hel,* comes Sheila's voice. *Your pen name is River Black.*

Shriek.

"Go! Git!"

Hoot. Shriek.

"Go! Go away! Leave me alone you stupid yeti! DEATH IS THE DEVIL'S BLESSING!"

"What the hell are you talking about?" Toby approaches from behind, on the opposite side of the murderous gang of apes. "Don't freak out, you'll just piss 'em off."

A second member of the murder trio starts to shriek at

me. Toby raises his arms and splays his fingers. I want to ask him why he's doing jazz hands at the moment of our de-limbing and de-facing.

"Show 'em you don't have any food," he says, so I imitate his gesture. Toby does something even weirder. He forms as "o" shape with his lips, raises his eyebrows, and leans slightly forward towards them. The main monkey's goons back up a step, while the O.G. monkey suddenly closes his mouth and starts to hoot to himself. Toby nudges me forward, and within a few seconds, they've retreated to the treeline, still making noises, but no longer on the advance.

"Oh my God. Oh my God. Oh my God." I'm shaking and laughing at the same time. I can feel the adrenalin coursing through everything, even my eyelids. "Oh my God. Oh my God. Oh my God."

"It's okay." Toby says. "They're gone."

"The monkeys in the hot springs are so nice," I opine. "How did you know?"

"I really do build cabins up here, sometimes," Toby replies. "There are monkeys. You learn how to scare 'em away."

"Oh my God. Oh my God. Oh my...thanks a lot, Masa, you jerk!"

Masa, that jerk, is a good thirty feet ahead, feeding himself from his precious, lethal bag of potato and dairy products.

"You still going to be okay with this?" Toby is referring to our descent into the heart of monkey darkness.

"Yeah. No. Yeah. I'm fine. No big deal. Just about chewed my face off..."

"Nothing chewed your—"

"—but every horrible thing you survive makes for a better story, right?"

"Sure," he says, looking unsure.

Hell Valley comes into view. It is named so, I imagine, for the molten fire underground that forces steam out between the rocks like smoke between Smaug's teeth. It looks slightly more hellish to me now because I have seen its demons, and those demons are monkeys. Monkeys quietly steeping in pools of hot water, pinkish-red faces peeking out from beneath greyish-brown fuzz with a kind of forlorn acceptance. Monkeys contemplating passers-by on the tops of walls, feeding their young, wandering into the hills. Black fences indicate where humans should and should not go. I should be asqueal with delight, but the attempted assassination has me wary of their simian eyes. They're clearly plotting against me.

We enter the blocky brick Hell Valley headquarters. Masa pays for three tickets and holds out two, his arm extended behind him as he's already moving forward. My eyes sweep the room for Reiko.

Toby stares at a display board; an overview of the habits of the Japanese serow, in *kanji* which I doubt he could possibly read. Masa is already gone outside, into the monkey mists.

"C'mon." Toby has wandered back to me. "Join us in the tourist crowd."

"You go ahead. They are amazing, adorable, fascinating creatures with black and treacherous hearts. I'll stay here."

Maybe it's the aftershocks of my adrenalin quake, but I feel spiky, irritable. Though he is generous, sometimes Masa barely registers our presence. Now is one of those times. Toby's acting as if we came to the monkey park to see monkeys. I just want to find Reiko and…

And what? Ask her to hop in the Mystery Machine with me to play amateur detective?

My eyes wander the room, and my mind follows. Placards cover half of the available wall space. Pictures and maps and *kanji* suspended on plexiglass, floating an inch above the wall. A taxidermy serow poses proudly, if stiffly, by the entrance. Its expression is set somewhere between the dull-eyed, slack-jawed stare of a Jersey cow and the slightly sinister smirk of a goat. I'm staring at the serow when a nondescript grey door behind the counter swings inward, and out steps a middle-aged woman in a park authority uniform. Her hair is cut in a bob now but remains coal black. I can't see if she still has those dimples because her face elongates as her jaw slides downward in disbelief.

Then she smiles. Yes, the dimples have endured.

"Kawa-chan?"

"*Hai*!" I fumble to project my old confidence, to locate and present the old River. "Rei-chan? *Ohisashiburi desu ne!*"

Rei squeaks at me, hopefully in delight, and rushes from behind the counter to give me a decidedly un-Japanese bear hug. A grin spreads across my face despite myself. The Japanese have a concept called *tatemae,* the public face, which is not always in sync with *honne,* your true feelings. Reiko's true feelings are immediately apparent. She clearly does not remember me as a selfish, ignorant child. Entirely unexpectedly, I find myself near tears.

"Kawa-chan!" She pulls back, hands on my biceps, to study my face, and I do the same. She's aged five years for my twenty. Her cheeks are still chipmunk-cute. Her front left incisor is still twisted perpendicular to the rest of her teeth. She still smells like an unnamed perfume.

"I can't belieeeeve this! It has been a long time!"

"About twenty years," I agree.

"Oh. My. God. Twenty years. *Shinjirarenai ne?*"

"I can't believe it either. My body believes it though. Believes it hard. But look at you! You look exactly the same!"

"Oh." She covers her face with one hand. "No no no. Make-up and hair dye. I'm old now."

"You look wonderful, Rei-chan, you look wonderful."

"Are you visiting Nagano?"

"Yes," I reply, "but this isn't an accident. I knew you were here, and we came to find you."

"We?"

"Me, Masa, and Toby."

"Oh my God." Her eyes widen again. "You are still talking to Toby?"

"Yes, well, not for a long time. We just reconnected."

The expression of surprise and incredulity returns to her

face every few moments, as it does when you're explaining twenty years of your exciting-on-paper life to someone you haven't seen for decades. She is a fountain of *wows* and *oh my Gods,* which I try to staunch with a series of *it's no big deals* and *it's not as good as you thinks.* Shooting a film on zero budget in Estonia, however, sounds interesting to her, and I start to feel slightly ungrateful about my life as I downplay it all.

"This is my job." She does a little turn with her palms out, as if to indicate the environs. "I started part-time and they hired me full-time two months ago. Nothing special. Only managing staff and schedules, hiring and *nan dake,* human re-resources? Yeah, human resources. Easy. I can't work in a bar for much longer."

She meant to use the word *couldn't,* but I don't correct her. Instead I take her arm, like the old friend I suppose I am, and lead her in a circle around the lobby.

"Reiko," I say, as conversationally as I can, "I have to be honest with you. I'm happy to see you, but I also had a question or two I wanted to ask."

"Oh! Okay, what do you need?"

"Well, I'm trying to solve a mystery."

"I don't understand."

"It's tough to explain."

"And Toby is helping you?" Rei's expression is quizzical, exaggerated, as many of her expressions are. "I'm sorry. I thought you maybe wouldn't be friends with Toby. I can remember you were angry."

"Yes." I see him out in the park, a full head-and-a-half taller than anyone else, motionless before a family of bathing apes. "Yes, I was."

"Sometimes he was rude to you."

"Yes, he was."

"And sometimes he was a liar."

I don't respond to that. We both know it is true.

LOVED AND CONFUSED

People warned me about Toby, but I didn't want to believe them. So I didn't—and oh, while I didn't, it was the best summer. The best summer. Even if I was in love with a mirage, shimmering in the August heat.

Nagano City was humid. It was like walking into one of those *oshiburi* ovens full of moist hot towels. There was no air conditioning at Sanyō, and there were no screen doors. Your options were to keep the apartment sealed and allow yourself to stew, or fling the balcony doors wide, rat population be damned. I chose the second option, welcoming the evening breezes and the sound of summer heat, the constant resounding chorus of cicadas and crickets from the hills, a continual chitter that swelled but never abated, subsuming all other noises until the thunderous hum became part of me. Though it was never silent, you stopped noticing it. It kept Babette awake, but it lulled me to sleep every night.

The Lifers were reunited at J.J.'s by then, everyone's vacations and visa-renewal-runs completed before high-season airline prices came into effect. To celebrate, Masa rented a cottage in the mountains, inviting us all to enjoy a respite from the humidity in the cool mountain air. We barbecued thin, squiggly strips of beef on a wire-mesh grill laid overtop a campfire, drank cold beer, and watched as Babette, exhausted from the humidity and frustrated by our carousing, sought refuge by sleeping the night away in a closet. To be fair, it was a big closet.

For the first time since childhood, summertime felt like adventure time again. The initial bliss of travel had faded, so we needed more. To see more, to do more, to dig deeper, not just into Japan, but into life itself. We climbed up a barren hillside to the lip of a volcano in Gunma to gawk at the crater lake, its water the colour of blue chalk. We took a bus to Gifu City where the Fantastic J.J. Band performed for one of Nax's wealthy clients. They asked us to sing. Those of us who could sing did solo numbers, while Daniel and I were relegated to the group numbers like "Take The A-Train" and "In The Mood." Daniel stood behind me and hummed. I mugged shamelessly for the room in lieu of singing on key. We frequented Nojiriko, or Lake Nojiri, gathering beforehand in Chitose Park, heads pulsing as the previous night's alcohol was extracted from our pores by the early-morning heat, making our way to the bus terminal hungover, sickly, yet grinning. At Nojiriko we swam and rowed boats across the lake under the enthusiastic summer sun. Toby pulled himself out of a rowboat and into a tree branch to snap a photograph of a giant insect. Allie and I shared sips of rum and coke from a giant paper cup. We ate mediocre pizza as though it was gourmet. We laughed and drank and smoked and slept and did it all again.

In August, during the Obon holiday season when Tokyo is least crowded, Toby and I took the train to Ueno Station to explore the comparatively empty city. We rode the Yamanote Line around its gigantic loop again and again, staring out the windows at the skyscrapers, the glittering glass giants that surrounded us. We took the elevator up the Tokyo Tower, shaped like the Eiffel Tower but painted orange and white like a traffic cone. We ate and ate and ate. We got drunk and walked down the narrow outdoor laneways of

Harajuku: wild, crowded Tokyo, snarling punks in pompadours, rock'n'roll blasting from every open door. We turned the corner to head back, up Omotesando, the opposite direction through an opposite world, with its wide boulevard and international brands, like a Japanese Champs-Élysées. We took photographs of the vast neon valleys of Shinjuku and pondered the carnal delights promised by pink signage in Soapland. From the second-floor Starbucks window, we watched hundreds of people mass and disperse, mass and disperse, mass and disperse with each change of the light at the scramble corner in Shibuya, as Sophia Coppola would stealthily do, sneaking cameras into that same Starbucks to film the scene for *Lost in Translation*.

We went to dance clubs in Roppongi, too, which appealed more to Toby than me. They were dark, shifty places where burly American servicemen seemed to perpetually straddle three or four simultaneous fistfights apiece. Toby seemed almost aroused by the danger of the whole thing, but my anxiety pinched me in place, left me scared to move. Toby acquiesced and took me back to the Hotel Ibis, where we had mad sex, missed our train, and had to appeal to the JR Rail staff's sympathies to get on a later one at no extra fee. We laughed and sang silly songs, and everything was gold.

Except on the train home, when suddenly it wasn't.

I laid my head against Toby's shoulder as the limited express lulled us with its rockabye rhythm. "This might be the last time we ride this train," I mused aloud.

"Hmmm." It didn't seem to move Toby as it did me.

"You don't find that a bit sad?"

"*Shinkansen's* faster," he replied, and immediately, though we'd just had four days of fun together, I found myself irritated.

"It is sad," I said, possibly with a bit of poutiness in my tone. "It's the end of an era."

"Did you have fun?" Toby changed the subject. He sounded like a father asking for a report at the end of a Disney trip. As if he needed the validation.

"Did you see a frown cross my face once?" I was willing to give him the validation, but not directly.

"You didn't look super pleased when we slept in," he said. This was true. We'd ranted and sworn as though it was the opening sequence in *Four Weddings and a Funeral,* the two of us spewing increasingly distressed variations of the F word.

"That wasn't a frown, that was abject terror at the hideousity of the situation."

"Hideousity is not a word."

"Hideousity is not a word, you are correct. It is an all-encompassing element of the dark side of existence, upon which you cannot look directly without going mad."

"Ah."

Now I frowned.

"Ah?"

No response.

"You know, only a few weeks ago, you'd have gone with me on that."

"On what?"

"Hideousity!" I said. "You'd have jumped on that. You'd have asked if there really was a dark side to the universe, one that human minds were not meant to envision let alone directly observe, or if, instead, each of us contains all elements of the universe, meaning that in the right circumstance, we can withstand such horrors, which is why the things humankind can endure are beyond horrific but, in many cases, nonetheless endurable."

"I didn't follow any of that," he replied.

"Wow, Toby, really? Because that's what you sound like when you're going off. You know that, right?"

I preferred that—his going off, the asinine antics—to this new, patronizing tone. As much as his nonsense made me roll my eyes, it was way better than the kindergarten-teacher-style correction of my grammar.

"I knew that, you know," I said, unable to let it go.

"You knew what." He continued to look out the window at the nothing of night.

"That it wasn't a word. I'm a writer. I won the English award in grade twelve. I know from words, Toby."

"I'm sure you do." Face to the window.

"Is it out there?" I asked.

"Is what out there?"

"The apology you're looking for? The one you meant to give to me?"

Toby closed his eyes and for a moment, a flash so brief it almost didn't exist, he looked frustrated and tired. By the time his eyes fluttered sideways towards me, however, he had filled them with penitence.

"Oh." He smiled meekly. "Sweetie, I'm really sorry. I didn't mean to suggest anything. I'm just, yes, I'm sorry. I'm very sorry. It's been a great weekend but it took a bit of a toll, I'm pretty tired, and when we get home, I have to head up to Hakuba."

"Tonight?"

"Yeah. I'm going to crash in one of the bunkies at the site. They've got us on extra-early shifts now, to get all those cabins finished before the full deluge of foreigners falls on the province."

It's a prefecture, I thought, but I didn't correct him.

At Nagano Station, Toby was back to his old self, though he was fidgety and impatient. We parted with a quick peck. I was disappointed by how unromantic the final notes of our romantic getaway had been.

It was a high August night, the air close as skin, moist as breath, and even there, on a major throughway, the textured, trilling drone of insects could be heard in the distance. I walked the cobblestone pathway I first took, almost a year ago, with my J.J.'s friends. Already, that feeling, the sense of wonder, of newness, some kind of near-transcendence, had diminished. Like a passionate romance settling into a true adult relationship, perhaps.

I emerged from the narrow corridor and passed a group of grinned-up drunk men in suits enjoying a smoke in front of the bar called Snack Donkey. The spicy smell of cigarettes combined with something honeyed and sweet, some sort of pork-cutlet sauce, that wafted from the door alongside the voice of a woman singing *enka* music with the karaoke machine. I smiled. Maybe wonder had diminished, but it was now balanced with warmth and familiarity. It felt like a hug. I could sink into it, forget about Toby, and remember that he was not the reason I was here.

The Gondō area was busy. Even on a Sunday, people drifted along the middle of the road in singles, duos, and small groups like errant waves, disturbed only by the cars that pushed them temporarily to the shore. Hostesses in impossibly tall-soled platform boots walked with varying degrees of stability behind middle-aged men, released from their salaryman suits for one more night. An umami aroma wafted from a stationary *takoyaki* truck.

A few blocks later, a less enjoyable sensory experience awaited. All at once I was struck with the sound of sobbing and the smell of vomit. I almost stumbled over Allie, who sat on the asphalt in front of the BOOM building, her back against a cigarette vending machine, her leg perilously close to what I presumed was a puddle of her prior alcohol intake. Nicolle leaned over her and spoke to her, but Allie clearly couldn't hear her through her violent, shuddery gasps and crying jags.

I loved them both. They always knew how to turn a bad situation into a half-decent one. But that love was also predicated on the fact that I avoided being ensnared by drama, and there was always drama. Beyond card games and letters home, the pre-customer workday usually included staff cattily sniping away at one another's reputations. We lived and worked together; it was going to happen. Anger, betrayal, et cetera. Someone would resent Reiko's authority, and there would be a low-grade argument. Someone else would burst into tears over some inaccessible boy.

I didn't need to overhear the conversation; they were in front of BOOM, Allie was crying, and that was enough. BOOM was ground zero for heartbreak if you didn't know the difference between fantasy and reality, and let's face it, alcohol can obliterate that line. Boys paid to look pretty and make women feel good about themselves whilst running up their drink tabs? BOOM boys were destined to marry proper Japanese women, find proper jobs, and raise proper families. Babette and Shinji were not the norm.

I spun on my heel and looped back, behind a parking garage, before they could recognize me.

I had my own drama now. I didn't need theirs.

REI-CHAN

Memory is a savvy editor. It reinforces your chosen narrative by conveniently clipping out the details. When I think of J.J.'s, I rarely think of Allie throwing up on the Gondō. Surely I must have a negative memory of Reiko somewhere, but none come to mind. I leave the monkey park with a warm glow, a stupid grin, and plans to meet Rei-chan at a Gondō coffee shop the following day.

She's already there when I arrive, a freshly squeezed orange juice in front of her, a smile on her face that reinforces my narrative of Rei as affable, enthusiastic, borderline joyous, despite the turmoil of her twenties and the soul-crushing reality of a job in the water trade. I feel as though I should hold fast to her buoyancy. She will be my strength. She will have answers.

Before I can expect answers, though, I have to explain this madness.

I tell her about Nax. Reiko hasn't seen or heard about him in a decade. Her reaction to his passing is one of sympathy, but not grief. Their relationship was no doubt more fraught than any of ours. I cannot imagine what it was like to work in that bar, under those circumstances, while being Japanese. If one of the owners of the House of Spirits passed away, I'd be bummed, but I'm not sure you'd call it "grief."

When I tell her about the book, she seems confused, so I hand it to her and shrug.

"Oh. My. God." She traces the cover image lightly with her fingers. "I remember drawing this."

"You were always so excited about Daniel and me working together."

"Of course," she says. "You wanted to be a writer, and Daniel needed...*nan dake...*"

"A hobby?" I ask.

"A distraction. Something to take his mind off his sickness. You were both doing something important for yourselves." Her pinky continues to follow the *kappa*'s outline. "So, this picture just...got here, on the cover of this book, somehow? And you really don't know where the book came from?"

"I really don't. And I can't explain why, exactly, but I need to find out."

"Maybe you are the one who needs a distraction now," she says. I want to protest. This feels too intense for a mere distraction, but I'm not sure that she's wrong.

"I want to know if you'll help us. Toby and me. Help us figure out this puzzle."

Reiko grins and clasps her hands together. "You. Want me. To help solve a mystery! It's so fuuuuun!"

Seriously, has she aged a day? After her casual acceptance of my situation, I'm convinced nothing is going to faze her. Maybe I could confide in her, tell her about Soba's visits? Ah, but, no. Mysterious books are one thing; otherworldly delusions are another. I decide to ask her normal questions that normal people might ask and skip right on by the legendary water beast in my bathroom.

"So what happened to J.J.'s after I left?" I sip black coffee from a small white mug. "I've heard from people on Facebook and stuff, but nothing...real, you know?"

"Oh boy," she says. "It's so long ago. Where can I start?"

She tells the story through a combination of Japanese, good English, bad English, and hand gestures. The gist of it is that our departures—Daniel's, Toby's and my own—marked the beginning of the end of an era, which confirmed what I'd learned from Nicolle and Allie. After we left, the dynamic shifted. It was a shock to J.J.'s internal ecosystem, and it cast a pall. New staff came and went. Many new staffers were there to party and make a quick buck; fewer had genuine interest in the customers, the culture, the country. Fewer customers came through the doors. This went on for a few years, Rei tells me, until Nax finally succumbed to the reality of his hobby. He could no longer handle the drain on his personal bank account. Hostesses resigned; Nax chose not to replace them. It was difficult to maintain the same level of service with fewer people; customers dwindled further still.

"No one ever cleaned the kitchen like you did." Rei shakes her head sadly. "They would barely vacuum the carpet."

So J.J.'s grew dingier, dirtier, sadder. Allie and Nicolle ran out their final few weeks. They withdrew the hundreds of thousands of yen they'd squirreled away in their Hachijuni Bank accounts and lit out for southeast Asia, where they spent time learning to be SCUBA instructors on Lombok Island in Indonesia.

"I stayed as long as I could stay," Rei says, but her tone suggests she stayed far longer than she should have. "The only person who stayed until the end was Babette. It got so bad. Even the regulars stopped coming in. Even Masa stopped coming in. I didn't care because I was tired of that job, but I'm glad you weren't around to see it. It would have made you sad."

"It makes me sad just hearing about it." And I do feel sad. It's as though Rei had told me about the tragic downfall of an old boyfriend about whom I had fond memories.

"Finally, I quit," Rei says. "I went to work in a café. It was much less money, but also, much less…"

"Depressing?"

"Yes."

Rei sips the last drops of her orange juice and squints into the cup as if hoping to uncover more beneath the half-melted ice cubes.

"I haven't thought about Nax in years," she says finally. "It was not always fun. But he was sometimes generous. He helped me. Are you hungry?"

"I could eat."

"Let's go to his restaurant. Do you remember?"

I do. She means Rokumonsen, the unassuming family-owned place at the end of the Gondō, where the street proceeds eastward, beyond the arcade with its curved glass ceiling.

"We can have lunch," she says. "It can be our own memory for him."

"A memorial lunch," I agree.

I like this idea. A memorial without tears. We will eat in his honour. I finish my coffee, and we head out along the Gondō, crossing Nagano-*odōri*. Along the streetscape, clothing shops and hostess bars give way to restaurant after restaurant.

"I never know what they serve or what's going on inside these places." I gesture to one of the wood-panelled shops on the roadside, ornamented with dangling paper ball lanterns. "Even reading these menus outside, even looking at photographs of the dishes, I don't know what's going on. I don't even know how to order regular ramen! There's *tonkotsu* ramen and *miso* ramen and curry ramen but what in hell do you call regular ramen?"

"*Shōyu* ramen?"

"That's it!" I shout. She laughs.

"Jesus, Rei, for twenty-two years I've just been saying 'ramen' and hoping they know what I'm talking about. Or else eating whatever they bring me."

Rei stops.

"I think we passed it."

"No," I say, surveying the shops behind us. "No, we'd have seen it."

"Rokumonsen," Rei says. "It was definitely called Rokumonsen, right?"

Now, though, we're not sure. We seem to share the memory of the name, the colour of the façade, the shape of the doorway. Yet here we are, and here it isn't.

"I don't understand. It should have been back there. Everything else looks the same."

"No!" Rei insists. "You really think so? I don't think anything looks the same."

"Maybe everything looks familiar, but nothing looks the same."

Familiar. *Kanji* on signs, red lanterns, blocky facades, tiled roofs, corrugated steel drop-doors, neon lights in windows, a busy grid of electrical wires that slices the sky into bright-blue blocks. Familiar. Yet I know that Rei is right. None of it is remotely the same. These storefronts didn't exist in 1996. This place is the same place, entirely different. The way we regenerate our cells every seven years until we technically consist of entirely different parts. The way a shot-for-shot remake of a film doesn't succeed because though the shots are the same, you can't perfectly recreate what lay in the frames themselves. The city was always here for me to revisit, but I was a fool to think I would be revisiting the same city.

"Oh, there it is."

"What?"

"There." Rei points at the sign a block down, which even I can read says Rokumonsen.

"Oh," I say. "It moved."

"Yeah," Rei agrees. "So…do we still want to go?"

"I don't know." Rokumonsen was Nax's favourite restaurant, and we went there with him regularly, downing tumblers of *shōchū* tinted green with lime cordial, luxuriating in mid-course cigarettes, laughing at Nax's wartime stories. For Nax, Rokumonsen was the sum of its parts: the family who owned it, the particularly good sushi, the company he kept at dinner, the years of enjoyment, the habit, the feeling of home. For me, Rokumonsen is about Nax, twenty years ago. I am struck again by the question. Is it still the same place if it's not the same place? It doesn't matter to him. He's gone. It matters to us.

Across the road, in front of a bakery, a gentleman leans forward in prayer.

"Maybe we can just eat ramen." Rei shrugs. "I think maybe Rokumonsen is expensive."

The fellow across the road isn't praying. He's just using two hands to light a cigarette.

"Yeah. Sounds good, Reiko."

Ramen, blessedly, has not changed. Ramen is a constant, every savoury slurp a perfect bite of happiness, and it erases some of this haunting metaphysical mist that had started to bum me out. People in North America try and replicate ramen and fail thanks to inferior recipes, middling ingredients, or, worst of all, a chef who tries to gussy it up, to elevate it beyond its intended station as accessible, affordable corner-shop soup. Soy base, slightly chewy noodles, not too thick, set against crunchy sprouts, tender bamboo shoots, salty seaweed, tangy slices of pork, and a halved hard-boiled egg. It tastes like the essence of place. Soup, of all things, has grounded me, stopped the world around me from shifting and folding in upon itself like *Dr. Strange* meets *Dark City* meets the streetscape-bending scene in *Inception*.

When the food is finished and our stomachs are suitably distended, we walk out into the afternoon sun once again. We talk less now, as both of us, through the power of food, seem to have been transported elsewhere. We wander towards the station, taking the back roads, eventually arriving at the Taisei Abinasu. Reiko surprises me, then, as she stops and squats on the sidewalk like a Japanese teenager, looking up to where the red windows used to be. There's no way in hell my ankles will flex enough for me to be in that position.

"I never got to say that I was sorry about what happened to Daniel," Reiko says.

I half-squat and lean against the wall of the parking garage behind us. "Thanks, Rei-chan. He was your friend, too, though."

"Yes, but not like you," she replies. "He was so quiet and shy, but you got through to him and became his real friend. It must have been hard when...."

I wait for her to find her words. Instead, she looks as though she wants to say more, but she doesn't. She shakes her head, more for her own benefit than mine, and sighs, staring across the road at the place that was once ours.

"Did I say, I used to be married?"

"No!" I'm genuinely shocked that this detail wasn't mentioned earlier.

"Yes," she says, as if to assuage my disbelief. "His name is Matsumoto Toshi."

"What was he like?" I give up the squat and plunk down on the curb beside her.

"Soooo niiiiice." She draws out the vowels in her Reiko way. "He has a kind face. He was a musician."

"You always had a thing for musicians."

"Yes, many girls have a thing for musicians."

"I hope that's not why you are no longer married."

"*Ee?*"

"I mean, he didn't...cheat on you or..."

"No, no, no, no," she assures me. "No, he was a musician. But then he got scared about his future and became a policeman. We got divorced a few years after that."

"Now *there's* a shift."

"Yes, big change. Big change that made him into a different person. He was very unhappy in his job. But doing a job you don't like is sometimes the Japanese way."

"Trust me, Rei-chan, that's not a strictly Japanese thing." I think of butterflies and pins and partial dentures. We stare quietly at the building some more. I listen to the ghosts, but their voices are muffled.

"So we can talk about our spy adventure? No, no. *Nan dake*...detective adventure!"

Her enthusiasm forces a smile to my face; like a ping-pong ball let go underwater, it rushes up and pops free.

"I want to find out where the book came from," I say. "My only clue is where I last saw the book, which is on my *wāpuro*. I thought Nax might have taken it, but he didn't. There's no way one of the girls who lived in that room took it, either—it was as heavy as a safe."

"It was safe?"

"No, *a* safe—never mind. It weighed a lot. No one would have taken it back to Brisbane or wherever. So the last person to be in that apartment, and who stayed in Nagano, was—"

"Babet*to*," she says, accentuating the Japanese pronunciation of the name.

"Yes."

"Will she be mad at you?"

I shrug, though I can't see how the answer is anything but "yes."

"It seems unlikely she'd send me the book," I say. "But... she's kind of where the trail of breadcrumbs ends."

"I haven't seen Babette since I quit," Reiko says.

"And Shinji?"

"No."

"Would you know where to look? Phone book? The internet? I can't read Japanese, but you can."

"We can try it," she says. "But maybe there's one easier way."

I cock my head and raise an eyebrow.

"Kogawa."

Even today, the name still provokes a mild shudder. I picture his terrible Jheri curl, his greasy-looking suits, his rage-contorted features, and I shudder again.

"Babette told me she knew him," I recall.

"Knew him?" Reiko laughs. "You don't know?"

She can see by my face that I don't.

"Kogawa is Shinji's uncle," she says. "They're family."

Family. All of the competing emotions inside me flare like

magnesium, followed by a burned-out numbness. I have no tools with which to process this information.

"Why wouldn't she have told me that?" I ask

"Why would she?"

"I...I just think it probably should have come up at some point."

"He is actually very close to here," Reiko says. "He has a shop."

"A shop?"

"Yes."

"In town?"

"Actually," she says, extending an arm and finger directly across the road, "It's right there."

THE COMPETITION

Kogawa was a horrible person who picked on the weak. Like girls in host bars. Like Babette. Like Daniel.

Daniel's illness had worsened that spring. Even a simple walk to work caused him to wheeze. When he told me he still went up to the *sakon inari* sometimes, to think and to write, I was horrified to think of this sickly boy all alone on the mountainside. Yet he never missed a day of work, still came to the ninja park, still meandered around Zenkōji with me in the summer-afternoon heat. He was still there, until he missed the Sanyō Heights Regatta. That should have been a warning sign to all of us.

I stood in front of the mirror in a black skirt, white blouse, and a lightweight black cardigan disinterred from the clothing graveyard of my closet. For the first time since my arrival, I'd even ironed the wrinkles from my clothes. I looked almost like a professional person, despite the bags under my eyes and unholy hangover breath. If you stood back and squinted, I could've passed.

"Where are you going?" Nicolle looked perplexed, as if I were her maid of honour who'd showed up at the church in jeans.

"Today is Sora's English competition."

Nicolle made a mock-sorrowful face and held up a small iced-coffee carton. It had been halved lengthwise and looked like a boat. A standard-issue chopstick, the kind you slide out of a narrow paper envelope and then split apart, stood perpendicular, like the ship's mast, secured by a wad of chewed gum. The removable part of a Kleenex box, the part you rip off to open them, was taped across the stick to mimic a sail. Tissue of Kitten, ahoy.

"The Sanyō Regatta is today?"

"Of course! All that rain yesterday, coming down out of the hills? The canals are way up, and the water's running like mad, mate. Weren't you listening yesterday?"

"I was too busy listening to a customer telling me my teeth were too big."

"Your teeth were too big? That's a new one. Weird thing to point out to someone who's lighting your cigarettes."

"Maybe it's the kind of thing you can only point out to someone who's lighting your cigarettes."

"Eh, your teeth aren't too big, mate. They're normal teeth. Regular-sized chompers."

"Anyway." I turned to finish stuffing some errant papers into my backpack. "I can't. This is a big deal for Sora, and I'm terrified because I'm the one who's been teaching her."

"Big event?"

"Huge. Olympic-themed, apparently."

"So, ten-year-olds talking about how much they love snowboarding."

"Six-year-olds talking about how figure skating is beautiful."

"Twelve-year-olds talking about how many new *gaijin* there are in town."

"Twenty-six-year-olds complaining about how many new *gaijin* there are in town," I pouted.

"Americans. Eating while walking." Nicolle said.

"Passing food to one another with chopsticks!" I cried.

"Not removing their shoes inside," Nicolle said.

"NOT LEARNING THE LANGUAGE," we shouted simultaneously, and laughed.

"I thought that skirt was a bit proper for a toy boat race."

Nicolle gestured towards my ensemble. "Well, we're about to go right now, so why don't you join us on your way?"

"Babette!" I called.

"Hey." Behind the door, the faint sound of knitting needles.

"I'm coming in."

"No, you're not coming in—"

"Already in." I slid the *shoji* behind me. Several of Babette's longtime students were part of this annual competition as well. It was our plan to sit together and crack inappropriate jokes about the children's poor language skills. She sat cross-legged on her futon in a pinstripe pantsuit, needles in hand. Beside her on the floor was a plastic water bottle, halved, with a spark plug taped inside and the words *S.S. Mizuwari* written in magic marker on the side.

"What?" Babette frowned at me. "You couldn't take ten minutes to make a boat?"

"I like your engine."

"It's *ballast,* you twit." She tapped the spark plug with her finger. "Found it on the road."

"Love ya, girl."

"Did you guys change brains or something?" Nicolle laughed from the kitchen. She wasn't wrong; normally, something like the boat race would have me zinging around the room, giddily gluing God-knows-what to God-knows-what, my creation decidedly unseaworthy. Making up silly race chants, decorating boats with glitter and macaroni, inviting the neighbours. I'd even saved a cold coffee carton of my own for the occasion. I'd simply lost track of the days.

Babette and I rushed down to the street. In front of Sanyō, along the side of the road, the four-foot-wide waterway ran southward, under the Zenkōji road, towards India Street and the Gondō. The clouds lay low, lower than the lowest mountains on the horizon, and the air was on the cusp of a dampness you could almost call drizzle. The water, often a few inches of trickle, was at least a foot deep, and the current gushed along like a real river. The boat race would be a rapids run.

Lined up along the rail, Babette and I found friends old and new: Allie, Nicolle, Rei, and three Canadians, Melissa and the twins Kristine and Marika. Babette walked up to Reiko and held her miniature craft out towards her.

"Sail her for me, Captain Reiko. Sail her well."

Reiko both protested and accepted with glee, as was her impossible way. We waved quickly to the others and started off towards the conference hall.

"I'm impressed with your boat-building skills."

"Piss off, yeah?"

"I mean, *ballast,* that shows some engineering knowledge and nautical wherewithal."

"Piss. Off." Babette was laughing, though. As we crossed the Zenkōji road, cheers rose behind us, followed by a delighted chant of *Go! Go! Go!* Someone moaned and cursed as their craft tipped or became tangled in weeds. The voices trailed behind us for several minutes and both of us grinned silently as we listened.

At the crowded downtown conference centre, a sprawling cube of enormous rectangular rooms, the hallways and foyer were packed with folding chairs and families. The rush of voices was like the water coursing along the canals.

"Do you see Toby?" I asked.

Babette grunted. "He's four feet taller than anyone else in the room, he'd be hard to miss."

I felt bad making Toby wait in the throng, but I needed to check in with my little champion. In the hallway on the left, the participants—twelve finalists in each of three categories—sat on the floor, backs to the wall, reading, mouthing words, some attended to by parents and teachers, others on their own. There, on her own as expected, was Sora. She wore a blue-striped dress with pink roses on the shoulders and hem, as well as her ear buds, her mouth moving silently as she stared intently at her notebook.

"Kawa-chan!" Sora sprang up, her disc player clattering to the ground, yanking the buds from her ears. She barely seemed to notice as she threw her arms around my neck. The distance between student and teacher, that respectful reserve, had long ago disappeared.

"Are you ready?"

"Yes, I am. Ready."

"How much did you practise?"

"I practised my…" She scanned her head for the word. "Face! I practised my face off!"

Babette sniggered beside me. I introduced the two of them, and then Babette wandered off down the hall in search of her own students.

"Practising hard today?" I asked.

"No." Sora sat down and picked up her notebook. "I'm bored. I have read my essay too much times."

"Too many."

"Too many times. I'm reading the next chapter in your story instead."

"Daniel's story," I reminded her. "If you're bored of reading your essay, why don't you just practise speaking by reading that aloud to me?"

Sora nodded, and I slid down the wall to land on my behind as she began to read.

The monster's hunger never seemed to end. Even while it was eating a cucumber, it would hiss at Kenichi that it wanted more, and if it didn't get more, the deal was off. Kenichi would be eaten instead.

So day after day, in rain or sun or snow, Kenichi climbed the hill with his satchel full of cucumbers. It was only a few days before his money was gone and he couldn't afford to buy them, so he began to steal them from neighbours' gardens, one at a time so as not to arouse suspicion. One time, he even stole from the grocer. He was afraid of being caught, but it was the only way to keep the *kappa* at bay until Kenichi could find some money of his own. A few stolen cucumbers were saving lives in the meantime.

The *kappa* insisted that Kenichi sit with it while it ate. After its meal, the *kappa* alternately ignored, abused, and dismissed him with a gurgly *mah* or a hissy *pfft*, yet it grew angry if Kenichi tried to leave. Kenichi felt as though the *kappa* was becoming his whole life, as if the monster were his best friend. Yet the thing was not friendly. The *kappa* was friend to no one. Kenichi knew if he stopped feeding it cucumbers, it would turn on him without hesitation. Even when it was happily and greedily devouring cucumbers, Kenichi was never sure how safe he truly was.

Kenichi imagined what it might be like to have a playmate. The *kappa* was stout and strong and, ultimately, magical—they could play games of catch, perhaps. He could toss a cucumber as high in the air as he could, and the *kappa* could launch itself from the stoop with a loud yyyyosh! The *kappa's* beak could snap the cucumber in half, in mid-air, and it could catch the two halves with one hand apiece. Then the *kappa* would land like a samurai or a dancer, on one knee, head bowed slightly, arms extended, each holding a half a cucumber as if they were hilts of swords, and then bounce to its feet and feed itself quickly, one hand and then the other, with a facial expression that combined pleasure and pride.

It was a fantasy. A modest fantasy, but impossible nonetheless. All the boy wanted to do was play, but the *kappa*, he had no doubt, would not allow it.

"More," the *kappa* barked at Kenichi one afternoon, after many months.

"I have no more." The boy was almost in tears as he said it, but the *kappa* didn't strike out or curse him. It merely blew air out its nostrils and turned away.

"Find more."

The boy turned, wondering how many gardens on the mountainside might contain *kyūri*. There were many daikon farmers. Perhaps the creature would accept daikon?

Then, as Kenichi turned, he saw her.

A girl about his age stood beneath the *torii* gates.

Instinctively, Kenichi laid his finger across his lips and said, "Shhhhh." He felt cold dread well up through his torso. If the *kappa* saw her, it might forget about its deal with Kenichi and, in the absence of more cucumbers, make itself another meal.

The girl raised a quizzical eyebrow.

"It might hurt you," the boy offered. "Be careful."

The girl walked slowly to Kenichi, reached out, and took him by the shoulders.

"Are you feeling okay?" she asked.

Then she bounced on her heels and skipped, actually skipped, right past the *kappa*, towards the shack. She did not react to the stench of rotten seaweed between the creature's cracked yellow talons. She did not scream at the sight of its horrible, evil eyes.

She didn't see it, and as far as he could tell, it didn't see her.

The girl plopped down onto the shack's wooden platform and placed her hands on her knees.

"I'm Sakura," she said, smiling brightly. "I know I'm not supposed to talk to strangers, but you're a kid, like me, and I don't think that counts. I live down the hill a ways, and there's no other kids anywhere near me. I'm so bored. Wanna play?"

Though I hadn't asked him outright, the girl, Sakura, still seemed represent me. A person who did not see the *kappa*, did not see Daniel's illness, the monster he felt he had to control in order to live. I admit it wasn't a perfect allegory, but it seemed to make sense. It made me wonder more than ever how this story was going to end.

At the end of the white-tiled hallway, a familiar figure appeared and waved. Sharky, Sora's father, whom I had not seen in person since that day on the limited express. Lifetimes ago.

"*Otōsan!*" Sora called. She ran to greet him, leaping on him with a delighted fervour that shocked me, given my experience with Japanese people and their lack of touchy-feelies.

Sora practically climbed him like a tree. Sharky laughed, and the two traded painfully adorable words I couldn't understand until she pointed at me and said "Kawa-chan!"

"Ah! Sora! You must call her *sensei*." Sharky grinned at me, amused.

"It's okay." I tried to think of something cutesy to do and settled on a good-old fashioned hair tousle. Sora shook her head away and squealed "*Yamete!*"

"We started with *sensei*, but I'm not really the *sensei* type. It disintegrated to *onēchan* and landed on Kawa-chan fairly quickly."

"The name you gave yourself."

"Not exactly," I corrected him. "I called myself River. It was *you* who came up with Kawa-chan."

Sharky laughed.

Someone somewhere rang what sounded like a tiny silver bell, and the children reacted as though trained. Sora joined them, sliding reluctantly from her father's embrace and gathering her disc player and papers together.

"Sora, *ganbatte!*" I called after her as she joined in the little row of uniforms.

"Yes!" Her voice came back to us as the line snaked into another room. "I will do my best!"

Once her tiny head bobbed through the door, Sharky and I turned back to one another.

"Sora talks about you every day." His smooth, untroubled gaze lulled me as it had on the train a year before. "She has been very excited about the story you've written."

"Well, I didn't write it, really."

"Sora says you always tell her you didn't write it, but she doesn't believe you." Sharky laughed. "Even if you didn't write it, I appreciate that you gave her something smart and difficult to read."

"Of course! It's been a pleasure. She's wonderful. She's smart, she's serious, she's thoughtful, she laughs at my jokes."

"How is River Black?" Somehow it was clear this wasn't the same question as "How are you?" Before I could answer, another bell sounded somewhere behind us.

"We'd better find seats if we want to sit down, Noguchi-san."

Sharky's expression changed, grin was mischievous. "Noguchi-san?"

"Uh…um…that's Sora's surname, right? Is that not your name?"

"If you want me to have a name, you can call me Tsuchi." Laughing, he bowed towards me. I bowed back.

In the theatre, Babette had saved me a seat. She'd even saved one for Toby, which was borderline miraculous given her opinion of him. Toby's continual lateness irritated me more after his behavior on the way home form Tokyo. The word *mikakedaoshi* haunted me now. I couldn't help but wonder if Toby's sketchy job and his pseudo-intellectual mumbo jumbo were all part of a front. Not a reinvention, as I'd imagined, but a redirection. Misdirection. I'd shake my head and try to dismiss it, but the possibility lingered in my brain.

A tiny woman the width of a string cheese stick came to the microphone to announce the start of the competition. Several men, presumably sponsors, followed. Everyone stood on stage at one time, and much bowing ensued. Then the parade of cuties began—adorable children who stumbled, stomped, bounded, danced, and shuffled their way to the podium, depending on their level of comfort and/or joy. The first participants were younger than Sora. Babette would make a face every time one of them said a particularly difficult word; as English teacher nerds, we had an ongoing list of words we insisted our students must properly enunciate. Our favourite was "ooo-mahn," woman, a word that was not an elocution high point for Japanese children. I poked Babette in the ribs after the first few grimaces, worried that parents might be watching and think we were making fun.

I could see Sora in the wings, stern and professional, a picture of the calm, controlled little girl I met over a year ago. This was a persona, though; I had learned she was really a playful goofball. When she wore this serious costume, though, she wore it well; she seemed to project herself forward into adulthood, to harness some gravity she shouldn't, by rights, have access to at this stage of her life.

I leaned towards Babette.

"Hey, Babs."

"I hate that name," Babette whispered as she punched my shoulder.

"Ow!" An eager mother several rows ahead of us looked back with annoyance; everyone else chose to ignore us.

"I met Sora's dad again today," I murmured. "Told me his name was Tsuchi, and then laughed and walked away. Am I missing a joke?"

Babette fixed me with a look of disdain, which, even at her friendliest, was her default expression. "*Sora* and *Tsuchi*. Sky and…Earth. It means 'soil.' He's screwing with you."

"Ah." To me, it seemed like more of an innocent joke than, you know, a *screw* per se, but her point was taken.

"Where's your boyfriend?" I asked.

"Shinji's coming later. Where's your dickhead?"

"Is that Kiwi for 'boyfriend?'" I twisted my body towards the door. Where *was* my dickhead? My satchel seemed rude, sitting arrogantly on an otherwise empty chair when it could be in my lap.

Tsuchi, the earth to Sora's sky, stood at the back of the auditorium as though it had never crossed his mind to find a seat. Further to the left, near the entrance, two out-of-place men caught my eyes. One was young, soft-haired, fine-featured, sporting a grey turtleneck and round wire-framed glasses. From photographs, I knew this was Shinji.

The other, however, looked like an outsized *yukuza* character in a Beat Takeshi film, in a shiny suit and sunglasses. He had what could only be described, from this distance, as a perm. Though I'd never seen him in the daylight, I recognized him immediately. His hairdo alone was hard to forget, let alone his countenance: a stern, bullying expression that remained on his face at all times, even at BOOM, where he usually lorded over the karaoke machine like a hostile tele-vision host, surrounded by whatever coterie of undesirables he'd dragged with him for the evening.

"Babs, why is Shinji with Kogawa?"

Babette looked over her shoulder and rolled her eyes. "Wannabe *yakuza* wanker. I wish Shinji would stop spend-ing time with him. He's an idiot. Glad I only saved one seat."

"Yeah, sure, but why—"

The name *Noguchi Sora* crackled from the PA system and distracted me from the question. Sora stepped onto the stage, her face intense, almost eerily focused. Before she could speak, though, I was distracted yet again, this time by the creak of the door. As I turned I saw Toby. There was a soft click as the door slid back into place. As Toby scanned the room for us, I turned and tried to wave discreetly, but it was difficult to be discreet yet also attract someone's attention.

Sora began to speak. I had heard her speech, about wom-en and the Olympic tradition, dozens of times. I was certain she chose it not because of budding feminist ideals, but be-cause she could say *woman* instead of *oooh-mahn*. Her speech was clear, her delivery sincere, her accent almost flawless.

I was glad I'd heard it so often, because at this moment, I was barely paying attention to her. Something strange was afoot behind me. I turned to wave to Toby again, and saw him squinting at the crowd. Then, suddenly, Kogawa looked in his direction. He narrowed his eyes and stormed towards Toby, moving brusquely through the audience, jostling peo-ple out of his way. Several people made disdainful faces, but no one complained aloud. As Sora said her thank you, mark-ing the end of her speech, I watched Toby spin in place, heave the door open, and disappear. Kogawa disappeared through the door after him. The door slammed shut, but the sound was lost in the thunder of enthusiastic parental applause.

What the hell had I just watched?

The contest proceeded. It was like a continuous feed of schoolchildren, a conveyor belt of cute. It went on for what seemed like hours, and when the conveyor belt ran out of children, it felt abrupt and unplanned, like a bobbin running out of thread. Adults returned to the podium in uniform beige suits that were not quite actual uniforms. They spoke interminably about interminable things, until someone arrived with an envelope and they began announcing the winners. In my estimation, seventy-five percent of the children won.

But only Sora won first place.

"Showoff," Babette said.

"Me or the kid?"

"Both of you." Babette laughed. "Congratulate her for me, I gotta go find Shinji in this chaos. I guess he noticed there was nowhere for Kogawa to sit and didn't want to leave him alone. Oh, and then I have to go and explain to my students the levels of shame they've brought on their families by not winning first place."

Almost immediately, the auditorium began to churn with bodies, parents rushing towards children, people taking photographs, children scattering throughout the room. Even though they were well behaved, it was still as if someone had freed a truckload of hungry ferrets. Every time I took a step, there was a kid under it. I managed to not actually crush anyone as I went. I could see Tsuchi grin at Sora, who headed in his direction, trophy clutched to her chest like a stuffed doll. We reached her father at the same time. She held up her miniature silver trophy cup, her notebook, and some sort of large envelope. Sharky scooped her up, beaming as brightly as she was.

"Sensei!" Sora shouted as I arrived. Her arms were still full, so I gave her an exaggerated bow, which she returned with a deep nod of her head.

"Thank you for helping me win."

"Nonsense. That was all you, kid."

Sora bashfully smooshed her face into her father's shoulder.

Suddenly, a hand gripped my shoulder from behind and pulled abruptly. I turned with the motion, staggering slightly, to face Kogawa. My stomach swelled and disintegrated at the same time.

"The *gaijin* with guitar."

' I blinked at him a moment.

Tsuchi said something softly in Japanese, aloud, but not directly to anyone.

"The *gaijin* with guitar!" Kogawa shouted over the commotion in the convention hall. "You know him."

Tsuchi spoke again, slightly louder, though still calmly. Kogawa glared over my shoulder, glanced at Sora and back up at her father. His eyes seemed to rattle in their sockets for an instant, as if recognition had set in and changed everything.

"*Moushiwake arimasen deshita*," he said, and nodded in approximation of a bow.

"Sorry," he said to me. "My mistake."

He hadn't made a mistake. The foreigner with the guitar. The eleven-foot white-headed foreigner who played guitar on the Gondō for spare change. There was only one of 'em.

I turned and flashed a weak smile at Sora, who now stood stock-still beside her father, clutching his hand, staring with a grin at the plastic prize in her hand. The weirdness of the grown-ups hadn't penetrated her bubble.

"Did he hurt you?" Tsuchi's voice was soft, as always, but his eyes looked firmer, more alert.

"No." I shored up my own smile. "He just startled me. I guess…I guess he's looking for someone and he's…dissatisfied. It's okay."

"That is Kogawa Genzō." Tsuchi pursed his lips into a peevish expression. "I know him. He is dissatisfied with most things. If he bothers you again, please, let me know. In the meantime, it's celebration day. Would you like to come for ice cream?"

That, apparently, did burst the bubble. Sora yelped and jumped up and down in place.

"Yes," I replied. "That sounds great!"

Ice cream would help me get my mind off the creep that was Kogawa Genzō.

BLESSÈD BLUE

Kogawa translates as "little river."

There's no deeper meaning there, just coincidence. I am tempted to shoehorn some meaning into it, to find some kind of parallel. The man who bullied River and assaulted her friend is also named River? Is there some irony in that he's the little River and I'm the regular-sized River? What about the fact that his given name is Genzō, same as a famous Japanese serial killer?

All right, that last one might be a stretch. There's plenty of people named Genzō. Ugh. I shouldn't be thinking about this anyway. I should be thinking about the meaning behind Leo Pardpeti continuing to exenterate women, three films after it stopped making sense. Assuming it ever did.

The computer is on and the document is open, a white blankness that regards me blindly as the cloudy eyes of a dead fish. I stare back, knowing that it will be me who blinks first. I've not typed a word. Not a single word.

That familiar Skype ringtone sounds. It's tempting to slam the laptop shut, and I almost do, but I see that it isn't Evvie this time.

"Hey, sis." Just saying the syllable *sis* makes me well up unexpectedly, but I bite it back, hard. I can't answer the call already crying.

"Hey, Hel." Sheila's at her kitchen table. She lives in one of those tall blue-green blockpiles we call condominiums, except in Toronto instead of Vancouver. They line the highway along the Lake Ontario waterfront now like an emerald corridor, except that sounds beautiful, when the reality is they form a steel-and-glass wall that blocks out the view of the lake.

"How's the weather, Hel?"

Behind her I can see the tacky macramé plant holder I bought her as a joke last Christmas. She has an actual plant in it. Her cupboards and fridge are also visible. On the fridge, notes, magnets, postcards, pictures. Most are of me.

"I miss you, Sheel."

"Hey. Hel? You okay?"

"Sure, why?"

"You're not usually that sappy that quickly. Often takes you at least ten minutes before you start begging me to move back to Vancouver."

"Well, I might not be going back to Van myself."

Sheila leans in, her face pixelating, separating and reforming before my eyes. "Something up?"

"Ah." I sit back, blow air at the bangs I don't have. "I dunno. I'm having a rough day, Sheel. I've been working on the new script."

"Oh. Not...not going so well?"

"What do you think?"

"I think it's time you let Evvie write his own bug-man movie, and you go write something for yourself."

"I know."

"Or direct!"

"You've said it a million times."

"Saying it again."

"Replying in the negative, again. I don't have any experience, I don't...I can't afford my apartment, let alone renting camera equipment or hiring actors. I have no producer interested in my work. Other than these rotten screenplays for Evvie, the only income I have is from guest columns for *Rue*

Morgue. I haven't been offered any script-doctor gig in years, and no one bit on the rom com pitches."

"What?"

"I shopped some rom coms," I admit sheepishly. "Under a pseudonym."

"What pseudonym?"

"Sheila Delaney."

"Hey!"

"Well, I wasn't going to use my name, obviously. A New Romantic Comedy From The Mind of River Black."

"No, no one wants to see *Murder, Actually.*"

"*10 Things I Hate About Monsters.*"

"Weak," Sheila scoffs. "*My Best Friend's Funeral.*"

"*When Freddy Met Sally.*"

"*When Freddy Met Jason?* It's been done, but it would have been better if they'd fallen in love."

"Oh my God," I gasp, "a love affair between iconic serial killers! That is brilliant."

"Google the fanfic," Sheila says. "I'm positive it already exists."

"It doesn't matter what name I use, Sheel. No one wants an unsolicited manuscript, and as I believe you know, I remain unsolicited in all ways, because Evvie talked me out of going with an agency."

"So go find an agent."

"Well, now, there's an idea. It's just that easy! You haven't lived my life, Sheel. You went through high school in a bowl cut and Bass Weejuns and Ralph Lauren Polo shirts and gifted programs and boyfriends' fathers' Lincoln Town Cars with car phones in 1986 when no one had car phones. You went through university in the young Conservatives and the tri-Delts, wrapped up in a warm blanket of scholarships and the promise of a bright future in law school."

"Yes, and then I graduated, went to law school, switched my allegiance to the Liberal Party, and became the first woman to make partner in her early forties. What's your point,

Hel? Jesus Christ, have you looked at yourself? You're every bit as privileged as I am. You just make less money."

"Far less. And my career is an issue. But even if I were midway through writing *Chinatown*, I wouldn't have the focus I need to finish. You have no idea what's going on around here."

"What's going on around there?"

"Nutshell? I've met up with Masa. Reiko. He Who Shall Not Be Named, even."

"He Who Shall Not Be Named?"

"Correct. Except, I guess he shall be named. I've called a temporary cease-fire."

"You haven't seen him in 20 years."

"Yeah, but I've been at war with him in my imagination the entire time."

"Imaginary cease-fire. Okay. So, this is good, no? You're catching up? You're seeing the sights? You're reliving the past a little?"

I sigh.

"Yeah, something like that." I pause, consider telling her that I am hunting for the origins of the mystery book, and stop myself.

"They actually ran an Evrard Frederich marathon on TV the other night."

"No way."

"All the *Pinned*s. "

"Seriously?" She chuckles. "You realize that's a River Black marathon, too, yeah?"

A sarcastic snort escapes me, but I suppose it's true.

"Maybe they'll do that and include *What Lurks Beneath*." says Sheila.

What Lurks Beneath was my screenwriting debut. A student film directed by a classmate named Lenny Kistermeyer. A much better opening than *Pinned III,* for sure. A black screen, a sombre woman's voice recalling some haunting moment from her past with the line "Even in the darkness, there are shadows." Then you realize that there is movement in the dark. The camera reveals the interior of a culvert, inside of which we see numerous gelatinous green pustules—with teeth. They hang from the top of the culvert like glutinous drops of condensation. Eventually they all drop, find their way into the city waterways, and Piranha-style antics ensue. Eviscerations, castrations, all the fun stuff. The underlying idea was unsettling—the creatures stood in for invasive species, which might be a little on-the-nose—but in my market, you don't sell a screenplay without the eviscerations and castrations.

"I don't think they're in the habit of airing student films. That's more like a DVD-extra sort of thing."

"It's good, though."

"Yeah. It is good," I admit.

"You could write something dark and utterly unsettling, like *Bite* or *Audition*."

"I tried, with *Pinned*. I really tried."

"And then, Evvie."

"And then, Evvie. You know, he used to tell me he'd given me the career I always wanted." I smile at the laptop, but it's a wan, wilted attempt. "This isn't the career I always wanted. I stopped trying, and I don't know how to go back, how to get to the place where I can start it all again. All I know is that I can't get there from here."

"Balderdash," Sheila half-yells into the computer. "River Black isn't scared of anything."

"Why do people think that? And when did you start saying balderdash?"

"And neither is Helen Delaney," she continues.

"Well, I talk a good game but..."

"No, Hel." Sheila looks into the camera with an expression that suggests she would place her hands on my shoulders if she could. "No. All the things you've done. The tenacity, the insistence on getting it right, on doing the best job, on being the best person. It's that annoying sense of duty you have. To others. To whatever. So think about your duty to Young River. To that part of yourself who would have wanted to do all these things."

I'm crying a little, and I don't want her to see, so I pretend to fiddle with the keyboard. It's not that I think she's right, though it's sweet of her to say. It's that I think she's wrong.

"I gotta get back to work, Sheel."

"Helen—"

"Call me soon, okay?"

Sheila sighs and regards me like a misguided child. "Okay, Hel. Call soon. Love ya, sis."

"Love ya, sis."

Young River. Young River would have talked about doing it all. Doing everything. Then she would have proceeded to do none of it. She's no different than me, except that I am no longer a child. I have bills to pay, and I have an obligation to that stupid bastard ex of mine. I know that he could replace me on a whim. He could dig up a creative writing group in Tallinn or Riga or just go home to his buddies in Leipzig and hire the one who spoke the best English. Or write it his damned self. He doesn't realize how dreadful a writer he is, that my scripts are written with his brain in mind. I had ways to trick him into using the shots I saw in my head. Directing the film off the page, as it were. Maybe that's why I cling to this. Maybe, even in the depths of depravity that constitute Leo Pardpeti's world, in the schlocky gore-strewn landscapes of Evvie's near-amateur film universe, I've developed a perverse, decidedly misplaced, pride. Maybe the only thing that rescues these films from true obscurity, lifts them to the slightly higher station of cult status, is me. And maybe he knows it.

My suitcase lies open on the bed beside me. Blessèd Blue pokes out from beneath a pile of hastily folded T-shirts. I reach over grab it between my thumb and forefinger, pull it into my lap.

Inside, spidery handwriting, crooked and tight, runs in

threadlike lines from margin to margin. There are no smears of silvery grey, no spots of wear, no erasure marks. Only fine mechanical pencil strokes. Daniel was so certain in his original draft. This notebook feels like a work of art. I am glad I didn't deface these pages with my crimson graffiti of half-baked editorial recommendations.

"*Pfft.*"

Christ, not this again. I want my brain to go back into its box, to stop its conjuring tricks. I don't have time to deal with myself right now.

"Mah." Another dismissive, unhuman grunt.

"What do you want, Soba?"

"What do you want, River. What do you want, Helen."

I cave and look over my shoulder, across the bedroom. Soba is cross-legged on the bed, its spindly tree-root legs dripping with what appears to be wet river weed, the faux-ceramic plastic cup from the bathroom in one snarled fist.

"Hey, you're dripping. I have to sleep on that, you know."

Soba doesn't reply. It just blinks at me like a frog, an amphibian gaze that possesses a contemptuous intelligence but no soul.

"Still write story about bad man."

"No," I correct it. "No, I haven't written a thing. I have opened my laptop and stared at the empty page and fantasized about eating blowfish until the law of averages takes over, and I have a poorly cut poisoned bite, and I die."

"This not help."

"No, this does not help. It only makes me hungry for sashimi. So instead of writing I picked up this." I hold the blue notebook out like a talisman. "Do you know what this is?"

Soba's eyes widen, a nearly invisible dilation, and for a moment it sits, slack-jawed.

"This is the Blessèd Blue Notebook," I explain. "This is the story the boy wrote. This is your origin. This is the universe that created you."

I expect scorn and a blaze of temper, but Soba is silent.

"This is your story. Though you seem to have taken on a life beyond it."

"This is boy's story," it agrees. "This is my story. This is your story."

"No, it's not. Daniel wrote it."

"Pfft." Soba shakes his head, shudders, and issues a loud fart. "Gross."

"You have forward," it says. "Only if take Soba advice."

"Jesus, your English is terrible. What do you mean, I have forward? How does one 'have' a 'forward'? Your grammar is so terrible it's confusing me."

"Maybe stupid."

"Maybe shut up." I put down the notebook and raise my hands in an exaggerated shrug as a teenager might when arguing with family. "I don't understand your advice anyway. If you're a god, why can't you find a way to speak that I can understand? Why do you talk like some ridiculous Buddhist martial-arts guru? What are you even talking about? Do you know what I'm looking for? I'm looking for a book. A book that shouldn't exist. A book that's about you."

Soba points at Blessèd Blue.

"Yes, it's this story, but no, not this book." I hold up the *Kenichi and the Kappa*. "It's this one."

Soba eyes the cover and its face softens. "Almost look like me."

I turn the book over and look at Reiko's sketch. Only then do I realize that it looks exactly like Soba. It's as if Soba had sat for the artist herself. Of course, it makes sense that Soba resembles the sketch, given that Soba exists in my head.

Soba shakes its head hard, once, as if to clear its thoughts. The water in its head sloshes about, one drop sidling downward across its temple. It reaches up and wipes the drop backwards into the oily black hair that hangs from is head like a row of dead spiders.

"Difficult to understand Soba," Soba says. "Soba not give advice before."

Humility? From a river god?

"Book," it says. "This not about book. But go through book to boy."

"I'm not looking for the boy," I reply, unsure what boy he means. Toby? Daniel? Kenichi, who doesn't exist? Actually, do any of them?

"Yes. You don't want find boy. You don't want remember. But must."

I shake my head.

"Unholy soup."

I shudder at those words again. "What does that mean?"

But when I turn back to the bed, Soba is gone. Not even an indentation on the bedspread. Which is probably fair, given that delusions don't have mass.

What is it? What's lying there, just out of my line of vision, just shy of my capability for understanding? It feels familiar. It feels like that instant before I'm struck by a plot twist I hadn't expected; it's that precognitive state. I'm aware there's something I should be seeing, but as of yet I cannot. Most people don't have green goblins providing them cryptic advice, though, so maybe it's no shock that I haven't nailed this down by now.

Soba's right about one thing: all of this is a distraction. A normal, undeluded, regular-acting human would simply finish the crappy screenplay or quit entirely. This script is a final essay, and I'm the sophomore trying to justify cleaning the grout in the shower the night before said essay is due.

At the same time, this isn't grout. Soba may be hallucinatory, but the book is not. There's a reason someone printed this book and sent it to me.

I stand, spin, and fall backwards onto the bed, staring at the ceiling. The back of my neck grows cold, clammy.

I swear this bedspread feels damp.

BIRTHDAY

After Sora won the competition, we went for ice cream, and I failed to shake the willies. Something about Kogawa Genzō slipped under my skin and stayed there, like a damp chill no matter how high the flame on your kerosene heater. He'd been looking for Toby for some reason. It was a new level of delinquency, with disturbing implications that involved illegal activity and mafia-managed shenanigans. I called him from the apartment phone that night.

"You didn't show up today." My voice was flat and tight.

"Yeah, yeah, sorry about that, I…" There was a pause. Toby didn't pause; he swung from word to word as smoothly as Spider-man swings from skyscraper to skyscraper. The only time he paused was when he hit the Hudson and ran out of skyscrapers. In other words, he paused when deliberating whether to spin more webs or, heaven help us all, tell the truth.

"I did show up," he said. "But there was someone there I didn't want to talk to. As soon as I saw him there, I split. I can't get into it right now, but believe me, it was best that I left the room. The guy is supposed to be *yakuza*."

"Hmmmmph," I grunted. What kind of shady nonsense could he possibly be involved with that connected him to

Kogawa? Yet I also didn't want to know, because he had told the truth. A little. *I did show up.* That meagre helping of truth was probably what kept me with Toby for the rest of 1997, even if I purposefully kept more distance between us. He claimed to have more early mornings on the work site. I was grateful for more time in front of my *wāpuro* with *Kenichi and the Kappa.*

The year tumbled forward into autumn, as though summer had sprinted too fast down a slope and was powerless against its own momentum. More western faces began to show up at J.J.'s: IBM employees, logisticians, media types. Some were pleasant, others disgusting and disrespectful. The good:bad ratio of customers, along eastern/western lines? About the same. I remember the spindle-thin white-haired programmer who, as Reiko took a group picture, said "Don't be afraid to touch me" and placed my hand on his ass. I shuddered and jerked my hand away. Somehow, coming from an American, it was twice as disgusting.

Masa took us to Togakushi for the best soba in Japan. The restaurant rested beneath an ancient tree, its diameter that of a small house, its branches disappearing into the bellies of clouds. We posed for pictures holding each others' noses with chopsticks. Masa pretended to be offended by our behavior and "stormed out" of the restaurant. We found him outside, smoking and chuckling to himself.

November landed with a soft but all-encompassing poof, the sound of a blanket of snow landing on everyone in one moment. Twentysomething snowboarders appeared en masse.

The less I saw Toby, the more I revelled in my time with Sora. *Kenichi and the Kappa* had become the backbone of our syllabus, even though it wasn't intended for young audiences. It wasn't really intended for any audiences.

The story had taken an optimistic turn after Daniel introduced Sakura, the little girl who couldn't see Kenichi's monster. Kenichi and Sakura became friends and played games on the hillside. As I worked, scratching out words here, scratching in words there, I thought about what it could all mean to Daniel. Was Sakura's inability to see the monster good or bad? Was a friend who could not see your burdens any kind of friend? And what did it mean that Sakura might be a stand-in for yours truly? Did he think I ignored his burden? Did he think I didn't care?

The story swung back towards grim a few days before my birthday.

Everything changed when Kenichi had a dream.

Kenichi was sitting on the steps of the shrine, bundled in his winter coat, hands and feet grown numb, when he heard a dry twig snap behind him.

Soba appeared, its eyes suggesting weariness or, strangely, grief. In its arms was an unearthly pale girl, her face darkened, yellow and purple discolouration above the thin pencil-line of her lips. Her sweatshirt, emblazoned with the image of Keroro the Frog, was streaked with grass and mud.

"Sakura," it moaned. "Soba find."

Soba lay the limp body on the stoop in front of the shrine. Her face was mottled by dirt, leaves, and bruises.

"What did you do?!" Kenichi screamed. Soba pointed to her white ankle socks, one of which was reddish-brown with dried blood.

"*Mamushi*," it said.

Despite the urge to run, despite the taste of blood in his mouth and a loosening in his stomach, Kenichi looked closer, gagging on the odour of decayed flesh. The skin on her leg looked blackened, as if charred, with blotches of red and a yellow crust formed along the edges.

"Why did you do this, Soba?" Kenichi choked, throat throttled by tears and the vile stench.

"Not Soba. *Mamushi*. Snake."

Sakura's tiny face, pale and purpling, seemed closed up, as if in death she had retreated into herself, nothing left to express to the world.

"I don't believe you," said Kenichi.

"Mah! Not kill. Not want eat." Soba straightens his back. "*Baka*."

"I'm not stupid," says Kenichi. "You eat children. What am I supposed to think?"

Soba sighed and looked down at the girl again.

"Used to eat children. Now eat *kyūri*."

A garbage truck on the road hissed and spat its way through the neighbourhood, waking Kenichi from the dream. He sat up, pressed himself into a corner, and clutched his pillow. He still felt it all, vividly: grief, fear, loss, horror. In the dream, the creature denied killing the girl. Yet for some reason, in the dream, Kenichi did not believe it. That fear and suspicion followed him out of the dream into the morning. Even as the dream faded, as the boy looked about his house for a few stray yen to purchase some cucumbers, he continued to think about it. There was nothing in the dream to suggest that Soba had killed the girl, yet Kenichi knew he had. He did not believe that it was a snake. It was Soba, simple and true. And even though it was only a dream, and even though Soba somehow could not see the girl in real life, it troubled him deeply.

Sora was thrilled at the dark turn, even if it was only in a dream. Her eyes lit up with emotion, though I couldn't have told you what emotions they were. Fear? Maybe a little. Empathy? Definitely. Excitement? Certainly. Surprise? Undoubtedly.

As we were more than simply teacher and student now, Sora asked if I would take her to the street festival along the Zenkōji road, as her father was busy. Three days later, a driver pulled up in front of Sanyō, and Sora stepped out of the car in pink rubber boots and a pink jacket with rainbow accents. Despite the wealth suggested by the Mercedes and uniformed chauffeur, she dressed like a normal little girl, in clothes you could find at any Japanese department store.

Vendor stalls had appeared overnight, vertical rectangles with orange curtains and long awnings to push back against the snow or rain. They sold sake in bottles shaped like white sows and little brown heads of Ebisu, the jolly fat god of fisherman and luck. The red heads of Daruma dolls dangled and swayed on thin ropes, strung above rows of plastic-wrapped porcelain *maneki neko* and paper flowers; three feet away, plastic Halloween-style masks hung in rows on suspended strings, along with flimsy likenesses of Mickey Mouse, Gojira, Doraemon, and Thomas the Tank Engine. Traditional Japanese music saturated the air, the occasional ripple of a cymbal ringing out with bright metallic resonance. A woman in a pink toque, clutching a mid-sized dog in her arms, smiled warmly at Sora. Another woman, a monk, hurried by, avoiding my gaze, her arms laden with paper bags. An older gentleman, with wide, nearly square spectacles and a mouth that opened in a similarly polygonic shape, accosted me and began to talk in my face. He wore a rolled-up kerchief headband that encircled his hairless head.

"*Ii kao shite iru!*" He said "*Bijin!*" Beauty.

"Hmmm." I ignored him, studying a towering display of floral ornaments fashioned out of reflective foil paper. Then the man jogged across the crowded road to his own kiosk, laden with reams of candy and *senbei*. He gestured for us to try some of the samples, which we did, but I didn't trust his intentions—he called me "beautiful" a few more times—so we continued forward, out of the crowd and through the first Zenkōji gate. Above us, workmen strode fearlessy across roofs they were retiling, rushing to finish now that the snow had come, their wide-legged pants flapping in the wind. Stone statues of stone-faced gods wore red hats and bibs. We passed through the gate, with its wooden Niō statues on either side, standing guard with their unsettling, white-eyed faces, swords poised at the apex of the killing arc, threatening even as they stood inanimate and locked within the pillars of the gateway.

At the temple I lifted Sora up so she could reach the statue of Binzuru the doctor and caress his smooth, blank face. We walked towards the *okaidan*.

"I'll give you *ichiman* yen if you go down there."

I turned to see Daniel, pale and winded, but with a grin on his face.

"I don't need *ichiman* yen." I grinned. "And slow yourself down, will you? Stop, take a breath."

Daniel smiled sheepishly and nodded, shoulders rising and falling as if he'd been sprinting.

"Sorry, I saw you ahead of me and walked too fast to catch up."

"Breathe, man! Breathe. Sora, this is Daniel."

Sora glanced up at him, unimpressed. "Hello," she said, her tone perfunctory. "Nice to meet you."

I thought of telling her that this was the boy who had invented her *kappa,* but I still hadn't told Daniel I was sharing it, and I didn't think he'd be pleased.

The three of us left through the east door of the main hall and walked to the pond, where we sat on the rocks and watched koi nibble the hem of the water. The clouds were a colour that you would expect if metals radiated light: hills of luminescent copper, bronze, and gold. At first glance the pond seemed muddy, murky, green-brown; after my eyes adjusted, it became a silver mirror of mercury, the fish orange ghosts on the other side, occasionally crossing into this dimension to mouth at the food atop the glass.

We skipped across the stepping-stone bridge, left the temple grounds, and headed up the steep road into the hills. An abandoned school lay in a valley to the west, looking forlorn next to its empty, dirt-caked swimming pool. Behind us, Zenkōji looked like some kind of remarkable living organism, existing in symbiosis with the trees and the mountains in an assortment of browns, greens, and whites.

"So, that last scene you gave me," I half-whispered. Sora was up ahead, kicking at stones along the side of the road. "That's...that's some grim stuff, buddy."

"Yeah." He grinned as though he'd been caught out in something. The sun cast orange rays that seemed to be holding on to the horizon, thinning, about to slide apart like soft toffee on the snow. "I think it's only going to get grimmer."

"You going through some stuff, Daniel?" I smiled but felt a rush of concern. If his story was heading down into the darkness, was he following? Or leading the way?

Daniel only laughed, a short, clean laugh that seemed to hide no secrets. That was the last he had to say on the subject. We snuck downward between the houses, along the cement steps that led towards Sanyō, and it was closing in on dark when we got to the doorway. Sora's driver was already idling on the other side of the building; she said goodbye as she skipped along the corridor towards him.

"She seems like a good kid," Daniel said as I turned the key in the lock.

"Yeah, she's the best. She's like a ray of sunshine is a world clouded with drunken—"

"*IRASSHAIMASE!*"

The lights came on and my larynx tightened as my lungs dropped into my stomach, creating a sound not unlike a kitten with hiccups. All the *shōji* were open, creating one big room out of our two bedrooms. Paper streamers were taped to the back wall, spelling out HAPPY BIRTHDAY RIVER, the paper thin and brittle so that the letters were adorably twisted and ripped as if they'd put too much passion into making them. The tangy aroma of something cooking filled the air.

"I can't believe your mindness!" I cried.

"I can't believe my mindness either!" shouted Masa from the back of the kitchen.

I immediately started to cry. No one had ever thrown me a surprise party before. It was as though the warmth and love of my friends were packaged and placed beneath the tree, an unexpected Christmas gift. I was overwhelmed. All the faces I wanted to see were before me, even Toby's, floating a full head above the rest of the crowd.

"I told Nax we were opening late tonight, mate." Babette poured approximately six fingers of bourbon into the Hello

Kitty mug and thrust it into my hand before turning back to a roiling pot of pasta on the stove. "He said that was fine as long as we don't show up too drunk. That's gonna work out great for him, I'm sure."

"This was your idea?"

Babette almost smiled. "I'm your bloody roommate, yeah?"

"Aw. You even let people go into your room! You like me."

"Piss off."

"You really, really like me."

"Yeah, shut up, Sally Field." She pulled the wooden spoon from the pasta and threatened to splash me with hot water. "We were afraid you'd come back early so we sent this one to make sure you didn't."

Daniel shrugged and smiled at the floor.

"Happy birthday, baby." Toby kissed the top of my head. I admit that I shrunk from it, ever so slightly, and didn't exactly understand why. He had fallen to a lesser place, in a way that I didn't consciously understand yet. I didn't want him hanging off me, one arm over my shoulders, as though his presence was inevitably the most magnetic. There were others with whom I wanted to talk: literally everybody else in the room.

I drained Hello Kitty of her bourbon in minutes, my tongue accustomed to the burnt sweetness, my throat more than used to the burn. Before long I was giddy, dancing in place during all my conversations, toasting everyone within arm's reach with a hearty *kanpai!* Toby grinned at me a lot, but mostly left me to my own, as if he could sense my uncertainty. At one point, when he thought I wasn't looking, he reached into his parka, pulled out a small prescription vial, and popped a pill into his mouth.

"Sick?" I asked a moment later.

"Allergies." He pulled the vial out of his pocket and shook the capsules with a smile.

I nodded at the orange plastic bottle. "There's no label."

"Don't need one. I know what it is."

"What is it?"

Toby didn't answer, but his smile disappeared.

Babette served us pasta, and Masa began making Babette-is-actually-Italian-not-Kiwi jokes, which weren't inherently funny, but we all laughed anyhow.

"You might wanna slow down on that." Babette nodded at my half-empty mug.

"Hey, you started it."

"Yeah, and I'm not gonna end it either, but just be careful."

"I will. I'll stop drinking when I get to work. I'll tell the customers I'm pregnant or I've converted to something orthodox, so no one buys me drinks."

"That's my girl."

We drank and laughed, and Reiko tried to teach us to play mah-jongg. Someone pulled out a disposable carboard camera and began taking photos. We posed in sunglasses and a boa, yet another random find from the back of the magic closet. We posed with our fingers splayed in peace signs, Japanese style. Babette and Rieko gave me a big woolly sweater for the coming season. I tried it on. It was as cozy as a *kotatsu*, one of those low Japanese tables with electric heaters underneath. It was as cozy as my Sanyō apartment with the kerosene heater on full blast. Our apartment, with its rats and its lack of central heating and its grime. Maybe the coziest place I'd ever known.

Masa drove some of us to J.J.'s, but Nicolle and Allie convinced me to walk. "You're going to need the air, Riv," Allie grinned "You powered through that Beam pretty quickly."

It didn't matter. I'd be fine. And if I wasn't fine, wasn't it worth it? All was aglow. I'd forgotten about Toby. In fact, I hadn't even seen him leave. I walked down the road, along the canals, on partially liquified knees, with a solid understanding that one day, sooner than later, this would all end. For now, though, these friends and experiences existed like a lucid dream. If I dreamed of a future, it was a future in which River Black always kept part of this in her heart, for warmth, for fuel, forever.

MAKE! EVERY DAY

Today my dreams are of little green monsters that drip water onto my bedspread. When I dream of a future, it is a future in which River Black isn't forced to take a job at Wal-Mart.

I should be writing. I just need to make up some stuff that I know Evvie will like. It isn't that hard. His tastes may be specific, but they're not exactly discerning. Pardpeti could drive around in a wood-paneled station wagon throwing javelins into the abdomens of random passers-by and Evvie would say *interesting! Let's have him spear his victims through the throat at least a few times, for variation!*

Instead, I am with my investigative team on our silly mission to find the origins of a book. It took Reiko a minute to find Babette and Shinji were not listed; a web search turned up nothing. The easiest and worst solution is to find Kogawa, whom no one has seen since that night he fulfilled everyone's worst fears and came into J.J.'s. And killed Daniel. Sort of.

So, we walk towards the Tokyū and Cher Cher department stores, where the streets curve and cross one another like a floppy boiled spaghetti. The coffee shop we used to visit, near Chitose Park, is gone, replaced by another, near-identical coffee shop. We pass a building that used to house Tower records and a clothing shop called Octopus Army. Neither remain.

Everything is different. Everything is the same.

The road curves around towards the train station, and we stop about halfway around its eastbound arc. In a row of modest storefronts, one is painted what was once upon a time a striking sunset pink. It's weathered and faded, but the façade still catches the eye. Set above the storefront window are tall blue letters that say *Make! Every Day*.

I stop. Rei and Toby, flanking me on either side, stop abruptly with me.

"Make! Every Day." I squint at the sign a moment.

"Like, maybe, make the most out of every day?" Toby offers. "Make every day count?"

"Maybe it means nothing," Reiko says. "I used to buy pants at a store called '...and meat.'"

"I used to buy stationary from a place called Purple Sugar, remember?" I say. "We used to think it would be a great name for a psyche band, but okay. Let's focus on making every day."

"Let's just focus on making the next ten minutes," Rei says.

"I'm not coming in," says Toby.

I stop, mid-advance, to turn and glare. "What the hell are you talking about?"

"He knows me," Toby says. "He won't remember you. He was always drunk and stupid at BOOM, and he was probably no different that night at J.J.'s. He won't remember you from that one night at J.J.'s. But he *knows* knows me."

"So you want us to go in and confront a violent criminal alone?"

"I'm not sure he's a violent—"

I stop listening, probably because I can't hear over the blood coursing through my ears, a roar like white water, like the constant hiss of Tokyo on fire.

"Listen, I'm not afraid of Kogawa," Toby explains. "I am worried that I'll piss him off and he won't help us. Why the hell would he tell me where his nephew lives?"

"It's fine." I stare hard at the windows of Make! Every

Day, but there's too much glare to see inside. "Since when have I needed a guy to do my dirty work? I went toe to toe with Evrard Fredrich, Herr Hegemonic Masculinity himself. And I won. I think. And Rei has always been a champion."

Rei poses like a weightlifter and grimaces.

"Biceps!" Toby laughs. "That's your new nickname, Rei. Biceps. Here."

Toby hands me a familiar-looking envelope, the kind that used to hold our wages.

"It's what I owe him," Toby explains. "Give it to him at some point. He wouldn't be happy to see me, but I'm sure he'll be happy to see his money."

"Okay," I sigh. "Me and Biceps here are going in. If you hear the smashing of glass, alert the authorities."

A metallic tinkle accompanies the slow creak of the door. Reiko leads, and I walk, almost tippy-toed, behind her. The shop is tiny, as expected—maybe 150 square feet. There is a rack of clothing against one wall, polo shirts and T-shirts, mostly in light colours, mostly striped in pattern. On the other wall, another rack: pants and shorts in colours that pair-bond them to shirts across the room. Pick one, see the other, buy twice as much. Recalling his glossy jackets and glossier hair curl, it's difficult to reconcile the fact that Kogawa seems to have a decent grasp on the basics of fashion. In the centre of the shop stands a delicate glass-and-tin display shelf that sparkles in the sunlight rebounding off the white walls. The items here seem unrelated to the clothing on display: wallets made from thick pale leather, clunky cube-like watches that appear ready to transform into robots; bullet-back cufflinks, despite the fact that none of the shirts he sells require cufflinks.

At the back of the room, Kogawa.

He stands behind an equally delicate-looking glass-and-tin counter bearing several rows of silk ties. Gone is the tacky gangster-junior suit, replaced by khakis and a golf shirt. I'm not sure what I expected after 20 years. I never saw him age, and in my mind, I expected a younger, more robust person than the frail, balding man before us. He could not be more than sixty, but he is slightly stooped, and his body is sunken in a way that suggests ill health, though his belly seems rounder and protrudes ahead of him. His arms, thin and spotted, rest atop the display counter, bony, with elbows like chocolate Turtles, all bulbous and lumpy. His neck is discoloured skin taut over sinew, and it reminds me of Soba, which only sharpens my discomfort.

He's halfway through muttering an *irrasshaimase* when he stops, mid-word, and begins to mutter something else entirely, his brow furrowed, his lips curled.

"Oh." Reiko stops in her tracks. "He definitely remembers us."

Instantly I am hurled backward twenty years to that awful evening. Kogawa's voice has a waver now, but he is still capable of a heated bellow. His sudden rage shocks Rei into immediate apologetic mode, and she begins to beg forgiveness, her pitch a few tones higher than her regular voice. Both spill sentences like a fisherman empties a net; words fall and pile up, flapping and silver, indistinguishable from one another, at least to me. There are a few key exceptions: *Shinji, gaijin, guitar,* and *keisatsu,* police.

"He's going to call the cops?" I ask. Reiko scrunches up one side of his face and nods.

"What the hell did we do? We just walked into a shop."

"It's not us," she says.

"That doesn't make any sense."

Kogawa continues to rant, rapping his bony knuckles against the counter for emphasis. Glass vibrates against metal and the row of ties shudders to the left, then back to the right. Kogawa trembles, but it seems less from rage and more from advanced Parkinson's. Now that the explosion is over and the shock waves have passed, he is anything but frightening. My fear now is that we're going to give him a heart attack. He jostles the glass counter; several boxes of ties tumble to the floor.

The word I hear most now is *dame,* which translates roughly to "it's no good" but really means "no way in hell." She must be asking him about Shinji now.

The door dingles behind us. I can feel Toby's head looming above me.

"I think he's telling us to get lost," I say.

Kogawa looks at me, and then gapes at Toby, before he responds, in English, "No. You go away. He get lost!"

God help me, but I laugh out loud.

Reiko keeps at it. She maintains that unrelentingly apologetic tone, somewhere just shy of high C, like an overly polite conflict negotiator. Kogawa, however, is impervious and has begun screaming directly at Toby. Reiko stops for a moment, breathes deeply, and squints as though she's trying to make sense of something.

"Kogawa-san, listen, come on," Toby says, but Kogawa has rallied his strength. He points at Toby accusingly and yells again, the shredding of his vocal cords almost audible beneath the tirade. I feel like I'm watching an NFL game: too many things are moving in too many directions, and I haven't got a clue what the game is all about in the first place. Then Toby's face contracts into a squint, as he stares at something on the countertop beside the cash register. Reiko resumes her pleading, Kogawa continues to repeat *dame* every few words, and Toby makes his way forward, around the delicate glass and tin cubes arranged into shelving, towards Kogawa.

"C'mon Toby, don't start anything," I plead. "Just leave, okay? He's obviously—"

"It's good, it's good." He snatches the envelope from me and continues to stare at something on the countertop. Kogawa glances downward, then back at Toby, and for a second their eyes lock.

Toby's foot comes to rest on one of the tie boxes, and he slips forward, knocking into the counter. Startled, terrified of what must surely be a calamitous miscalculation, Rei and I scream. We shriek. Kogawa adds a third harmony to the screeching chorus before he swings one scrawny forearm in front of him. His hand lands with a loud thump and a clatter on the countertop, and for a second I think the glass is going to explode into a shower of shards. Instead, more boxes of ties skitter left and right as the cash-register drawer pops open with a thump and the clang of a bell. Toby has dropped the envelope in front of Kogawa, but it does not seem to have placated him in any way.

"*Yamete!*" Kogawa is frantic now, and he charges around the counter—or he attempts to, but the cash-register drawer catches his belly. There's a yelp of pain as his belly pushes the register forward. It revolves almost 90 degrees on the countertop before tottering on the edge of the glass. Kogawa winces and grabs for the ancient machine, but his attempt to slide it back onto the counter causes him to lose his balance. He staggers and tumbles forward. The entire counter topples and crashes to the floor, the bell of the cash register protesting with a winded, pathetic-sounding *ping*. One of the glass panels shatters. Ties and sharp glass fragments spray across the floor at our feet. The envelope falls through the glass, tilts, and lands in the debris below.

Kogawa can barely move, he is so consumed with anger. His head seems to pulse as if it's about to rupture. I imagine it ballooning and bursting and soaking the room with carnage, because I have watched *Scanners* an unhealthy number of times.

The door behind us dingles yet again; Toby has made a break for it. We take advantage of Kogawa's rage paralysis and scramble after Toby. The apoplexy is short-lived; Kogawa regains responsiveness and resumes his shouting and cursing. As he steps over the shattered counter, his foot slips in the wreckage, and on my way out the door I see him slide sideways, his hand extended in an appeal to gravity's mercy. The hand strikes the three-dimensional glass case of cubes with the wallets and watches, and though it wavers, it doesn't fall. His shouts penetrate the glass and follow us up the street.

"What. Was. That. All. About?" I say through gritted teeth as we power walk towards Nagano *o-dōri*.

Toby grins, a self-satisfied grin that, aside from the yellowed teeth, looks very familiar to me, and my heart actually twitches for a second. *Toby, I really do think I loved you, you ridiculous man.*

"I paid him back," Toby says. "He was saying he didn't want the money after all these years, he only wants me to go to jail, but he's got his money. I finally did it."

Another 12-step moment, I want to say, but Toby grows genuinely reflective, almost serene. "This," he says, holding the purloined object above our heads between thumb and forefinger, "was tucked below the corner of his cash register. I liberated it."

"What is it?" Reiko asks.

"It's what we came for." He lowers the object to eye level. It's a business card.

"My Japanese is just good enough for me to make it out."

The card is beige with dark-brown characters and a small logo—an abstract line drawing of some sort of blossom.

"Ah!" Rei claps her hands together. "Toby, your eyes are so good!"

"I don't get it." I say, as we cross in the direction of Taisei Abinasu.

"It's a soba blossom." Rei taps the image with her index finger. My eyes gloss over all the *kanji* and focus on the *katakana* that I can read. *Katakana*, usually reserved for words of foreign origin. Computer becomes *kon-pyū-taa*; McDonalds becomes *Ma-ku-don-a-ru-do*.

And Babette becomes *Ba-bet-to*.

"Well done, tall man." I snatch the card away and study it. *Tanaka Babetto*, with her husband's name above.

田中 真治

田中 バベット.

Rei's finger returns to the card, rests against the lines of *kanji* in the bottom corner.

"It's a soba restaurant," she says. "It's called Hisoka. I have heard of this place! It's supposed to be very good."

"They sell *soba*."

"Yes!"

Soba keeps popping its head up in the most unexpected places.

"Well, there we go." I put on a chipper, forging-forward tone, but I'm unsettled. Visiting Kogawa was bad enough. Visiting Babette might be worse.

"It's on the highway to Hakuba," explains Rei. "We can't get there on the train or bus, though. We'll have to take my car. We're lucky Toby can see so good!"

Toby grins but doesn't respond.

"Yeah, easy," I say. "All we had to do was cause minor property damage and give an old gangster a stroke. No big."

Rei barks out a laugh. "What do you mean?"

"Didn't you see him? He looked like he'd just snorted a three-foot line of wasabi. His head—"

"No, what do you mean, gangster?"

"What do you think I mean?" I stop and turn to Reiko, just as we reach the shadow of the former J.J. International. "Kogawa was *yakuza*. He worked for Takahashi."

"Not *yakuza*," she chuckles. "Asshole yes. Such an asshole. But not *yakuza*."

"What are you talking about? That night he came to J.J.'s, we were all so scared to do or say anything because we thought he was *yakuza*!"

"Yes," Rei agrees with an emphatic nod. "Yes, we thought so. He liked bad tailored suits and had that haircut like a curly squid on his head. But he's just mean, not a criminal."

Kogawa is not a criminal. My brain locks with the introduction of this new information. Not a figure from a shadowy and unpredictable world. Just an asshole.

"You told me he was the mob!" I smack Toby as hard as I can on his bicep.

"Ouch!" Toby pulls away like I'm a dog about to bite.

"I did not! Never said anything of the sort. What are you talking about?"

"You told me you left the English competition because there was a guy you didn't want to talk to! And that he might be a gangster!"

Toby frowns at me.

"Yeah, I remember saying that," he says. "But River, I wasn't talking about Kogawa."

KOGAWA

Kogawa killed Daniel, sort of. It's an intentionally ambiguous statement. I realize now, looking back, that Kogawa did nothing of the sort, but that night at J.J.'s marked a decline in Daniel that ended in his death. Trying to make sense of it was impossible. Kogawa gave me someone to hate other than myself.

It was a slow work night. Daniel made me some instant coffee and a plate of frozen French fries. Reiko picked up an acoustic guitar left behind by our jazz band and performed an extremely intense version of Skid Row's "I Remember You," of all things. After she finished, Daniel picked up the guitar and noodled around as best he could. When he stood up to clear the plates, he walked around with the guitar strapped over his back like Bruce Springsteen in that famous photo, the one taken from the back, with the guitar slung low over his ass, headstock pointed downward. Our sweaty, pale, purple-fingered Springsteen.

Two uniformed men in green Nagano Electric jumpsuits came through the door. We sat them in the corner at table one. The entire staff crowded in around them, desperate for a break in the monotony.

It was about thirty minutes later that Kogawa arrived.

"Arrived" is the wrong word. He barged into the room as though challenging it to a fistfight. There was an immediate chill, deep and still, where the air thickened until it could dampen sound. His uneven curls dripped wetly over his forehead. A weak *irrasshaimase* trickled from our mouths and spilled on the floor, where the man seemed to slip in it. He wobbled and blinked before he unleashed a stream of barbed Japanese at Reiko, who immediately began to nod and mumble apologies. It seemed we had not given him a suitably enthusiastic welcome. When Reiko glanced at me, her eyes were watery; she was shocked and embarrassed.

Bad customers were not uncommon, but a dick like Kogawa filled us with a nauseating dread. He would be an appalling customer, obviously, but his connection to organized crime seemed to eliminate the possibility of telling him off or kicking him out. The problem was clear in Reiko's fake smile, affixed to her face as though strapped on with overtight rubber bands. She made rambling apologies as she led Kogawa inside. He was followed by a hesitant entourage—two nondescript young men who seemed half-ashamed to be there and a woman in a blue evening suit decorated with a gaudy ribbon lapel fringe. Her pursed lips drew her features inward from forehead to chin, as if her entire face had been sucking on a lemon. She glanced with distaste at us white girls and ignored Reiko entirely.

At his table, Kogawa collapsed roughly on his ass and rested his hands on his knees. He was not an attractive man. He resembled a bushel of root vegetables stuffed into a suit jacket. He had strong eyebrows, as arched as the high cheekbones that suspended his narrow lips. His ridiculous permdo sprouted ringlets like the tentacles of a deceased octopus. No, a dying octopus, because his ringlets twitched with his facial movements, and his face was in constant motion, electrified by some rage we couldn't understand. His eyes had the sick shimmer of someone on the prowl for violence.

Reiko dashed across the room to retrieve a drink menu, while Kogawa reloaded and fired off another stream of abuse in her direction. His voice was jagged, the cutting edge of a chipped and nicked hacksaw blade; hers was nervously musical, frenetic but lilting, humble, and apologetic. I could follow the conversation well enough. Reiko wasn't good enough for him; he wanted to sit with the *gaijin* women.

Daniel stood blankly at the bar. Our two other customers, the ones in Nagano Electric jumpsuits, studied their hands. Kogawa's young gentlemen friends similarly took an interest in the swirls of skin on their knuckles.

"They already have customers," I heard Reiko say, in the politest, humblest Japanese. "Very important customers. Sensei would be angry if they did not pay them attention."

"I am angry now!" Kogawa bellowed.

Any of us could have joined Kogawa; these two salarymen didn't need the attention of four hostesses, and Nakadaira-sensei would not have been angry if some of us left the table. Reiko was just trying to take the bullet for us. Kogawa, though, would have none of it. His two underlings looked uncomfortably at the tabletop and at their reflections in the black ceramic ashtrays. Daniel looked queasy. Kogawa's voice rose.

Reiko approached us with an expression that was equal parts apologetic and incensed.

"Nicolle and Babette, you must come and sit with new customers." She barely looked them in the eye as she asked.

"I can't," Babette said, looking uncomfortable and, I thought, shifty. "I just can't."

"Ah, to hell with it." I splayed my fingers out on the table before me for balance. "I'll go."

I picked up a lighter off the table and straightened my skirt. There was no plan, no reason for me to do this, but the jumpsuits had bought us a drink or two, so I was not sober. I was, however, ticked off. Possibly a poor foundation on which to make a decision.

"*Ojama shimasu,*" I said to the salarymen, then perched on a stool with my back to the bar. "River *de gozaimasu.*" I even added a bow for extra politeness. The woman smirked.

Kogawa clearly did not recognize me from our brief interactions at BOOM and the convention centre, or if he did, he did not care. He continued to shout over my head at Reiko. *I want the curly-haired blonde,* he said, *not this ugly gaijin.* Why go out in public for the sole purpose of acting like a giant turd? What was the possible endgame?

Babette understood him. She glared at him and shook her head. This seemed to enrage him further. Most of my buzz-borne bravado quickly deflated. I had presumed the first thing this gargantuan horse's ass would do was to start in on me for not being pretty enough, for being Western, for whatever problem he decided to invent. What I did not expect is that he would completely ignore me. After he finally disengaged from Reiko, he turned his attention to lemonlips, whose countenance had been curdling all the while. When he finally spoke to her, some of the pucker around her mouth relaxed. Why she responded to his attention was a mystery, especially since he still looked and sounded furious. His voice was ashy, almost scorched, the sound of a burning cigarette that talked. No one else said a word.

For a few minutes a sort of woozy, nervy equilibrium held. It felt as though a bomb had walked into the room and everyone was trying to pretend they didn't know it was there. The steadiness ended when he wanted a smoke.

Kogawa pulled out a package of Peace cigarettes, withdrew one, and put it in his mouth. The woman went for her lighter, but dammit, ignore me as much as he wanted, I was the hostess. I was fed up with sitting in tense silence, so I thrust my lighter forward towards him. In my frustration, I didn't adhere entirely to protocol. Instead of raising both hands politely, one to light, one to cup around the flame, I lit it with one hand.

"*Bakayarō!*" He grabbed my wrist with surprising quickness and whipped my arm downward, where my knuckles smacked hard against the ice bucket.

"Ow!" I stood, kneading my injured knuckles with the other hand. "You dick!"

I spun toward the others, looking for backup. Almost immediately, there was a clamour and crash behind me, as though the ceiling had collapsed. I turned to see the table on its side, the floor strewn with ashes and whiskey, ice sinking into craters in the carpet, *ebi* chips floating in gelatinous-looking puddles of water. The two quiet men had drawn into themselves, hunched together and staring at the rug. The woman's pursed lips had pursed further and seemed to ooze and wriggle on her face. Kogawa stood, shouting at Reiko, who bowed deeply and intensified the speed and volume of her apologies.

"A table flip?" Nicolle shouted. "Are you serious? Who does that?"

Babette shrank into herself and said nothing.

"Someone do something," Allie shouted. "Kick him out of here."

But none of us moved. We knew that by doing something, we could be entering uncharted territory. As if to silently express our thoughts, one of the Nagano Electric men drew his pinky downward across his cheek and raised his eyebrows in query. The other customer shrugged as if to say, I don't know, maybe.

Daniel approached the wreckage and eyed Kogawa cautiously. The guitar was still strapped across his back like he was Johnny Cash.

"*Yamete itadakemasen ka?*" As politely as possible. Would you stop this, please? Reiko's eyes, however, screamed *no* in his direction, as if to tell him stand down, to leave this to her. Daniel's words made no difference; Kogawa went volcanic, but in Reiko's direction. The pitch of argument and apology rose as Kogawa demanded justice or recompense or whatever it was he obstinately wanted from Rei. Daniel stood silently, unsure of himself, well aware that his role as the only male staff member was to stand up to this idiot.

Kogawa growled and gestured with his hands, and as we watched, Reiko's face shaded with embarrassment. She began to bend at the knees, slowly, until her kneecaps touched the soggy floor. The two young men's faces fell from awkwardness into shame. Even the woman seemed suddenly uncomfortable. Reiko clearly wanted to end the entire spectacle, even if it meant this humiliation, prostrating herself, forehead-to-the-floor, *dogeza*-style, in deep apology.

That's when something in Daniel snapped. No; that's wrong. Nothing came untethered, and he didn't lose control. It was the opposite. The tangle of ties that bound him didn't let go; he let go of them.

Daniel reached down and gently took Reiko's arm.

"Don't," he said. "He doesn't deserve it."

Kogawa leapt to his feet and shouted at Daniel, inches from his nose. Daniel kept his arm on Reiko's, while Reiko, frustrated and uncertain, continued to kneel. Daniel let go of her arm to stand straighter, pushing his face closer to the torrent of verbal fire. I'd say he met Kogawa's gaze, but Daniel had no gaze. His eyes were blank. Here he was, a kid who wanted to cower when asked about the weather, looking almost unfazed, almost welcoming an assault.

Which is what he got.

Kogawa's arm zipped upward and he slapped Daniel across the face with the back of his hand. Taken by surprise, Daniel lost his balance and fell to the carpet, just shy of shards of broken glass. The guitar made a hollow, discordant bonging sound on the rug.

Nicolle and Allie rushed to my side. The three of us screamed at Kogawa, almost hysterical. Sourpuss finally looked suitably self-conscious. Kogawa barked something at the two quiet men, who leaped to their feet and scrambled past us. One of them mumbled an apology to Nicolle as he passed; Nicolle shoved him and muttered under her breath. The woman followed, eyes on the floor, followed by Kogawa, who either had gotten what he came for or else had, at last, realized he had overstepped the bounds of decency. He tossed a few thousand-yen bills into one of the puddles on the floor.

No one made a move to pick them up.

When they reached the door, Kogawa turned to the woman and raised a finger in Babette's direction. He said something I didn't understand and laughed. The group disappeared into the florescence of the hallway, and the door settled shut with a calm hiss.

Allie burst into tears almost immediately.

"I...called...Sensei..." she sniffed. "I snuck to the...coat room and called...he should..."

"What just happened?" I knelt on the mushy carpet next to Daniel. He was propped on his elbow, eyes closed, breathing deeply as if to calm himself.

"You all right, bud?" I asked. Daniel nodded, but something in the set of his teeth said otherwise.

"My heart's a little...palpitate-y." He grimaced once, and then manufactured an effort-filled smile. "Help me up. I just need to drink some water and calm down."

I helped him to his feet, and when I made to support him on his way to the kitchen, he brushed my arm off and shook his head.

"I'm good," he panted. "Let me just go sit down a minute."

I was about to argue when the door flew wide and there was Nax, head swiveling like an owl, mottled grey hair stuck up in tufts, dressed in a western-style bathrobe with grey and blue stripes. In his hands, God bless him, he gripped a wooden baseball bat, held upward in front of him as if he were about to bunt his way to first. Nobody laughed, but I felt the tension fracture enough for us to catch our collective breath.

Nicolle and Allie tag-teamed the explanation to Nax while Reiko sopped up whiskey puddles with dishtowels and Tissues of Kitten. When he realized the perpetrators were gone, Nax seemed almost disappointed. Before long, he had us all gathered around the table with a drink (including free ones for the jumpsuits, who seemed as traumatized as the rest of us).

"You must...learn karate!" Nax's eyes glinted with joy. "We can be Nagano's only western-girl karate jazz bar!"

We all laughed lightly.

"We didn't know how to react," said Nicolle. "We didn't know if he had, you know, friends."

"She means we were afraid he might be a gangster," Allie clarified.

Nax raised his eyelids without really opening his eyes any wider. "Maybe," he replied. "I...don't know."

Babette stared at the tabletop.

"Sometimes men are very angry," Nax said. "Why? I don't know. They can shout and yell and wave hands. You might think they are criminals or important men because they try to act...superior? Yes, superior. But really, they are just regular people. Not criminals, not important. Just angry people. Why? I don't know."

"Daniel should have kicked them out," Nicolle said in a whisper, though Daniel was not in the room.

I smirked and sipped my whiskey. "We should have done it. The situation shouldn't have reached that table-flipping crescendo. We should have ousted that belligerent moron immediately. We were *all* too scared."

"Yeah, leave Daniel alone." I was surprised, not only that Babette had finally spoken, but spoken in defense of Daniel. "He got hurt, too."

She reached for my hand and pressed her fingertips gently against my wrist. My second and third knuckle were bruised and swollen.

"You need to get some ice on that," she said. I nodded and headed to the ice machine. As I filled a silver bucket, I could see Daniel's legs and feet through the crooked curtains. He paced the confined space of the kitchen in a continuous pirouette. He had thrown open the window, since no degree of cleanliness could make up for the room's oppressive confinement. I peeked through the curtain to see his pinched face, jaw quivering, though not as though he were about to cry; it was more like he was trying to stop grinding his teeth and failing. I pulled back the curtain and stood in the doorway.

"Here." He took the ice bucket, distracted, glancing at it shakily. Then he held it against his chest. Took a deep breath.

"Daniel, you look awful." I tried to say it conversationally, but his skin was alarmingly pallid, except for his lips, which had taken on the bluish tinge often found in his fingers. I was scared, and my tone must have begun to border on true panic. I took the ice bucket back from him, placed it on the stovetop, and laid my hands on his shoulders.

"I'm just shaken," he said. "I'm fine."

I shook my head.

"You are not fine. I'm taking you to the hospital."

"No!" Daniel didn't just look me in the eye, he glared at me. "I'm not going to the hospital. I can't afford to go to the hospital."

"Nax would pay for it," I insisted.

"It's okay. My heart's just racing, that's all. This isn't the first time this has happened, you know. It happens all the time. Just…just take me home, maybe. Take me home, draw me a bath, and get me some water, if you want to help. I just need to relax."

Daniel never looked you in the eye. Daniel never told you what to do. Daniel never insisted on anything. What was I going to do? I took him home by taxi, which Nax paid for, and walked him into his living room. I poured him some water over some freezer-burned ice cubes. I turned on his bathtub. I turned on his kerosene heaters. I sat there until his room was warm.

"You all right in there?" I asked through the door.

"I'm good," he replied. His voice was smoother, calmer than before. "It's okay. You can head home. Please."

So I went home, where I opened up the latest pages of *Kenichi and the Kappa.* Instead of editing, though, I screwed off the cap of a half-full Jim Beam bottle and stared at the screen, fretting about Daniel, his health, and that gangster Kogawa.

STITCH

Who, I am now told, was not a gangster after all.

This was not something I wanted to hear.

If he wasn't a gangster, and we were all wrong, there was no reason—*no reason*—we couldn't have tossed his ass to the curb long before he hit Daniel.

"Why would you have assumed I meant Kogawa?" Toby asks.

"I...I just..." Why did I assume he meant Kogawa?

"Well, because...because he saw you and headed straight for you! Because everyone kinda thought he was a gangster? So I put two and two together and—"

"Riv." Toby's voice reaches for soothing but misses and lands on patronizing. "I never would have told you Kogawa was a mobster. I left that day because I was nervous about someone, but it wasn't Kogawa, trust me."

"So you had secret goings-on with Kogawa and some other gangster?"

"I, uh....I'm not sure what you're even asking me, really, Riv. I'm not sure why you're so upset."

"I don't know!" I turn to Rei, desperate for backup, support, something. Rei, for her part, looks equally confused.

"Why on earth would we jump to that conclusion?" I

yell at Toby. "He was a pushy grumpy man in a ridiculous suit with a dumb haircut and we all just assumed he was in the mob? Because all Japanese men are salarymen, farmers, or *yakuza*?"

"That's a specific kind of diversity there—"

"That's the point," I fume, but mostly at myself, at my stupidity. "What kind of weirdo racists were we? What kind of exotic fantasies were we making up about this place?"

"Whoa, River, I'm not sure—"

"I'm just saying it was a stupid, naïve conclusion to reach, and I've spent two decades thinking that Daniel died and blaming Kogawa, only to find out he was just some random goof and we could easily have stopped him and none of this would have happened."

Wait. There was someone in the room who would have known Kogawa wasn't a criminal.

"Babette!" I say. "Surely, if Kogawa was Shinji's uncle, she would have known about any *yakuza* connections, or lack thereof. She could have at least told us that, no, he wasn't going to strap dynamite beneath Nax's car or leave a severed horse's head in someone's bed. She could have told us he wasn't a gangster, just an idiot. Instead, she said nothing."

Reiko puts her hand on my arm, but I shake it off. I'm not able to explain to Reiko that, for all this time, I have blamed that pot-bellied, bitter little man for the death of my friend. I'm not able to explain that, now that I know there was another course of action, another way it could have played out, the blame has shifted.

"Babette knew," I say. I want to focus my blame on her, now, but it doesn't want to shift. It doesn't want to exist.

Reiko's face softens.

"Kawa-chan, Daniel was very sick." Her voice is calm and steady, with short pauses for thought. She's trying to be precise in her language. "I don't think what happened to Daniel was because of Kogawa. Even if it was, even if Kogawa got Daniel's heart too excited and that eventually gave him a heart attack, he was not going to live for a long time. He was always trying to tell us this. He was always saying he was lucky."

"Babette knew," I repeat.

"Babette avoided Shinji's family like the plague," Toby says. "She hated them and was afraid they'd find out about her. Don't you remember how secretive they were? Hell, nobody met Shinji. Kogawa knew, though. She was always afraid Kogawa would tell Shinji's father. I bet he came to J.J.'s just to mess with her, because he's just that kind of person. Also, Reiko's right. You've put way too much weight on this one event. Getting knocked onto the carpet couldn't have been any worse for him than climbing Asahi all those times."

I glare at Toby again. I'm confused. I'm angry, but I'm angry at a ghost. No, it's worse. I'm angry at a ghost that we're trying to find to solve a mystery. It's illogical and selfish and I don't know what to think anymore.

"Come," Rei says, as if to distract me. "Let's go for a walk."

We walk a few feet, but Toby doesn't join us.

"You coming or not?" I say.

"You two go on without me," he replies. I think he can sense that I want to pick a fight, which I do. Then he simply turns and walks away. As he leaves, I feel the water fill my lungs, almost literally; my lungs are stiff, they won't inhale, and a psychic pressure seems to come from above, from all around me, and the sky becomes too low, the sun too close. *The feeling.*

It's a warm day for mid-October. My clothes are like a gummy coating on my skin. We walk silently across the road to the train station, through it, and out the east entrance. In front of the station there are busses and taxis and a neon cascade; here, behind the station, there is only a footbridge over a four-lane road. Somewhere in the distance is the house where I used to teach Sora. Somehow, beyond the station, Nagano diminishes, crumbles into low-lying houses and highways and sprawl. Short grey buildings and train tracks beneath open skies, like an urban prairie.

"Are you all right to find Babette?" Reiko asks.

"What do you mean?"

Reiko gives me a bit of side-eye. "I think she was maybe a little upset that you left without saying goodbye."

"Reiko, I left without saying goodbye to anyone. Were you mad at me? I mean...wait...were you mad at me?"

"No!" Reiko laughs. "But I wasn't your roommate and best friend."

"Oh, I don't know about best friend..." Something about this statement rings true. True enough that I want to change the topic.

"You know the other day, when we couldn't find Rokumonsen?" I say.

"Yes."

"It really bothered me."

"Why?"

"I don't know if I can explain," I sigh. "Have you ever heard the English saying, 'you can't go home again?'"

"Maybe? Is it like, you can't live again in the past?"

"Yeah, that's it. You can't go back because the past is no longer there. Not the way you remember it. Nagano was the best time of my life, in so many ways, you know? Then what happened with Daniel and Toby made me run home. For twenty years I held on to this narrative I'd created, but so far on this trip, all I've learned is that nothing is the way it was, and nothing was the way I thought it was. Does that make sense?"

Rei nods, and though I can't know if she understands, I feel like she does.

"Isn't that just how memory works?" Rei gestures vaguely to the city spread out in front of us. "Probably half the things you think are different are the same, and half the things you think are the same are different."

I don't respond. We start down the stairwell that leads to the street below.

"You know what I think?" Rei says. "I think time is kind of changing, constantly, but kind of never changing at the same time. J.J.'s and now—they are not far apart because they are both inside you. Years are like loops that are all one line."

"Like an infinite Spirograph, interlocking circles on and on forever," I offer.

"Ah," Reiko replies, "I'm going to say, sure, if you think so? I don't know what a Spirograph is. But I think your memory, your life, is wool. One long line of wool you knit together. The sleeves, the collar, they're all part of the same thing."

"Yeah, totally. But now that I'm back, I kinda feel like I'm looking for a dropped a stitch."

"You can't drop stitches in your life! You're not making a jumper."

I laugh at her use of the word, so different from the meaning we ascribe to it in North America.

"You can't drop stitches in your life," she repeats. "You can't spread out your life and find one small mistake that ruined everything. And even if you can, even if one small mistake changed the direction of your life, you can't go back and pick up that stitch again. You can't undo life."

"I didn't know you knit."

"Babette taught me," she grins.

"What? She did not!"

"Yes. We were good friends for a short time. After you left, you know, she was very sad."

"I find that hard to believe."

Rei has the good sense to let that one go. I don't find it hard to believe. It's simply easier if I don't consider it.

"I'm sorry we weren't better friends, Rei-chan," I tell her when we reach ground level. "It must be weird hanging out with me now, after all these years, after the way we all acted."

Rei looks at me with a furrow of her brow. "What do you mean?"

"Us. All of us. Here, pretending this was a real life, while you were, you know, living a real life."

"Wait." Reiko stops and studies me. "Do you mean, you think it was a vacation for you, but real life for me?"

"Uh."

"That was my early twenties. Same age as all of you."

"Oh."

"Yes, sometimes I was serious at work, but that was my job. Just because I did my job doesn't mean I wanted to be a Mama-san for life."

"No, I didn't—"

"I hated the customers sometimes. I was just the same as you. I was only twenty-two."

"Rei-chan, I didn't mean anything by it. I just assumed you thought we were stupid *gaijin.*"

"Why would I think you were stupid?" Rei says with disbelief and, unexpectedly, an undercurrent of anger. "Didn't you think we were all friends? Because I thought we were all friends. All in the same situation *deshō.* But maybe you didn't think of me like a friend because I was Japanese."

"No! Rei, no, that's not—"

"I'm not...what's the word...sentimental. I am very bad, sooooo bad, at making phone calls and writing letters. And then years went by and I was embarrassed to try and get in touch. I am sad that all of you are gone and never came back. Sometimes I Google you, to see where you are in your life."

"You Google me?"

"I Google everybody!" Reiko says. "I don't go on Facebook because I don't want my private life to be in the public, but I want to know that everyone was doing well, because that part of my life was very important. All of you were important to me, and now you think I wasn't the same as you because I was Japanese? Maybe you think we weren't even friends?"

"Rei." I approach her cautiously, unsure just how upset I've made her. "You're my friend. You were always my friend. I just thought...we behaved so badly sometimes. I thought maybe you wished we had a bit more respect, a bit more responsibility. We were in your country, and we treated it like a playground."

"Kawa-chan." Rei suddenly looks weary of the conversation. "We were in our twenties and didn't have careers. Life was a playground. You worry too much."

She doesn't know the half of it. I'm stuck on the image of life as a sweater. Stuck trying to figure out how to undo past mistakes. What if there are dozens of mistakes? What if the resulting sweater is an ungodly, unravelling mess? How do you start from scratch? Didn't I already do that, twenty years ago? I thought I'd succeeded. Now I think I failed.

I messed up somewhere. I'm doing what I thought I wanted to do, and I'm unhappy. I wrote movies. I had movies produced and released. I dated the sociopath who directed those movies. I moved to Berlin for a spell. I travelled around the world and signed 8 x 10 glossies of myself posing with Meelis Kuusk. I loved my life until one day I didn't. I am unsatisfied and I feel ungrateful for feeling that way. It's too much to bear and too hard to fix. I can't face my present, and now I can't revel in my past, either.

Maybe I can at least find out about the stupid book.

I stand up, head back up the stairs, back across the footbridge, back into Nagano Station. Reiko follows wordlessly. I hear the sound of amplified voices on the loudspeaker: familiar cadences, unfamiliar meanings, as always. Some teriyaki-ish smell wafts from the doors as I reach the top of the escalator.

Reiko tells me she has to go, and I don't question it. I apologize again, but she waves it off as if it was nothing. I wander down the cobblestone alleyway, past the illuminated signs in front of the shops. J.J.'s looms above me, its windows dark. It is filled with more memories than any I've made in the 20 years since.

Except that thought is as foolish as it is untrue. Memories are not in short supply. I've been to Estonian movie sets and watched Evrard Frederich feed Meelis Kuusk chocolate bars laced with caffeine because Evvie didn't think Kuusk was "fidgety enough." I've discussed the finer points of the practical effects in the *Puppet Master* series with a fourteen-year-old farm kid from Saskatoon, only to have the same conversation in halting English with a schoolteacher from Ulsan six months later. I've engaged in soul-sucking online arguments with disgusting *otaku* douchebags. I drank wine in a hotel on the Danube while the director of *My Bloody Valentine* and his wife recounted how they met at a screening of *A Serbian Film* which, well, Christ, what a place to meet, but they're very happy together. The bassist from Goblin and I are Facebook friends. I have grown up to be a low-level success in my chosen field. My *chosen field*.

Yet I feel like I haven't chosen a damn thing.

The pale-green elevators are stoic and silent at the base of the Taisei Abinasu building. The sign outside lists the businesses within, including a restaurant called Meaters, which is either a singles hangout or a barbecue place, though possibly neither. Maybe they sell men's jeans. No businesses are listed on 3F, where J.J.'s used to be.

I cross the plaza and press the elevator button. One of the elevator doors jitters open. I can almost hear Allie yelling *mate, hold the elevator.* I can almost see Daniel sloping towards me with a sheepish grin.

The doors slide shut. My hand trembles when my fingers pause over the button marked 3F.

You're going into the haunted house, River. Not a nice polite county-fair one, either. An extremely haunted house. This is the House of 1000 Corpses.

Except when I press the button, nothing happens. No sound, no movement, no indicator light. 3F is empty, so 3F has been locked out of the public elevators. Dammit. I press 5F instead; maybe I can find a stairway down to the third floor. Yet when the doors shake open on the fifth floor, they reveal a wood-and-glass-walled reception area. I jam my thumb on the "close" button before someone can dart into the lobby and shout *irrashaimase!*

Back on the ground, I circle the building. This, now, is a mission. I need to get inside. There are spiral fire stairs hooked to the side of the building like the hose on a fire extinguisher, but their entrance is barricaded by green plastic netting, some kind of ersatz construction barrier.

What does it matter? The door to J.J.'s itself will be locked, no doubt. If something else had taken J.J.'s place, another bar, a restaurant, a clothing shop, I could find an excuse to get inside. Instead, it feels like the space has been blocked, shut away, as if it was never there at all. Some higher power, perhaps, has a benevolent hand in this—

Take it easy, brain.

Or maybe it's not benevolent at all! Maybe it's against me. Maybe there's some entity trying to hide facts from me! Some elder god who doesn't want me to know mysterious truths. Maybe Daniel's ghost reached out to me through the book, and now something else doesn't want him to be found.

Or maybe I'm a complete maniac.

I pull at the green netting, but it's thick and well-secured. No elevators, no stairs. No J.J.'s.

Here you go, Soba. I'm trying to walk into darkness and see death, but something won't let me.

But I can't stop here. I can't. I have to find him. I have to find Daniel.

Mount Asahi. The *sakon inari* shrine. That's where I'll go.

Waiting for the traffic signal pains me physically, but I do it. I've waited at crosswalks at three a.m. with no other vehicles or pedestrians in sight. It's what you do. Once the light changes and the friendly audio chirp fills the air, I walk westward with a speed that causes my shins to burn. Soon, the slightly asymmetrical peak of Asahi-yama appears.

The low mountains ring Nagano entirely, distant and hazier on one end of the city, smaller but immediate, almost within grasp, on the other. They impressed upon us a sensation of insignificance and immensity in equal measure, beautiful and ageless. Today, when I see them rise three hundred sixty degrees around the city, I am simply reminded of a bowl, a birdbath, or the skull of a *kappa*.

The bridge over the Susobana is narrow. The river flows down from the north, a greenish-grey murmur. Rocks dot the shallow water's surface; naturally, I peer at them intently, as if one of them might stand up and reveal itself to be something other than a stone.

A set of concrete stairs cuts a pedestrian path directly through the winding roads. I'll come to the forest path, hang a right around the small apple orchard, and keep moving upward until I find the route to the shrine. I'm two decades older, but my lungs are clear and my shoes sensible enough. Let's do this.

At the top of the hill, there is a plateau where the houses separate and drift apart. All roads lead up. Yet only one leads to the orchard. And…huh.

Wait, am I going the right way?

There's no way I've forgotten the route. I know this place. I know the way. Up the concrete stairs, to a few winding streets where the roads spread out like splayed fingers. There's a narrow path, no more than three feet wide, of crumbled asphalt and broken rock. I never failed to find it.

Yet nothing looks familiar. But, okay, everything looks familiar, just reversed and tilted as though I'm looking at it from the wrong angle. The road arcs to the south, which is wrong; by now, I should have found the path.

I turn back, my heart and lungs thankful for the temporary respite of descent. All the way back to the bottom, back to the cement steps lined with oblong cedars like fat cocoons. My heart thuds persistently as I turn around and reconsider my upward trajectory. I take off my jacket and tuck it under the strap of my satchel. Sweat begins to gather in my bra, which has already begun to chafe.

This time, I take a different splayed finger, one that points westward. Looking up towards Asahi, though, is like that final shot in *Raiders of the Lost Ark*—everything looks the same—how can I possibly find the Ark in this warehouse? Fields and orchards and garden plots and houses and roads and paths. What if, like the Ark, like J.J.'s, the *sakon inari* was intentionally hidden? Or what if I've simply forgotten?

Ridiculous. Nothing is ever forgotten, I tell myself, despite the proof of phone numbers and Japanese words and what I ate last Tuesday, all gone, inaccessible to me. The tall horizon holds no clues, so I simply began to walk upwards, my heart thumping like an angry downstairs neighbour. A pulse and surge of blood in my ears. Paths wind through the apple orchards, around shacks and homes and makeshift garages covered by tarps. They lead up into the forest, promising the way.

Yet every time I turn down one of these three-foot wide trails, it weakens underfoot, dissolves into grass and dirt and, eventually, impassable overgrowth. I double back, triple back, quadruple back. My feet begin to swell. An initially promising route turns in the wrong direction, and I find myself in a hamlet I've never seen before, a collection of homes nestled into the hills. Gardens sit on steep hillsides, and middle-aged men water these gardens, filling pots from thin hoses that snake their way up into their houses through sliding doors. Dogged and with few options, I walk. *I have forward.* Even though I know that, here, forward is the wrong direction. On my left, more buildings, temples, full-sized and towering, above me in the trees. I have either circled around the *sakon inari* or climbed above it. I begin to feel like a character in a Murakami novel; I've traversed some entranceway into another plane, and my Asahi is gone, vaporised, or, more succinctly, denied me; moved by the gods, disappeared like Brigadoon.

Out of the greenery leaps a large white sign. I can't read too many of the characters, but I recognize the *kanji* for *chūi*, caution, and the *katakana* syllables that sound out *kuma*.

Kuma means bear—this is further edified by the black silhouette of a bear prominently included in the design. *Caution: you are entering bear country.*

River Black, creator of the dark, inventor of monsters, is scared to death of bears.

I don't care if this sign is merely a better-safe-than-sorry warning, a form of risk management, whatever. I cannot find the shrine and I will not be eaten alive trying. Forget bears. There's a reason I won't go father north than Squamish.

You're not meant to find your way.

Suddenly, like a lost child, I burst into tears. It's over. Whatever forces that are against me have prevailed. I tried to march directly into my past and instead I stumbled around like an idiot.

I turn back the way I came. The sun is already starting to drop, though it's only late afternoon. I haven't got a clue what I need to do. I haven't got a clue where I need to go.

Before long I'm back on the crooked streets of Zenkōjishita, looking at Sanyō Heights. Those rooms house others now; I can't go knocking on doors or barging into private spaces, a deranged white woman with a Godzilla tattoo. Instead, I sit on the railing beside the canal where the Sanyō regattas once sailed. Toby used to call the canals Little Rivers, saying that somehow they were all my offspring, borne from my imagination, snaking their way from me throughout the city, collecting the stories of those who passed alongside them. "If you fall into a Little River," he would say, "you would live forever as a character in one of your stories." It was a wonky idea, which is why I loved it so much. Toby, trying to create his own mythology; me, trying to create myself. I sit on the orange metal railing that follows the water, these gullies that stream from my imagination, staring at the stream as it sparkles its way beneath the sunlight, brownish yet somehow also clean, unpolluted, as if it had come directly from the tops of the Alps into this rivulet.

"Stitch," comes the croak.

I can't pretend I didn't know he'd come. Extreme stress, frustration, depression, alone in front of water. I can't pretend I didn't hope, either.

"That's what she said, yeah," I answer. "Stitch. You like that analogy, do you?"

"Stitch," it repeats. It takes me a moment to locate Soba, as its voice seems to echo along the canal. Then I see it, crouched in the water, on its haunches, as if ready to pounce at something unseen. It's looking up at me from twenty feet away.

"Yeah. Stitch. Thanks, you're helpful."

It sloshes its way forward a few feet, towards me, almost floating, though there's no way the water is deep enough for that. It's as though the lower half of its body is not in this world.

"I come from little river," it says.

"No. You're *in* a little river. You come from the Susobana."

It blinks its amphibian blink and regards me with its head cocked slightly to one side.

"Boy. Book. River."

"Yes, thank you for the nouns. Now let's try some adjectives. Dumb. Stupid. Smelly. Pointless."

"Mah." Soba shakes its head. "Can't undo life. Move forward."

"What did you say?" I know full well what it said, but I want to hear more. I want to know why this figment of my imagination keeps referencing my conversation with Reiko.

"*Pfft.* You have no idea what is real and what is not!"

"There's an enormous irony in *you* saying that, Soba."

"No!" Soba leaps from the water and lands a few feet away from me, alighting on the top of the canal wall. It's startling, but then again, it's not really here, so I don't react.

"Maybe too late! Soba warn you!"

"I want closure," I moan. "I want to find out where this book came from. I want to find Daniel. I want it all to be okay."

"Find Daniel!" Soba spits into the canal as if warding off the evil eye. "Stupid thing. How find dead person? What do you mean?"

I start to answer but realize I don't have an answer. That statement didn't really make any sense. Yet that's what was on my mind all afternoon, trying to revisit all those old places.

"Not you!" Soba screams now and hops closer to me. *"Not you, not Kogawa, not stitch! Not! Empty!"*

At this distance, I can see the soggy, meaty sway of the loose flesh under its face. I can smell the reek, like rotten fish. The look on its face is, reliably, one of mild disgust and extreme disdain, but it tilts its head one way and the other, as if trying to decide what to do with me—teach me, taunt me, devour me from the inside out. Then Soba dives into the water with the grace of a cormorant on the hunt, disappearing from this world and into another one, in my mind or wherever it may be. The surface of the water leaves me no clues.

But this time, to my surprise, I feel shaken. My imagination has taken things too far. In my hotel room, in an *onsen*, in places where I drifted near to dreaming—all these visits took place on the flickering border between wakefulness and sleep. This time, it appeared on the side of the road, something I could reach out and touch. There was something too real about Soba, something too believable about its stink, its hiss.

And, most disturbingly, its words. It's my subconscious, telling me that no matter what I have learned about Kogawa, this still isn't anyone's fault. Daniel didn't die because of some uncompleted due diligence. Beneath the weight in my chest, there is a light spot, a bubble of air, where I know this to be true. What worries me, however, is the other thing it said.

Not. Empty.

BABETTE KNITS A JUMPER

Daniel took a couple nights off work. Kogawa had shaken up his heart and opened the floodgates into the arteries of his lungs. My mild concerns about his health exploded; I was in full-fledged mother mode. I came by twice a day—once in the late morning to see what he needed for the day, and once before work to make sure he was feeling all right (read: still alive). More often than not, I stayed for the hours in-between, too. We ate 7-11 *oden* and watched imported VHS tapes of *The Simpsons.* I considered lugging my *wāpuro* to his apartment, but its weight dissuaded me. Instead, I continued to spend time at home, with a beer and the late-night quiet, when I worked on *Kenichi and the Kappa.* Daniel, for his part, remained propped up on pillows on his futon, surrounded by pens, his notebook, his TV remote, multiple glasses of water, and some medication whose origin I could only imagine was the United States, as Daniel had no Japanese drug plan and no way to accurately communicate with a Japanese medical professional.

Nax had offered again to take Daniel to the hospital; Daniel had declined.

Those afternoons were fun, despite my anxieties. As winter wore on and the Olympics drew closer, the city around us was whipping itself into a frenzy of enthusiasm and excitement. I was content to step back from all of it and watch the snow falling softly onto Daniel's windowsill.

The rest of my routines didn't change. We were, as we always were, inside our own boozy bubble, floating up and over our own lives, hoping it would, somehow, return us to earlier days, days when the future held such promise.

Or that might have just been me.

One afternoon when I was waking up after yet another night at India, a voice amplified into a crushing, spiky assault blasted from beyond the glass of the balcony doors. It grew louder until it sounded as though someone had a megaphone inserted into my cranium. Then it grew louder still, as though a rough hand had taken hold of that megaphone and was using it to wrench my grey matter free from my skull.

"What in actual hell, Babette," I moaned.

Babette slid the *shoji* open and poked her head through.

"Elections. Right-wingers in campaign trucks, shouting shit. You've been here a year and a half—you've never heard them?"

"Never had the pleasure. What are they saying?""

"I don't know, mate. Right-wing things."

"Of course."

As I lay face-down on my own futon, I noticed that not only was I still dressed, I was still in my winter jacket. When the crackle and jibber of the election truck finally faded into silence, I felt my jaw unclench.

"I think I drank too much, Babette."

"Mate, this differs from another day how?"

"I don't know." I pushed myself up on my elbows and ignored the pain as best I could. "Do you ever think we need to get out of J.J.'s and find normal jobs?"

"Bloom's off the drunken rose, huh?"

"The rose died months ago. It's just a sad-looking wilted brown dead head that I should have thrown away."

Babette sighed, and there was a moment or two of silence.

"That's not really true," I said, realizing how grim it had sounded. "I just need to look at going about my days differently. I'm late to go see Daniel, and I've got writing to do, and whatnot."

Babette appeared not to have heard me. "I'm never going home," she eventually said.

"Why not?"

"There's nothing there for me. My family in Christchurch are the worst, and my family in Wellington are not much better."

"Jesus, Babette."

"Not my fault my family sucks."

"Probably not, no. But you do like it here."

There was another short pause. The sound of car tires rose and fell beyond the windows.

"I do," she said. "I badmouth work a lot, the *sukebe* customers and all that, but I like it well enough. I can't keep drinking vodka tonics with salarymen for much longer, though. God knows if it's viable for me to find a regular job here. My Japanese is good. I'd be content even working as a bank teller or something. That would seem like a nightmare back home, yeah? But for some reason, it's different for me here. It seems... possible. Shinji and I have talked about things."

Babette rarely talked about Shinji. I hoped she'd keep talking, so I rolled onto my side and gazed up at her.

"You know, that could even have been Shinji's dad's truck that woke you. He's been going hard lately."

"Is he running for office?"

"Maybe? I think the prick campaigns steadily, regardless."

Babette disappeared from the doorway, and I heard the soft *whump* of her body falling on the *tatami*. My feet made a light *shish* on the mats as I forced myself to shuffle into the kitchen, remove my jacket, and fill Hello Kitty with water.

Babette didn't flinch when I came into her room. Instead, she reached over towards the nicked and dented kerosene heater, fumbled for a lighter, and flicked it against the circular wick.

"What about you? What grand ambitions are you harbouring? Are you going home?"

I coughed, and a bit of water sloshed onto my lap.

"I don't know. I feel like coming here was...a necessity."

"The whole River reinvention."

"No." I sat cross-legged in the doorway and felt the warmth begin to emanate from Babette's heater. "No. Just...I needed to get out of a rut. It took a tragedy to make it happen, but it happened. I just didn't expect..."

"To leap out of the rut into a rut."

"Bingo. I have no complaints, you gotta understand. But...it doesn't feel like real life anymore."

"It isn't."

"I need to get writing. Working on Daniel's story is amazing—he's really incredible—but it's not what I'm going to do forever."

"You're really serious about the movies, aren't you?" Babette said.

"Not serious enough." I gesture vaguely to the air.

"You're no different than anyone else here, River." She was chiding me, but she was gentle about it. "This is a way station. Some of us are here to stall. Some of us are here to recalibrate. Some of us are here to take the money and run. It won't work out for all of us, but with you, mate, I don't have a lot of doubt. Keep yourself off the sauce and put the pen to the paper, you'll be fine."

I wanted to tell her that was a lovely thing for her to say, but she would have just told me to piss off, embarrassed. Instead, out of the blue, I said something else.

"I don't know what to do about Toby."

"Oh *God*, River."

"Yeah. I know. These last couple of months, I've barely seen him, and when I do see him, I can barely stand to talk to his stupid face. And I still can't bring myself to break it off, because I...love the guy, maybe?"

"Convincing."

"Yeah, that's the thing. I'm not convinced." I took a long pull on my water. "At my birthday party, there, he was taking some pills in an unmarked vial."

Babette looks at me with sympathy.

"You finally figured that out, yeah?"

"Figured out what?"

"You couldn't see it? The hyperactivity, the speech patterns, the weird hours..."

"...the vial of pills that somehow I'd never seen until my birthday party."

Babette rolled onto her side and seemed to study me. "River, I told you he was an ass."

"I know."

"You didn't want to believe me."

"Why would I want to believe you?"

"Good point." She nodded to herself. "All of this is transitory. We, you and I, anyway, fell in love with this place. We fell in love with people, too. I fell in love with Shinji, and you fell in love with...everyone. Everything. The idea of it all. But what you see and love is not sustainable. It's going to end, and it's probably not going to end well unless you end it on your own terms. Toby, he's something you should end on your own terms."

I sipped more water while Babette gathered her knitting bag. She removed her latest project, which at this stage appeared to be a baby blanket wrapped in a massive web of unspooled wool.

"He's involved with Kogawa somehow, too," I said, as if the conversation hadn't stopped entirely already.

Babette rolled her eyes and sighed. "Kogawa is involved in a lot of things."

I leaned closer, reaching for the tangle of knitting to get a closer look, but she slapped at my hand.

"Hey! My knuckles are still bruised." I picked up the clump of wool and straightened out what appeared to be the front part of a sweater.

"That was weeks ago. Bruised, my ass."

"Why did he show up that night?" I ask Babette.

"Kogawa?"

"No, the Emperor. Of course Kogawa."

Babette shrugged.

"This sweater is going to take you a long time," I said.

"I have all the time in the world."

"For Shinji, yeah?"

"No, I'm knitting this for you."

"Shut up! You are not!"

Babette laughed. "No, I am in fact not. Of course it's for Shinji."

I rubbed the fabric between my thumb and forefinger, felt its heavy gauge. "Why do you keep him away from us?"

"Have you met us?"

"I'm serious."

Babette reached over and took the embryonic sweater away from me. "His family can't know about me." She took one of her needles and began poking at the ball of yarn, expanded and loose from use. "Right-wing wannabe politicians, and right-wing wannabe politicians' wives, would prefer their sons don't date *gaijin* hostesses. Imagine a family of evangelical Christians with a history of racism, then make them Japanese. That's his family. One of his uncles found out and threatened to tell his father, and I've been scared shitless ever since, so now we're twice as careful. We meet somewhere discreet, and we drive. We head up into the mountains, stop at little soba restaurants. It's nice. Maybe one day, that's what we'll do. Open a soba restaurant in the mountains. Is that too much of a dream, do you think?"

I was certain that had to be sarcasm, in some way, but Babette looked at me with genuine hope.

"No, man, not at all. In fact, that's a pretty modest dream. Kind of a beautiful one, too."

"Sometimes you just gotta run your dreams by a friend, you know?" Babette said. "Not a friend who'll shoot you down, tell you your ideas as stupid and unrealistic, but a friend who'll just kinda give you the perfect answer. No matter what you say, River, somehow you always say the right thing."

"Oh, piss off," I replied in my best Babette voice. We both laughed..

"A soba restaurant in the mountains," I repeated.

"Just don't tell anyone, all right?" Babette said. "Everyone thinks I'm this hard-ass, and I prefer to maintain the illusion. Let's just keep it a secret."

HISOKA

Hisoka means "secret."

It's not the conversational word for "secret," which is *him-itsu*. *Hisoka* means the same, except it's not a word you use in conversation. It's a proper noun. It's also a unisex given name; I knew a girl named Hisoka.

Shinji and Babette. Their secret relationship. Their secret future, come to pass. In tribute, they've built a restaurant and named her Hisoka.

Babette may not appreciate that I've discovered their secret.

The drive from Nagano to the mountains by Hakuba takes under an hour. We pass flashing red lights, hear the faint chime and clang of the train signals. Snub-nosed trucks, compact cars, schoolchildren with tiny square navy-blue backpacks, men in baggy grey coveralls idling on scooters: all are held back by metal arms, striped red and white, as trains pass.

Toby stares at the scenery, alone with his thoughts. Rei, too, is quiet; I hope it's not because she's still sore from our conversation, and my stupidity, just yesterday. This whole Kogawa situation, too. I wanted to blame him, because blame takes some of the power out of grief. Anger feels directed;

you can almost control it. Grief feels like part of the environment; you can't control it, you can only live in it. Anger can make sense. Grief never does.

Learning we could have stopped Kogawa made me feel complicit in his actions. Twenty years of blame, redirected at myself, would destroy me. For a moment, I wanted to blame Babette. I still don't understand why she didn't speak up to allay our fears, or why she never told me Kogawa was Shinji's uncle. Today, though, my heart is too listless to lift blame in any given direction. There's emptiness where the anger once burned. New emotions are stirring, ones I don't entirely understand. I'm still unsettled by Soba's words. Words that mean nothing to me, but make me deeply, inexplicably uncomfortable nonetheless. *Unholy soup. Not empty.* Oh, and the fact that I'm seeing that gnarly green freakshow in the daylight now. That can't be a good sign.

West of the city the distance between buildings widens, and fewer vehicles cross the intersections. I stare out the window as Reiko picks up speed, perhaps unnecessarily so, and I am reminded of driving with Masa, both twenty years ago and again only last week. Whirling our way upward into the hills, his face inscrutable, on a mission as always, speed so intense you swear if the car tilted sideways it would spin out over the abyss and never find ground. It's good to get lost in memory, to pretend I am not on this mission. I've been so fixated on the book that I haven't thought of what might happen when I see Babette again. It won't be a reunion of old souls—not if Babette is still Babette. If Babette is still Babette, it might be more of a confrontation. I left with her with no roommate, a closet's worth of flotsam and jetsam, and one less co-worker to share the load.

And I did all that without telling her.

The road we're on curves upward into the peaks, but we don't follow it there. Instead, we turn onto a narrow strip of asphalt that splits sideways around a small building. It's an unassuming structure, a new build, an approximation of antiquity built with modern supplies. Reiko pulls into the tiny parking lot, and we march single-file towards the door. The sign above it says *Hisoka*.

Inside, the rice paper on the *shoji* is so crisp and white it looks like pressed mountain snow. The kitchen, visible though a horizontal opening in the wall, is impeccable; in a decades-old restaurant, the kitchen would look lived-in, maybe even comfortably grimy. A young woman with a substantial gap in her teeth greets us at the door, seats us at a table in the corner. I see faces float from one side of the kitchen to another, but no one is blonde enough to be Babette or old enough to be Shinji.

Rei grins at the menu as our greeter brings us earthy brown tea in earthy brown earthenware.

"It is supposed to be very good, the best soba noodles in the area," Reiko whispers, as though the praise were actually nasty rumour. I trust the gossip and order a simple soba noodle set: a bamboo plate of buckwheat noodles with a soy-based dipping sauce, a bowl of nearly-clear miso soup, and some pickled vegetables on the side. It's remarkably good, fresh, the perfect texture, the blissfully umami-rich sauce so tasty that I wish I could just upend its ceramic bowl and drink. Sometimes they'll bring you the water in which the soba is boiled; you add it to the bowl and do exactly that.

We don't make small talk. I am too busy staring into the kitchen. It isn't until I finally see Shinji that I am overwhelmed by the understanding that this whole thing has been a mistake. What in God's name are we doing here? What do we expect to find out?

Shinji's face hasn't aged so much as it has set. He's become oddly rugged and handsome now, the intervening years having relaxed the pores of his formerly fresh face. He wears needle-thin wire-framed glasses and an expression of locked and immutable focus as he glides from counter to counter, cooking and chopping, his attention scattered across various stages of food preparation. It's as if he's reading a story by flipping to random pages, yet he's following the plot perfectly fine, reassembling it chronologically in his mind. It's fascinating to watch, and I find myself entranced even though I can only see the top half of his body and none of what his hands are doing.

Our server crosses to our table, apologizes for some imagined transgression, refills our water. When she walks away, I see a door is open, and in that doorway stands Babette.

What strikes me immediately is not the way the skin around her face has settled around her cheekbones, nor the fact that her hair has gone from blonde to an almost sunlight white. It's that she is, in the instant before she recognizes us, peaceful. The hooded look of her eyes is gone, the look that suggested she faced life with a protective wall of distaste to disguise her uncertainty and fear.

Then she recognizes us and morphs into old Babette, like a benevolent ghost suddenly transforming into a screaming, gape-mouthed terror. She doesn't register recognition, or shocked recognition, or delighted recognition, or any other form of recognition. It's immediate disgust, as if she'd been force-fed a mouthful of *natto*. In the next moment, she is gone.

"Babette!" I call after her. Every head in the building turns towards me in surprise. Before Toby or Rei-chan can react, I charge over to the counter, only to trip on my own feet and, in the process of righting myself, interrupt an older gentleman mid-noodle-slurp. The soba disappears through his lips as his head thrusts forward, and he seems otherwise unharmed, so I don't bother with the usual apologetics. I lob him a "sorry" and run towards the kitchen.

She's gone.

Shinji stares at me. His eyes narrow like a camera lens until he realizes who I am. When he does, the tiniest smile ticks the corner of his mouth upward. Beside him, I see the door to outside is ajar. I raise my eyebrows. With the same economy of movement, he nods. I point at myself, finger to my nose. Same faint nod, as though he wants his agreement to be as neutral as possible for maximum plausible deniability.

I come around the counter and cross through the kitchen. Through the door I see her. She crouches about ten metres away, at the back of the property, where the ground slopes upwards into the skirt of the mountains. She wears black slacks and a white blouse covered by a white apron. Beside her on the ground towers a pile of foot-long daikon, dirt-caked, fresh from the soil. She uses a paring knife to slice off the greens at impressive speeds, tossing them onto a rapidly rising pile in front of her knees. As automatically and carelessly as she tosses the waste, she gently and carefully places the radishes in a new row, as if it were a woodpile made of crystal logs.

"Babette."

She doesn't respond, but her hands flutter more quickly.

"Babette, hey."

"Ah! Shit!" she exclaims as the vegetable-based commotion comes to an immediate halt. She drops the knife and studies her finger.

"Look what you fuckin' made me do." She turns about a quarter of a revolution. Blood spills out of her finger, and a splatter of red droplets dot the white and brown daikon.

"Here." I reach into my shoulder bag and pull out a few napkins. I lean over, and she snatches them without making eye contact.

"You probably shouldn't drink and slice," I say.

"That's your joke? That I've been drinking?"

"I...I thought a terrible non-sequitur-type wisecrack was about the best I was going to do. I figure you might not be happy to see me."

The napkin is already soaked, and it clings to her finger like a bloody, misshapen growth. After a brief scrounge, I find another deck of napkins in another section of my bag and hand them to her. She looks at me this time, her face like a kid I've just pushed off a bicycle, pained and angry.

"What do you want." It's more a statement of dismissal than a question.

"I wanted to say hi," I reply. Already, it seems impossible to ask her the questions I want to ask, to admit this unexpected reunion is a selfish means to a selfish end. Guilt surges up my esophagus and stops halfway to burn against the inside of my throat.

"I had something I had to do, here, and…while I'm here I'm seeing…I'm talking to…"

"You're here with Toby."

I nod. "It's a little bit against my will, but yeah. He's been…okay. He's changed, he says. It seems legit. No long-winded philosophical diatribes."

"How about amphetamines and lies?"

"Definitely no speed. Only time will tell about the lies."

Babette frowns, or doubles down on the current frown, and turns back to her finger.

"Kogawa told us you were looking for us."

"So you've been waiting."

"I've been preparing," she corrects me. "Thinking about all the ways I can tell you to piss off."

"Babette, I—"

"Don't." She squeezes her injured digit tighter and stands, still not quite facing me. "Just don't, yeah? I don't care what weird realization you've come to, or what twelve-step program you're in, or what news you thought you'd share. You deserted me."

I did, I think.

"I did not!" I say.

"You abandoned me and didn't even tell me you were going."

"Babette, I was a mess! I was distraught. I—"

"You were never the same after Daniel, but in the end, you left just like Toby did. Didn't say goodbye, didn't write a letter, didn't care. You just left."

"Babette…"

"For Christ's sake, stop saying my name."

"I was scared. I couldn't take it. I'm sorry that I didn't say goodbye. I didn't say goodbye to anyone, not even Nax, and he was expecting me at work that night."

This is like telling someone it's okay that you punched them in the face because they weren't the only person you punched in the face. I stop talking. Babette stares at the gore-saturated napkins wrapped around her finger and shakes her head repeatedly, even though I've stopped speaking. She's angry that I betrayed our friendship. Babette. Babette, who never had a nice word to say about anyone, who I practically had to bully into friendship. Another difficult personality, another hard case, consistent with the friends I had made all my life. I endured the serrated edge of her sarcasm, pretended her *piss off*s were *please*s and *thank you*s. It wasn't just because I had to live with her. It was because we had become friends. Then I went to a train station, rode a train to an airport, and flew home. I never said goodbye. Yeah, I did abandon her.

"We were friends," is all I can think to say.

Babette snorts, but her head stops shaking. "Yeah."

She turns around then and faces me, though her eyes are trained on my chin, the way Daniel used to approximate eye contact without making it.

"You were the only person there I could relate to," she says. She seems so much younger as she speaks, her voice a blend of a sucky petulance and genuine pain. That pain reaches out of her voice and closes a hand around my heart. "Everyone else wanted to drink and be stupid and complain about the way the post office operates or gush about BOOM boys or save all their money to go party in Thailand. They'd come and suck it up like mosquitoes and then fly away. I cared about that place. I was in love with Shinji. You seemed to get it, and I liked that. I liked you. Then you just left. You hurt me, River, you really did."

"I'm sorry," I say.

Babette straightens her back, and her eyes finally meet mine.

"Great. You're forgiven, I guess. But seeing you reminds me of all that stuff, all that happened, and I don't want to be reminded. I have a life now, a very different life. I don't mix *mizuwari* for philandering idiots who ought to be at home with their families. I grow food, cook food, I wake up every day in a little house on the side of a mountain with my husband and our children. It's the life I set out to achieve here, and it means a lot to me. Seeing you just reminds me of the terrible parts. So, you know, all that to say, even with the forgiveness, I'd be a lot happier if you'd just go away."

I'm crying now, but she can't see it because she's already gone, walking past me towards the kitchen door. I want to call after her, to apologize again, but what's the point? It would feel better to express it again, and again, and perhaps again after that, but for her, the transaction is done. I don't even want to ask her about the *wāpuro* or the book or any of it. I never meant to hurt Babette; I only needed to leave Japan, to forget. I could have called. Written. Something. Instead, I did nothing.

I can't face going back inside the restaurant. I walk around the side, past a rusty barrel, some plastic beer crates filled with empty bottles, and a cardboard box overflowing with slimy brown vegetable matter. In front of Hisoka Soba-ya, there's nowhere to go, and Reiko's car is locked, so I can't even hide away and finish my cry. I go to a corner of the parking lot and find a stone just about the size of my rear, which I plant there. Rear on stone, elbows on knees, chin in hand, I shudder with tears, shaken out by the force of a realization that has come decades too late.

A few minutes later, Toby emerges from the front door. He overcompensates in his stoop as he does so. As he always did. He is a redwood in a country built for maples. Reiko follows behind. They both approach me with something like caution.

"Hey," he says.

"Hey."

"Are you okay?" Rei-chan asks.

"I've been better. Sorry I skipped out on the bill."

No one knows what to say, now, so no one really says anything. It seems insane, to have come this far for what we need and then just skip out because she hates me. Maybe with time? Maybe with another day or something? But, okay. No.

The door to the restaurant slides open, and Shinji steps out, his apron immediately caught by the breeze. He looks over his shoulder once and then jogs across the parking area towards us.

"Kawa-chan," he says. It is, impossibly, the first time we have ever spoken.

"Hi, Shinji. Good to see you."

Shinji nods. I have no idea if he speaks English; Babette was fluent in Japanese, even in those long-ago days of J.J.'s. I speak to him in English anyway, because I don't have the energy to do otherwise.

"I'm sorry to upset her, Shinji. I didn't know she was so mad at me. I didn't know I hurt her feelings so bad."

Shinji nods again, a kind of sadness in his eyes. When he speaks, his uncertainty in my tongue makes some of his statements sound like questions. "Back then? At J.J. Back there, she still loves you."

"Oh, Shinji." I hope I don't start crying again, because in reality I'm not sure how a Japanese guy is going to deal with a strange foreigner blubbering in front of him. I stifle a sob into a kind of hitching snort and clear my throat.

"*Dōmo,* Shinji-san."

"You're welcome," he replies.

Reiko's car chirps like a robot chickadee as she unlocks it. Toby and I walk towards it, but Reiko shouts for Shinji, crosses to him, and takes him by the elbow—a very un-Japanese gesture, it seems to me. I slump into the back seat, shuffle across it, and lean my head on the window on the far side. Toby makes to climb in beside me but thinks better of it; he slips into the passenger seat wordlessly. A moment later, Reiko arrives. Her eyes disappear into her face as she grins that face-consuming grin of hers. "I have good news."

"Good news," I repeat.

"Yes!" Reiko's eyes widen like she's about to tell us an unbelievable tale. "Shinji feels bad about Babette. He says she still has a lot of anger, and he is a good guy, loyal, he doesn't ask questions. He can only agree and help her to feel better."

"Good husband."

"But also a good guy," Reiko says. "Because I told him, Kawa-chan is sad, maybe you can help us. We are trying to find out what happened to things after she left."

I sit up and stare at her.

"He said after you were gone, everything just stayed there, in your room. Then one day two men came. They said they were police, but Babette knew they weren't. She argued with them, but Shinji let them in. They left with some of your notebooks, some papers off your dresser, and then...."

"The *wāpuro*." I inhale and hold my breath.

Reiko nods. "Babette tried to stop them, but Shinji said to let them."

"Who were they? What did they want?"

"He says they did not say, but he knew. It was people looking for Toby."

The colour in Toby's face seems to retreat.

"Then we know what happened to your *wāpuro*," he manages, softly.

"We do?"

"Yeah," Toby says. "Takahashi."

JŌHATSU

Takahashi. He was, by all accounts, the very picture of an upstanding citizen and a gentle soul. Real bosses, they always said, were like this; it was the upstarts who were loud, boorish, and acted as though they had something to prove. No wonder we were suspicious of Kogawa.

Takahashi, however, was a phantom. I'd never heard his name connected to any real-world news. No one seemed to know what he'd done, what he did, and what, exactly, he was likely to do. We heard his name and feared it, even though he might not even exist. A fable, a cautionary warning. Sort of like a *kappa*. Or maybe more like Kaiser Soze.

The last time the name Takahashi crossed my mind, it was at the Sochi Winter Olympics. Someone on set (*Pinned II,* I believe) made a crack about the number of Russian mobsters cashing in, both legitimately and illegitimately, on the games. It reminded me that as Nagano began to swell and creak under the deluge of white faces, many businesses posted signs that specifically disavowed any connection to the mob. It seemed an odd thing to do—just how many businesses in town were connected to the *yakuza*, anyway? Why was it important we let people know we were clean? What was stopping any mob businesses from just posting the sign anyway?

And who knew people selling commemorative Olympic pins was a thing? They set up tables from the centre of downtown in a long line like dominoes laid end to end, down to the train station and through it, until the tiles spilled out onto the east side. Pin stalls were everywhere.

When we tried to go for drinks after work, bars were already swollen with customers. What a strange irony that all I could think, in the early months of 1998, was that I couldn't wait for all the foreigners to go home.

With our drinking spots crowded out by men in golf shirts and I.D. lanyards, we went out more infrequently. Toby flitted in, flitted out, but there seemed to be an unspoken moratorium on sleeping in the same bed. I wasn't interested in sex for the sake of it, either. What I really wanted was for everything to work out—to refocus his attention, to pull the spotlight back in my direction, to forget the cracks in his façade and what I'd seen through them. I wasn't equipped to break up with him. I'd never done that before.

I didn't retreat, exactly. Instead, I recommitted to other things. I went by Daniel's, goaded him to write more, watched television, and felt dismayed when he inevitably told me he wasn't ready to go back to work. I spent time with Babette. I taught Sora, took her to Obuse to eat chestnuts. On the street, on my way to the post office, looking down from my balcony window, I paid attention to the little things, made them bigger things. A frail question-mark-shaped octogenarian in an Olympics tuque, a particularly sweet chunk of *yakiniku* roast, a slant of sunlight that projected trapezoids onto my *tatami* on sunny afternoons—these moments were, if tallied, worth the price of admission. I guess I was practising mindfulness, years before I had ever heard the term.

Yet it was so easy to get bogged down by the bickering between the new staff. There seemed to be a new person every day. Easy to worry about Reiko, who seemed fed up with our *gaijin* antics and just wished we'd behave a little more Japanese. It was easy to be bummed by Daniel's health. It was definitely easy, unavoidable, in fact, to be dismayed and distressed because I knew my boyfriend was taking speed, and was probably up to some other monkeyshines in the mountains, but I was too afraid to talk to him about it. I'd never had a real boyfriend before, and it seemed easiest to believe this was all just an alcoholic Disneyland, and that eventually, the park would close, so why shouldn't I jump on another ride?

To stay on the ride, however, I needed a new ticket. My tourist visa was almost expired. Babette and I had planned a five-day run to Seoul, which, if customs didn't suspect shenanigans and deny us re-entry, would give me three more months.

Before we got on the bus to Tokyo, which was far cheaper than the shiny new *shinkansen* that cost close to $100 one-way, I called Daniel to check in. He had seemed cheery the last time I'd seen him and had even suggested he was ready to head back to work.

The phone rang seven times before there was a click.

"Hey, bud! Aren't you back today?"

"Oh." It was a distracted reply, as if he had forgotten entirely. "Yeah. Sorry, I."

Long pause.

"Daniel?"

"I'm feeling off again, Riv. Can you just tell Nax and Reiko that I can't make it? I think I'm going to have another bath and get to sleep early."

"Daniel, you'll have to do it, I'm about to hop on a bus. I'm going to Seoul, remember?"

"Oh. Yeah. Right."

"Are you—"

"I feel really terrible," he added, in a too-bright tone contradicting his words. "I'm sorry, I should have called. I just need to stay here. I'm gonna ask Nax for a few extra days off, come in again Monday. Work on the story a bit and rest. I could be done the last chapter by the next time you see me."

"Amazing!" I said, in a too-bright tone for someone who felt uneasy.

"You know what we should do to celebrate?" he asked.

"Squid pizza and beer?"

"No."

"Green tea ice cream?"

"No. We should go down into the *okaidan*." He said it with what I would describe as casual conviction. "We should do it. Face down our fears together."

"You mean, we give each other *ichiman* yen?"

"Yes." His laugh was brusque, barely a laugh at all. "I could only do it with you. It might sound weird, but I think it would be a pretty good way to celebrate. Rites and rituals."

"Rites and rituals," I agreed, though my throat clenched around the words, my emotions piqued with both worry and gratitude for his sweetness. "Okay, Daniel, we'll do it. Want me to call you from Korea?"

"Nah, I'm all right. Call me when you get back."

So Babette and I flew to Korea. We went to the opening of a dance club in Itaewon, dared one another to eat silkworms in Insadong, convinced the hesitant proprietors of a run-down corrugated-steel *makkoli* shack to let us come in to eat fish and drink Korean rice wine with old men from the neighbourhood. It was another fun adventure in a life that had become, in part, a series of small adventures strung together like popcorn on a garland. I spent the entire week pretending I wasn't worried sick about Daniel.

When we got back, I called, but got his answering machine. That wasn't surprising; it was late; I assumed he was asleep.

The next day I called and got the machine again. I thought about walking over but had to get ready for work. I'd already taken a week off; I couldn't be late on my first day back. I had just enough time to ride to Itō Yōkadō—slowly, lest icewater from the slushy sidewalks spray up my back—to buy dinner and slush my way home again. I planted my icicle butt in front of the kerosene heater briefly. Babette and I dumped the sushi I'd bought into a pan, which was likely some sort of sacrilege, but neither of us was in the mood for the flavor of raw fish and wasabi. We took the train three stops to J.J.'s so the slush wouldn't ruin our shoes. By seven, I'd shaken off my ice-incurred melancholy, and a vodka tonic helped loosen the rest. Yet as it fell from my shoulders, a fresh anxiety began to form in my stomach like a jewel. Everyone was there except Daniel.

"Where's Handler been lately?" Allie asked. "You two are still a thing, yeah?"

I put down the vodka tonic and absently adjusted my bra. "Sure," I said.

"Have you noticed he doesn't, you know, do all that Toby stuff anymore?" Nicolle noted. "The long speeches about our auras being the energy that our souls exude to draw the power of the universe into our hearts and give us power to climb to the greatest heights and commune with one another on a higher plane of existence, the way Brahma meant us to do?"

"Christ, that's…alarmingly accurate," Babette laughed.

"Yeah, he seems to have gone off that," I agreed. "Though he still says *namaste*."

"Yes, he does," Babette seconded.

"When we see him," Allie said. "He doesn't come around the same."

"No," I replied. "Of course, Babette's usually already in bed when he does come around, because she's a princess who needs her beauty sleep."

"I'm old, River."

"You're 28!"

"Whatever."

The conversation continued, though I lost track of it, as if the discussion was happening in another room. Toby was not on my mind. Daniel was.

"Hey, so, how was Daniel last week?" I asked.

Everyone raised their eyebrow or shrugged.

"He isn't back yet," Reiko said.

"What?" I sat forward and looked from one person to the next. "He hasn't come back yet? What did he say?"

Nicolle shrugged.

"You mean none of you, not one of you, bothered to check in on him?" Babette seemed as floored as I was. "Bloody hell, guys."

I picked up the telephone receiver, watched a baby cockroach dart from underneath the phone across the counter. There was still no answer. There was nothing I wanted less than to drink with strangers. I made a second call.

"*Ee, moshi moshi.*"

"Hi, Sensei, it's River. Sorry to bother you. I know I was away for a week already, but no one seems to have heard from Daniel, and I'd like to go check on him if that's okay. If he's fine, I'll come right back, I promise."

"Please," he said in his languid way. "Take care. Of him. He needs a mother, or someone like one!"

The slush had hardened into icy ruts and grooves. I made my way across Chitose Park, along the diagonal sidestreets to Chūo Dori, and up the street towards Zenkōji, hands out at waist level for balance. My feet continually slid out from under me, sideways and apart, the ground trying to split me like a wishbone.

Daniel's building was slender and neat, painted an unusual blue somewhere between Egyptian and navy. It was in the shape of something constructed from Lego bricks, his apartment at the back of the first floor.

There was no answer to my knock. The lights were on, but the curtain was drawn; through it I could only see yellow haze. I turned to knock again, and when there was still no answer, I pressed my ear against the door. I tried the handle. It was unlocked.

Everything about the apartment appeared normal. His books stood in prim rows like a reverential congregation at mass. His white sheets were pulled tight around his futon. His dishes were tucked away. His shoes were lined up at the door.

Maybe he felt so sick that he made his way to a hospital, I thought. Called an ambulance, stepped out into the street for a taxi. Maybe he'd gone down to the Lawson convenience store for some tea, some lozenges, a meal. Maybe he'd gone for a walk for no reason whatsoever; maybe his brain had begun to broil and he needed to cool it down on the dark, quiet streets by Zenkoji.

That was when I saw, on top of the *kotatsu*, the Blessèd Blue notebook. It was lined up at right angles in one corner. My heart free-fell for a moment, lost in that suspension of new information, unable to discern if this was a good or bad omen. I picked it up and opened it, flipped to the back. He had written a dozen or more new pages, and sure enough, on the last page, in his trademark scrawl, he had written in caps, THE END.

I rushed to the bathroom, wondering, almost hoping, that he had been suffering a fever or some other illness. I envisioned him slumped over the toilet bowl or unconscious in the bathtub.

I checked both rooms. I couldn't find him.

Everything after that is a blur. I couldn't shout his name; I couldn't scream. I wanted to. Tears rolled down my cheeks, and I stood in one spot, arms wrapped around myself, shaking. Where had he gone?

Instead of screaming, I left. I wanted to shout his name aloud to the streets, but the idea was ridiculous; he wasn't a dog that had broken its chain. I ran for Zenkōji, up the darkened street, the silence like a headwind, thickening the air, dissuading me, warning me. The sound of my feet pounded from the pavement below, flew into the trees, dropped like stones in front of the sleeping structures at the side of the road. Through the Niōmon gate, where the guardians tried to ward me off with their mad white stares and threatening swords. Up through the gauntlet of shops, steel doors rolled down against the night; beneath the main gate, straight up the steps to what I already knew was, at this time of day, a temple locked and darkened.

I leaned against the doors for a second, burst into tears, and stood there until the crying stopped.

I should have gone home after that, but I needed comfort. I wanted someone who would wrap their arms around me, tell me it was okay, stroke my hair. I wanted Toby, but Toby from months ago, not Toby now. Why I thought I would find a person who no longer existed was beyond me, but I went for him anyhow, back down through the gates, all the way to the Gondō, hoping that maybe, just once more, that old Toby would be there.

I thrust my extra key into the lock and bounded up the steps towards his apartment. His door was unlocked. Toby sat cross-legged on the bed, facing the window, an open bottle of Cutty Sark beside him. The slam of the door jolted him upright, as if his spine had tried to eject itself from his body but met resistance at his thick skull. Though the bed itself only shifted a little bit, the bottle toppled sideways. Whisky poured onto the mattress, and Toby didn't seem to notice, even when he turned towards me. His thigh came to rest in the puddle pooling there.

"What the hell, Riv."

Toby didn't look good.

"Sorry. Sorry. I didn't mean to startle you."

"You didn't. The whole Gondō heard you coming. You were like a stampede of horses on those stairs."

His voice sounded odd, as though someone had pitched it down a semitone or two.

"I just took a sleeping pill," he said, apparently noticing me noticing. "I'm feeling a bit drowsy."

"A sleeping pill? It's 8:30 pm. And mixing that with whisky is a terrible idea." I walked towards him and stooped to pick up the bottle, which had now deposited most of its contents deep within the bedsprings. In front of him was the toiletry kit of pill bottles.

"For God's sake, Toby, what are you doing?" I snatched away the kit as well. "I need you to focus. Something's happened to Daniel."

"What do you mean?" Suddenly, his eyes lost their watery

reflection, and his voice turned irritable, almost angry. "What do you mean something happened to Daniel?"

"I mean something's happened. He's gone. I don't know what to do."

"Oh, damn." Toby wobbled to his feet and stared out onto the nighttime Gondō, which was unnaturally quiet and still. He seemed to be scanning the empty arcade for signs of life.

"Toby, how long have you been taking these pills?"

"A while."

I'd expected him to bark at me, to tell me not to mother him, to tell me he'd needed them because of his crazy schedule, but none of that came out of him. He stood in silence.

"Toby."

"Why do you keep saying my name." It was more statement than question.

"Because you're scaring me, Toby."

"Stop saying my name!" He shouted as he turned. "Just shut up! Get out of here! I don't want you here anymore, okay?"

Tears came again, even more violently than the last time. "I need to be with someone, Toby, I need you to help me, I need—"

"Go home!" He shouted again and turned to the window. This time he leaned his forehead directly against the glass.

If I had the wherewithal, I would have questioned my reality, but instead I accepted it as if in a nightmare. Dreams where Sheila would refuse to speak to me; dreams where my father would be alive again, hurling drunken insults; dreams where human monsters chased me through ghastly galleries and displays of death. At some point, in all my nightmares, my conscious brain would stir and begin to whisper *no, these are not things that can happen. You are dreaming.*

There were no whispers now.

I thought if I reached out and touched him, maybe I could close the gap between that world and this, I could make the situation whole again, but when my hand reached his sleeve, I was suddenly afraid that touching him would make him disappear.

"Just go home," he muttered once more. He didn't seem to notice, or care, that my sobs were racking my entire body.

"Fuck you, Toby," I spat between sobs as I headed for the door.

"Stop saying my name," I heard him mumble, as the door closed behind me. I flung myself down the stairs recklessly, four at a time, and burst out onto the pale glow of the Gondō. I stopped to catch my breath but wasted it again on a primal scream cut short by an involuntary sob. My bellow streaked along the galleria, all the way to a man in a suit at the far end. He looked back over his shoulder without stopping.

COWBOY BOOTS

"What in the name of—"

"Hey, River, c'mon, let go of my sweater."

"Why on earth would Takahashi have my *wāpuro*?"

"River, just, listen, c'mon, *ow*, seriously, you're stretching the fabric."

I twist harder, as though I'm trying to heft him over the headrest and into the back seat with me. Reiko drives, quietly amused, until I smack Toby on the top of his head. The threat of actual violence causes her vertebrae to align, and she leans towards us slightly, square-shouldered.

"Kawa-chan." She says it softly, and I know she's right, so I let go, but not before I use both hands to shove him hard from behind. He bounces against the restraint of his seat belt.

The car swerves around cliffs and encircles entire mountains. I struggle to keep my mouth shut, as emotional and impetuous is not always my finest state. Impetuous, like last week, lighting out to solve a mystery in Asia on a day's notice. Emotional, like twenty years ago, lighting out for home without notice whatsoever, ignoring my responsibilities, my job, my friends.

We drive back from the country, passing by orchards, farmhouses, and—always in the distance—mountains. I look up at it all with disinterest. I fix my gaze on myself, reflected in the glass. I think back to how I pressed my face against the window and saw Sharky—Tsuchi—behind me in the reflection on that first Limited Express to Nagano.

I don't even look in the general direction of Toby or Reiko. I feel for Reiko; none of this is her fault; none of this is her business, even, and I should be nicer to her, but I can't find it within me. Not at the moment.

We glide back into central Nagano, and Reiko pulls up to the corner of India Street and the Gondō. Its shops are modest, mundane, ordinary, devoid of the promise of commercial delight and discovery. They probably never held this promise. They're just ramen shops and drugstores and karaoke bars and pachinko parlours. They're just everyday life for those who live here every day.

Reiko and Toby sit in silence as I take a moment to gather myself.

"I need some time alone." I alternate between looking at Reiko apologetically and Toby accusingly. "Meet me here at eight, when India opens. I want to talk about this, but I need a bit of time to cool down."

"*You* are going to buy me a bottle of bourbon." I thrust a forefinger at Toby. "Then you're going to make this make sense."

I exit the car and head to the hotel. Between the sets of glass doors, I pause to scrape a few yen coins off the bottom of my shoulder bag and slide them into the tobacco machine, selecting a brand named Mevius. I take the cigarettes up to my room, then notice it's a non-smoking room. I lie on the bed and stare at the ceiling, thinking of nothing, considering everything.

I am not surprised to hear a liquid slosh behind me, as though someone had tossed a water-laden mop back into the bucket.

"Not now, Soba."

"Come to tub," it hisses from around the corner.

"I am not getting off the bed to talk to myself in the bathroom," I mutter.

"Soba give you *ichiman* yen."

I wouldn't write a cliché as weak as "my blood runs cold" if it wasn't exactly what happened.

Soba sits, only the top half of his face visible over the high tub wall. His eyes are less intense than usual. Not quite a different colour, but a different vibrancy; the striking, terrifying, supernatural quality, like the eyes of a monster under the bed, is gone. His eyes seem like the eyes of an animal that has seen as much pain as the rest of us.

"What did you say?"

"River heard Soba."

"Yes, I did!" I grab the nearest item, a plastic razor off the sink, and toss it. It whizzes past Soba's ear, clicks against the wall like, well, like a cheap plastic razor, and *plooops* into the water. There are no recriminations from the creature this time. No *pfft* or *mah*. Just those sad eyes. The tension I've held in my shoulders breaks, and they slump. I slump with them against the wall, where I slide slowly to the floor and hang my head.

"Almost ready." With this less hostile tone, it could almost be the sound of a human larynx, albeit one owned by an eighty-year-old Brooklyn woman with a two-pack-a-day habit.

"For what." I don't look up at him.

"Ready to find."

"What?" A jolt of electricity hits my brain, and I look up quickly enough to pull a neck muscle. "I'll find out where the book came from?"

"Yes. You will find book. You will also find boy again."

"Dammit, Soba." I let my head loll backwards, this time with a special new pain as it strikes the cheap ceramic tile. "There's no boy to find."

"No. There has always been a boy."

"There has *always* been a *boy*?" I want to stand up and approach this thing, but I can't seem to make my legs work, so I crawl towards it like an actor in a cheesy death scene. Horror, revulsion, fear: none of these exist any longer. I have created more monstrous things, and they wear human faces. This kelp-faced little frog is not going to scare me.

"What do you mean," I ask, inches from its face, "there has always been a boy?"

Soba looks down.

"Okay. Enough of the boy, the boy, the boy. The boy you knew was named Kenichi, but we aren't talking about him, are we? No. We are talking about Daniel. Daniel Truman. From Missoula, Montana. You are saying, now, Daniel Truman exists. There is a Daniel to find."

Soba moves back ever so slightly, as if it's afraid I'm going to smack it. "There is no Daniel to find."

"Because he's dead."

"And you will find him. Very close."

"Screw you, Soba, and your Zen koans, too."

I let my chin sink to my chest, scratch the top of my neck at the hairline. I don't know what kind of hallucinatory revelations Soba promises me. I don't understand.

Soba blinks at me. There is a watery shimmer in its eyes.

"You will find book now," it says. Its expression is one of someone giving you bad news. "But book not matter. Find boy and be finished."

With that, it disappears downward with a soft splash.

Standing above the bath, I have a brief but vivid flashback to that film scene, that corpse in the bathtub. I imagine the brownish-red slush on the water, the body bloated and water-logged, and despite my usual detachment from such imagery, an urge to vomit overwhelms me. I inhale slowly, clutch my stomach, and notice that the tub is actually filled with water. I don't recall having drawn a bath at all since I arrived here.

The nausea subsides.

Find boy and be finished. An imperative or a prediction? But Soba can't predict the future, because Soba is only me, and I am not a soothsayer.

I return to my position on the matchbox-sized bed, where I spot a rippled beige-and-brown ring on the ceiling, suggesting the room has not always been designated non-smoking. I doze, perhaps, though it's one of those naps that merely flicks the hands of the clock ahead a few minutes and provides no rest.

My phone dings. It's a text from Reiko.

R U OK. COMING TO INDIA NOW.

Eventually I head for the elevator, stroll past the middle-aged man at the desk, and head next door.

The bar is empty, so I head for "our" old table, beside the batwing doors that lead to the bathrooms. Master-san is still not here; the bartender is the same woman from before. She brings me my bottle of bourbon. My name is scrawled in pen on the label.

川

The door opens and Reiko comes in. She grins and waves at me, though it's one of those weird sad grins that says "Hiiiiiii, how are you feeeeeeeling?"

Reiko slides a chair out and sits.

"So, just so I'm clear," I say. "All we have to do is find the head of the city's biggest crime syndicate, and we should be golden."

"I think he is retired."

"That does not make it easier."

"I think maybe Toby can help," she replies. Toby. I stare upward at the pair of cowboy boots suspended from the ceiling. Reiko follows my gaze. They're soft leather, a medium brown. Tentative-looking Japanese characters have been scrawled down the sides of them.

"Oh. My. God. The boots are still here."

"Yeah." Just like everything else. I am still here, in this place that is the same and almost not the same at all. We sit in silence, the sound of Quicksilver Messenger Service, thick with dusty pops and snaps, filling the unused space.

A few minutes later, the door pulls wide, and there is the length of Toby, all legs and torso. He stoops to peer through, spots us, and passes beneath the doorjamb. He remains bent at the neck, head low, as the various decorative items dangling from chains or mounted to posts present a concussion risk to someone his height. He eyes me warily. I look away, study the boots that dangle above.

"Sit," I say, and he does. He tries to fold his praying-mantis appendages into as small a space as possible and fidgets. His hand reaches out for a peanut from the snack tray.

"Why would Takahashi have my stuff?" I ask, if only to interrupt his annoying jittery movements.

"I don't know." He runs a hand from the back of his neck, over his face, to his chin. I want to scream at him but somehow lack the will. We sit in silence until he gathers his thoughts. His hand returns to the back of his neck and pats it gently, as if checking the severity of a sunburn.

"So maybe try this one, then. Why was Takahashi in my apartment looking for clues to your whereabouts?"

Toby doesn't answer right away. He waves over the Mamasan, orders a bottle of Jim Beam, ice, and water. When it arrives, he places the glass in front of himself, adds two ice cubes from the hotel-style ice bucket, and pours the water from a dented bronze urn. He places it in front of me like an accomplished hostess.

"I really did come here to build cabins," he begins.

"Oh, Jesus, this is going to be full-on biography, isn't it?

Toby doesn't respond. His face is pointed squarely at the tray of *sembe* snacks on the centre of the table.

"My friend Robbie did it the year before," he continues. "Came here, lived in Nagano, went up to the mountains every day to build. Told me it was amazing pay, physically intensive work but not difficult. I thought okay, that sounds good. I'd been…floundering, let's say. MLM schemes, selling weed. Not really a lot of forward motion down the career track. Halifax was just finished for me. For years I'd been the life of the party, the wise life guru, dispensing the advice, preaching the gospel, all the stuff you remember. But the show was finite. There was a running time. Mine was up."

I am not surprised by this admission.

"Turned out, though, cabin construction was difficult work," he continues. "Robbie told me you didn't need experience, but without it and without Japanese, it was just frustration for me and everyone else. Robbie hadn't mentioned the sixteen months he'd spent teaching at an English school in Saitama or the Japanese classes he took every Saturday morning. I ended up working long days and weekends to make up for it. After a while, I decided the best way to keep up with the pace was to start doing drugs."

"Toby!" Reiko looks alarmed. "Okay, I don't want to be rude, but that was sooooo stuuuupid."

"I know." Toby pours a mouthful of bourbon into another glass, skipping the ice-and-water ritual. He takes a pull, grimaces, and adds water to his glass. "I know. The penalties for that kind of thing are bananas here. I could have gone to jail for a very long time. When I asked around for the most trustworthy source, and by asked around I mean asked the two guys on my shift who were already using speed, they referred me to dudes who were supposedly involved with Takahashi."

"So, you bought drugs from the head of the Nagano mafia," I say.

"Oh, Christ, no." Toby laughs. "No, I would see him on the Gondō when I was busking. One of my work buddies pointed him out. I'm sure someone told him about me, though. I was memorable."

"A seven-foot white dude," I say.

"Are you really seven feet tall?" Reiko asks.

"No, Reiko, River's just being facetious."

"What does that word mean?"

"It means she's being mean. Anyway, my idiocy prevailed and I got into debt with these guys. That's where Kogawa comes in. Kogawa was basically just this shifty businessman that no one liked. He'd been wanting to suck up to Takahashi for years, but Takahashi knew Kogawa was a loud, bullying unpleasant experience of a man.

"Back then, Kogawa's entrepreneurial endeavors included co-owning a small *izakaya* restaurant," Toby continues. "He was a blowhard, but for me, he was also a mark. I'd eat my rice bowls and nod while he railed on about this and that. I don't even know what he said; he mostly spoke Japanese, even though I'd told him a dozen times that I couldn't speak Japanese. He thought I was a good guy just because I agreed with him on everything. I waited until I was sure he liked me, and then I told him I needed some money—I was in heavy with these criminal cats, and if he'd only loan me the money this one time, I could arrange for him to meet Takahashi. As he wanted to do. He fell for it. I took the money and then never ate another rice bowl in his presence again."

Toby takes one of the spicy soy snacks, the little ones that look like tiny dried seed pods, and proceeds to hold it between his thumb and forefinger, tapping it on the table. "Of course, I was too stupid to just pay off my dealer and quit the drugs. No, I had to pay off my dealer, and then go right back into debt with him. By this time, I could barely wake up in the morning without those pills—if I could sleep in the first place. Hiding it from you was tricky, but then we started to drift apart, and it became a lot easier."

Reiko leans forward and raises her eyebrows. "This explains a lot of you, Toby."

I lean back. "I'll say."

"How did you get away from the *yakuza*?" Reiko asks.

"I just left." Toby's eyes find the edge of the table and stay there, flitting along its edge. "I just went *jōhatsu*."

"Yes," I agree. "You evaporated. Gone. Thanks for the forwarding address. You were such a..."

And I stop, because I realize, I'm talking about myself, too.

RIVER LEAVES TOWN

I don't remember everything that led to my evaporation. There's no timeline, no sense of sequence, only one memory laid on top of another on top of another. I can pull them out, isolate them, recall one at a time, but have no idea where to put them back in the stack. It doesn't really matter, in the end. It began with crying at the temple; it ended with an airplane.

Scene: Distraught young woman wakes up after a fitful sleep, wants to know what happened to Daniel, is afraid, confused, uncertain where she is.

Montage: There are police. There are questions that don't really make any sense, questions about water, questions about death, questions about places. There are weird offhand remarks from detectives that she doesn't quite understand, but they anger her roommate so much that she actually tells them to *bakayarō* and spends at least fifteen minutes holding a trembling River and stroking her hair, the way Sheila used to when River was a young and frightened girl. The roommate makes miso soup. She lets River rail and moan.

Cut to: a morning. A morning when suddenly, it is all made clear; the haze disperses, the lens focuses on the boy, found in the water, his heart stopped.

Throughout, there are blurry, poorly-lit sequences, indistinct and ill-framed, like something out of an Evrard Frederich film. The cold blue air of the police station, the late nights at the *wāpuro,* first transcribing the blue notebook, then editing—fleshing out sentences, rethinking word choices, delving as deeply as possible into the river of text where I could neither see nor be seen. It was, I think, my way of dealing with all of it, finding those brief stretches of time where I could be with him again. I also wanted to do it for Sora, because Sora needed to know the rest of the story. I did not see Sora, though. I remember I called her father on one of the blurry nights, that first night or that last night or any one in-between, to explain that Sora's lessons were over until I could manage again.

No. No, that's not true. I remember, now, for reasons I cannot explain, that I spoke to him the night before they found Daniel in the canal. This...this seems right. Yes. Details like this float freely around my brain, yet the core memory is solid. It's as though I'd spent an hour in front of a remarkable work of art. The details of the painting— brush strokes, exact shades, expressions on faces—were gone, but the impression never dimmed. I remember confusion, sadness, anxiety, and, for the first time since the Limited Express had burrowed through mountains and deposited me here, a sense of unwelcome enclosure. A sense of claustrophobia.

I returned to Toby's apartment. My anger with him was a separate fire that had crept along the block and fused with the raging blaze of my grief. I went back to find his pills spilled on the *tatami.* The top dresser drawer, where he kept his driver's license, bank card, immigrant card, and passport, sat open. I didn't need to look inside. Toby had fled. Toby had taken the final step in his abandonment of me, which had started many months before. It wasn't until my shock over Daniel began to subside that my rage at Toby surfaced, coming from the same scorched region of my soul.

No one expected me to work. I couldn't make small talk and drink with customers. Instead, I drank alone or with a chaperone. Nicolle and Allie were down the hall, Babette in her room, one ear tilted towards me, listening for whimpers, listening for sniffles, listening for tears.

The only time I could focus and feel calm was in the glue, the glue of words, words that held my mind when it wanted to unravel or ignite. Words, a glue that held my friendship with Daniel intact in some ways. We were friends, but the bond, the creative bond, was what really cemented that friendship. I transcribed page after page, stopping at the end of each section to return to the beginning of it and edit, to chip and chisel, to flatten and smooth. I typed and wrote and read. Read about a boy who tumbles backwards over the shell of a *kappa*. He saves the *kappa* by replenishing its water, by feeding it cucumbers. He begins to lose hope—when the girl enters his life.

While I was in Korea, Daniel had finished the story. In the conclusion, the boy becomes convinced that Soba will kill his new friend, so he tells her to go away and never come back. She is confused and upset. After a few more weeks of misery and loneliness, Kenichi finally decides he has to undo what he did. He has to kill the river god.

"Can't kill," it spat. "Kill me, kill yourself. One and same."

"Well, then," Kenichi said as he stepped forward. "Maybe it's time for both of us to die."

Kenichi leapt towards Soba and whacked the back of its knees with a stout stick. The *kappa*, startled, tumbled backwards, shell banging against the steps. The *kappa* rolled off the step and onto the ground. Water splashed like blood against the snow. Soba reached for the water bottle Kenichi had strung around his neck, but the boy yanked the bottle away.

Kenichi stepped back from the *kappa*, which lay thrashing and spasming in the white, its face a grimace of fear and pain. It threw its head back, knotty neck twisting back and forth, its face pained, its breath beginning to hitch in its chest.

"Mi," it gargled. "Mi!"

"No more water," the boy said. "No more cucumbers. Let it be done, then."

The creature began to stiffen, but as it did so, Kenichi felt his own muscles spasm one limb at a time. A great thirst filled him, and he felt weak, suddenly exhausted. The truth of what lay before him settled into his heart.

"Ah," it said, eyes rolled upward. "Ah."

"I'm sorry, Soba." Kenichi felt the need to rest. He knelt beside the dying creature and felt a surprising sadness at the end of their coexistence.

"Ah," it replied, making the smallest motion with its finger. The boy came closer. It spoke, almost inaudibly, with an otherworldly croak.

"Touch."

It opened its hand and, with what seemed to be a last reserve of strength, held the hand towards the boy. He took the *kappa*'s hand and closed his eyes.

There, in the darkness of his mind, he could see what appeared to be a distant galaxy, a jumble of light. As it drew closer he could see the lights were stones, not black and white stones but stones of all colours, stones made of light, countless combinations, countless reflections. The stones trailed tails that grew brighter as they crossed one another. From this asymmetrical yet perfect confusion of incandescence a pulse seemed to emerge, a rhythm that rose higher as the stones turned to flashes that popped and crackled, each a number, each a combination of numbers, each infinite, and the boy felt as though he was propelled through them, down a tunnel through a mountain of impossible immensity, and he could not understand the tunnel or the light but absolutely understood its vastness, its immeasurability, and in this space between beasts and beings, he held tighter to the *kappa*'s hand, exhilarated. He felt as though he understood it all, and he felt as though he understood nothing. His pulse quickened until finally it stopped and his heart burst into his veins, filling his body with heat and wonder.

Later that day, a young girl passed beneath the old *torii* gates. Sakura, looking for answers, wanted to know why Kenichi had been so mean to her, had ended their friendship. Yet on this snowy day, she discovered Kenichi was not there. She saw only a blackish, brackish outline on the crystalline white snow.

And that was how it ended. A vision of infinity, and an evaporation. Just like Daniel. Like Toby.

Was there anything else I could do but follow?

I tapped out the final words, THE END, and printed the remaining few pages. Then I took them and added them to the manuscript, completed the book, but instead of delivering them to Sora, I threw them in a trash can and lit them on fire when everyone else was at work. A moment later, I fuelled the fire with the edit notes. I burned it all, made it evaporate into the air. My version wasn't Daniel's version. Daniel was gone. This book, this blue notebook, was the last of Daniel—his true, authentic, unpolluted spirit, his words, not his bastardized by my own edits. I burned every edited page that I had touched, packed a suitcase as full as I could, and called Masa.

Masa tried to talk me out of it, but seeing there was no dissuading me, he drove me to the train station. He promised to explain to Nax that I was sorry, that I couldn't be here any longer. I remember floating into Narita on a dark cloud of doom, so late for my flight that they stuck on my arm a big purple sticker in the shape of a cartoon airplane. A sticker that screamed *make way for this foreign idiot!* A JAL staffer ran ahead of me, her legs shuffling in her narrow skirt like she was in a kimono. I remember thinking *that is not a uniform intended for jogging.* She led me to the ramp; I got on the plane, swallowed some sleeping pills I'd liberated from Toby's apartment, and was gone.

Evaporated.

Jōhatsu.

TAKAHASHI

I went *jōhatsu* on everyone. I hurt people.

It's not fair. I lost my friend, I lost my boyfriend, I lost a new life that I loved. I'm supposed to be the victim in all this, not just another selfish perpetrator. But there it is.

I've missed whatever Reiko and Toby are talking about. "I wasn't exactly a priority," he is saying. "I've been back in Nagano for years now, and no one's even blinked at me."

Apparently, they talking about whether or not the mob has come after him since he returned.

"They certainly recognize you," I say. "You're a like an Aryan Ent."

"Yes."

"Like a lemon on the end of a yardstick."

"Sure."

"Like Big Bird after a long struggle with a horrible disease."

"Great, River, thanks. We get it."

All I want to do is give Toby grief. I want to return him to the role of villain in my story.

"Maybe he's biding his time." I say, just to mess with Toby. "Maybe Takahashi knows you're here indefinitely, and he wants you to be nice and comfortable before he comes for your thumbs."

"Kawa-chan!"

I grin at Reiko. I don't care if I'm being mean. Toby is my villain. It just feels right. To see him visibly blanch makes me smile like a cartoon shark. Anger roils up my esophagus like magma from the centre of the earth, and it won't be swallowed back down. I have to let the steam escape through cracks, or the whole thing's going Vesuvius.

"Maybe they won't do that," I sneer. "Maybe it'll just be a mild beating and then they'll send you on your way with your tail between your legs."

Toby doesn't look at me. He simply stands up. His calves slide the chair backward, a chalky scrape across the floor.

"It's not funny." His voice is not upset, but rather flat, emotionless. He walks for the door, ducks as he pushes.

"River." It's the first time I've heard Reiko use my English name in decades. "Why are you being like this?"

I sigh.

"Sorry, Rei-chan. I know. I know. I'm just...it's hard to... let me go apologize."

I clamber over several chairs, leaving poor Reiko on her own. I open the door to see Toby halfway along India Street towards the Two Horses Boning Store. Which is now a café, the *in flagrante delicto* horses replaced by watercolour orchids.

"Toby!" I call out. "I'm sorry, okay? And I'm wrong. I'm sure no one gives a damn about you."

"Oh, thanks," he calls over his shoulder. "That's much better."

"Toby, I know, you're trying to help me and I'm being an asshole. I'd walk away from me, too. But come on, I'm apologizing here."

He refuses to answer me, just keeps walking. His stride is twice the length of mine; I start to jog.

"Come on, Handler! I'm sorry!" All the rage has diffused again, morphed into something else. I'm starting to feel untethered.

Toby wheels around, walking backward now, finally shouting back.

"I'm sorry I left you, okay?" There is a quiver in his bottom lip that doesn't suggest tears so much as a lifetime of regret resurfacing. "I was a wreck, and I'm sorry you were sucked into that, but it's not my fault Daniel died. It's not your fault Daniel died. It's not Babette's fault Daniel died. It's not even Kogawa's fault that Daniel died. He died, you found him, it was an absolute mess—"

"What do you mean, I found him?" I scream. I feel as though the sky has darkened and the earth has folded up around me in an attempt to snuff me out like a candle flame. Toby stares at me as if I've lost my mind. I fly at him, my fists smashing into his chest and neck as he tries to ward me off. Inside me, though, the magma spreads, threatens to take all of me, threatens to stop surging up my throat but instead to explode sideways, engulfing my lungs, vaporizing my heart. I swing and punch and think *this is no one's fault but my own.*

Suddenly, there is someone behind me, a muscular, barrel-shaped chest pressing into my back. Ropy-muscled arms snake under mine and pull me into a full nelson. I see Toby now, almost sprinting, loping like a drunken gazelle, with a dark figure behind him, trying in vain to catch up. Then another shadow appears from out of nowhere, fast enough to catch Toby off guard; Toby dekes to his left, only to have his hip connect with the guardrail. I see him stumble, topple, and fall over the railing and into the miniature river below; beneath the rush of blood through my ears, I hear the splash.

Someone mutters in my ear in Japanese. *Please be quiet,* he is saying, *you are disturbing the neighbours.* The dark shadows ahead are now in focus: two middle-aged men in dark suits. They have created a two-link human chain, one gripping the handrail, the other extending his arm down into the gulley. Together they hoist and grunt until Toby's head appears, blond locks plastered to his water-slicked face. He looks at me sheepishly a second before the two men each grab an arm and help him, then one another, back over the rail and onto the road.

Toby stands, his sweater dripping onto his shoes. He looks like a crane or some other kind of spindly waterfowl, something that dove for dinner and came up empty. Sad, embarrassed, and agitated. Someone's cell phone rings, a muffled tinkle of bells; one of the dark-suited men answers, listens intently, says *hai* several times, and hangs up. His suit is a dark grey, mottled, obviously bespoke, as it seems to move with him like a second skin.

"Sorry for what happened to your friend." He speaks to me in a slow, foreigner-friendly Japanese. "*Shatchō* would like to invite you to come see him, Miss Black. He says he can give your friend some dry clothes."

He knows my name. I glance at Toby. He doesn't look cold or embarrassed now, merely stricken with panic.

"*Shatchō* heard your voice from over there," explains the bespoke-suited man. He points to a high wall on the other side of the *dobugawa,* over which we can see a light in a window. A shadow within raises a hand, a near-motionless but nevertheless friendly wave. I bow towards the figure and turn back to the bespoked one.

"Who is your *shatchō*?"

The man smiles. "He wants it to be a surprise."

Toby shakes his head.

"Toby, it's someone we know."

"No," Toby says as his head continues to pivot from side to side. "No, it's not someone you know. It's someone I know. It's Takahashi."

"So why do they know my name? Why are they talking to me instead of you?"

Toby shrugs.

"A few minutes ago, I was taunting you about the mob, and apparently I taunted loudly enough to attract the attention of the actual goddamn mob. You have to admit, it's kind of amazing."

"Amazing," Toby whispers. "Sure, yeah, what a wonderful irony."

"More like remarkable poetic justice, no?"

The men walk around the corner with us, back past the former sexy-stallion shop, through a parking lot, and up the street to a gated yard. We walk through the gate beneath dark Japanese maples that block out the stars above. I have passed this place hundreds of times, probably passed it a dozen times this week alone. I always assumed it was a temple, with its solemn wooden structure hidden by trees and stone walls.

Inside one of the men huffs *kutsu o noide*—"take off your shoes." As if this is our first rodeo. I kick off my shoes, don the slippers that lie on the step, and we continue down a hallway. There is nothing on the white walls other than a row of windows that look out on the front yard. There is no sound other than pillowy footsteps and breathing. We come to a stop as Mr. Bespoke slides a *shoji* open. The man gestures for me to enter, but the others continue forward with Toby, presumably for the aforementioned change of clothes.

It is a 16- or 18-mat room, which for a downtown Nagano home seems absurdly spacious. The white negative space gives the room a Kubrickian quality, had Kubrick been Japanese. White walls and white *shoji* and only the slightest hint of décor—a scroll of calligraphy, a delicate *ikebana* arrangement in a slim blue vase atop a slim black pedestal. A legless chair rests behind a low table. In film and video games, the *yakuza* lair always has a red rug, a massive ceremonial sword, and maybe a dragon serving tea to a gaggle of geisha or some ninjas playing mah-jongg. Here, in corporeal reality, there is only a horizon of white, softly reflecting the yellow glow of several traditional-style lamps.

The man behind the desk appears, at first, to be stooped, as if he's suffering osteoporosis from working in rice fields. Then I realize he's just leaning forward, texting. Once he is finished, he rises to full height, shoulders pinned back, chin aloft, eyes focused. He must be seventy, but maybe he's sixty or eighty. When his eyes pan sideways and catch me in their lenses, the unexpected happens: his face expands with glee.

His eyebrows raise and a clipped *ah* escapes his throat.

"Kawa-chan," he says, and my heart stops.

"*Hai*," I reply, though I know I should use more formal language. Formal Japanese, however, is immediately lost to me, as if my shock has dropped it through a trap door. I know, instinctively, that I'm looking at four people at once. I'm looking at Takahashi; I'm looking at Tsuchi. I'm looking at Sharky.

Jesus Christ, I'm looking at Sora's father.

The light quickens, as if the chemical composition of the atmosphere has changed. The room itself seems to quicken, too, as if objects in the room instantaneously gain mass, more presence. Time doesn't stop, but my brain stays in that pocket of consciousness, lags behind the real world just a moment.

Sora's father is Takahashi. The man whose name was spoken with hushed, reverential fear, whose name hinted at menace and mystery, whose presence was felt but whose face was never seen…and who took me out for ice cream.

The look on his face can only be described as delight.

Takahashi's stride is sure-footed; he doesn't seem sixty now, but forty, as he crosses from behind the desk and stands in front of me and—sweet mother of all that is holy—he bows. Deeply. I bow in return.

"*O-hisashiburi desu ne*," I mutter.

Takahashi's eyes flicker and his temples spiderweb as he laughs, an affectionate laugh, the laugh you would use when a child says something cute but incorrect.

"*O-hisashiburi desu yo!*" His eyes are as rich and otherworldly as they always have been. "Kawa-chan, I wasn't sure you would remember me. We met on a train."

"I remember," I reply. "And then at the competition. Sora won. We ate ice cream together twenty years ago. You remember me."

Takahashi nods.

"Sora told me her surname was Noguchi," I say. "That's not your name, though, is it?"

"She has her mother's name," he replies.

Safer for her not to share the name Takahashi, most likely.

"Even if you hadn't become my daughter's *sensei*, you would be difficult to forget," Takahashi continues. "A young *gaikokujin* on a train tells me she has come to my country to escape her father's ghost! I never forgot that. Actually, I think of you quite often."

That's a weird thing to say.

The door slides open, and I glance over my shoulder. Toby is barefoot, clad only in a bright-blue *yukata*. It is, however, a *yukata* made for a regular Japanese person; on Toby, it stops just short of his knees, like a miniskirt. His hair clings to his forehead like seaweed. The moment he sees me, humiliation mushrooms across his face.

If Takahashi recognizes Toby, that recognition does not spread to the old man's face. We haven't been left alone; the lieutenants are still behind us, and while they seem unarmed, their presence is foreboding. Mind you, Takahashi could force any other personality out of a room with just his smile and a nod. His charisma has not diminished.

"This is unbelievable." Takahashi shakes his head. "I know your former boss passed away—my condolences—so you've been on my mind this week. When I heard your voice outside the window, I thought my mind was playing tricks on me, or I'd fallen asleep and was having a dream. Then I looked out the window and there you were in the streetlight! I sent Ikeda-san over to greet you, but then there was screaming and hitting, and a few of my other associates decided to investigate. I hope they didn't scare you."

"I was a bit nervous," I say. "This one, on the other hand, tried to swim to safety."

This makes Takahashi laugh. "He spun in circles and fell into the water! It was like a comedy routine."

Toby doesn't find it comedic. He swallows hard, gulping like a cartoon character.

"You remember me, Takahashi-san?" he asks.

Takahashi, a half-smile on his serene face, barely raises his eyebrows.

"You are the tall boy I used to see with Kawa-chan," Takahashi replies. "You used to play guitar on the Gondō."

"My name's Tobias Handler. I used to—"

I glare at Toby. It is clear that Takahashi remembers Toby, but not whatever infraction Toby committed. Toby reads my glare to mean "shut up," which is accurate.

Most of my unease has dissipated, fallen away like marbles through holes in my pockets. I almost feel relaxed by his sonorous voice and the lamplight that expands gently across the enormous room.

"You are an excellent writer, Kawa-chan."

This I did not expect.

"You...you've seen my movies, then," I stammer.

"Evrard Frederich?" It's a name full of letters that should throttle a Japanese tongue, but Takahashi says it effortlessly. "No! I do not like, what is the term in English...torture porn? He is a terrible filmmaker. Sorry."

"No, no. He *is* a terrible filmmaker. Just the worst, really."

"I understand why you left him. He pretends to be a tough guy. Every day, for much of my career, I was surrounded by men pretending to be tough guys. They are filled with bad ideas about what makes them men. But no. *Pinned*, I think the idea is interesting. But I think your idea was ruined by him. The murderer should realize his mistake and then die at the end of the first film. But if he dies—"

"—there are no sequels," we say in unison.

I laugh at the absurdity. "You must read a lot of horror movie blogs," I joke.

He laughs again, a rich, generous laugh. "Oh no. I hear about you from Sora."

"Sora." Hearing her name aloud causes a sudden tension that pulls at my esophagus. I recognize this as the sensation of guilt.

"She follows your career very closely."

"And how is Sora-chan?"

"Sora is excellent. She has grown up to be beautiful and brilliant. She is finishing her Ph.D. at the Chan School of Public Health. Harvard."

"That's...that's wonderful."

"You must contact her and say hello."

"I...I will, of course, but..." I look down at the straw mat below me. "I...I don't know if she'd want to hear from me. I didn't mean to disappear on her. I didn't mean to disappoint her, to disappoint you both. I was young and upset and—"

"No apology needed," Takahashi's grin softens into a sympathetic smile. "Without you, Sora might not have learned English well enough to attend Harvard. As for disappointing her, well, yes, you did. Sora was very sad, which was upsetting, but you were young. I was surprised you stayed in Nagano as long as you did. *Gaijin* come and go, English teachers come and go. Sora has only fond memories of you. She was very excited when you began to write films. She even has one of your earliest stories."

I knit my brows and lift my head to indicate a lack of understanding.

"The boy and the monster. She has a copy of *Kenichi and the Kappa*."

Toby turns to me in utter disbelief, but I barely notice. I'm too busy falling backward. Takahashi's smile falters a moment, and I realize it's concern—he thinks I might actually swoon. I close my eyes and focus my balance until I can open them again.

"You sent people to my old apartment," I say. "They took my *wāpuro*."

"That was wrong." Takahashi turns and begins to pace smoothly across the floor. "I should not have done that. But I would do anything for Sora. As I said, she was very sad. She told me about the story. She wanted to finish reading it, to find out how it ended. So I sent some associates to your apartment. Your roommate and her boyfriend were there.

My employees may or may not have claimed to be police looking for clues."

"Clues to what?"

"Where this one went." Takahashi gestures vaguely in Toby's direction. "You called me, and you told me he had gone missing, remember? It seemed like a good cover story. I don't think your roommate believed a word of it."

Takahashi chuckles to himself. "I'm sorry, I crossed a line. I never should have gone looking for *Kenichi and the Kappa*, or stolen your *wāpuro* to find it."

I am not sure what to think. Should I be furious that the man lied, stole my property, invaded my privacy? Probably. But what did it matter? He'd known, probably more than I had, that I would never be back. I'd left my life behind, a newspaper forgotten on a park bench.

"Sora loved the end of this story," Takahashi says. "It was a fun story for a child, especially. I remembered that Sora would come home from lessons and tell me about it."

"With all due respect, Takahashi-san, there's a dead kid and a slow, painful torture in there."

"Folk stories are always grim. Nothing in your story is as gruesome as Hansel and Gretel."

"True."

"I took your words from the *wāpuro* and had them put into a book," Takahashi says. "I told her it was a present from you. She knows now that isn't true, though."

I flip the flap of my satchel. Behind me one of the associates starts to protest, but Takahashi furrows his brow and shakes his head at him. I wonder if I almost got shot just now. *Jesus God, no sudden moves, River.*

"Did she send me this?" I hold it out towards him, with two hands and a polite bow. The smile on his face shoots out electricity like a Tesla coil. It touches everything in the room. Even Toby manages a slight grin. I bet even the bozos in the shiny suits are enchanted.

Takahashi takes the book with both hands and a bow

of his own. I have never been treated as graciously as I am being treated by this man, who no doubt has ruined lives, severed body parts, or at least ordered body parts to be severed. Ugh, my imagination and Miike Takashi films are a bad combination. Still, it's like staring into the face of a character I would invent.

"It went into the world," I say. "It found me, and it brought me back." My knee joints begin to fill with jelly, a gelatinous goop like pummeled pork fat, and suddenly it takes concentrated effort to stand without trembling. "I bring it back to you, and you can return it to Sora-san."

"I don't know what you mean." Takahashi eyes the cover. "You had it published? Sora didn't know you had this published."

"This...this isn't Sora's book?" For what feels like the thousandth time this hour, I'm confused and vertiginous.

"No." He frowns at the *kappa* on the cover, who looks back at him.

"It was sent to me a few weeks ago, postmarked Nagano—" Then it hits me. My emotions are a murmuration of starlings, a flutter and swoop that changes direction abruptly. "—But she's still in America, isn't she?"

"Yes." He opens the front cover, peers at the title page. "Even so. All I did was print your story and put it in a binder. This is a published book. You don't know where it came from?"

My ankles and hips are jellying up, too. My lower jaw begins to quiver as I talk. "This story, Takahashi-san. These words are mine, but the story, that belonged to someone else, someone I knew and loved very much. The boy who died. He told me this story, and I wrote it down, and then he died. I came to Nagano to pay my respects to Nakadaira-sensei and to find out where the book came from. I wanted to know why it was sent to me, and I wanted to find Daniel."

It's the second time I've said that out loud. I don't know what part of my mind it comes from.

"But you did find him." Takahashi returns the book to me. I take it in my left hand, which now begins to tremble. "You called me and told me all about it. Don't you remember? I suppose maybe you don't. You were very upset. Hess…hiss…"

"Hysterical?" offers Toby, but Takahashi ignores him.

"I don't know what you're talking about," I whisper.

"Yes, you do." Takahashi's face is angled towards the book, but his eyes are tilted upward towards mine, as though he were talking to a waiter over top of a dinner menu. "You phoned me, very upset. You told me you would have to cancel Sora's lessons indefinitely. You told me about the boy. The more you talked, the more upset you were. You didn't seem like you could help yourself. It seemed like you needed to talk to someone, to tell someone what happened, and you chose me. This is what I assumed. You first told me that he was found outside, but then as you started to cry, you told me that when you arrived, you found his story on the table and the bathroom door closed—"

"No."

"and when you opened it, you said you couldn't—"

"What are you talking about?!" It's a shout smothered by a sob. It's the sound of fear, exhaustion, and globules of phlegm. It doesn't seem to come from my own larynx. Toby jumps at the sound of it, but Takahashi merely approaches me, holds the book in one hand, and places the other gently on my shoulder. I swing my arms wildly to shake it away. I lose my balance, my head turns to air, and I drop to my knees before I can fall. Black tunnels begin to close around my line of vision, and I am afraid I will faint. I am afraid I will scream. I am afraid I will remember.

RIVER FIND

When really, I've never forgotten.

There are always monsters. Not zombies, or *kappa*, or *kaiju*. Monsters more sinister, monsters more unknowable, beasts banished to the ocean floor or beneath the bulk of mountains, dead memories that lie dreaming until something shakes them awake, the reek of their breath like decay and flowers.

There is no answer at his apartment. The lights are on, but the curtain is pulled over the window. Everything about the apartment appears normal. His books stand in prim rows like a reverential congregation at mass. His white sheets are pulled tight around his futon. His dishes are tucked away. His shoes are lined up at the door. The Blessèd Blue notebook is atop the *kotatsu*.

Yet nothing is normal, because there is a putrefaction in the air that I have never smelled before.

The toilet is empty, but I know the bathroom is not. Yet I open the door anyway. Yet forward I step, even as I retch at the stench that threatens to pull my insides out through my throat. Beneath this smell, a hint of kerosene. The heater had kept the room warm until the fuel tank was empty. Now a thin layer of ice has formed, and it clings to the cold edges around what remains of—no, this is not what remains, this is...

The ice on the water is a slush the colour of runny mud or watery feces, a sickening broth in which he, no, *the body* half-floats, his head, Daniel's head, pushed up and over the back of the tub, limbs and torso fat with bloat, flesh mottled like chicken skin, blackened, yet almost translucent in other places, yeilding a view of other blues and blacks underneath, the result of days floating in his own death like a scene from a film, skin stuck to the edges of the plastic tub as though glued, a rotten gaping wound in his neck where the flesh has begun to pull apart with the weight of his head, a putrid soup of rot and *unholy* smell.

I lurch and vomit onto the frosty tile floor; steam rises from it as I hold my hands on my knees and will it to stop but cannot. I heave again and again and begin to panic because I can't breathe. I am retching and sobbing and screaming and finally I back out of the room with one last look up at his face, distended, discoloured, unrecognizable, ended.

AFTER THE FLOOD

"River."

The voice is familiar. It is gentle, kind, grounding. It is Toby and it is twenty years late, but I welcome it without reproach, because what is the point anymore? I'm blubbering and shaking, and mucus creeps out of my left nostril. My arms are wrapped around him, and as my head clears, I realize I feel as though my life depends on it.

Takahashi kneels beside Toby and gives me a tender look, the look of someone who is worried but knows everything will be all right. His knees are on the *tatami* and his hands are on his knees. Neither he nor Toby needs to ask what was just unearthed. They both knew. Everyone knew.

Somewhere, I knew.

The block, the misremembrance, the emotionally-self-preserving fiction, whatever you want to call it—it was all in service of obscuring this truth buried in a corner of my mind, a corner that made itself felt without making itself known. The exhumation of this memory, now that the initial shock and horror have begun to subside, makes the world clearer. Soba warned me about this place, but insisted I come to it. As sickened and weak as I feel, I believe I should be grateful.

Shakes settle into tremors; tremors settle into sighs. Toby continues to hold me. I wish he would say my name again.

"Thank you," I whimper at him.

"It's all right, River." His voice feels good, and at this moment, at least, it makes up for the old Toby's mistakes.

"Are you okay?" he asks.

A snotty sniffle is my response. Takahashi pulls a handkerchief out of the breast pocket of his suit. I take it but only stare at it.

"Please, *dōzo*," he says, clearly not expecting it back. I blow my nose and feel the relief of being able to breathe.

"Well," I say, "that was unexpected."

"Oh, look who's back," snickers Toby.

"I found Daniel in the bathtub," I tell them.

"We know," Toby says as I pull back from our hug and wipe my cheeks with my palms. "You don't have to revisit it again, Riv."

"It was always there," I tell them. "I told myself he'd vanished, that the cops found him in a canal afterward. I don't...I don't understand where...where that came from. At some point, my mind buried the memory. But you all knew."

"You told us," Toby agrees. "Riv, I'm sorry. You came to me, telling me you'd just found Daniel dead, but I was...I was pretty messed up by that point. Tired, strung out, confused, and you freaked me out. I was afraid, too, afraid that I'd..."

Toby glances sideways at Takahashi, who looks back at Toby with interest.

"I was in too deep and completely paranoid," Toby continues. "I didn't see any future other than the one where I dug my own hole far, far deeper than I could ever escape. You showed up, and I couldn't deal. I ran. I'm sorry."

I shrug and sniffle.

"It's okay," I say. I can't use the word "forgive" yet. Maybe one day I will forgive him. I almost do. I'm sure I will. Eventually.

the ice on the high water is not ice, a slush, the colour of runny mud or

I clutch at my forehead as if I can press the imagery back

into the dank basement where it's been hiding, posing as part of a picture show. It stands its ground, paused, frozen, immovable.

I am suddenly self-conscious, snotty and sniveling on the floor. I make to stand up, and Takahashi offers me an arm. The three of us stand a moment, silent but for my rough breathing.

"Tsuchi-san." I turn towards Takahashi and reach to hold his hands in mine, even though it's probably inappropriate. "I'm sorry you had to see me lose my mind."

"I've seen worse," he grins.

I can barely stand. My head aches. My eyes feel salted like a winter sidewalk. Grief, repeated, sudden and shocking. A blast, a burn, and now emptiness. I feel outside of myself. Split in two—not down the centre, but through the core.

"I'd very much like to catch up with you for real, in a normal way," I hear myself tell Takahashi. "Can we do that? I haven't figured out when I'm leaving yet. I may or may not have plenty of time."

"I would like that too, Kawa-chan," he says. "For now, you should go home and rest."

"I sincerely doubt sleep wants me today, but I will try. Call me at the Hotel New Yama; leave a message tomorrow. Will you do that?"

"I will," he replies. "I definitely will."

One of Takahashi's staff leads us back to the entrance. Toby clutches a plastic shopping bag full of his wet clothes as he slides his bare feet into squishy shoes. Before we leave, I turn back to Takahashi.

"Can I ask you a question?"

Takahashi nods.

"Are you really a crime boss?"

He squints at me a moment.

"A crime boss?" He smiles teasingly. "River Black, you watch too many movies."

Which doesn't really answer the question.

THANK YOU, RIVER

Toby and I don't speak until we reach the hotel door. "I'd invite you in, but you'd barely fit in the lobby. Even if I were willing to share a bed with you, which I'm not, your feet would stick out the door."

"The tall jokes never fail to entertain you, do they?"

"Not. Ever."

Toby's expression settles into concern again, albeit milder. "Are you sure you're all right?"

"Lord, no," I reply. "Are you kidding me?"

But I smile at him anyway.

Toby leaves me and I wander to my room, finally alone. When I open my door, I am certain that a particular little freak frog monkey bird will be waiting, *tsk tsk*-ing and telling me it told me so, but no, I am still alone. This is good, because I have already cried in front of a bunch people. I don't need to cry in front of a *kappa*.

Sleep swallows me whole before I can even undress. Before I am aware what has happened, I am stirring on the microbe farm that is the bedspread, still in my clothes. The light outside is liquid sun that burns at the edges of the blackout shades as it tries to bubble through. When I open them, my puffy eyes can barely handle the brightness. Outside, in the vibrant sunlight, India Street looks like a photograph from many years ago.

A new day. A new memory.

The picture-perfect world outside my window, the streetscape of my youth, makes me feel warm, almost content, but I can't trust that. I feel fine here and now, but there's something deeply wrong underneath. I need to talk to someone about what happened yesterday. Someone who can help me make sense of it, guide me back. I feel as if I've been shattered and glued back together.

Before I can think about my next course of investigation, the familiar bouncy *blip-bloop* ringtone emanates from my laptop.

Ugh.

"Hello, Evrard."

Evrard doesn't respond. He is staring at me—or he thinks he is, but doesn't seem to know, as usual, how a webcam works, so his granite forehead and sunken eyes glare at the wall behind me, which is more disorienting than intimidating.

"Here, Evvie. I'm over here. Look into the stupid camera."

Evrard's eyes dart as though he's following the flight of a mosquito, until they land in the approximate scope of the lens. His expression does not change.

"I have not heard from you," he chides, as if I'm a schoolgirl.

"No, you have not." I can't think of a worse day for him to hector me. "You said Monday."

"I believe you need some encouragement."

"You call this encouragement?"

"Yes!" Evrard's jaw is slightly out of alignment with his denture in. He still hasn't learned to speak with it; he looks less feral, but there's a wetness to his words. "I must crack the whip! Make sure you are on time."

"That's a terrible way to foster employee loyalty and get results, Ev. It works on set because you can replace everyone if you have to. It doesn't work with me."

"Did we use the Winnebego?"

"You asked me that last time." I want to be righteously furious with him, but hearing him slurp around the word Winnebago, watching him try so hard to keep his facial expression stern, saps me of the energy. The idea of writing for Evrard leaves me depleted, entirely devoid of resentment or frustration. Simply filled with nothing.

"Evvie," I say, enjoying the way his eyebrows bump together every time I say his hated nickname. "Evvie, I'm just yanking your chain. It's done. I'll send it to you now."

"It's done."

"Yes."

Evrard grins, a hyena from a Disney movie. "Send it to me now. I will get in touch after I read it. Thank you, River."

"Oh no," I reply. "Thank *you.* Evrard."

When he hangs up, I open a file. My fingers smatter the keyboard with quick strokes, the rhythm of steady rain, the sound of a stream of consciousness running its course. When I finish, I save, I title, and I send.

With a smile.

PINNED IV

INT. HOTEL ROOM – DAY

A small but functional room in a Japanese business hotel.
There is a small television on a small table, a plain, likely
germ-bespattered bedspread, and a desk better suited to a
pre-teen girl than an adult woman. RIVER BLACK sits at
the desk, knees pressed against the wall beneath, writing on a
laptop computer. There is something in her face that suggests
weariness, but inside, she is simply too empty to be weary.

SHOT: A close-up of RIVER's face. She is in her forties—
charitably, her "mid" forties—but is still pretty, she thinks, in a
plain way; it has never been important to her, prettiness versus
ugliness, because her concept of what is pretty and what is
ugly does not always coincide with society's. She realizes that,
to grow up unconcerned with make-up and fashion and boys,
she was not the average woman. This has never bothered her,
though at times it bothers her that this has never bothered
her. She has had better days than this, without a doubt, but
something in her eyes speaks to a recent epiphany. Suddenly,
something exists in the void she previously felt. Something
terrifying, a realization of something that must be done. Her
mind begins to wander forward, through space and time.

MONTAGE: Movies. Movie after movie, scene after scene, shot after shot, frame after frame. The history of cinema projected on the backs of her closed eyelids. The possibilities of now, the daunting prospect of trying to jump into the stream of celluloid, to leap in and go against the current, when she only has the vaguest notion of how to swim. She has watched EVRARD FREDERICH swim and has learned many techniques to avoid. EVRARD FREDERICH has succeeded despite himself, and RIVER BLACK will not have that as her fate, not anymore. No more succeeding in spite of herself. Now it will be with herself, because of herself. Failures and successes hers.

CUT TO: A close shot of her eyes when she realizes she's about to jump out of an airplane with a shoddy parachute but knows it's better to free-fall than to stay on this aircraft one minute longer and be taken on this journey she can no longer stand.

RIVER
Fuck you, Evvie.

THE END

RIVER TO RIVER

I have solved a mystery I didn't know existed, but the mystery I have been trying to solve remains unsolved. This book. Why does this book exist? Did it exist only to lead me deeper into myself, to exhume the dead?

Right on the Gondō. Left on Chūō-odori. Right again, along sidewalks, paved shoulders, past chain-link fences surrounding schoolyards, chest-high walls surrounding gardens. There is a cool undercurrent to the breeze as October suggests the season to come. I reach the Susobana, whose concrete banks are being reclaimed by tufts of grass and weeds that widen the cracks. The river flows unhurried, but not lazily; there is too much sparkle and skip on its surface for it to seem idle.

Across the bridge, up through the winding streets. I try and flow uphill as water would flow down, to let go of my doubts, to use instinct instead of memory. Or perhaps a combination of both, as if every recognizable thing in the world is a doorway rather than an impenetrable wall. Onward to the past. There are ways in. There are ways out. The *sakon inari* is still up there, and today I will find it.

Floating along on instinct, it's the same as my last attempt; paths that look familiar dissolve into scrub grass and crumbled asphalt. A stone wall shoulders a modest field, a small crop of daikon. Beyond the field is an equally modest home. An elderly gentleman stands, dirt caked onto his knees and gardening gloves. He calls to me and asks if I would like some fresh daikon. From a bag at his feet he produces a white root the size of my forearm. I grin back at him and tell him I am staying at a hotel, I've nowhere to cook it, but thanks anyway.

"*Sakon inari ni ikimasu*," I say politely. "*Dochira desu ka?*"

He grins harder, somehow, though his face doesn't change. Right there, he says, and points to a façade of foliage into which the stone wall disappears.

"*Sō desu ka?*"

"*Hai*," he replies with an emphatic nod, arm still extended towards the dead end. That's when it slowly comes into view. The overgrowth is simply that; overgrowth, cascading down over what I can now see, thanks to the farmer's direction, is the old path, hidden by nothing more than a few branches and leaves.

"*Dōmo!*" I practically skip towards the brush. It isn't machete-level scrub; all I do is pull at some branches and sweep them aside. It's as though I've fallen through some hole in my own brain, tumbled down through a time vortex. I can almost see Allie and Nicolle off ahead, Daniel at my side. A few metres farther and there's a dilapidated shed, greying from sun on one side, darkened with damp rot on the others. An ewe lived there once.

The shrine grounds are almost derelict. The steel bench has been flattened into rusty scrap metal and lies in the overgrown grass. The towering red *torii* gates are missing; I spy them a moment later, in segments, lying in a valley on the other side of the shrine. The rust-mottled flagpole sways in the wind, loose within the moorings at its base. The inscribed metal pole still aspires, its words *May peace prevail upon the earth* more antiquated and urgent than ever, given the state of things. It has not crumbled or crumpled with time, nor has the lone building; it is spotless, has been freshened up with pockets of new paint, its interior swept and dusted.

This place was special to Daniel. He built an entire story around it; he built an entire mythology of sorts, one that surrounded us as the grey bulwarks of cloud surround Nagano, almost like a lid over the plateau. As I stand here, I can imagine Soba, our imaginary mutual friend. Perched like Spider-man on the stairs of the shrine, arms straight, hands flat on the ground between his feet, knees apart, ready to pounce. I can hear Kenichi and Sakura giggle. Kenichi, who I always imagined to be Daniel. Sakura, who I always imagined to be me.

I sit on the meticulously swept step of the shrine when there is a rustle from below the shrine's little plateau on the hillside. In all my times coming here, I have never seen another person unless they were with me. I wait for the little *kappa* to croak at me.

"You are so predictable, mate, even after twenty years."

She stops and stands, hands on hips, a few metres away, where the *torii* gates once stood. Her posture is matriarchal and sarcastic and questioning and concerned all at once. That she's here at all seems impossible.

"Hey," I try to say, but a sudden tightness grips my throat and I only manage to hiccup. Babette crosses the grounds and sits wordlessly next to me on the stoop. After a moment or two, she sighs.

"I stood there on the Gondō and stared at the Hotel New Yama for at least a half hour." Babette stares at her knees as she speaks. "I must have looked like a bloody stalker. I chickened out when you walked through the door, though. Ducked into a doorway. As soon as you walked west, I knew you were coming here. So I followed you. Got my nerve back."

I don't know what to say, so I don't say anything.

"I'm still upset," Babette says. "But I'm sorry I told you to piss off." I notice that she is still short of breath, her voice gaspy, her shirt splotched with perspiration. Sweat darkens her white-blonde hair; the damp strands along her hairline are streaks of silver against her skin. Babette blows a moist clump of errant curls off her forehead. It promptly sinks back to where it began; she tucks it up into her other curls with a middle finger.

"I'm still working this all out in my head, yeah?" She absently raises one hand to swipe moisture from her brow. "Reiko told me where you were staying. I talked to her this morning. She says you and Toby had some kind of adventure yesterday."

I don't respond. I can't respond. I have not even begun to process what happened to me yesterday, to contend with the fact that one of my horrific celluloid memories was not from a film. Something beyond terror existed on a screen, and then suddenly it noticed me and stepped through, into the real world, to destroy me. It's like that Italian horror flick *Dèmoni*, which is pretty damned obscure, but it's the only analogy I've got. Leave it to me to make this trauma seem meta.

Part of me wants to run from Babette, but another wants to hug her, and another to beat her with the meat of my fists and scream, yet another to beg her forgiveness. My heart doesn't know what to make my body do.

Babette stares at the stone foxes perched like guardian dogs from mythology, almost regal. I follow her gaze as a numbness inside me starts to thaw.

"Came all the way across the planet to solve a mid-life crisis, I bet."

"I wasn't having a mid-life crisis until I got here." My voice sounds emotionless. Flat. I wonder if my face looks equally vacant.

Babette clears her throat, sniffles a little, but I don't look to see if she is crying. Babette doesn't cry. Didn't, anyway.

"If it makes you feel any better, I went through one, too." She pauses. The wind sizzles in the trees, a fizzy rustle, and dies down again.

"I haven't felt myself the last few years," she continues. "I didn't understand it, because Japan still feels like home. Shinji is wonderful. The restaurant is everything we ever wanted. And yet...I started looking at old photos, walking by J.J.'s, wondering what happened to people. I only had one real friend, though, and I missed her, suddenly, after all these years."

Babette missed me. Why is this a surprise? Why is it so hard for me to imagine that our friendship had two halves?

"You're not hard to find." Babette is trying to talk to me without talking to me, using her hands as though tracing cursive in the air, but she still speaks around me, not at me. A little like Daniel used to do. "In fact, given the creepy types who like your movies, maybe you should make yourself a little harder to find?"

"They're mostly very nice," I say.

"Whatever, mate. Anyway, I found you. Instead of ringing you or emailing you, I sort of kept tabs. I wanted to know you were still out there, that River Black still existed. I was...I *am...so angry* with you, even after all these years. You know, you were the kind of person I hated. Always so chipper, this stupid ray of sunshine that I couldn't block out. I'd managed to be an island until then, except for Shinji. I didn't want any friends, didn't need any friends, especially eighteen-year-old drunks saving up their yen to pay for months of debauchery in Phuket. Then you burst into my room, without my permission I might add, and goddammit, I liked you, so I let you in."

"I used to barge in on you all the time." Now there is, at least, a sliver of River back in my voice. "I'm sorry for that."

Babette turns her head in my general direction but stares forward, kind of over my knees, at the grass below the stone foxes. "I hated it at first. You fought hard to make sure everyone liked you. I thought you were one of those unbearably needy types who would try and wear down my resolve. Then I realized it wasn't wearing down resolve. It was tearing down walls. You wanted to be friends with me, the most raging *gaijin* bitch in Nagano. So I let you in, and you left."

"I'm sorry, Babette." My eyes well up, surprising me. "I don't know what happened."

"You lost your shit, is what happened," Babette says, though not unkindly. "You were dazed and scared and just mental about everything, and sometimes what you said didn't even make sense. Which is fair, considering what happened didn't make sense. You tried to understand it, but there was nothing to understand. What happened just happened."

"Why didn't you tell me Kogawa wasn't a criminal?" I ask before I can think better of it. "If we'd kicked Kogawa out before he hit Daniel, maybe Daniel would have lived."

"Are you serious, mate?" Babette finally looks directly at me, now that she has something to say in her old, familiar tone. "I always made fun of him for not being a gangster. Called him 'wannabe *yakuza*' and such."

"I guess we kinda missed that nuance, Babette. That's why we were all so scared to kick him out when he got belligerent."

"Jesus." Babette looks down a moment, kicks the toes of her shoes together. "You know he came there just to see me, yeah? Just to be a prick. Let's go see the Kiwi tramp at work, make her feel bad about her life choices. God, I just wanted to disappear."

"I don't understand. Why would he do that?"

She fidgets with her sock a moment, pulls it up from behind, as if they were slipping into her shoe. "Kogawa acted like I was disgusting. White girl, hostess, what kind of wife would I be, what kind of mother would I be, all that. The truth is, when Shinji wasn't around, he was always coming on to me. He liked me."

"Ick."

"A thousand icks, mate. One time, he threatened to tell Shinji's parents about us if I didn't go to dinner with him. Creepy as hell. The only way to deal was to disengage. Not talk to him. Any time he showed up where I was, he acted twice as badly. On purpose. To show me what a man he was. Or maybe just because he was a wanker."

"And now?"

"A mellower wanker. Still not a charmer. I didn't want people to know he was Shinji's uncle because I didn't want anyone to think Shinji was like that. You're the only one who even knew they knew each other."

She pauses and places a hand on the step, near but not touching me.

"So, wait. You wish I'd clarified that he wasn't a gangster. Do you…did you…blame me for Daniel dying?"

Babette should sound indignant, but instead, she sounds concerned.

"No," I say. "No, I blamed Kogawa, and for a split second I wanted to blame you, but by that point, I didn't know what to think anymore. Daniel…nothing killed him except for his own body. I know that. Always should have always known that."

"Eisenmenger's," Babette says. "When you don't treat a hole in the heart, whatever a hole in the heart is called."

"Atrioventricular septal defect."

"Sure. I read up on it once. Daniel lived about as long as most people with that syndrome used to live. So much easier to treat now. He probably would have survived, nowadays."

"Probably not," I say. "They had treatments then, too. The family didn't have health insurance."

"So even today, things might have been the same," says Babette. "Some things are just going to happen. It wasn't a matter of Kogawa or mistaken identity or anything. It was just a thing that happened. If you hadn't imagined Ultraman giving you the thumbs up, would you have come to Japan? If Nax didn't have a fascination with American soldiers, would he have gotten into jazz? If he hadn't gotten into jazz, would there have been a J.J.'s to come to? Every minute you live, any minute you live, can be split into a billion universes. You can't know what leads to what. You can't spend your energy looking for causes to blame. You have to accept what happened as what happened. Deal with it directly. Turn the lights on and face it. Finding the light switch, though, that's the hardest part."

"Wow."

"Piss off, yeah?"

"No," I insist. "I mean, really, honestly, a sincere wow."

"I told you, I've been on my own trip."

We sit another moment in silence, the trees shushing in the background.

"You said you talked to Reiko." I say.

"Yeah. I haven't been in touch in years, but I knew where to find her."

"Toby must have filled her in on our, ah, adventures."

"She told me a pile of things that made no sense. You and Toby went to Takahashi's house because Takahashi was Sora's dad? Something about Toby falling into a canal?"

"Did she mention my brain cracked open and flooded me with memories?"

"Of finding Daniel in the bathtub, yeah." Babette's voice softened. "Yeah, mate. You...blocked it out, I guess?"

"The images were there, but I'd convinced myself it was something I'd seen in a movie."

"Holy crap."

"Holy crap indeed."

"Mate, I'm sorry." She actually seems sorry.

"Well." I grit my teeth a little, trying to stem another waterfall. "She tell you about the book?"

"She said something about the book you wrote with Daniel. That part didn't make a lot of sense, either."

"Trust me, nothing was lost in translation.," I said. "It doesn't many sense in any language. Long story short, I thought maybe you had printed out a copy of Daniel's story, put Reiko's *kappa* drawing on the cover, and then mailed it to me."

"Why would..."

"I know, I know."

Babette shrugs and looks at the ground.

"You were so weird about letting me read that story," she sighs. "You wouldn't let anyone near it. After you left, when I was still telling myself you were going to come back,

I grabbed a bunch of stuff from your room to keep aside for you. The stuff on your wall, like Reiko's art, some letters, some clothes. I left your *wāpuro* where it was. But then some gangster-looking guys came, said they were cops, and—"

"Yeah, I know. That's a whole other story, probably for another time."

"I printed *Kenichi and the Kappa* before they took it away, though," Babette continues. "I probably shouldn't have. Sorry."

"Yeah, well. I wasn't around to ask, so what the hell."

"Well. When I had my own mid-life crisis, I wanted to sever all ties to my past. As if I hadn't done that already. I threw a whole box of J.J.'s-era, Sanyō Heights shit away. I'm sorry. I didn't think we'd be sitting here on Mount Asahi together twenty years on."

"Neither did I. It's okay. You got through your crisis intact?"

She shrugged. "Men buy sports cars and have affairs with young girls. Women develop a general sense of dissatisfaction and existential dread."

"I don't know if men and women are so different. I think the dissatisfaction and dread is what leads to the cars and the girls."

"Then let's just say women don't act out like idiots."

"Fair."

"Maybe I did act out a bit," Babette smiles sadly. "Throwing that J.J.'s shit away was symbolically tossing my past in the bin, you know? I threw out photos, stuff salvaged from your room, the story, everything. I thought it would mark a new beginning. Rites and rituals, yeah?"

"Rites and rituals. That was my thing."

"Well," Babette says, "it didn't do much of anything, really. I destroyed some memories for no reason."

"Sorry to hear it didn't work."

"I regret doing it," Babette continues. "In the end, I just went back to resenting you until, I don't know. Yesterday, I guess."

Even after all these years in another country, she says *giss*.

"What'd you do, burn it all and scatter the ashes? That's what I did."

"I went down behind the restaurant and threw it in the river," she says, rolling her eyes at herself.

Rites and rituals and symbolic gestures and whatnot.

"River to river," I say. "That's a bit on the nose, isn't it?"

"Shut it, yeah?" She's obviously a bit embarrassed by her admission.

"Sorry," I say. "*Namaste.*"

Babette sits up straight, pushes me over sideways. We both laugh a little. A bird-banger pops in the distance.

"Wait, Babette." The wind seems suddenly still, but I think it's because my mind has stopped. "You...threw it all in the river? My story, the *kappa* picture, all of it?"

"Yeah."

"What river runs up that way?"

Babette points through the trees. "That one. The Susobana. It's longer than you think."

I sit upright, take her hands in mine, like we're small children in an old timey movie, and I laugh. She looks at me with one eyebrow raised, a half-smirk on her face.

"Of course you did!" It can't be, it isn't real, it can't be real...but now, there's a through line. Hope isn't extinguished. The map didn't run out. The investigation hasn't met a dead end. Merely an impossible one.

"Come on." I stand, hands on my creaky knees, still throbbing slightly from the climb up. I extend a hand to her with faux gallantry, which she immediately smacks away.

"Ow. You still don't know your own strength, Babette. Let's go. I suddenly realize I need to do something."

"Now? I follow you up a mountain and you've decided to run errands?"

"No," I say. "It's a bit more important than that. But walk with me. I don't know why I'm up here, really. It was Daniel's place, and it doesn't seem interested in giving up any more secrets."

"More?"

I don't respond. *Kenichi and the Kappa*, the McGuffin that set this whole story in motion. If it hadn't weirded me out so badly—if I hadn't been actively avoiding it—I would have read the book before Nax died. When I called, it might have been Nax who answered, not his grieving daughter. He would have explained he had nothing to do with the book. He would have been blissfully ignorant of the fatal stroke that lurked around the corner, and I would not have made it to the funeral. If it wasn't for the book, it's possible I never would have known that Nax died, reconnected with all these people, or unearthed the trauma from the basement of my brain.

It's just an urge right now—vague, undefined, but taking shape. Shadows have begun to emerge, even in the darkness. Shapes. Terrifying, elemental, nonsensical by any normal, rational standards.

But I've never had normal, rational standards. I'm River Black.

HEAT AND WONDER

There are stairs now.

They were invisible to me while I searched for a route up to the *sakon inari,* but now that I am here, they are immediately observable. Fate wasn't keeping me away from my destiny, though that was the narrative I'd chosen to create for myself. No. The trail was just overgrown, hidden from view, because people don't use the trail anymore. They use these new stairs, little more than plateaus of earth shaped into steps by rails of rebar. This place had not disappeared at all. In fact, someone has made it *easier* to reach. It was my dogged adherence to that faultiest of human traits, memory, that made it vanish. I clung to memory as those adorable baby macaques cling to the bellies of their mothers (while their fathers, obviously, mutilate the shrieking).

The stairs descend into greenery and terminate in one of the grassy fields that, coming in the opposite direction, I had mistaken for a dead end. If I'd just walked a few metres farther, I would have seen the bottom step. Babette and I descend and then follow two asphalt lines, mere ruts fortified like a road, that lead out onto a proper street.

"Nax died," I say.

"Reiko mentioned that too." Babette walks behind me. "I haven't seen him since the J.J.'s days. Sorry to hear it. The old bugger was all right."

"Yeah. That's the real reason I came here, or at least the reason I gave myself."

We circle around, we circle down, mostly in silence. We gaze at the plots of land laden with green leafy daikon tops, apple trees now stripped of their bounty. We circumnavigate the water-treatment facility with its smooth beige prison-like walls. Down winding roads, concrete stairs, to the bridge over the river, a shallow flow in a deep bed that ripples and dances its way down from the mountains and out of the city. The rocks that surface are dry on top, sand-coloured turtles basking in the sun. I look for one wet stone, and in fact, I see several scattered throughout the current, coloured a blackish, brackish green. Just like someone I know.

"You still hate Toby?" I ask.

"Ah." Babette makes a sour face. "I never hated him. I just kinda hated him. I don't know. I knew he was back in town. He's hard to miss."

"Like an ambulatory sunflower."

"Like a great big, enormous white guy."

We reach Chuō-*odōri* and stroll past *kanji* signs, red lanterns, blocky facades, tiled roofs, corrugated steel drop-doors, neon lights in windows, a busy grid of electrical wires that slices the sky into bright-blue blocks. Familiar. Regenerated, but still the same organism. Don't look too closely, don't look too hard. You don't have to. I was a fool to think this was not the same city.

"We should get together, then," I tell Babette. "Me, you, Reiko, Toby, Masa. Go for *yakiniku*. Drink too much draft beer. Reminisce. Really dive headlong into the thing. It might raise up some zombies, but it might just be what you need."

"Masa." Babette smiles. "I admit I miss his talk-singing."

"He still does it."

"Does Toby still say *namaste*?"

"Not so far."

"Well, I can't believe I'm saying this, and I might change my mind, and this might make me hate your stupid face forever, but I think I'm in. So how long are you here for, then?"

"I don't know when I'm going home," I say. "I don't know if I'll *stay* stay, but I don't have to be anywhere. I was working on a screenplay, but I hated it. So I quit. Sort of."

"When?"

"This morning."

"After what you went through last night?" Babette laughs. "You idiot. Re-experiencing trauma is probably not a good basis for making major life decisions, mate."

"I know." I laugh, surprised that in my own twisted way, I honestly find it funny. "I'll spend tomorrow on the Internet convincing myself I'm not as old as I think I am. That there has never been a better time for a female horror writer to take hold of her own vision. I know people who know people, and I know that I'll have a huge swell of support from just about every woman in the industry when they find out what I did to Evvie."

"What did you do to Evvie?"

"Let's just say I delivered a script, but it wasn't the script he wanted. So yeah. It'll be hard for a while. I can go back to Toronto and stay with Sheila, the way she's always insisting."

I can do what I want now. Create whatever begs for creation. *Kappa*, giant snake, things that I have yet to imagine. I have enough inside me for a thousand stories, told to a thousand worlds. It's terrifying. It's exhilarating.

We stop on the corner where Chuō-*odōri* transitions into the temple road. Stone-forged statues of stone-faced, serene O-jizō-sama appear, wearing red hats and bibs, greenish stone figures dressed for purposes I still don't understand.

"I have to go up this way," I say, as vaguely as possible. "You have Reiko's number now, yeah?"

"I do."

"Call her. Or call me at the New Yama. We'll set up something. And I swear, if we don't hear from you, we're coming back to your restaurant, eating our faces off, and leaving a cheapskate tip."

"You don't tip in this country."

"I know. It was a joke."

Babette rolls her eyes.

"I didn't know how much I missed you, Babette."

Babette mimes sticking a finger down her throat and mouths *baaaaaarf.* "Twenty years later and you're still a weirdo, River Black. But whatever. Okay. I'll call. Today, even. I promise."

She reaches out and before I know what's happening, she hugs me around the neck and pulls me to her.

"I missed you too, ya nitwit." She pulls back, and lo and behold, we're both tearing up. "Go do your weird mystery errand. I'll see you soon."

Babette turns and walks away. The wooden Niō statues watch me as I watch her go. The statues who stand guard with their unsettling, white-eyed faces, swords poised at the apex of the killing arc, threatening even as they stand inanimate and locked within the pillars of the gateway. They are enmeshed in a sheet of steel webbing like chicken wire. Tied to wooden slats near the bottom of the pillar box are dozens of blond straw sandals, prayer boards attached to each: wishes to the departed, messages to the deceased. Each one reaching out to a past that cannot be reached—or so we believe. When I am finished this, I can go to one of the shops I pass now, along the walkway that leads to the temple, and buy a pair of *waraji,* the ones with the white straps. I don't know what the prayer boards say or how to choose one, but it doesn't matter. I can write Daniel's name on a scrap of paper and tie it to the sandals. Tie the sandals to the gate. The way it is supposed to be done.

I walk up towards the main temple building, but I do not go up the worn wooden steps and stroke the smooth face of Binzuru the doctor. Instead, I head right, almost at a skip now, along the path of loose stones, to the pond. I sit on the rock I always sit on, sort of in the corner where the walkway of smooth stones halves the water. There are no people in sight. It is not high tourist season; it is not a special occasion. I think, in fact, it is a simple Tuesday in October.

I wait.

The sky has thickened, lowered, flattened. Small raindrops flick at the surface of the water here and there. It looks as if it is being kissed by motes of dust. A whitish, translucent head bobs to the surface, the simultaneously dumb and serene face of a koi billowing its mouth open and closed at the edge of the water.

In the centre of this half of the pond, the dark bowl of a turtle's shell seems to hover beneath the reflections of grey sky and green leaves. It grows, darker, broader, until I am quite sure it isn't a turtle.

Soba's hair sticks slimily to its skull, its head-concavity filled with pond water. Its beak-maw still looks harsh, still threatens violence, but I know there's nothing to be afraid of.

I look around. The droplets are pinging more frequently now, though it is still nothing like a downpour. Just enough to ensure there's no one around to see this creature surface—though I have no idea if anyone else would see it if they were here. Sakura never saw it, even when Kenichi did.

Soba comes closer to me as though propelled by something other than its own body, its head above the water; it doesn't swim so much as it simply moves. When it reaches me, it clambers up onto the first rock below me. It smells of decades-old logs broken down into soft disarray, of salamanders in the creeks in Ontario, of rot that is not disgusting but rather elemental, more fuel for the future than decay. And it looks like Dr. Moreau got his hands on Gollum and went to town.

It stands there a moment, in front of me, and I notice for the first time it is entirely out of the water. The only water it touches are the raindrops that make the mirrored surface of the pond dance behind it, tiny pulses that propel concentric circles out towards the edges.

As Soba looks at me, its face softens. Its eyes are too black, too impenetrable, for me to say it looks at me with empathy, but certainly it is the friendliest look the thing has had on its face since we met.

"The boy is dead," it says.

"The boy is dead," I agree.

"You went back."

"I went back. Through the book, I found the boy. He was always here, in my head." I tap my temple. "I saw death. Like you told me to. But why? Why did you help me, in your creepy little way?"

"Boy create me, Kawa-chan. Boy, you, me, we create book."

"That didn't answer my question."

Its nostrils swell in and out, its neck pulses like bellows. "Boy is Kenichi."

"Daniel was Kenichi, yes."

"Soba is what."

I frown. "Soba is...his disease. Or his anxiety about his disease. Or the ugliness that comes with that anxiety. I don't think it was meant to be cut and dried."

"And what is girl."

"Sakura? She's me."

Soba grins, inasmuch as its facial structure allows it to grin, and shakes its head softly.

"Girl is *life*," it says. "Kawa-chan is part of life. Not meant for cut and dry."

I laugh at its attempt at aphorism.

"I guess that makes sense. But why? How does this book exist? Babette threw the story into the Susobana. I can only presume you and your river-god magic are responsible. I've come a long way to get to the end of this mystery, and I gotta be honest, I don't know if 'river god magic' is really a satisfactory resolution for me."

"McGuffin," it says, and to my surprise, I laugh again.

"Why funny? Your word."

"Yes, it's...my word, sort of. I just don't expect film-crit lingo to come out of the mouth of…something such as yourself."

"Mah. Words. Matter so much, matter not at all."

"You said it."

"Book, me, you, boy, all same. I am born of book but exist before book. You and boy create book, but book exist before book. Book come to river, book come from river. Book? Book not come. Book is."

"That's not an answer either," I say, as I hold the book out. "This book is your origin story. This book is where you came to be."

"And you."

"No. No, I know you're trying to tell me that all is one and one is all and et cetera, which I find really weird because that sounds vaguely Buddhist and you are not a Buddhist. But being a self-professed river god, I suppose you'd know more about the nature of existence than I do. You're a water god created by someone's mind. You're a projection, you're a ghost, you're elemental, you're not real, and you exist."

"All these are true."

"Yeah, and that's more than a little perplexing. But answers, even some answers, would be helpful."

"No answers."

"Well then." I shake the book a little, in its face. "Whatever you are, you wanted me to have a minor nervous breakdown and remember what happened. Maybe you wanted me to reconcile with my past. When I think of it that way, I realize you exist, but only in my head. But then there's this. This physical, very real book, which my head doesn't have the power to create. So, here."

I hold the book out with one hand.

"If I can't have answers, I don't want the book. Take it. It's probably more yours than mine."

Soba reaches out one snaggle-fingered claw, its nails a crusty yellow, and takes hold of the book. It pulls it closer to its chest, turns it around, glances at the cover and laughs—a dry, hacking sound, but unmistakably a laugh.

"Me," it says, eyes still on the cover.

"You," I agree. "I have no need for that anymore. Take it with you."

It steps back into the water and begins to sink until only visible from the neck up. Suddenly, Soba stops sinking.

"For boy," it says. "You know what Soba is for boy. But what is Soba for you?"

And it disappears with a splash.

By now, the rain is strong enough that I cannot tell if the ripples are from the *kappa* or from the raindrops. Either way, it's as though Soba was never there at all. But it was there. It took the book. Back to whatever. Back to wherever. The book may never have existed, either, though the story existed. The story continues to exist. That much I know.

What is Soba for me? A hallucination that has taken on corporeal form? Manifestation of my pain, my darkness, my own imagination? The best way for the universe to get River Black's attention?

I know one thing—there's a lot to do, tomorrow perhaps, and in the days to follow. But there's only one thing left to do today, and it's not utilizing critical theory to deconstruct my life story and the role of an imaginary creature within it. I'm simply going to listen to the imaginary creature's words.

I saw death. Now I have to walk into darkness.

Entering the main hall from the eastern door, I kick off my shoes. The *tatami* is smooth beneath my feet and well kept. The hall is empty; the day is done, and pilgrims have gone. One monk and one temple staff member shake their heads at me when I move to slide a ¥500 coin into the ticket machine.

"No," says the staff member. "It's closing time. Go ahead, you don't have to pay."

"Okay," I say in Japanese. "But one moment please."

I walk over to Binzuru, the doctor. From my bag I pull my wallet; from my wallet, I pull a ten thousand yen bill.

"*Ichiman* yen," I tell Binzuru, as I slide the bill into the offering tray. Daniel is not here to pay me for what I am about to do, but someone has to make this offering.

I place my shoes in a plastic bag and leave it by the exit.

I don't know when I will be leaving, but before I go, I will talk to them all. Toby, Masa, Reiko, Babette. Maybe I'll even call Sora in Boston.

The shrine, in full light, would gleam like daybreak. Here in the dim it is murky, the promise of gold shadowed, as if under cloudy water. I can make out small pillars and an image of the Buddha, small but central, on a platform.

Beside me are the stairs that lead into the dark. Another statue of Buddha guards a stone or metal bowl beneath it, smoke wafting out, the smell of incense. To my left is a pillar of sorts, except it hangs from the ceiling; it supports nothing. Twenty-five bodhisattvas welcome me, as they welcome the spirits of the dead.

An impressive red-lacquered rail descends along the left wall, while on the right there is a smaller gold rail, more practical for pilgrims to hold. There is nothing ahead of me. It should feel like looking into the mouth of my greatest fear, but all told, I'm River Black. I don't scare easily. I have no greatest fear other than the fear that I will no longer be able to tell stories. That, and the fear that when the light goes out, the stories I told will no longer be remembered.

Tomorrow I will remember the living, but now I will remember the dead who haunt me. After twenty years, I will think about Daniel. After twenty years, I may even think about my father.

As I approach the bottom of the stairway, the light does not so much disappear as it weakens and dies. The stairs are steep, and it feels like going down into a cellar. At the bottom I take three steps forward, and there is only darkness. No shadow. No hand in front of my face. No walls. No mooring. No claustrophobic swell, no tension or anxiety or fear. The room could be as closed as a coffin or the vast open blackness of the abyss. There is no size: Toby was right. The dark is so complete that

I no longer see it; I do not feel constricted, trapped, buried. A low-grade hum fills the air, a furnace or some machinery located in an undefined centre, but it soon fades, blends itself into the blackness. Only the inside of my head and the feeling of wood on my palm remain, the wood of the wall beneath my right hand, smooth as glass but light as air. I nudge myself forward, short steps, though I know there's nothing here to trip over. After a few feet there is a wide, round pillar half-embedded in the wall. I keep my hand on the wall, sliding it up and down, feeling the smooth surface and around the pillar, which seems at once smallish and impossibly large. After the pillar, a sharp turn, as if the hallway is triangular or hexagonal, which perhaps it is. The keyhole is here, somewhere, in the nothing. If I find it, I break the wheel of *samsara*; I ascend directly to Nirvana after this life.

Wood smoothed by thousands, maybe millions of hands. A square of roughness, the end of a post or joist.

Then something else.

It is metal, fashioned to fit the curves of a human hand. It is iron, yet not cold; in fact, it is warmer than the wood that surrounds it. I stop. Something inside me swells, and I feel as though I want to burst into tears, but I quell it.

So it is not a keyhole after all, but the handle to a door. I don't pull it so much as push it forward on its hinge, so it goes from flat in its casing to perpendicular to the door. This is where I should finish. Normally, pilgrims would be shuffling in the dark behind me, forcing me to continue forward. There is no one here now, though. No sounds of plastic shoe bags, no sniffles or murmurs. I am not sure what this means. I feel as though this door is not mine to find. I am not Buddhist, and I am not Japanese. I squeeze the handle, concentrate on the sensation of it in my hand.

The door creaks and slides, almost imperceptibly, a few millimetres forward.

It is impossible. The door should not open. This handle is a prop, not an access point. Yet the door opens farther. This door—in this world or merely in my mind—opens at my touch. I am uncertain if it's the right thing to do, but I'm also uncertain that it's really happening. I push further, peer inside, compelled to step inward, compelled by the sound I hear now, the pulse of drums and the chant of voices, *so-rei, so-rei,* swelling in from the background, the sound of ten thousand hands coming together, rising and falling into a thunderous clap. But this time there is no neon, there is no fountain, there are no dancers in blue-and-white kimonos. There is, instead, everything. A distant galaxy, a jumble of light. Stones of every colour, stones made of light, countless combinations of reflections.

This is not the secret chamber beneath Zenkōji. This is someplace else.

The stones turn to flashes that pop and crackle, each a number, each a combination of numbers, each infinite, and this is what Daniel and the *kappa* wanted me to see, this perfect moment of creation, swinging with abandon on Nagano streets, grinning with anticipation at the first words to flow from deep inside of me, to the tips of my fingers and out, into the world. Words as doorway, combinations of doorways, doorways between worlds and doorways between beasts and beings, this flight of fancy that sees me standing in a dark hallway having faced a fear that pursued me half my life, a fear of darkness, a fear of loss, a fear of death, a fear of moving forward, and though these thoughts make me feel as though I've lost my mind, make me roll my eyes at myself, they are real. This moment, this instant, in the dark tunnel somewhere in my brain, where suddenly I feel as though everything is possible, a feeling I've felt once before, at a train station a lifetime ago in the mountains of foreign country. My pulse quickens and then falls silent as my heart bursts into my veins, filling my body with heat and wonder.

THE END

ACKNOWLEDGEMENTS

This is a work of fiction. None of the characters are real, and none of the events took place.

Well, almost none. Sensei, or Nax (Nakadaira Yoshihiro, 中平 嘉弘), passed away in 2009. I kept his name, as well as the name of his bar, as a tribute. His family and home, however, are fictional creations like the rest.

J.J. International was a real place. It's my nostalgic ritual to walk past the Taisei Abinasu building every time I visit Nagano. I could never name all the people I worked with at J.J.'s, but they all had lasting impacts on my life. Bits of them can be spotted in these characters, though they've been deconstructed and re-amalgamated again and again.

River stole the film title *Legacy of Brutality* from an album by The Misfits. "Telephone Call to Nagano-shi" was inspired by Tom Waits's "Telephone Call from Istanbul." "Limited Express (Has Gone)" is taken from the Kansai rock band Limited Express (Has Gone?). "Loved and Confused" is taken from a song off *Electric Heavyland* by Nagoya collective Acid Mothers Temple and the Melting Paraiso UFO.

I would like to recognize the Ontario Arts Council for their continued support of the arts and literature in this province. Their assistance made much of my research possible.

Thanks to those who helped with that research—Katagiri Masahiro, Noguchi Yuko, the good folks at Zenkōji, Melissa Smeets and Keisuke Kubo, Kristine Misfud, and Marika Viger. Thanks also to Ashley Gazda for the assistance with the gruesome bits.

Thanks must go to my beta readers, Jan Steinberg, Sherri Vanderveen, the aforementioned Melissa Smeets, and Teresa Caterini. Thanks to Jaime Krakowski for her vast knowledge of all things literary. Thanks to Noelle Allen from Wolsak & Wynn for her never-ending support of writers new and old. Thanks to Yukari Peerless for her thoughtful read (and for fixing my many Japanese-language errors) and to Theo

Hummer for her wonderfully thoughtful edit (and for dealing with my countless grammatical errors). Huge thanks to Ellie Hastings for her amazing cover design. An enormous thank you to my editor and publisher Aimée Parent-Dunn and everyone at Palimpsest Press. Aimée, your faith in me is greatly appreciated.

If I forgot you, it's because I'm forgetful, not because you're not important. My apologies.

Last but not least, my endless gratitude to my family, especially my partner Teresa Caterini and my son Jordan Tennant. Both allowed me to drag them across the Pacific and show them glimmers of my memories on another continent. Love you both.

Jamie Tennant is a writer, editor, and broadcaster in Hamilton, ON. He is the Program Director at 93.3 CFMU at McMaster University and the host/producer of GET LIT, a books-and-literature program. His debut novel, *Captain of Kinnoull Hill*, was published in 2016. It was shortlisted for the 2017 Hamilton Literary Award for Fiction and the 2017 ReLit Award. *River, Diverted* is his second book.